One of the longest runnii "The Bobbsey Twins" and it ha parents for over a hundred years now. Follow the adventures of two sets of young twins at the turn of the Twentieth Century when there were no telephones, radios, or televisions, and horses and carriages were common-place.

When the series begins (1904), Bert and Nan are eight, and Flossie and Freddie are four. The twins enjoy wonderful days filled with sunshine and love with their playmates, Grace, Nellie, and Charlie, and get into and out of trouble as only little kids can manage. Their cat, Snoop, (and after book #4, "The Bobbsey Twins at School," their dog Snap, too) goes along on many of their adventures as they build snow houses, ice boats and kites, and find a mysterious ghost wandering in their house at night. Then they take a trip to the country to visit their Uncle Daniel and make their own circus, celebrate the Fourth of July, almost burn down their uncle's barn, and then help save a neighbor's henhouse from washing away in a flood! Finally they travel to the seashore to stay at Uncle William's house where they have more exciting adventures.

"The Bobbsey Twins" is one of the many book series written in the early 20th Century by the Stratemeyer Syndicate. The first book in each series was written by Edward Stratemeyer, who then produced outlines for the other books in the series and hired writers to produce the actual books using a pseudonym. For the Bobbsey Twins' series this was Laura Lee Hope.

"The Bobbsey Twins, or Merry Days Indoors and Out" was published in 1904 and written by Edward Stratemeyer. "The Bobbsey Twins in the Country" and "The Bobbsey Twins at the Seashore" were both published in 1907 and written by Lilian C. Garis.

THEY WENT UP INTO THE AIR AND SNOOP WITH IT.

THE BOBBSEY TWINS COLLECTION

VOLUME 1

CONTAINING THE BOOKS:
... MERRY DAYS INDOORS AND OUT
... IN THE COUNTRY, &
... AT THE SEASHORE

By Laura Lee Hope

Flying Chipmunk Publishing
Bennington, NH

The Bobbsey Twins Collection, Volume 1
The Bobbsey Twins, Merry Days Indoors and Out
The Bobbsey Twins in the Country
The Bobbsey Twins at the Seashore
by Laura Lee Hope
Editing and Format Copyright © 2010 by Terry Kepner.

Please Help Fight Internet Piracy!
Scanning and uploading this novel to the internet without the editor's
permission is not an act of flattery. It is an act of *theft*. It not only
disrespects the editor; it violates the editor's copyright and literally
takes money from the editor's paycheck by distributing copies of this
book for which the editor gets no payment.

The Bobbsey Twins Collection, Volume 1

Published by Flying Chipmunk Publishing
162 Onset Road
Bennington, NH 03442

ISBN: 978-1-60459-980-0
           1-60459-980-4

Cover Design by Terry Kepner
First Flying Chipmunk Publishing edition: June 2010.

TABLE OF CONTENTS

THE BOBBSEY TWINS,
MERRY DAYS INDOORS AND OUT

Chapter I. The Bobbsey Twins at Home 3

Chapter II. Rope Jumping, and What Followed 6

Chapter III. The First Snow Storm 10

Chapter IV. The Broken Window 14

Chapter V. Bert's Ghost 18

Chapter VI. Coasting, And What Came Of It 23

Chapter VII. Freddie and Flossie's Snow House 28

Chapter VIII. Fun on the Ice 32

Chapter IX. Freddie Loses Himself 35

Chapter X. Lost and Found 39

Chapter XI. The Cruise Of The "Ice Bird" 43

Chapter XII. Tige—Playing Theater 47

Chapter XIII. Nan's First Cake-Baking 51

Chapter XIV. Christmas 55

Chapter XV. The Children's Party 59

Chapter XVI. A Grand Sleigh Ride 64

Chapter XVII. The Race and the Runaway 68

Chapter XVIII. A Quarrel in the Schoolyard 72

Chapter XIX. Nan's Plea 76

Chapter XX. St. Valentine's Day 79

Chapter XXI. The Rescue of Snoop, the Kitten 84

Chapter XXII. The Last Of The Ghost—Good-Night 88

THE BOBBSEY TWINS IN THE COUNTRY

Chapter I. The Invitation 97
Chapter II. The Start 100
Chapter III. Snoop on The Train 103
Chapter IV. A Long Ride................................ 106
Chapter V. Meadow Brook 109
Chapter VI. Frisky 112
Chapter VII. A Country Picnic 118
Chapter VIII. Fun in the Woods 124
Chapter IX. Fourth of July............................. 129
Chapter X. A Great Day 133
Chapter XI. The Little Gardeners 137
Chapter XII. Tom's Runaway 144
Chapter XIII. Picking Peas 149
Chapter XIV. The Circus 155
Chapter XV. The Chariot Race 160
Chapter XVI. The Flood 167
Chapter XVII. A Town Afloat 174
Chapter XVIII. The Fresh-Air Camp 179
Chapter XIX. Sewing School 185
Chapter XX. A Midnight Scare 192
Chapter XXI. What the Well Contained 200
Chapter XXII. Little Jack Horner.—Good-Bye 204

THE BOBBSEY TWINS AT THE SEASHORE

Chapter I. Chasing The Duck 215

Chapter II. A Traveling Menagerie 221

Chapter III. Railroad Tennis 226

Chapter IV. Night In A Barn 231

Chapter V. A Queer Stage Driver 235

Chapter VI. The Ocean 240

Chapter VII. Nellie 247

Chapter VIII. Exploring—A Race For Pond Lilies 251

Chapter IX. Fun On The Sands.................... 256

Chapter X. The Shell Hunt 261

Chapter XI. Downy On The Ocean 265

Chapter XII. Real Indians 269

Chapter XIII. The Boat Carnival 273

Chapter XIV. The First Prize 278

Chapter XV. Lost On An Island 281

Chapter XVI. Dorothy's Doings 287

Chapter XVII. Old Friends 291

Chapter XVIII. The Storm 296

Chapter XIX. Life-Savers 300

Chapter XX. The Happy Reunion 305

Chapter XXI. Good-By................................ 308

ILLUSTRATIONS

THE BOBBSEY TWINS ,

MERRY DAYS INDOORS AND OUT

The kite went up into the air
and Snoop with it............... *frontispiece & 83*

Down the hill swept the two sleds. 21

"Dat chile dun gwine an' buried himself alive." 27

At seven o'clock a supper was served............................. 62

THE BOBBSEY TWINS IN THE COUNTRY

"Whoa, Frisky! Whoa!" 113

"Dinner served in the dining car!" 123

"Hurrah! hurrah!" shouted everybody. 161

The boys were dashing out now right in the stream. 177

THE BOBBSEY TWINS AT THE SEASHORE

They rode along the sandy driveway. 242

He had only gone a few strokes when Bert
appeared with Nellie under his arm. 258

Toward this little island the children's boat
was now drifting. 283

"There's a man in it!" exclaimed the boys. 302

THE BOBBSEY TWINS

MERRY DAYS
INDOORS AND OUT

Chapter I

The Bobbsey Twins at Home

The Bobbsey twins were very busy that morning. They were all seated around the dining-room table, making houses and furnishing them. The houses were being made out of pasteboard shoe boxes, and had square holes cut in them for doors, and other long holes for windows, and had pasteboard chairs and tables, and bits of dress goods for carpets and rugs, and bits of tissue paper stuck up to the windows for lace curtains. Three of the houses were long and low, but Bert had placed his box on one end and divided it into five stories, and Flossie said it looked exactly like a "department" house in New York.

There were four of the twins. Now that sounds funny, doesn't it? But, you see, there were two sets. Bert and Nan, age eight, and Freddie and Flossie, age four.

Nan was a tall and slender girl, with a dark face and red cheeks. Her eyes were a deep brown and so were the curls that clustered around her head.

Bert was indeed a twin, not only because he was the same age as Nan, but because he looked so very much like her. To be sure, he looked like a boy, while she looked like a girl, but he had the same dark complexion, the same brown eyes and hair, and his voice was very much the same, only stronger.

Freddie and Flossie were just the opposite of their larger brother and sister. Each was short and stout, with a fair, round face, light-blue eyes and fluffy golden hair. Sometimes Papa Bobbsey called Flossie his little Fat Fairy, which always made her laugh. But Freddie didn't want to be called a fairy, so his papa called him the Fat Fireman, which pleased him very much, and made him rush around the house shouting: "Fire! fire! Clear the track for Number Two! Play away, boys, play away!" in a manner that seemed very lifelike. During the past year Freddie had seen two fires, and the work of the firemen had interested him deeply.

The Bobbsey family lived in the large town of Lakeport, situated at the head of Lake Metoka, a clear and beautiful sheet of water upon which the twins loved to go boating. Mr. Richard Bobbsey was a lumber merchant, with a large yard and docks on the lake shore, and a saw and planing mill close by. The house was a quarter of a mile away, on a fashionable street and had a small but nice garden around it, and a barn in the rear, in which the children loved at times to play.

"I'm going to cut out a fancy table cover for my parlor table," said Nan. "It's going to be the finest table cover that ever was."

"Nice as Aunt Emily's?" questioned Bert. "She's got a—a dandy, all worked in roses."

"This is going to be white, like the lace window curtains," replied Nan.

While Freddie and Flossie watched her with deep interest, she took a small square of tissue paper and folded it up several times. Then she cut curious-looking holes in the folded piece with a sharp pair of scissors. When the paper was unfolded once more a truly beautiful pattern appeared.

"Oh, how lubby!" screamed Flossie. "Make me one, Nan!"

"And me, too," put in Freddie. "I want a real red one," and he brought forth a bit of red pin-wheel paper he had been saving.

"Oh, Freddie, let me have the red paper for my stairs," cried Bert, who had had his eyes on the sheet for some time.

"No, I want a table cover, like Nanny. You take the white paper."

"Whoever saw white paper on a stairs—I mean white carpet," said Flossie.

"I'll give you a marble for the paper, Freddie," continued Bert.

But Freddie shook his head. "Want a table cover, nice as Aunt Em'ly," he answered. "Going to set a flower on the table too!" he added, and ran out of the room. When he came back he had a flower-pot in his hand half the size of his house, with a duster feather stuck in the dirt, for a flower.

"Well, I declare!" cried Nan, and burst out laughing. "Oh, Freddie, how will we ever set that on such a little pasteboard table?"

"Can set it there!" declared the little fellow, and before Nan could stop him the flower-pot went up and the pasteboard table came down and was mashed flat.

"Hullo! Freddie's breaking up housekeeping!" cried Bert.

"Oh, Freddie! do take the flower-pot away!" came from Flossie. "It's too big to go into the house."

Freddie looked perplexed for a moment. "Going to play garden around the house. This is a—a lilac tree!" And he set the flower-pot down close to Bert's elbow. Bert was now busy trying to put a pasteboard chimney on his house, and did not notice. A moment later Bert's elbow hit the flower-pot and down it went on the floor, breaking into several pieces and scattering the dirt over the rug.

"Oh, Bert! what have you done?" cried Nan, in alarm. "Get the broom and the dust-pan, before Dinah comes."

"It was Freddie's fault."

"Oh, my lilac tree is all gone!" cried the little boy. "And the boiler to my fire engine, too," he added, referring to the flower-pot, which he had used the day before when playing fireman.

At that moment, Dinah, the cook, came in from the kitchen.

"Well, I declar' to gracious!" she exclaimed. "If yo' chillun ain't gone an' mussed up de floah ag'in!"

"Bert broke my boiler!" said Freddie, and began to cry.

"Oh, never mind, Freddie, there are plenty of others in the cellar," declared Nan. "It was an accident, Dinah," she added, to the cook.

"Eberyt'ing in dis house wot happens is an accident," grumbled the cook, and went off to get the dust-pan and broom. As soon as the muss had been cleared away Nan cut out the red table cover for Freddie, which made him forget the loss of the "lilac tree" and the "boiler."

"Let us make a row of houses," suggested Flossie. "Bert's big house can be at the head of the street." And this suggestion was carried out. Fortunately, more pasteboard boxes were to be had, and from these they made shade trees and some benches, and Bert cut out a pasteboard horse and cart. To be sure, the horse did not look very lifelike, but they all played it was a horse and that was enough. When the work was complete they called Dinah in to admire it, which she did standing near the doorway with her fat hands resting on her hips.

"I do declar', it looks most tremend'us real," said the cook. "It's a wonder to me yo' chillun can make sech t'ings."

"We learned it in the kindergarten class at school," answered Nan.

"Yes, in the kindergarten," put in Flossie.

"But we don't make fire engines there," came from Freddie.

At this Dinah began to laugh, shaking from head to foot.

"Fire enjuns, am it, Freddie? Reckon yo' is gwine to be a fireman when yo' is a man, hey?"

"Yes, I'm going to be a real fireman," was the ready answer.

"An' what am yo' gwine to be, Master Bert?"

"Oh, I'm going to be a soldier," said Bert.

"I want to be a soldier, too," put in Freddie. "A soldier and a fireman."

"Oh, dear, I shouldn't want to be a soldier and kill folks," said Nan.

"Girls can't be soldiers," answered Freddie. "They have to get married, or be dressmakers, or sten'graphers, or something like that."

"You mean stenographers, Bert. I'm going to be a stenographer when I get big."

"I don't want to be any stenogerer," put in Flossie. "I'm going to keep a candy store, and have all the candy I want, and ice cream——"

"Me too!" burst in Freddie. "I'm going to have a candy store, an' be a fireman, an' a soldier, all together!"

"Dear! dear!" laughed Dinah. "Jess to heah dat now! It's wonderful wot yo' is gwine to be when yo' is big."

At that moment the front door bell rang, and all rushed to the hallway, to greet their mother, who had been down-town, on a shopping tour.

Chapter II

ROPE JUMPING, AND WHAT FOLLOWED

"Oh, mamma, what have you brought?" Such was the cry from all of the Bobbsey twins, as they gathered around Mrs. Bobbsey in the hallway. She had several small packages in her hands, and one looked very much like a box of candy.

Mrs. Bobbsey kissed them all before speaking. "Have you been good while I was gone?" she asked.

"I guess we tried to be good," answered Bert meekly.

"Freddie's boiler got broke, that's all," said Flossie. "Dinah swept up the dirt."

Before anything more could be said all were in the dining room and Mrs. Bobbsey was called upon to admire the row of houses. Then the box of candy was opened and each received a share.

"Now you had better go out and play," said the mother. "Dinah must set the table for dinner. But be sure and put on your thick coats. It is very cold and feels like snow."

"Oh, if only it would snow!" said Bert. He was anxious to try a sled he had received the Christmas before.

It was Saturday, with no school, so all of the boys and girls of the neighborhood were out. Some of the girls were skipping rope, and Nan joined these, while Bert went off to join a crowd of boys in a game of football.

"Let us play horse," suggested Freddie to Flossie. They had reins of red leather, with bells, and Freddie was the horse while his twin sister was the driver.

"I'm a bad horse, I'll run away if you don't watch me," cautioned Freddie, and began to prance around wildly, against the grape arbor and then up against the side fence.

"Whoa! whoa!" screamed Flossie, jerking on the reins. "Whoa, you naughty horse! If I had a whip, I'd beat you!"

"If you did that, I'd kick," answered Freddie, and began to kick real hard into the air. But at last he settled down and ran around the house just as nicely as any horse could. Then he snorted and ran up to the water bucket near the barn and Flossie pretended to give him a drink and some hay, and unharnessed him just as if he was a real steed.

Nan was counting while another girl named Grace Lavine jumped, Grace was a great jumper and had already passed forty when her mother called to her from the window.

"Grace, don't jump so much. You'll get sick."

"Oh, no, I won't," returned Grace. She was a headstrong girl and always wanted her own way.

"But jumping gave you a headache only last week," continued Mrs. Lavine. "Now, don't do too much of it," and then the lady closed the window and went back to her interrupted work.

"Oh, dear, mamma made me trip," sighed Grace. "I don't think that was fair."

"But your mamma doesn't want you to jump any more," put in another girl, Nellie Parks by name.

"Oh, she didn't say that. She said not to jump too much."

It was now Nan's turn to jump and she went up to twenty-seven and then tripped. Nellie followed and reached thirty-five. Then came another girl who jumped to fifty-six.

"I'm going a hundred this time," said Grace, as she skipped into place.

"Oh, Grace, you had better not!" cried Nan.

"You're afraid I'll beat you," declared Grace.

"No, I'm not. But your mamma said——"

"I don't care what she said. She didn't forbid my jumping," cut in the obstinate girl. "Are you going to turn or not?"

"Yes, I'll turn," replied Nan, and at once the jumping started. Soon Grace had reached forty. Then came fifty, and then sixty.

"I do believe she will reach a hundred after all," declared Nellie Parks, a little enviously.

"I will, if you turn steadily," answered Grace, in a panting voice. Her face was strangely pale.

"Oh, Grace, hadn't you better stop?" questioned Nan. She was a little frightened, but, nevertheless, kept on turning the rope.

"No!" puffed Grace. "Go—go on!"

She had now reached eighty-five. Nellie Parks was counting:

"Eighty-six, eighty-seven, eighty-eight, eighty-nine, ninety!" she went on. "Ninety-one-, ninety-two——"

"No—not so—so fast!" panted Grace. "I—I—oh!"

And then, just as Nellie was counting "Ninety-seven," she sank down in a heap, with her eyes closed and her face as white as a sheet.

For a moment the other girls looked on in blank wonder, not knowing what to make of it. Then Nan gave a scream.

"Oh, girls, she has fainted!"

"Perhaps she is dead!" burst out Nellie Parks. "And if she is, we killed her, for we turned the rope!"

"Oh, Nellie, please don't say that!" said Nan. She could scarcely speak the words.

"Shall I go and tell Mrs. Lavine?" asked another girl who stood near.

"No—yes," answered Nan. She was so bewildered she scarcely knew what to say. "Oh, isn't it awful!"

They gathered close around the fallen girl, but nobody dared to touch her. While they were there, and one had gone to tell Mrs. Lavine, a gentleman came up. It was Mr. Bobbsey, coming home from the lumber yard for lunch.

"What is the trouble?" he asked, and then saw Grace. "What happened to her?"

"She was—was jumping rope, and couldn't jump any more," sobbed Nan. "Oh, papa, she—isn't de—dead, is she?"

Mr. Bobbsey was startled and with good reason, for he had heard of more than one little girl dying from too much jumping. He took the limp form up in his arms and hurried to the Lavine house with it. "Run and tell Doctor Briskett," he called back to Nan.

The physician mentioned lived but a short block away, and Nan ran as fast as her feet could carry her. The doctor had just come in from making his morning calls and had his hat and overcoat still on.

"Oh, Doctor Briskett, do come at once!" she sobbed. "Grace Lavine is dead, and we did it, turning the rope for her!"

"Grace Lavine dead?" repeated the dumfounded doctor.

"Yes! yes!"

"Where is she?"

"Papa just carried her into her house."

Without waiting to hear more, Doctor Briskett ran toward the Lavine residence, around which quite a crowd had now collected. In the crowd was Bert.

"Is Grace really dead?" he asked.

"I—I—guess so," answered Nan. "Oh, Bert, it's dreadful! I was turning the rope and she had reached ninety-seven, when all at once she sank down, and——" Nan could not go on, but leaned on her twin brother's arm for support.

"You girls are crazy to jump rope so much," put in a big boy, Danny Rugg by name. Danny was something of a bully and very few of the girls liked him.

"It's no worse than playing football," said a big girl.

"Yes, it is, much worse," retorted Danny. "Rope jumping brings on heart disease. I heard father tell about it."

"I hope Grace didn't get heart disease," sobbed Nan.

"You turned the rope," went on Danny maliciously. "If she dies, they'll put you in prison, Nan Bobbsey."

"They shan't do it!" cried Bert, coming to his sister's rescue. "I won't let them."

"Much you can stop 'em, Bert Bobbsey."

"Can't I?"

"No, you can't."

"I'll see if I can't," answered Bert, and he gave Danny such a look that the latter edged away, thinking he was going to be attacked.

Doctor Briskett had gone into the house and the crowd hung around impatiently, waiting for news. The excitement increased, and Mrs. Bobbsey came forth, followed by Freddie and Flossie, who had just finished playing horse.

"Nan, Nan! what can it mean?" said Mrs. Bobbsey.

"Oh, mamma!" murmured Nan, and sank, limp and helpless, into her mother's arms.

Just then Mr. Bobbsey came forth from the Lavine residence. Seeing his wife supporting their daughter, he hurried in that direction.

"Grace is not dead," he announced. "She had a fainting spell, that is all. But I think after this she had better leave rope skipping alone."

Chapter III

THE FIRST SNOW STORM

Nan felt greatly relieved to learn that Grace was not dead.

"Oh, mamma, I am so glad!" she said, over and over again.

"I am glad too," answered Mrs. Bobbsey. "Her mamma has told her several times not to jump so much."

"Yes, I heard her." Nan's eyes dropped. "I was wicked to turn the rope for her."

In the end Nan told her mother the whole story, to which Mrs. Bobbsey listened very gravely.

"It was certainly wrong, Nan," she said. "After this I hope my little girl will try to do better."

"I shall try," answered Nan.

It was long after the dinner hour before the excitement died away.

Then it was learned that Grace was resting quietly in an easy chair and the doctor had ordered that she be kept quiet for several days. She was very much frightened and had told her parents that she would never jump rope again.

The time was the fall of the year, and that Saturday evening there was a feeling of snow in the air stronger than before.

"Oh, if only it would snow!" came from Bert, several times. "I like winter better than anything."

"I don't," answered Nan. "Think of the nice flowers we have in the summer."

"You can't have much fun with flowers, Nan."

"Yes, you can. And think of the birds——"

"I like the summer," piped in Freddie, "'cos then we go to the country where the cows and the chickens are!"

"Yes, and gather the eggs," put in Flossie, who had gathered eggs many times during the summer just past, while on a visit to their Uncle Daniel Bobbsey's farm at Meadow Brook. All of the Bobbsey children thought Meadow Brook the finest country place in all the world.

Bert's wish for snow was soon gratified. Sunday morning found it snowing steadily, the soft flakes coming down silently and covering the ground to the depth of several inches.

"Winter has come after all!" cried the boy. "Wish it was Monday instead of Sunday."

"The snow is not quite deep enough for sleighing yet," returned his father.

Despite the storm, all attended church in the morning, and the four children and Mrs. Bobbsey went to Sunday school in the afternoon. The lady taught a class of little girls and had Flossie as one of her pupils.

To the children, traveling back and forth through the snow was great sport, and Bert couldn't resist the temptation to make several snowballs and throw them at the other boys. The other boys threw back in return and Bert's hat was knocked off.

"Bert, this will not do on Sunday," said Mrs. Bobbsey, and there the snowballing came to an end.

All through that night the snow continued to come down, and on Monday morning it was over a foot deep. The air was crisp and cold and all of the children felt in the best of spirits.

"Nan and Bert can go to school," said Mrs. Bobbsey. "But I think Freddie and Flossie had better stay home. Walking would come too hard on them."

"I want to go out in the snow!" cried Freddie. "I don't want to stay indoors all day."

"You shall go out later on, in the garden," replied his mother.

"They can watch Sam shovel off the snow," put in Mr. Bobbsey. Sam was the man of all work. He and Dinah, the cook, were married and lived in some pleasant rooms over the stable.

"Yes, let us watch him!" cried Flossie, and soon she and Freddie were at the window, watching the colored man as he banked up the snow on either side of the garden walk and the sidewalk. Once Sam made a motion as if to throw a shovelful of snow at the window, and this made them dodge back in alarm and then laugh heartily.

The school was only a few blocks away from the Bobbsey home, but Nan and Bert had all they could do to reach it, for the wind had made the snow drift, so that in some spots it was very deep.

"Better look out or we'll get in over our heads," cried Bert.

"Oh, Bert, wouldn't it be terrible to have such a thing happen!" answered his twin sister. "How would we ever get out?"

"Ring the alarm and have the street-cleaning men dig us out," he said merrily. "Do you know, Nan, that I just love the snow. It makes me feel like singing and whistling." And he broke into a merry whistle.

"I love it because it looks so white and pure, Bert."

They were speedily joined by a number of other boys and girls, all bound for school. Some of the girls were having fun washing each other's faces and it was not long before Nan had her face washed too. The cold snow on her cheek and ear did not feel very nice, but she took the fun in good part and went to washing like the rest.

The boys were already snowballing each other, some on one side of the street and some on the other. The snowballs were flying in all directions and Bert was hit on the back and on the shoulder.

"I'll pay you back!" he cried, to Charley Mason, who had hit him in the back, and he let fly a snowball which landed directly on Charley's neck. Some of the snow went down Charley's back and made him shiver from the cold.

"I wouldn't stand that, Charley," said Danny Rugg, who was close at hand. "I'd pitch into him if I were you."

"You pitch into him," grumbled Charley. "You can throw awfully straight."

Danny prided himself on his throwing, which, however, was no better than the throwing of the other lads, and he quickly made two hard snowballs. With these in hand he ran out into the street and waited until Bert's hands were empty. Then he came up still closer and threw one of the snowballs with all his might. It struck Bert in the back of the head and sent him staggering.

"Hi! how do you like that?" roared Danny, in high glee. "Have another?" And as Bert stood up and looked around he let drive again, this time hitting Bert directly in the ear. The snowball was so hard it made Bert cry out in pain.

"For shame, Danny Rugg, to hit Bert so hard as that!" cried Nan.

"Oh, you keep still, Nan Bobbsey!" retorted Danny. "This is our sport, not yours."

"But you shouldn't have come so close before you threw the snowball."

"I know what I'm doing," growled the big boy, running off.

The whack in the ear made that member ache, and Bert did not feel near so full of fun when he entered the schoolyard. Several of his friends came up to him in sympathy.

"Did he hurt you very much, Bert?" asked one.

"He hurt me enough. It wasn't fair to come so close, or to make the snowballs so hard."

"Let us duck Danny in the snow," suggested one of the boys.

This was considered a good plan, but nobody wanted to start in, for, as I have said before, Danny was a good deal of a bully, and could get very rough at times.

While the boys were talking the matter over, the school bell rang and all had to go to their classrooms. In a little while Bert's ear stopped aching, but he did not forget how Danny Rugg had treated him.

"I'll pay him back when we go home to dinner," Bert told himself, and laid his plans accordingly.

As soon as Bert got out of school he hurried into a corner of the yard and made three good, hard snowballs. These he concealed under his overcoat and then waited for Danny to appear.

The big boy must have known that Bert would try to square matters with him, for as soon as he came out he ran in the direction of one
of the main streets of Lakeport, just the opposite direction to that
which he usually pursued.

"You shan't get away from me!" cried Bert, and ran after him.
Soon he threw one snowball and this landed on Danny's back. Then
he threw another and knocked off the bully's cap.

"Hi! stop that!" roared Danny, and stooped to pick up the cap.
Whiz! came the third snowball and hit Danny on the cheek. He let
out a cry of pain.

"I'll fix you for that, Bert Bobbsey!" he said, stooping down in the
street. "How do you like that?"

He had picked up a large chunk of ice lying in the gutter, and now
he threw it at Bert's head with all force. Bert dodged, and the ice went
sailing past him and hit the show window of a small shoe store, shat-
tering a pane of glass into a hundred pieces.

Chapter IV

THE BROKEN WINDOW

Neither Danny nor Bert had expected such an ending to the snowball fight and for the moment neither knew what to do. Then, as the
owner of the shoe store came running out, both set off on a run.

"Stop! stop!" roared the shoe dealer, coming after them. "Stop, I say!"

But the more he cried stop the harder they ran. Both soon reached
the corner, and while Danny went up the side street, Bert went down,
so the boys soon became widely separated.

Reaching the corner, the owner of the store did not know which
boy to go after, but made up his mind to follow Bert, who could not
run as fast as Danny. So after Bert he came, with such long steps that
he was soon close to the lad.

Bert was greatly scared, for he was afraid that if he was caught he
might be arrested. Seeing an alleyway close at hand, he ran into this.
At the back was a fence, and with all speed he climbed up and let

himself down on the other side. Then he ran around a corner of a barn, through another alleyway, and into a street leading home.

The shoe dealer might have followed, but he suddenly remembered that he had left the store unprotected and that somebody might come in and run off with his stock and his money. So he went back in a hurry; and the chase came to an end.

When Bert got home he was all out of breath, and his legs trembled so he could scarcely stand. Nan had just arrived and the family were preparing to sit down to lunch.

"Why, Bert, why do you run so hard?" protested his mother. "You must not do it. If you breathe in so much cold air, you may take cold."

"Oh, I—I'm all right," he panted, and started to drop into his seat, but Mrs. Bobbsey made him go up to the bathroom and wash up and comb his hair.

Poor Bert was in a fever of anxiety all through the meal. Every instant he expected to hear the front door bell ring, and find there a policeman to take him to the station house. He could scarcely eat a mouthful.

"What's the matter? Do you feel sick?" asked the father.

"No, I'm not sick," he answered.

"You play altogether too hard. Take it easy. The snow will last a long time," went on Mr. Bobbsey.

After lunch Bert did not dare to go back to school. But he could think of no excuse for staying home and at last set off in company with Nan. He looked around for Danny, but the big lad did not show himself.

"What's the matter with you, Bert?" questioned his twin sister, as they trudged along.

"Nothing is the matter, Nan."

"But there is. You act *so* strange."

"I—I don't feel very good."

"Then you did run too hard, after all."

"It wasn't that, Nan." Bert looked around him. "Do you see anything of Danny Rugg?"

"No." Nan stopped short. "Bert Bobbsey, did you have a fight with him?"

"No—that is, not a real fight. I chased him with some snowballs and he threw a big chunk of ice at me."

"Did he hit you?"

"No, he—he—oh, Nan, perhaps I had better tell you. But you must promise not to tell anybody else."

"Tell me what?"

"Will you promise not to tell?"

"Yes," said Nan promptly, for she and her twin brother always trusted each other.

"When Danny threw the ice at me it flew past and broke Mr. Ringley's window."

"What, of the shoe store?"

"Yes. Mr. Ringley came running out after both of us. I ran one way and Danny ran another. I ran into the alleyway past Jackson's barn, and got over the fence, and he didn't come any further."

"Does Mr. Ringley think you broke the window?"

"I guess he does. Anyway, he followed me and not Danny."

"But you had nothing to do with it. Oh, Bert, what made you run away at all. Why didn't you stop and tell the truth?"

"I—I got scared, that's why. I was afraid he'd get a policeman."

"Danny ought to own up that he did it."

"He won't do it. He'll put it off on me if he can,—because I chased him in the first place."

"Did Mr. Ringley know it was you?"

"I don't know. Now, Nan, remember, you promised not to tell."

"All right, Bert, I won't say a word. But—but—what do you think Mr. Ringley will do?"

"I don't know."

When they reached the school Danny Rugg was nowhere to be seen. The boys continued to have fun snowballing, but Bert had no heart for play and went to his classroom immediately. But he could not put his mind on his lessons and missed both in geography and arithmetic.

"Bert, you are not paying attention," said the teacher severely. "You just said the capital of Pennsylvania was Albany. You must know better than that."

"Philadelphia," corrected Bert.

"After this pay more attention."

Danny Rugg did not come to school, nor did he show himself until an hour after school was out. Bert had gone home and brought forth his sled, and he and Nan were giving Freddie and Flossie a ride around the block when Danny hailed Bert.

"Come here, I want to talk to you," he said, from across the street.

"What do you want?" asked Bert roughly.

"I've got something to tell you. It won't take but a minute."

Bert hesitated, and then leaving Nan to go on alone with the sled, he crossed to where Danny was standing, partly sheltered by a tree box.

"You can't blame that broken window off on me, Danny Rugg," he began.

"Hush!" whispered Danny, in alarm. "I ain't going to blame it off on you, Bert. I only want you to promise to keep quiet about it."

"Why should I? It was your fault."

"Was it? I don't think so. You began the fight. Besides, if you dare to say a word, I'll—I'll give you a big thrashing!" blustered Danny.

He clenched his fists as he spoke and looked so fierce that Bert retreated a step.

"I haven't said anything, Danny."

"Then you had better not. Old Ringley doesn't know who broke his window. So you keep quiet; do you hear?"

"Are you sure he doesn't know?"

"Yes, because he has been asking everybody about it."

There was a pause and the two boys looked at each other.

"You ought to pay for the window," said Bert.

"Huh! I'm not going to do it. You can pay for it if you want to. But don't you dare to say anything about me! If you do, you'll catch it, I can tell you!" And then Danny walked off.

"What did he have to say?" questioned Nan, when Bert came back to her.

"He wants me to keep still. He says Mr. Ringley doesn't know who did it."

"Did you promise to keep still, Bert?"

"No, but if I say anything Danny says he will give it to me."

A crowd of boys and girls now came up and the talk was changed. All were having a merry time in the snow, and for the time being Bert forgot his troubles. He and Nan gave Freddie and Flossie a long ride which pleased the younger twins very much.

"I wish you was really and truly horses," said Flossie. "You go so *beautifully!*"

"And if I had a whip I could make you go faster," put in Freddie.

"For shame, Freddie!" exclaimed Nan. "Would you hit the horse that gave you such a nice ride?"

"Let me give *you* a ride," answered the little fellow, to change the subject.

He insisted upon it, and soon Nan was on the sled behind Flossie, and Bert and Freddie were hauling them along where pulling was easy. This was great sport for Freddie, and he puffed and snorted like a real horse, and kicked up his heels, very much to Flossie's delight.

"Gee-dap!" shrieked the little maiden. "Gee-dap!" and moved back and forth on the sled, to make it go faster. Away went Freddie and Bert, as fast as the legs of the little fellow could travel. They went down a long hill and through a nice side street, and it was a good half hour before they reached home,—just in time for a good hot supper.

Chapter V

BERT'S GHOST

Bert felt relieved to learn that Mr. Ringley did not know who had broken the store window, but he was still fearful that the offense might be laid at his door. He was afraid to trust Danny Rugg, and did not know what the big boy might do.

"He may say I did it, just to clear himself," thought Bert. "And if Mr. Ringley comes after me, he'll remember me sure."

But his anxiety was forgotten that evening, when some of the neighbors dropped in for a call. There was music on the piano and some singing, and almost before Bert and Nan knew it, it was time to go to bed. Freddie and Flossie had already retired, worn out by their play.

But after Bert had said his prayers and found himself alone in the small bed chamber he occupied, he could not sleep. The talk of the folks below kept him awake at first, and even after they had gone to bed he could not forget the happening of the day, and he could still hear the crash of that glass as the chunk of ice went sailing through it.

At last he fell into a troubled doze, with the bright light of the moon shining across the rug at the foot of the bed. But the doze did not last long, and soon some kind of a noise awoke him with a start.

He opened his eyes and his gaze wandered across the moon-lit room. Was he dreaming, or was that really a figure in white standing at the foot of his bed? With a shiver he ducked down and covered his head with the blankets.

For two or three minutes he lay quiet, expecting every instant to have something unusual happen. Then, with great caution, he pushed the blankets back and took another look.

There was nothing there!

"But I saw something," he told himself. "I am sure I saw something. What could it have been?"

Ah, that was the question. For over an hour he continued to lie awake, watching and listening. Nan was in the next little chamber and he was half of a mind to call her, but he was afraid she would call him a "'fraid-cat!" something he despised.

Bert had heard of ghosts and now he thought of all the ghost stories he could remember. Had the thing in white been a ghost? If so, where had it come from?

After a while he tried to dismiss the thing from his mind, but it was almost morning before he fell asleep again. This time he slept so soundly, however, that he did not rouse up until his mother came and shook him.

"Why, Bert, what makes you sleep so soundly this morning?" said Mrs. Bobbsey.

"I—I didn't get to sleep until late," he stammered. And then he added: "Mamma, do you believe in ghosts?"

"Why, of course not, Bert. What put that into your head?"

"I—I thought I saw a ghost last night."

"You must have been mistaken. There are no ghosts."

"But I saw *something*," insisted the boy.

"Where?"

"Right at the foot of the bed. It was all white."

"When was this?"

"Right in the middle of the night."

"Did you see it come in, or go out?"

"No, mamma. When I woke up it was standing there, and when I took a second look at it, it was gone."

"You must have been suffering from a nightmare, Bert," said Mrs. Bobbsey kindly. "You should not have eaten those nuts before going to bed."

"No, it wasn't a nightmare," said the boy.

He had but little to say while eating breakfast, but on the way to school he told Nan, while Freddie and Flossie listened also.

"Oh, Bert, supposing it was a real ghost?" cried Nan, taking a deep breath. "Why, I'd be scared out of my wits,—I know I'd be!"

"Mamma says there are no ghosts. But I saw something—I am sure of that."

"I don't want to see any ghostses," came from Flossie.

"Nor I," added Freddie. "Sam told about a ghost once that was as high as a tree an' had six heads, to eat bad boys and girls up. Did this have six heads, Bert?"

"No."

"How many heads did it have?"

"I don't know—one, I guess."

"And was it as high as a tree?" went on the inquisitive little fellow.

"Oh, it couldn't stand up in the room if it was as high as a tree," burst out Flossie.

"Could if it was a tiny *baby* tree," expostulated Freddie.

"It was about as high as that," said Bert, putting out his hand on a level with his shoulder. "I can't say how it looked, only it was white."

"Perhaps it was moonshine," suggested Nan, but at this Bert shook his head. He felt certain it had been more substantial than moonshine.

That day Danny Rugg came to school as usual. When questioned about his absence he said he had had a toothache. When Bert looked at him the big boy merely scowled, and no words passed between the pair.

Directly back of Lakeport was a long hill, used during the winter by all the boys and girls for coasting. After school Nan and Bert were allowed to go to this hill, in company with a number of their friends. They were admonished to come back before dark and promised faithfully to do so.

Among the boys there was a great rivalry as to who could go

DOWN THE HILL SWEPT THE TWO SLEDS.

down the hill the fastest, and who could make his sled go the farthest after the bottom was reached.

"I'll try my sled against yours!" cried Charley Mason to Bert.

"Done!" returned Bert. "Are you going down alone, or are you going to carry somebody?"

"You must carry me down," insisted Nan.

"Then I'll take Nellie Parks," went on Charley.

Nellie was close at hand and soon the two sleds were side by side, with a girl on each. Bert and Charley stood behind.

"Are you ready?" asked Charley.

"Yes."

"Then go!"

Away went both lads, giving each sled a lively shove down the hill. Then each hopped aboard, and took hold of the rope with which to steer.

"A race! A race!" shouted those standing near.

"I think Charley will win!" said some.

"I think Bert will win!" said others.

"Oh, let us win if we can!" whispered Nan to her twin brother.

"I'll do my best, Nan," was the answer.

Down the long hill swept the two sleds, almost side by side. Each was rushing along at a lively rate of speed, and those aboard had to hold on tightly for fear of being jounced off.

"Whoop!" roared Charley. "Clear the track, for I am coming!"

"Make room for me!" sang out Bert. "We are bound to win!"

The bottom of the hill was almost reached when Charley's sled began to crawl a bit ahead.

"Oh, Bert, they are going to beat us after all," cried Nan disappointedly.

"I knew we'd beat you," cried Nellie Parks. "Charley's is the best sled on the hill."

"The race isn't over yet," said Bert.

His sled had been running in rather soft snow. Now he turned to where the coasting was better, and in a twinkling his sled shot forward until he was once more beside Charley and Nellie.

"Here we come!" shouted Bert. "Make room, I say! Make room."

On and on they went, and now the bottom of the hill was reached and they ran along a level stretch. Charley's sled began to slow up, but Bert's kept on and on until he had covered a hundred feet beyond where Charley had come to a stop.

"We've won!" cried Nan excitedly. "Oh, Bert, your sled is a wonder."

"So it is," he answered, with pride. "But it was a close race, wasn't it?"

When they came back to where Charley and Nellie stood they found Charley rather sulky.

"Nellie is heavier than Nan," said he. "It wasn't a fair race. Let us try it alone next time."

"I'm willing," answered Bert.

Chapter VI

COASTING, AND WHAT CAME OF IT

It was a long walk back to the top of the hill, but Nan and Bert did not mind it.

"So you won, did you?" said one of the boys to Bert. "Good enough."

"We are going to try it over again," put in Charley. "Come on."

In the crowd was Danny Rugg, who had a brand-new sled.

"I guess I can beat anybody!" cried Danny boastfully. "This new sled of mine is bang-up."

"What slang!" whispered Nan, to Bert. "If I were you I shouldn't race with him."

"I'm going to race with Charley," answered her twin brother, and took no notice of Danny's challenge.

Bert and Charley were soon ready for the test, and away they went amid a cheer from their friends.

"I think Charley will win this time," said Nellie.

"And I think that Bert will win," answered Nan.

"Oh, you think your brother is wonderful," sniffed Nellie, with a shrug of her shoulders.

"He is just as good as any boy," said Nan quickly.

Down the hill swept the two sleds, keeping side by side as before. They were but a foot apart, for each owner wished to keep on the hardest part of the slide.

"Keep on your side, Bert Bobbsey!" shouted Charley warningly.

"And you keep on yours, Charley Mason!" returned Bert.

All of the others on the hill had stopped coasting to witness the contest, but now with a whoop Danny Rugg swept forward with his new sled and came down the hill at top speed.

The bottom of the hill was barely reached when Charley's sled made an unexpected turn and crashed into Bert's, throwing Bert over on his side in the snow.

"What did you do that for?" demanded Bert angrily.

"I—I—didn't do it," stammered Charley. "I guess you turned into me."

"No, I didn't."

Bert arose and began to brush the snow from his clothes. As he did so he heard a rushing sound behind him and then came a crash as Danny Rugg ran into him. Down he went again and his sled had a runner completely broken off. Bert was hit in the ankle and badly bruised.

"Why didn't you get out of the way!" roared Danny Rugg roughly. "I yelled loud enough."

"Oh, my ankle!" groaned Bert. For the moment the wrecked sled was forgotten.

"I didn't touch your ankle," went on the big boy.

"You did so, Danny—at least, the point of your sled did," answered Bert.

"You ran into me in the first place," came from Charley.

"Oh, Charley, you know better than that." Bert tried to stand, but had to sit down. "Oh, my ankle!"

"It wasn't my fault," said Danny Rugg, and began to haul his sled away. Charley started to follow.

"Don't leave me, Charley," called out Bert. "I—I guess I can't walk."

Charley hesitated. Then, feeling in his heart that he was really responsible for running into Bert in the first place, he came back and helped Bert to his feet.

"The sled is broken," said Bert, surveying the wreck dismally.

"That was Danny's fault."

"Well, then, he ought to pay for having it fixed."

"He never pays for anything he breaks, Bert,—you know that."

Slowly and painfully Bert dragged himself and his broken sled to the top of the hill. Sharp, hot flashes of pain shooting through his bruised ankle. Nan ran to meet him.

"Oh, Bert, what is the matter? Are you hurt?" she asked.

"Yes,—Danny ran into me, and broke the sled."

"It wasn't my fault, I say!" blustered the big boy. "You had a right to get out of the way."

"It was your fault, Danny Rugg, and you will have to have my sled mended," cried Bert.

Throwing down the rope of his own sled, Danny advanced and doubled up his fists as if to fight.

"Don't you talk like that to me," he said surlily. "I don't like it."

Bert's ankle hurt too much for him to continue the quarrel. He felt himself growing dizzy and he fell back.

"Let us go home," whispered Nan.

"I'll ride you home if you can't walk," put in Charley, who was growing alarmed.

In the end Bert had to accept the offer, and home he went, with Charley and Nan pulling him and with the broken sled dragging on behind.

It was all he could do to get into the house, and as a consequence Mrs. Bobbsey was much alarmed. She took off his shoe and stocking and found the ankle scratched and swollen, and bathed it and bound it up.

"You must lie down on the sofa," she said. "Never mind the broken sled. Perhaps your papa can fix it when he comes home."

Bert detested playing the part of an invalid, but he soon discovered that keeping the ankle quiet felt much better than trying to walk around upon it. That night Mr. Bobbsey carried him up to bed, and he remained home for three days, when the ankle became as well as ever. The broken sled was sent to a nearby cabinet maker, and came back practically as good as new.

"You must not have anything to do with Danny Rugg," said Mrs. Bobbsey to her son. "He is very rough and ungentlemanly."

"I'll leave him alone, mamma, if he'll leave me alone," answered Bert.

During those days spent at home, Nan did her best to amuse her brother. As soon as she was out of school she came straight home, and read to him and played games. Nan was also learning to play on the piano and she played a number of tunes that he liked to hear. They were so much attached to each other that it did not seem natural for Nan to go out unless her twin brother could go out too.

The first snow storm had been followed by another, so that in the garden the snow lay deeper than ever. This was a great delight to Freddie and Flossie, who worked hard to build themselves a snow house. They enlisted the services of Sam, the stableman, who speedily piled up for them a heap of snow much higher than their heads.

"Now, chillun, dar am de house," said the colored man. "All yo' hab got to do is to clear out de insides." And then he went off to his work, after starting the hole for them.

Flossie wanted to divide the house into three rooms, "dining room, kitchen, and bedroom," as she said, but Freddie objected.

"'Taint big enough," said the little boy. "Make one big room and call it ev'rything."

"But we haven't got an *ev'rything*," said Flossie.

"Well, then, call it the parlor," said Freddie. "When it's done we can put in a carpet and two chairs for us to sit on."

It was hard work for such little hands to dig out the inside of the heap of snow, but they kept at it, and at last the hole was big enough for Freddie to crawl into.

"Oh, it's jess *beautiful!*" he cried, "Try it, Flossie!" And Flossie did try, and said the house was going to be perfect.

"Only we must have a bay window," she added. "And a curtain, just like mamma."

They continued to shovel away, and soon Freddie said he could almost stand up in the house. He was inside, shoveling out the snow, while his twin sister packed what he threw out on the outside, as Sam had told them to do.

"Where shall I put the bay window?" asked the little boy, presently.

"On this side," answered Flossie, pointing with the shovel she held.

At once Freddie began to dig a hole through the side of the pile of snow.

"DAT CHILE DUN GWINE AN' BURIED HIMSELF ALIVE."

"Be careful, or the house will come down!" cried Flossie, all at once, and hardly had she spoken when down came the whole top of the snow pile and poor Freddie was buried completely out of sight!

Chapter VII

FREDDIE AND FLOSSIE'S SNOW HOUSE

"Freddie! Freddie!" shrieked Flossie, when she saw her twin brother disappear. "Do come out!"

But Freddie could not come out, and when, after a few seconds he did not show himself, she ran toward the kitchen door, screaming at the top of her breath.

"Oh, Dinah! Dinah! Freddie is buried! Freddie is buried!"

"Wot's dat yo' say, Flossie?" demanded the cook, coming to the door.

"Freddie is buried. The ceiling of the snow house came down on him!"

"Gracious sakes alive, chile!" burst out Dinah, and without waiting to put anything on her head she rushed forth into the garden. "Gib me dat shovel quick! He'll be stuffocated fo' yo' know it."

She began to dig away at the pile of snow, and presently uncovered one of Freddie's lower limbs. Then she dropped the shovel and tugged away at the limb and presently brought Freddie to view, just as Mrs. Bobbsey and Nan appeared on the scene.

"What in the world is the matter?" questioned Mrs. Bobbsey, in alarm.

"Dat chile dun gwine an' buried himself alive," responded the colored cook. "De roof of de snow house cabed in on him, pooh dear! He's 'most stuffocated!"

In the meantime Freddie was gasping for breath. Then he looked at the wreck of the snow house and set up a tremendous roar of dismay.

"Oh, Flossie, it's all spoilt! The bay window an' all!"

"Never mind, Freddie dear," said his mother, taking him. "Be thankful that you were not suffocated, as Dinah says."

"Yes, but Flossie and me were makin' an *ev'rything* house, with a parlor, an' a bay window, an' *ev'rything*. I didn't want it to fall down." Freddie was still gasping, but now he struggled to the ground. "Want to build it up again," he added.

"I am afraid you'll get into trouble again, Freddie."

"No, I won't, mamma. Do let us build it up again," pleaded the little fellow.

"I kin watch dem from de doah," suggested Dinah.

"Let me help them, mamma," put in Nan. "Bert is reading a book, so he won't want me for a while."

"Very well, Nan, you may stay with them. But all of you be careful," said Mrs. Bobbsey.

After that the building of the snow house was started all over again. The pile of snow was packed down as hard as possible, and Nan made Flossie and Freddie do the outside work while she crept inside, and cut around the ceiling and the bay window just as the others wanted. It was great sport, and when the snow house was finished it was large enough and strong enough for all of them to enter with safety.

"To-night I'll poah some water ober dat house," said Sam. "Dat will make de snow as hard as ice." This was done, and the house remained in the garden until spring came. Later on Bert built an addition to it, which he called the library, and in this he put a bench and a shelf on which he placed some old magazines and story papers. In the main part of the snow house Freddie and Flossie at first placed an old rug and two blocks of wood for chairs, and a small bench for a table. Then, when Flossie grew tired of the house, Freddie turned it into a stable, in which he placed his rocking-horse. Then he brought out his iron fire engine, and used the place for a fire-house, tying an old dinner bell on a stick, stuck over the doorway. *Dong! dong!* would go the bell, and out he would rush with his little engine and up the garden path, looking for a fire.

"Let us play you are a reg'lar fireman," said Flossie, on seeing this. "You must live in the fire-house, and I must be your wife and come to see you with the baby." And she dressed up in a long skirt and paid him a visit, with her best doll on her arm. Freddie pretended to be very glad to see her, and embraced the baby. But a moment later he made the bell ring, and throwing the baby to her rushed off again with his engine.

"That wasn't very nice," pouted Flossie. "Dorothy might have fallen in the snow."

"Can't help it," answered Freddie. "A fireman can't stop for anything."

"But—but—he doesn't have to throw his baby away, does he?" questioned Flossie, with wide open eyes.

"Yes, he does,—ev'rything."

"But—but supposing he is—is eating his dinner?"

"He has to throw it away, Flossie. Oh, it's awful hard to be a real fireman."

"Would he have to throw his jam away, and his pie?"

"Yes."

"Then I wouldn't be a fireman, not for a—a house full of gold!" said Flossie, and marched back into the house with her doll.

Flossie's dolls were five in number. Dorothy was her pride, and had light hair and blue eyes, and three dresses, one of real lace. The next was Gertrude, a short doll with black eyes and hair and a traveling dress that was very cute. Then came Lucy, who had lost one arm, and Polly, who had lost both an arm and a leg. The fifth doll was Jujube, a colored boy, dressed in a fiery suit of red, with a blue cap and real rubber boots. This doll had come from Sam and Dinah and had been much admired at first, but was now taken out only when all the others went too.

"He doesn't really belong to the family, you know," Flossie would explain to her friends. "But I have to keep him, for mamma says there is no colored orphan asylum for dolls. Besides, I don't think Sam and Dinah would like to see their doll child in an asylum." The dolls were all kept in a row in a big bureau drawer at the top of the house, but Flossie always took pains to separate Jujube from the rest by placing the cover of a pasteboard box between them.

With so much snow on the ground it was decided by the boys of that neighborhood to build a snow fort, and this work was undertaken early on the following Saturday morning. Luckily, Bert was by that time well enough to go out and he did his fair share of the labor, although being careful not to injure the sore ankle.

The fort was built at the top of a small hill in a large open lot. It was made about twenty feet square and the wall was as high as the boys' heads and over a foot thick. In the middle was gathered a big pile of snow, and into this was stuck a flag-pole from which floated a nice flag loaned by a boy named Ralph Blake.

"Let us divide into two parties of soldiers," said Ralph. "One can defend the fort and the others can attack it."

"Hurrah! just the thing!" cried Bert. "When shall the battle begin?"

The boys talked it over, and it was decided to have the battle come off after lunch.

The boys went home full of enthusiasm, and soon the news spread that a real soldiers' battle was to take place at the lot.

"Oh, Bert, can't I go and look on?" asked Nan.

"I want to go, too," put in Flossie.

"Can't I be a soldier?" asked Freddie. "I can make snowballs, and throw 'em, too."

"No, Freddie, you are too little to be a soldier," answered Bert. "But you can all come and look on, if you wish."

After lunch the boys began to gather quickly, until over twenty were present. Many girls and a few grown folks were also there, who took places out of harm's way.

"Now, remember," said a gentleman who was placed in charge. "No icy snowballs and no stones."

"We'll remember, Mr. Potter," cried the young soldiers.

The boys were speedily divided into two parties, one to attack and one to defend the fort. It fell to Bert's lot to be one of the attacking party. Without loss of time each party began to make all the snowballs it could. The boys who remained in the fort kept out of sight behind the walls, while the attacking party moved to the back of the barn at the corner of the big lot.

"Are you all ready?" shouted Mr. Potter presently.

A yell of assent came from nearly all of the young soldiers.

"Very well, then; the battle may begin."

Some of the boys had brought horns along, and now a rousing blast came from behind the barn and then from the snow fort.

"Come on and capture the fort!" cried Bert, and led the way, with his arms full of snowballs.

There was a grand cheer and up the hill rushed the young soldiers, ready to capture the snow fort no matter what the cost.

Chapter VIII

Fun on the Ice

"Oh, the fight is going to start!" cried Nan, in high excitement. "See them coming up the hill!"

"Will they shoot?" asked Flossie, just a bit nervously.

"Course they won't shoot," answered Freddie. "Can't shoot snowballs. Ain't got no powder in."

The attacking party was still a good distance from the fort when those inside let fly a volley of snowballs. But the snowballs did not reach their mark, and still the others came up the hill.

"Now then, give it to them!" cried Bert, and let fly his first snowball, which landed on the top of the fort's wall. Soon the air was full of snowballs, flying one way and another. Many failed to do any damage, but some went true, and soon Bert received a snowball full in the breast and another in the shoulder. Then he slipped and fell and his own snowballs were lost.

The attacking party got to within fifty feet of the fort, but then the ammunition gave out and they were forced to retreat, which they did in quick order.

"Hurrah! they can't take the fort!" cried those inside of the stronghold, and blew their horns more wildly than ever. But their own ammunition was low and they made other snowballs as quickly as they could, using the pile of snow in the middle of the fort for that purpose.

Back of the barn the attacking party held a consultation.

"I've got a plan," said a boy named Ned Brown. "Let us divide into two parties and one move on the fort from the front and the other from the back. Then, if they attack one party, the other party can sneak in and climb over the fort wall and capture the flag."

"All right, let us do that," said Bert.

Waiting until each boy had a dozen or more snowballs, half of the attacking force moved away along a fence until the rear of the fort was gained. Then, with another cheer, all set out for the fort.

It was a grand rush and soon the air was once more filled with snowballs, much to the delight of the spectators, who began to cheer both sides.

"Oh, I hope they get into the fort this time," said Nan.

"I hope they don't," answered another girl, who had a brother in the fort.

Inside the fort the boys were having rather a hard time of it. They were close together, and a snowball coming over the walls was almost certain to hit one or another. More than this, the pile of snow around the flag was growing small, so that the flag was in great danger of toppling over.

Up the two sides of the hill came the invaders, Bert leading the detachment that was to attack the rear. He was hit again, but did not falter, and a moment later found himself at the very wall.

"Get back there!" roared a boy from the fort and threw a large lump of soft snow directly into his face. But Bert threw the lump back and the boy slipped and fell flat. Then, amid a perfect shower of snowballs, Bert and two other boys fairly tumbled into the fort.

"Defend the flag! Defend the flag!" was the rallying cry of the fort defenders, and they gathered around the flag. The struggle was now a hand-to-hand one, in which nothing but soft snow was used, and nearly every boy had his face washed.

"Get back there!" roared Danny Rugg, who was close to the flag, but as he spoke two boys shoved him down on his face in the snow, and the next moment Bert and another boy of the invading party had the flag and was carrying it away in triumph.

"The fort has fallen!" screamed Nan, and clapped her hands.

"Hurrah!" shouted Freddie. "The—the forters are beaten, aren't they?"

"Yes, Freddie."

A cheer was given for those who had captured the fort. Then some of the boys began to dance on the top of the walls, and down they came, one after another, until the fort was in ruins, and the great contest came to an end.

"It was just splendid!" said Nan to Bert, on the way home. "Just like a real battle."

"Only the band didn't play," put in Freddie disappointedly. "Real soldiers have a band. They don't play fish-horns."

"Oh, Freddie!" cried Flossie. "They weren't fish-horns. They were Christmas horns."

"It's all the same. I like a band, with a big, fat bass-drum."

"We'll have the band next time—just for your benefit, Freddie," said Bert.

He was tired out and glad to rest when they got home. More than this, some of the snow had gotten down his back, so he had to dry himself by sitting with his back to the sitting-room heater.

"Danny Rugg was terribly angry that we captured the fort," said he. "He is looking for the boys who threw him on his face."

"It served him right," answered Nan, remembering the trouble over the broken show window.

The second fall of snow was followed by steady cold weather and it was not long before the greater part of Lake Metoka was frozen over. As soon as this happened nearly all of the boys and girls took to skating, so that sledding and snowballing were, for the time being, forgotten.

Both Nan and Bert had new skates, given to them the Christmas before, and each was impatient to go on the ice, but Mrs. Bobbsey held them back until she thought it would be safe.

"You must not go too far from shore," said she. "I understand the ice in the middle of the lake, and at the lower end, is not as firm as it might be."

Freddie and Flossie wanted to watch the skating, and Nan took them to their father's lumber yard. Here was a small office directly on the lake front, where they could see much that was going on and still be under the care of an old workman around the yards.

Nan could not skate very well, but Bert could get along nicely, and he took hold of his twin sister's hand, and away they went gliding over the smooth ice much to their combined delight.

"Some day I am going to learn how to do fancy skating," said Bert. "The Dutch roll, and spread the eagle, and all that."

"There is Mr. Gifford," said Nan. "Let us watch him."

The gentleman mentioned was a fine skater and had once won a medal for making fancy figures on the ice. They watched him for a long while and so did many of the others present.

"It's beautiful to skate like that," cried Nan, when they skated away. "It's just like knowing how to dance everything."

"Only better," said Bert, who did not care for dancing at all.

Presently Nan found some girls to skate with and then Bert went off among the boys. The girls played tag and had great fun, shrieking at the top of their lungs as first one was "it" and then another. It was hard work for Nan to catch the older girls, who could skate better, but easy enough to catch those of her own age and experience on the ice.

The boys played tag, too, and "snapped the whip," as it is termed. All of the boys would join hands in a long line and then skate off as fast as they could. Then the boy on one end, called the snapper, would stop and pull the others around in a big curve. This would make the boys on the end of the line skate very fast, and sometimes they would go down, to roll over and over on the ice. Once Bert was at the end and down he went, to slide a long distance, when he bumped into a gentleman who was skating backwards and over went the man with a crash that could be heard a long distance off.

"Hi! you young rascal!" roared the man, trying to scramble up. "What do you mean by bowling me over like that?"

"Excuse me, but I didn't mean to do it," answered Bert, and lost no time in getting out of the gentleman's way. The gentleman was very angry and left the ice, grumbling loudly to himself.

Down near the lower end of Mr. Bobbsey's lumber yard some young men were building an ice-boat. Bert and Charley Mason watched this work with interest. "Let us make an ice-boat," said Charley. "I can get an old bed-sheet for a sail, if you will get your father to give you the lumber."

"I'll try," answered Bert, and it was agreed that the ice-boat should be built during the following week, after school.

Chapter IX

Freddie Loses Himself

Christmas was now but four weeks away, and the stores of Lakeport had their windows filled with all sort of nice things for presents. Nan and Bert had gazed into the windows a number of times, and even walked through the one big department store of which the town boasted, and they had told Freddie and Flossie of many of the things to be seen.

"Oh, I want to see them, too!" cried Flossie, and begged her mother to take her along the next time she went out.

"I want to go, too," put in Freddie. "Bert says there are *sixteen* rocking horses all in a row, with white and black tails. I want to see them."

"I am going to the stores to-morrow," answered Mrs. Bobbsey. "You can go with me, after school. It will be better to go now than later on, when the places are filled with Christmas shoppers."

The twins were in high glee, and Freddie said he was going to spend the twenty-five cents he had been saving up for several months.

"Let us buy mamma something for Christmas," said Flossie, who had the same amount of money.

"What shall we buy?"

That question was a puzzling one. Flossie thought a nice doll would be the right thing, while Freddie thought an automobile that could be wound up and made to run around the floor would be better. At last both consulted Nan.

"Oh, mamma doesn't want a doll," said Nan. "And she ought to have a real automobile, not a tin one."

"Can't buy a real auto'bile," said Freddie. "Real auto'biles cost ten dollars, or more."

"I'll tell you what to do," went on Nan. "You buy her a little bottle of cologne, Freddie, and you, Flossie, can buy her a nice handkerchief."

"I'll buy her a big bottle of cologne," said Freddie. "That big!" and he placed his hands about a foot apart.

"And I'll get a real lace handkerchief," added Flossie.

"You'll have to do the best you can," said practical Nan, and so it was agreed.

When they left home each child had the money tucked away in a pocket. They went in the family sleigh, with Sam as a driver. The first stop was at Mr. Ringley's shoe store, where Mrs. Bobbsey purchased each of the twins a pair of shoes. It may be added here, that the broken window glass had long since been replaced by the shoe dealer, and his show window looked as attractive as ever.

"I heard you had a window broken not long ago," said Mrs. Bobbsey, when paying for her purchases.

"Yes, two bad boys broke the window," answered the shoe dealer.

"Who were they?"

"I couldn't find out. But perhaps I'll learn some day, and then I mean to have them arrested," said Mr. Ringley. "The broken glass ruined several pairs of shoes that were in the window." And then he turned away to wait on another customer.

Soon the large department store was reached and Mrs. Bobbsey let Freddie and Flossie take their time in looking into the several windows. One was full of dolls, which made the little girl gape in wonder and delight.

"Oh, mamma, what a flock of dolls!" she cried. "Must be 'bout ten millions of them, don't you think so?"

"Hardly that many, Flossie; but there are a good many."

"And, oh, mamma, what pretty dresses! I wish I had that doll with the pink silk and the big lace hat," added the little girl.

"Do you think that is the nicest, Flossie?"

"Indeed, indeed I do," answered the little miss. "It's too lovely for anything. Can't we get it and take it home?"

"No, dear; but you had better ask Santa Claus to send it to you," continued her mother with a smile.

Some wooden soldiers and building blocks caught Freddie's eye, and for the time being his favorite fire engines were forgotten.

"I want wooden soldiers," he said. "Can set 'em up in a row, with the sword-man in front, an' the man with the drum."

"Perhaps Santa Claus will bring you some soldiers in your stocking, Freddie."

"Stocking ain't big enough—want big ones, like that," and he pointed with his chubby hand.

"Well, let us wait and see what Santa Claus can do," said Mrs. Bobbsey.

Inside of the store was a candy counter near the doorway, and there was no peace for Mrs. Bobbsey until she had purchased some chocolate drops for Flossie, and a long peppermint cane for Freddie. Then they walked around, down one aisle and up another, admiring the many things which were displayed.

"Bert said they had a lavater," said Freddie presently. "Mamma, I want to go in the lavater."

"Lavater?" repeated Mrs. Bobbsey, with a puzzled look. "Why, Freddie, what do you mean?"

"He means the stairs that runs up and down on a big rope," put in Flossie.

"Oh, the elevator," said the mother. "Very well, you shall both ride in the elevator."

It was great sport to ride to the third story of the store, although the swift way in which the elevator moved made the twins gasp a little.

"Let us go down again," said Freddie. "It's ever so much nicer than climbing the stairs."

"I wish to make a few purchases first," answered the mother.

She had come to buy a rug for the front hallway, and while she was busy in the rug and carpet department she allowed the twins to look at a number of toys which were located at the other end of the floor.

For a while Freddie and Flossie kept close together, for there was quite a crowd present and they felt a little afraid. But then Flossie discovered a counter where all sorts of things for dolls were on sale and she lingered there, to look at the dresses, and hats, and under-wear, and shoes and stockings, and chairs, trunks, combs and brushes, and other goods.

"Oh, my, I must have some of those things for my dolls," she said, half aloud. There was a trunk she thought perfectly lovely and it was marked 39 cents. "Not so very much," she thought.

When Freddie got around to where the elevator was, it was just coming up again with another load of people. As he had not seen it go down he concluded that he must go down by way of the stairs if he wanted another ride.

"I'll get a ride all by myself," he thought, and as quickly as he could, he slipped down first one pair of stairs and then another, to the ground floor of the store. Then he saw another stairs, and soon was in the basement of the department store.

Here was a hardware department with a great number of heavy toys, and soon he was looking at a circular railroad track upon which ran a real locomotive and three cars. This was certainly a wonderful toy, and Freddie could not get his eyes off of it.

In moving around the basement of the store, Freddie grew hopelessly mixed up, and when he started to look for the elevator or the stairs, he walked to the storage room. He was too timid to ask his way out and soon found himself among great rows of boxes and barrels. Then he made a turn or two and found himself in another room, filled with empty boxes and casks, some partly filled with straw and excelsior. There was a big wooden door to this room, and while he was inside the door shut with a bang and the catch fell into place.

"Oh, dear, I wish I was back with mamma," he thought, and drew a long and exceedingly sober breath. "I don't like it here at all."

Just then a little black kitten came toward him and brushed up affectionately. Freddie caught the kitten and sat down for a moment to pet it. He now felt sleepy and in a few minutes his eyes closed and his head began to nod. Then in a minute more he went sound asleep.

Long before this happened Mrs. Bobbsey found Flossie and asked her where Freddie was. The little girl could not tell, and the mother began a diligent search. The floor-walkers in the big store aided her, but it was of no avail. Freddie could not be found, and soon it was time to close up the establishment for the day. Almost frantic with fear, Mrs. Bobbsey telephoned to her husband, telling him of what had occurred and asked him what had best be done.

Chapter X

LOST AND FOUND

When Freddie woke up all was very, very dark around him. At first he thought he was at home, and he called out for somebody to pull up the curtain that he might see.

But nobody answered him, and all he heard was a strange purring, close to his ear. He put up his hand and touched the little black kitten, which was lying close to his face. He had tumbled back in the straw and this had proved a comfortable couch upon which to take a nap.

"Oh, dear me, I'll have to get back to mamma!" he murmured, as he struggled up and rubbed his eyes. "What can make it so awful dark? They ought to light the gas. Nobody can buy things when it's so dark as this."

The darkness did not please him, and he was glad to have the black kitten for a companion. With the kitten in his arms he arose to his feet and walked a few steps. Bump! he went into a big box. Then he went in another direction and stumbled over a barrel.

"Mamma! Mamma!" he cried out. "Mamma, where are you?"

No answer came back to this call, and his own voice sounded so queer to him that he soon stopped. He hugged the kitten tighter than ever.

He was now greatly frightened and it was all he could do to keep back the tears. He knew it must be night and that the great store must be closed up.

"They have all gone home and left me here alone," he thought. "Oh, what shall I do?"

He knew the night was generally very long and he did not wish to remain in the big, lonely building until morning.

Still hugging the kitten, he felt his way around until he reached the big wooden door. The catch came open with ease, and once more he found himself in that part of the basement used for hardware and large mechanical toys. But the toy locomotive had ceased to run and all was very silent. Only a single gas jet flickered overhead, and this cast fantastic shadows which made the little boy think of ghosts and hobgoblins. One mechanical toy had a very large head on it, and this seemed to grin and laugh at him as he looked at it.

"Mamma!" he screamed again. "Oh, mamma, why don't you come?"

He listened and presently he heard footsteps overhead.

"Who's there?" came in the heavy voice of a man.

The voice sounded so unnatural that Freddie was afraid to answer. Perhaps the man might be a burglar come to rob the store.

"I say, who's there?" repeated the voice. "Answer me."

There was a minute of silence, and then Freddie heard the footsteps coming slowly down the stairs. The man had a lantern in one hand and a club in the other.

Not knowing what else to do, Freddie crouched behind a counter. His heart beat loudly, and he had dim visions of burglars who might have entered the big store to rob it. If he was discovered, there was no telling what such burglars might do with him.

"Must have been the cat," murmured the man on the stairs. He reached the basement floor and swung his lantern over his head. "Here, kittie, kittie, kittie!" he called.

"Meow!" came from the black kitten, which was still in Freddie's arms. Then the man looked in that direction.

"Hullo!" he exclaimed, starting in amazement. "What are you doing here? Are you alone?"

"Oh, please, I want my mamma!" cried Freddie.

"You want your mamma?" repeated the man. "Say!" he went on suddenly. "Are you the kid that got lost this afternoon, youngster?"

"I guess I did get lost," answered Freddie. He saw that the man had a kindly face and this made him a bit braver. "I walked around and sat down over there—in the straw—and went to sleep."

"Well, I never!" cried the man. "And have you been down here ever since?"

"Yes, sir. But I don't want to stay—I want to go home."

"All right, you shall go. But this beats me!"

"Are you the man who owns the store?" questioned Freddie curiously.

At this the man laughed. "No; wish I did. I'm the night watchman. Let me see, what is your name?"

"Freddie Bobbsey. My papa owns the lumber yard."

"Oh, yes, I remember now. Well, Freddie, I reckon your papa will soon come after you. All of 'em are about half crazy, wondering what has become of you."

The night watchman led the way to the first floor of the department store and Freddie followed, still clutching the black kitten, which seemed well content to remain with him.

"I'll telephone to your papa," said the watchman, and going into one of the offices he rang the bell and called up the number of the Bobbsey residence.

In the meantime Mrs. Bobbsey and the others of the family were almost frantic with grief and alarm. Mr. Bobbsey had notified the police and the town had been searched thoroughly for some trace of the missing boy.

"Perhaps they have stolen Freddie away!" said Nan, with the tears starting to her eyes. "Some gypsies were in town, telling fortunes. I heard one of the girls at school tell about it."

"Oh, the bad gypsies!" cried Flossie, and gave a shudder. The idea that Freddie might have been carried off by the gypsies was truly terrifying.

Mr. Bobbsey had been out a dozen times to the police headquarters and to the lake front. A report had come in that a boy looking like Freddie had been seen on the ice early in the evening, and he did not know but what the little fellow might have wandered in that direction.

When the telephone bell rang Mr. Bobbsey had just come in from another fruitless search. Both he and his wife ran to the telephone.

"Hullo!" came over the wire. "Is this Mr. Bobbsey's house?"

"It is," answered the gentleman quickly. "What do you want? Have you any news?"

"I've found your little boy, sir," came back the reply. "He is safe and sound with me."

"And who are you?"

"The night watchman at the department store. He went to sleep here, that's all."

At this news all were overjoyed.

"Let me speak to him," said Mrs. Bobbsey eagerly. "Freddie dear, are you there?" she asked.

"Yes, mamma," answered Freddie, into the telephone. "And I want to come home."

"You shall, dear. Papa shall come for you at once."

"Oh, he's found! He's found!" shrieked Nan. "Aren't you glad, Bert?"

"Of course I am," answered Bert. "But I can't understand how he happened to go to sleep in such a lively store as that."

"He must have walked around until he got tired," replied Nan. "You know Freddie can drop off to sleep very quickly when he gets tired."

As soon as possible Mr. Bobbsey drove around to the department store in his sleigh. The watchman and Freddie were on the look-out for him, the little boy with the kitten still in his arms.

"Oh, papa!" cried Freddie. "I am so glad you have come! I—I don't want to go to sleep here again!"

The watchman's story was soon told, and Mr. Bobbsey made him happy by presenting him with a two-dollar bill.

"The little chap would have been even more lonely if it hadn't been for the kitten," said the man. "He wanted to keep the thing, so I told him to do it."

"And I'm going to," said Freddie proudly. "It's just the dearest kitten in the world." And keep the kitten he did. It soon grew to be a big, fat cat and was called Snoop.

By the time home was reached, Freddie was sleepy again. But he speedily woke up when his mamma and the others embraced him, and then he had to tell the story of his adventure from end to end.

"I do not know as I shall take you with me again," said Mrs. Bobbsey. "You have given us all a great scare."

"Oh, mamma, I won't leave you like that again," cried Freddie quickly. "Don't like to be in the dark 'tall," he added.

"Oh, it must have been awful," said Flossie. "Didn't you see any— any ghosts?"

"Barrels of them," said Freddie, nodding his head sleepily. "But they didn't touch me. Guess they was sleepy, just like me." And then he dropped off and had to be put to bed; and that was the end of this strange happening.

Chapter XI

THE CRUISE OF THE "ICE BIRD"

The building of the ice boat by Bert and Charley Mason interested Nan almost as much as it did the boys, and nearly every afternoon she went down to the lumber yard to see how the work was getting along.

Mr. Bobbsey had given Bert just the right kind of lumber, and had a man at the saw-mill saw the sticks and boards to a proper size. He also gave his son some ropes and a pair of old iron runners from a discarded sleigh, so that all Charley had to provide was the bed-sheet already mentioned, for a sail.

The two boys worked with a will, and by Thursday evening had the ice boat completed. They christened the craft the *Ice Bird*, and

Bert insisted upon it that his father come and see her.

"You have certainly done very well," said Mr. Bobbsey. "This looks as if you were cut out for a builder, Bert."

"Well, I'd like to build big houses and ships first-rate," answered Bert.

The sail was rigged with the help of an old sailor who lived down by the lake shore, and on Friday afternoon Bert and Charley took a short trip. The *Ice Bird* behaved handsomely, much to the boys' satisfaction.

"She's a dandy!" cried Bert. "How she can whiz before the wind."

"You must take me out soon," said Nan.

"I will," answered Bert.

The chance to go out with Bert came sooner than expected. On Monday morning Mrs. Mason made up her mind to pay a distant relative a visit and asked Charley if he wished to go along. The boy wanted to see his cousins very much and said yes; and thus the ice boat was left in Bert's sole charge.

"I'll take you out Monday afternoon, after school," said Bert to his twin sister.

"Good!" cried Nan. "Let us go directly school is out, so as to have some good, long rides."

Four o'clock in the afternoon found them at the lake shore. It was a cloudy day with a fair breeze blowing across the lake.

"Now you sit right there," said Bert, as he pointed to a seat in the back of the boat. "And hold on tight or you'll be thrown overboard."

Nan took the seat mentioned, and her twin brother began to hoist the mainsail of the *Ice Bird*. It ran up easily, and caught by the wind the craft began to skim over the surface of the lake like a thing of life.

"Oh, but this is lovely!" cried Nan gleefully. "How fast the boat spins along!"

"I wish there were more ice boats around," answered Bert. "We might then have a race."

"Oh, it is pleasure enough just to sail around," said Nan.

Many other boys and girls wished a ride on the ice boat, and in the end Bert carried a dozen or more across the lake and back. It was rather hard work tacking against the wind, but the old sailor had taught him how it might be done, and he got along fairly well. When the ice boat got stuck all the boys and girls got off and helped push the craft along.

"It is 'most supper time," said Nan, as the whistle at the saw-mill blew for six o'clock. "We'll have to go home soon, Bert."

"Oh, let us take one more trip," pleaded her twin brother.

The other boys and girls had gone and they were left alone. To please Bert, Nan consented, and their course was changed so that the *Ice Bird* might move down the lake instead of across.

It had grown dark and the stars which might have shone in the sky were hidden by heavy clouds.

"Not too far now, remember," said Nan.

The wind had veered around and was blowing directly down the lake, so, almost before they knew it, the *Ice Bird* was flying along at a tremendous rate of speed. Nan had to hold on tight for fear of falling off, and had to hold her hat, too, for fear that would be blown away.

"Oh, Bert, this is too fast!" she gasped, catching her breath.

"It's just glorious, Nan!" he cried. "Just hold on, it won't hurt you."

"But—but how are we to get back?"

Bert had not thought of that, and at the question his face fell a little.

"Oh, we'll get back somehow," he said evasively.

"You had better turn around now."

"Let us go just a little bit further, Nan," he pleaded.

When at last he started to turn back he found himself unable to do so. The wind was blowing fiercely and the *Ice Bird* swept on before it in spite of all he could do.

"Bert! Bert! Oh, why don't you turn around?" screamed Nan. She had to scream in order to make herself heard.

"I—I can't," he faltered. "She won't come around."

Nan was very much frightened, and it must be confessed that Bert was frightened too. He hauled on the sail and on the steering gear, and at last the *Ice Bird* swung partly around. But instead of returning up the lake the craft headed for the western shore, and in a few minutes they struck some lumpy ice and some snow and dirt, and both were thrown out at full length, while the *Ice Bird* was tipped up on one side.

Bert picked himself up without difficulty and then went to Nan's aid. She lay deep in the snow, but fortunately was not hurt. Both gazed at the tipped-up ice boat in very great dismay.

"Bert, whatever shall we do now?" asked Nan, after a spell of silence. "We'll never get home at all!"

"Oh, yes, we shall," he said, bravely enough, but with a sinking
heart. "We've got to get home, you know."

"But the ice boat is upset, and it's so dark I can't see a thing."

"I think I can right the ice boat. Anyway, I can try."

Doing his best to appear brave, Bert tried to shove the *Ice Bird*
over to her original position. But the craft was too heavy for him, and
twice she fell back, the second time coming close to smashing his toes.

"Look out, or you'll hurt your foot," cried Nan. "Let me help you."

Between them they presently got the craft right side up. But now
the wind was blowing directly from the lake, so to get the *Ice Bird* out
on the ice again was beyond them. Every time they shoved the craft
out the wind drove her back.

"Oh, dear, I guess we have got to stay here after all!" sighed Bert,
at last.

"Not stay here all night, I hope!" gasped Nan. "That would be
worse than to stay in the store, as Freddie did."

It began to snow. At first the flakes were but few, but soon they
came down thicker and thicker, blotting out the already darkened
landscape.

"Let us walk home," suggested Nan. "That will be better than
staying out here in the snow storm."

"It's a long walk. If only we had brought our skates." But alas!
neither had thought to bring skates, and both pairs were in the office
at the lumber yard.

"I don't think we had better walk home over the ice," said Bert,
after another pause. "We may get all turned around and lost. Let us
walk over to the Hopedale road."

"I wish we had some crullers, or something," said Nan, who was
growing hungry. They had each had a cruller on leaving home, but
had eaten them up before embarking on the ice-boat voyage.

"Please don't speak of them, Nan. You make me feel awfully hollow," came from her twin brother. And the way he said this was so
comical it made her laugh in spite of her trouble.

The laugh put them both in better spirits, and leaving the *Ice Bird*
where she lay, they set off through the snow in the direction of the road

which ran from Lakeport to the village of Hopedale, six miles away.

"It will take us over an hour to get home," said Nan.

"Yes, and I suppose we'll catch it for being late," grumbled Bert. "Perhaps we won't get any supper."

"Oh, I know mamma won't scold us after she finds out why we were late, Bert."

They had to cross a pasture and climb a fence before the road was reached. Here was an old cow-shed and they stood in the shelter of this for a moment, out of the way of the wind and driving snow.

"Hark!" cried Bert as they were on the point of continuing their journey.

"It's a dog!" answered Nan. "Oh, Bert, he is coming this way. Perhaps he is savage!"

They listened and could hear the dog plainly. He was barking furiously and coming toward them as fast as he could travel. Soon they made out his black form looming into view through the falling snow.

Chapter XII

Tige—Playing Theater

Nan dearly loved the dogs with which she was well acquainted, but she was in great terror of strange animals, especially if they barked loudly and showed a disposition to bite.

"Bert! Bert! what shall we do?" she gasped as she clung to her twin brother's arm.

Bert hardly knew what to say, for he himself did not like a biting dog. He looked around for a stick or a stone, and espied the doorway to the cow-shed. It was open.

"Let us get into the shed," he said quickly. "Perhaps we can close the door and keep the dog out."

Into the shed sprang Nan and her twin brother after her. The dog was almost upon them when Bert banged the door in his face. At once the animal stopped short and began to bark more furiously than ever.

"Do you—you think he can get in at the window?" faltered Nan. She was so scared she could scarcely speak.

"I don't know, I'm sure. If you'll stand by the door, Nan, I'll try to guard the window."

Nan threw her form against the door and held it as hard as if a giant were outside trying to force it in. Bert felt around the empty shed and picked up the handle of a broken spade. With this in hand he stalked over to the one little window which was opposite the door.

"Are there any cows here?" asked Nan. It was so dark she could see next to nothing.

"No cows here, I guess," answered Bert. "This building is 'most ready to tumble down."

The dog outside was barking still. Once in a while he would stop to catch his breath and then he would continue as loudly as ever. He scratched at the door with his paw, which made Nan shiver from head to feet.

"He is trying to work his way in," she cried.

"If he does that, I'll hit him with this," answered her twin brother, and brandished the spade handle over his head. He watched the window closely and wondered what they had best do if the dog leaped straight through and attacked them in the dark.

The barking continued for over quarter of an hour. To Nan and Bert it seemed hours and hours. Then came a call from a distance.

"Hi, Tige, what's the matter? Have you spotted a tramp in the shed?"

"Help! help!" called out Bert. "Call off your dog!"

"A tramp, sure enough," said the man who was coming toward the cow-shed.

"I am not a tramp," answered Bert. "And my sister isn't a tramp, either."

"What's that? You've got your sister with you? Open the door."

"Please, we are afraid of the dog," came from Nan. "He came after us and we ran into the shed for shelter."

"Oh, that's it?" The farmer gave a short laugh. "Well, you needn't be skeert! Tige won't hurt ye none."

"Are you sure of that?" put in Bert. "He seems to be very savage."

"I won't let him touch ye."

Thus assured Nan opened the door and followed Bert outside. At a word from the farmer Tige stopped barking and began to wag his tail.

"That dog wouldn't hurt nobody, 'ceptin' he was attacked, or if a person tried to git in my house," said Farmer Sandborn. "He's a very nice fellow, he is, and likes boys and gals fust-rate; don't ye, Tige?" And the dog wagged his tail harder than ever, as if he understood every word.

"I—I was so scared," said Nan.

"May I ask what you be a-doin' on the road all alone and in this snowstorm?"

"We are going home," answered Bert, and then explained how they had been ice-boating and what had happened on the lake.

"I do declare!" cried Farmer Sandborn. "So the boat up an' run away with ye, did she? Contrary critter, eh!" And he began to laugh. "Who be you?"

"I am Bert Bobbsey and this is my twin sister Nan."

"Oh, yes, I know now. You're one pair o' the Bobbsey twins, as they call 'em over to Lakeport. I've heard Sary speak o' ye. Sary's my wife." The farmer ran his hand through his thick beard. "You can't tramp home in this storm."

"Oh, we must get home," said Nan. "What will mamma say? She will think we are killed, or drowned, or something,—and she isn't over the scare she got when Freddie was lost."

"I'll take you back to town in my sleigh," said Farmer Sandborn. "I was going to town for some groceries to-morrow morning, but I might just as well go now, while the roads are open. They'll be all closed up ag'in by daylight, if this storm keeps up."

He led the way down the road to his house and they were glad enough to follow. By Nan's side walked Tige and he licked her hand, just to show that he wanted to make friends with her.

"I guess you are a good dog after all," said she, patting his head. "But you did give me *such* a scare!"

Both of the twins were very cold and glad enough to warm themselves by the kitchen fire while the farmer hitched up his horse. The farmer's wife wished to give them supper, but this they declined, saying they would get supper at home. But she made each eat a big cookie, which tasted exceedingly good.

Soon Farmer Sandborn drove around to the door with his sleigh and in they piled, on the soft straw, with several robes to keep them warm. Then the horse set off on a brisk trot for town.

"It's a nice enough sleigh ride for anybody," declared Bert. And yet they did not enjoy it very much, for fear of what would happen to them when they got home.

"Where in the world have you been?" exclaimed Mrs. Bobbsey as she ran to the door to let them in. "We have been looking all over for you. Your papa was afraid you had been drowned in the lake."

An evening dinner was in waiting for them, and sitting down to satisfy their hunger, they told their story, to which all of the others listened with much interest.

"You can be thankful you weren't blown clear to the other end of the lake," said Mr. Bobbsey. "I think after this you had better leave ice-boating alone."

"I know I shall!" declared Nan.

"Oh, I'll be more careful, papa, after this," pleaded Bert. "You know I promised to go out again with Charley."

"Well then, don't go when the wind is strong," and Bert promised.

"I'm so glad the dog didn't bite you," said little Flossie. "He might have given you hy—hydropics."

"Flossie means hydrophobics," put in Freddie. "Ain't no hydropics, is there, Bert?"

"Oh, Freddie, you mean hydrophobia!" burst out Nan, with a laugh.

"No, I mean hydrophobics," insisted the little fellow. "That's what Dinah calls them anyway."

After the adventure on the ice boat matters ran smoothly with the Bobbsey twins for two weeks and more. There was a great deal of snow and as a consequence Freddie and Flossie stayed home from school most of the time. Nan and Bert also remained home two separate days, and during those days all of the children had great fun in the attic, where there was a large storeroom, filled with all sort of things.

"Let us play theater," said Nan, who had been to several exhibitions while at home and while visiting.

"All right," said Bert, falling in with the plan at once. "Let us play Rip Van Winkle. I can be Rip and you can be the loving wife, and Flossie and Freddie can be the children."

Across the storeroom a rope was placed and on this they hung a sliding curtain, made out of a discarded blanket. Then at one side they arranged chairs, and Nan and Flossie brought out their dolls to be the audience.

"They won't clap their hands very much," said Bert. "But then they won't make any disturbance either."

The performance was a great success. It was their own version of Rip Van Winkle, and Bert as old Rip did many funny things which caused Freddie and Flossie to roar with laughter. Nan as the loving wife recited a piece called "Doughnuts and Daisies," pretending to be working around the kitchen in the meantime. The climax was reached when Bert tried to imitate a thunderstorm in the mountains and pulled over a big trunk full of old clothes and some window screens standing in a corner. The show broke up in a hurry, and when Mrs. Bobbsey appeared on the scene, wanting to know what the noise meant, all the actors and the doll audience were out of sight.

But later, when mamma went below again, Bert and Nan sneaked back, and put both the trunk and the screens in their proper places.

Chapter XIII

NAN'S FIRST CAKE-BAKING

"Let's!" cried Nan.

"Yes, let's!" echoed Flossie.

"I want to help too," put in Freddie, "Want to make a cake all by my own self."

"Freddie can make a little cake while we make a big one," said Bert.

It was on an afternoon just a week before Christmas and Mrs. Bobbsey had gone out to do some shopping. Dinah was also away, on a visit to some relatives, so the children had the house all to themselves.

It was Bert who spoke about cake-making first. Queer that a boy should think of it, wasn't it? But Bert was very fond of cake, and did quite some grumbling when none was to be had.

"It ought to be easy to make a nice big plain cake," said Bert. "I've seen Dinah do it lots of times. She just mixes up her milk and eggs and butter, and sifts in the flour, and there you are."

"Much you know about it!" declared Nan. "If it isn't just put together right, it will be as heavy as lead."

"We might take the recipe out of mamma's cook-book," went on Bert; and then the cry went up with which I have opened this chapter.

The twins were soon in the kitchen, which Dinah had left spotlessly clean and in perfect order.

"We mustn't make a muss," warned Nan. "If we do, Dinah will never forgive us."

"As if we couldn't clean it up again," said Bert loftily.

Over the kitchen table they spread some old newspapers, and then Nan brought forth the big bowl in which her mother or the cook usually mixed the cake batter.

"Bert, you get the milk and sugar," said Nan, and began to roll up her sleeves. "Flossie, you can get the butter."

She would have told Freddie to get something, too—just to start them all to work—but Freddie was out of sight.

He had gone into the pantry, where the flour barrel stood. He did not know that Nan intended to use the prepared flour, which was on the shelf. The door worked on a spring, so it closed behind him, shutting him out from the sight of the others.

Taking off the cover of the barrel, Freddie looked inside. The barrel was almost empty, only a few inches of flour remaining at the bottom. There was a flour scoop in the barrel, but he could reach neither this nor the flour itself.

"I'll have to stand on the bench," he said to himself and pulled the bench into position. Then he stood on it and bent down into the barrel as far as possible.

The others were working in the kitchen when they heard a strange *thump* and then a spluttering yell.

"It's Freddie," said Nan. "Bert, go and see what he is doing in the pantry."

Bert ran to the pantry door and pulled it open. A strange sight met his gaze. Out of the top of the barred stuck Freddie's legs, with a cloud of flour dust rising around them. From the bottom of the barrel came a succession of coughs, sneezes, and yells for help.

"Freddie has fallen into the flour barrel!" he cried, and lost no time in catching his brother by the feet and pulling him out. It was hard work and in the midst of it the flour barrel fell over on its side, scattering the flour over the pantry and partly on the kitchen floor.

"Oh! oh! oh!" roared Freddie as soon as he could catch his breath. "Oh, my! oh, my!"

"Oh, Freddie, why did you go into the barrel?" exclaimed Nan, wiping off her hands and running to him. "Did you ever see such a sight before?"

Freddie was digging at the flour in his eyes. He was white from head to feet, and coughing and spluttering.

"Wait, I'll get the whisk-broom," said Bert, and ran for it.

"Brush off his hair first, and then I'll wipe his face," came from Nan.

"Here's the wash-rag," put in little Flossie, and catching it up, wringing wet, she began to wipe off Freddie's face before anybody could stop her.

"Flossie! Flossie! You mustn't do that!" said Bert. "Don't you see you are making paste of the flour?"

The wet flour speedily became a dough on Freddie's face and neck, and he yelled louder than ever. The wash-rag was put away, and regardless of her own clean clothes, Flossie started in to scrape the dough off, until both Nan and Bert made her stop.

"I'll dust him good first," said Bert, and began such a vigorous use of the whisk-broom that everybody began to sneeze.

"Oh, Bert, not so hard!" said Nan, and ran to open the back door. "Bring him here."

Poor Freddie had a lump of dough in his left ear and was trying in vain to get it out with one hand while rubbing his eyes with the other. Nan brushed his face with care, and even wiped off the end of his tongue, and got the lump out of his ear. In the meantime Flossie started to set the flour barrel up once more.

"Don't touch the barrel, Flossie!" called Bert. "You keep away, or you'll be as dirty as Freddie."

It was very hard work to get Freddie's clothes even half clean, and some of the flour refused to budge from his hair. By the time he was made half presentable once more the kitchen was in a mess from end to end.

"What were you doing near the flour barrel?" asked Nan.

"Going to get flour for the cake."

"But we don't want that kind of flour, Freddie. We want this," and she brought forth the package.

"Dinah uses this," answered the little boy.

"Yes, for bread. But we are not going to make bread. You had better sit down and watch Bert and me work, and you, Flossie, had better do the same."

"Ain't no chairs to sit down on," said Freddie, after a look around. "All full of flour."

"I declare, we forgot to dust the chairs," answered Nan. "Bert, will you clean them?"

Bert did so, and Freddie and Flossie sat down to watch the process of cake-making, being assured that they should have the first slices if the cake was a success.

Nan had watched cake-making many times, so she knew exactly how to go to work. Bert was a good helper, and soon the batter was ready for the oven. The fire had been started up, and now Nan put the batter in the cake tin.

The children waited impatiently while the cake was baking. Nan gave Freddie another cleaning, and Bert cleaned up the pantry and the kitchen floor. The flour had made a dreadful mess and the cleaning process was only half-successful.

"'Most time for that cake to be done, isn't it?" questioned Bert, after a quarter of an hour had passed.

"Not quite," answered Nan.

Presently she opened the oven door and tried the cake by sticking a broom whisp into it. The flour was just a bit sticky and she left the cake in a little longer.

When it came out it certainly looked very nice. The top was a golden brown and had raised beautifully. The cake was about a foot in diameter and Nan was justly proud of it.

"Wished you had put raisins in it," said Freddie. "Raisins are beautiful."

"No, I like plain cake the best," said Bert.

"I like chocolate," came from Flossie.

"And I like layer cake, with currant jelly in between," said Nan. "But I didn't dare to open any jelly without asking mamma."

"Let us surprise her with the cake," said Bert.

"Want cake now," protested Freddie. "Don't want to wait 't all!"

But he was persuaded to wait, and the cake was hidden away in the dining-room closet until the hour for the evening meal.

When Dinah came home she noticed the mussed-up kitchen, but Nan begged of her to keep quiet.

"All right, honey," said the colored cook. "But I know youse been a-bakin'—I kin spell it in de air."

When they sat down to the evening meal all of the children produced the cake in great triumph.

"Oh, Nan, a real cake!" cried Mrs. Bobbsey. "How nice it looks!"

"We've got some real housekeepers around here," said Mr. Bobbsey. "I'll have to try that sure."

When the cake was cut all ate liberally of it. They declared it just right and said it could not be better. Even Dinah was tickled.

"Couldn't do no better maself," she declared. "Bymeby Dinah will be cut out of a job—wid Miss Nan a-doin' ob de bakin'."

"No, Dinah, you shall stay even if I do do the baking," answered Nan; and went to bed feeling very happy.

Chapter XIV

CHRISTMAS

As the time for Christmas drew shorter all of the Bobbsey children wondered what Santa Claus would bring them and what they would receive from their relatives at a distance.

Freddie and Flossie had made out long lists of the things they hoped to get. Freddie wished a fireman's suit with a real trumpet, a railroad track with a locomotive that could go, and some building blocks and picture books. Flossie craved more dolls and dolls' dresses, a real trunk with a lock, fancy slippers, a pair of rubber boots, and some big card games.

"All I want is a set of furs," said Nan, not once but many times. "A beautiful brown set, just like mamma's."

"And all I want is some good story books, some games, a new pocket-knife, a big wagon, and some money," said Bert.

"Mercy, you don't want much, Bert," cried Nan. "How much money—a thousand dollars?"

"I want money, too," piped in Freddie. "Want to start a bank account just like papa's."

By dint of hard saving Bert and Nan had accumulated two dollars and ten cents between them, while Freddie and Flossie had each thirty-five cents. There was a wonderful lot of planning between the twins, and all put their money together, to buy papa and mamma and Dinah and Sam some Christmas presents. Freddie and Flossie had not yet purchased the cologne and handkerchief before mentioned, and now it was decided to get Mr. Bobbsey a new cravat, Mrs. Bobbsey a flower in a pot, Dinah a fancy apron, and Sam a pair of gloves. Nan and Bert made the purchases which, after being duly inspected by all, were hidden away in the garret storeroom.

As the time for Christmas came on Flossie and Freddie grew very anxious, wanting to know if Santa Claus would be sure to come. Flossie inspected the chimney several times.

"It's a dreadfully small place and very dirty," said she. "I am afraid Santa Claus won't be able to get down with a very big load. And some of his things will get all mussed up."

"Santa Claus can spirit himself wherever he wants to, dear," said Mrs. Bobbsey, with a quiet smile.

"What do you mean by *spirit* himself, mamma?"

"Never mind now, Flossie; you'll understand that when you grow older."

"Does mamma mean a ghost?" asked Flossie, later on, of Nan.

"No, Flossie; she means the part of a person that lives but can't be seen."

"Oh, I know," cried the child, brightening. "It's just like when a person is good. Then they say it's the *spirit* of goodness within him. I guess it's the good spirit of Santa Claus that can't be seen. But we can feel it, can't we? and that's what's best."

On the day before Christmas the sitting-room door was closed and locked, so that none of the children might enter the room. Freddie was very anxious to look through the keyhole, but Bert told him that wouldn't be fair, so he stayed away.

"We are to hang up our stockings to-night," said Nan. "And

mamma says we must go to bed early, too."

"That's to give Santa Claus a chance to get around," said Freddie. "Papa said so. He said Santa Claus had his hands more than full, with so many boys and girls all over the world to take care of."

"Santa Claus must be a twin, just like you and me," said Flossie. "Maybe he's a twin a hundred times over."

At this Freddie roared. "What a funny twin that would be—with each one having the same name!"

The stockings were hung up with great care, and Freddie and Flossie made up their minds to stay awake and watch Santa Claus at his work.

"Won't say a word when he comes," said the little boy. "Just peek out at him from under the covers." But alas! long before Santa Claus paid his visit that Christmas Eve both Freddie and Flossie were in dreamland, and so were Bert and Nan.

It was Flossie who was the first awake in the morning. For the moment after she opened her eyes and sat up she could not remember why she had awakened thus early. But it was for some reason, she was sure of that.

"Merry Christmas!" she burst out, all at once, and the cry awoke Freddie. "Merry Christmas!" he repeated. "Merry Christmas, ev'rybody!" he roared out, at the top of his lungs.

The last call awoke Nan and Bert, and before long all were scrambling out to see what the stockings might contain.

"Oh, I've got a doll!" shrieked Flossie, and brought forth a wonderful affair of paper.

"I have a jumping-jack!" came from Freddie, and he began to work the toy up and down in a most comical fashion.

There was some small gift for everybody and several apples and oranges besides, and quantities of nuts in the stockings.

"We must get the presents for the others," whispered Nan to Bert and the smaller twins, and soon all were dressed and bringing the things down from the storeroom.

It was a happy party that gathered in the dining room. "Merry Christmas!" said everybody to everybody else, and then Mr. Bobbsey, who was in the sitting room, blew a horn and opened the folding doors.

There, on a large side stand, rested a beautiful Christmas tree, loaded down with pretty ornaments and apples and candies, and with many prettily colored candles. Around the bottom of the tree were four heaps of presents, one for each of the children.

"Oh, look at the big doll!" screamed Flossie, and caught the present up in her arms and kissed it.

"And look at my fireman's suit!" roared Freddie, and then, seeing a trumpet, he took it up and bellowed: "Bring up the engine! Play away lively there!" just like a real fireman.

Bert had his books and other things, and under them was hidden a real bank book, showing that there had been deposited to his credit ten dollars in the Lakeport Savings Bank. Nan had a similar bank book, and of these the twins were very, very proud. Bert felt as if he was truly getting to be quite a business man.

"Oh! oh!" cried Nan, as she opened a big box that was at the bottom of her pile of presents, and then the tears of joy stood in her eyes as she brought forth the hoped-for set of furs. They were beautiful, and so soft she could not resist brushing them against her cheek over and over again.

"Oh, mamma, I think they are too lovely for anything!" she said, rushing up and kissing her parent. "I am sure no girl ever had such a nice set of furs before!"

"You must try to keep them nice, Nan," answered the mother.

"I shall take the very best of care of them," said Nan, and my readers may be sure that she did.

"And now we have something for you, too," said Bert, and brought out the various articles. Flossie gave their mamma her present, and Freddie gave papa what was coming to him. Then Nan gave Dinah the fancy apron and Bert took Sam the new gloves.

"Well this is truly a surprise!" cried Mr. Bobbsey, as he inspected the cravat. "It is just what I need."

"And this flower is beautiful," said Mrs. Bobbsey as she smelt of the potted plant. "It will bloom a long while, I am sure."

Dinah was tickled over the apron and Sam with his gloves.

"Yo' chillun am the sweetest in de world," said the cook.

"Dem globes am de werry t'ing I needed to keep ma hands warm," came from Sam.

It was fully an hour before the children felt like sitting down to breakfast. Before they began the repast Mr. Bobbsey brought forth the family Bible and read the wonderful story of Christ's birth to them, and asked the blessing. All were almost too excited to eat.

After breakfast all must go out and show their presents to their friends and see what the friends had received. It was truly a happy time. Then all went coasting until lunch.

"The expressman is coming!" cried Bert a little later, and sure enough he drove up to the Bobbsey house with two boxes. One was from their Uncle Daniel Bobbsey, who lived at Meadow Brook, and the other from their Uncle William Minturn, who lived at Ocean Cliff.

"More presents!" cried Nan, and she was right. Uncles and aunts had sent each something; and the twins were made happier than ever.

"Oh, but Christmas is just the best day in the whole year," said Bert that evening, after the eventful day was over.

"Wish Christmas would come ev'ry week," said Freddie. "Wouldn't it be *beautiful?*"

"If it did I'm afraid the presents wouldn't reach," said Mrs. Bobbsey, and then took him and Flossie off to bed.

Chapter XV

THE CHILDREN'S PARTY

The little black kitten that Freddie had brought home from the department store was a great friend to everybody in the Bobbsey house and all loved the little creature very much.

At first Freddie started to call the kitten Blackie, but Flossie said that wasn't a very "'ristocratic" name at all.

"I'll tell you what," said Bert jokingly, "Let's call him Snoop," and in spite of all efforts to make the name something else Snoop the cat remained from that time to the day of his death.

He grew very fat and just a trifle lazy, nevertheless he learned to do several tricks. He could sit up in a corner on his hind legs, and shake hands, and when told to do so would jump through one's arms, even if the arms were quite high up from the floor.

Snoop had one comical trick that always made both Flossie and Freddie laugh. There was running water in the kitchen, and Snoop loved to sit on the edge of the sink and play with the drops as they fell from the bottom of the faucet. He would watch until a drop was just falling, then reach out with his paw and give it a claw just as if he was reaching for a mouse.

Another trick he had, but this Mrs. Bobbsey did not think so nice, was to curl himself on the pillow of one of the beds and go sound asleep. Whenever he heard Mrs. Bobbsey coming up one pair of stairs, he would fly off the bed and sneak down the other pair, so that she caught him but rarely.

Snoop was a very clean cat and was continually washing his face and his ears. Around his neck Flossie placed a blue ribbon, and it was amusing to see Snoop try to wash it off. But after a while, having spoilt several ribbons, he found they would not wash off, and so he let them alone, and in the end appeared very proud of them.

One day, when Snoop had been in the house but a few months, he could not be found anywhere.

"Snoop! Snoop!" called Freddie, upstairs and down, but the kitten did not answer, nor did he show himself. Then Flossie called him and made a search, but was equally unsuccessful.

"Perhaps somebody has stolen him," said Freddie soberly.

"Nobody been heah to steal dat kitten," answered Dinah. "He's jess sneaked off, dat's all."

All of the children had been invited to a party that afternoon and Nan was going to wear her new set of furs. After having her hair brushed, and putting on a white dress, Nan went to the closet in which her furs were kept in the big box.

"Well, I never!" she ejaculated. "Oh, Snoop! however could you do it!"

For there, curled up on the set of furs, was the kitten, purring as contentedly as could be. Never before had he found a bed so soft or so to his liking. But Nan made him rouse up in a hurry, and after that when she closed the closet she made quite sure that Snoop was not inside.

The party to be held that afternoon was at the home of Grace Lavine, the little girl who had fainted from so much rope jumping. Grace was over that attack, and was now quite certain that when her mamma told her to do a thing or to leave it alone, it was always for her own good.

"Mamma knows best," she said to Nan. "I didn't think so then, but I do now."

The party was a grand affair and over thirty young people were present, all dressed in their best. They played all sorts of games such as many of my readers must already know, and then some new games which the big boys and girls introduced.

One game was called Hunt the Beans. A handful of dried beans was hidden all over the rooms, in out-of-the-way corners, behind the piano, in vases, and like that, and at the signal to start every girl and boy started to pick up as many as could be found. The search lasted just five minutes, and at the end of that time the one having the most beans won the game.

"Now let us play Three-word Letters," said Nan. And then she explained the game. "I will call out a letter and you must try to think of a sentence of three words, each word starting with that letter. Now then, are you ready?"

"Yes! yes!" the girls and boys cried.

"B," said Nan.

There was a second of silence.

"Boston Baked Beans!" shouted Charley Mason.

"That is right, Charley. Now it is your turn to give a letter."

"F," said Charley.

"Five Fat Fairies!" cried Nellie Parks.

"Four Fresh Fish," put in another of the girls.

"Nellie has it," said Charley. "But I never heard of fat fairies, did you?" and this question made everybody laugh.

"My letter is M," said Nellie, after a pause.

"More Minced Mushrooms," said Bert.

"More Mean Men," said another boy.

"Mind My Mule," said one of the girls.

"Oh, Helen, I didn't know you had a mule," cried Flossie, and this caused a wild shriek of laughter.

"Bert must love mushrooms," said Nellie.

"I do," said Bert, "if they are in a sauce." And then the game went on, until somebody suggested something else.

AT SEVEN O'CLOCK A SUPPER WAS SERVED.

At seven o'clock a supper was served. The tables were two in number, with the little girls and boys at one and the big girls and boys at the other. Each was decked out with flowers and with colored streamers, which ran down from the chandelier to each corner of both tables.

There was a host of good things to eat and drink—chicken sandwiches and cake, with cups of sweet chocolate, or lemonade, and then more cake and ice-cream, and fruit, nuts, and candy. The ice-cream was done up into various fancy forms, and Freddie got a fireman, with a trumpet under his arm, and Nan a Japanese lady with a real paper parasol over her head. Bert was served with an automobile, and Flossie cried with delight when she received a brown-and-white cow that looked as natural as life. All of the forms were so pleasing that the children did not care to eat them until the heat in the lighted dining room made them begin to melt away.

"I'm going to tell Dinah about the ice-cream cow," said Flossie. "Perhaps she can make them." But when appealed to, the cook said they were beyond her, and must be purchased from the professional ice-cream maker, who had the necessary forms.

There were dishes full of bonbons on the tables, and soon the bonbons were snapping at a lively rate among the big girls and boys, although the younger folks were rather afraid of them. Each bonbon had a motto paper in it and some sort of fancy article made of paper. Bert got an apron, which he promptly pinned on, much to the amusement of the girls. Nan drew a workman's cap and put it on, and this caused another laugh. There were all sorts of caps, hats, and aprons, and one big bonbon, which went to Flossie, had a complete dress in it, of pink and white paper. Another had some artificial flowers, and still another a tiny bottle of cologne.

While the supper was going on, Mr. Lavine had darkened the parlor and stretched a sheet over the folding doors, and as soon as the young people were through eating they were treated to a magic-lantern exhibition by the gentleman of the house and one of the big boys, who assisted him. There were all sorts of scenes, including some which were very funny and made the boys and girls shriek with laughter. One was a boy on a donkey, and another two fat men trying to climb over a fence. Then came a number of pictures made from photograph negatives, showing scenes in and around Lakeport. There were the lake steamer, and the main street, and one picture of the girls and boys rushing out of school at dinner time. The last was voted the best of all, and many present tried to pick themselves out of this picture and did so.

After the exhibition was over one of the largest of the girls sat down to the piano and played. By this time some of the older folks drifted in, and they called for some singing, and all joined in half a dozen songs that were familiar to them. Then the young folks ran off for their coats and caps and wraps, and bid their host and hostess and each other good-night.

"Wasn't it splendid?" said Nan, on the way home. "I never had such a good time before."

"Didn't last half long enough," said Freddie. "Want it to last longer next time."

"I wanted my cow to last longer," said Flossie. "Oh, if only I could have kept it from melting!"

Chapter XVI

A GRAND SLEIGH RIDE

For a long while all of the Bobbsey children had been begging their parents for a sleigh ride into the country.

"The winter will be gone soon, papa," said Nan. "Won't you take us before the snow is all gone?"

"You may as well take them, Richard," said Mrs. Bobbsey.

"Well, if I do, Mary, you must go along," answered Mr. Bobbsey, and so it was arranged that they should take the ride on the following Saturday, weather permitting.

You may well suppose that all of the twins were very anxious about the weather after that, for Mr. Bobbsey said he would not go if it rained or if it snowed very hard.

"What does it say in the newspapers?" asked Freddie. "They always know what the weather is going to be."

"Not so far ahead as that," answered his brother.

But Friday evening the paper said cold and clear, and sure enough, on Saturday morning it was as nice as one would wish. From behind masses of thin clouds the sun peeped shyly, lighting up the snow until it shone like huge beds of diamonds.

They were to drive to Dalton, twelve miles away. Mr. Bobbsey had learned that the road to Dalton was in good condition, and the family had friends there who would be pleased to see them and have them remain to dinner.

By half-past nine the big family sleigh was at the door, with Sam on the front seat, driving. Into the sleigh piled the four children, and Mr. and Mrs. Bobbsey followed.

"Want to sit by Sam and help drive," said Freddie, and he was lifted over to the desired position. Then off they went, with a crack of the whip and jingling of sleigh-bells that could be heard a long distance.

"Oh, but isn't this just too splendid for anything!" exclaimed Nan, who sat at one side of the seat, with her mamma on the other and Flossie between them. "I do love sleigh riding so much!"

"See me drive!" cried Freddie, who held the very end of the reins, the part dangling from Sam's hands.

"Well, Freddie, don't let the team run away," said Mr. Bobbsey, with a laugh.

"I shan't," answered the little fellow soberly. "If they try to run away, I'll whip them good."

"You'll never stop them that way," said Bert. "You want to talk gently to them."

On and on they went, over the smooth snow. The horses were fresh and full of spirit, and mile after mile was passed with a speed that pleased all of the twins very much. They passed several other sleighing parties, and every time this was done the children set up a merry shout which was sure to call forth an equally merry answer.

A large part of the ride was through the country, and often the country folks would come to the doors to see them pass. Once they met a boy on the road and he asked for a ride to his home, half a mile away.

"Yes, jump in," said Mr. Bobbsey, and the boy got in and was taken to his house almost before he knew it.

"Much obliged," he said on leaving them. "You're fine people, you are," and he took off his hat at parting.

"It was nice to give him a ride," said Nan. "It didn't cost us anything and he liked it a great deal, I am sure."

"We must never forget to do a kindness when we can, Nan," said her mamma.

Before noon Dalton was reached and they drove up to the home of Mr. Ramdell, as their friend was named. Immediately Bob Ramdell, a youth of sixteen, rushed eagerly out to greet Bert.

"I'm glad you've come," he cried. "I've been watching for you for an hour."

"It isn't noon yet," answered Bert.

All were soon into the house and Sam drove the sleigh around to the barn. Bob Ramdell had a sister Susie, who was almost Nan's age, and a baby brother called Tootsie, although his real name was Alexander. Susie was glad to see Nan and Flossie, and all were soon playing with the baby, who was just old enough to be amusing.

"I've got a plan on hand," whispered Bob to Bert, just before dinner was served. "I've been wondering if your father will let us carry it out."

"What is it?" questioned Bert.

"You are not to drive home until late this afternoon. I wonder if your father won't let you go down to Long Lake with me after dinner, to see the hockey match."

"Is it far from here?"

"About two miles. We can drive down in our cutter. Father will let me have the cutter and old Rusher, I'm sure."

"I'll see about it," said Bert. "I'd like to see the hockey match very much."

As soon as he got the chance Bert questioned his parent about going.

"I don't know about this," said Mr. Bobbsey slowly. "Do you think you two boys can be trusted alone with the horse?"

"Oh, yes, papa. Bob has driven old Rusher many times."

"You must remember, Rusher used to be a race horse. He may run away with Bob and you."

"Oh, but that was years ago, papa. He is too old to run away now. Please say yes."

Bert continued to plead, and in the end Mr. Bobbsey gave him permission to go to the hockey match.

"But you must be back before five o'clock," said he. "We are going to start for home at that time."

The dinner was a fine one and tasted especially good to the children after their long ride. But Bert and Bob were impatient to be off, and left the moment they had disposed of their pieces of pie.

Old Rusher was a black steed which, in years gone by, had won many a race on the track. He had belonged to a brother to Mr. Ramdell, who had died rather suddenly two years before. He was, as Bert had said, rather old, but there was still a good deal of fire left in him, as the boys were soon to discover to their cost.

The road to Long Lake was a winding one, up one hill and down another, and around a sharp turn where in years gone by there had been a sand pit.

In the best of spirits the two boys started off, Bob handling the reins like a veteran driver. Bob loved horses, and his one ambition in life was to handle a "spanking team," as he called it.

"Old Rusher can go yet," said Bert, who enjoyed the manner in which the black steed stepped out. "He must have been a famous race horse in his day."

"He was," answered Bob. "He won ever so many prizes."

The distance to Long Lake was covered almost before Bert knew it. As the hockey game was not yet begun they spent half an hour in driving over the road that led around the lake.

Quite a crowd had gathered, some in sleighs and some on foot, and the surface of the lake was covered with skaters. When the hockey game started the crowd watched every move with interest.

It was a "hot" game, according to Bert, and when a clever play was made he applauded as loudly as the rest. When the game was at an end he was sorry to discover that it was after four o'clock.

"We must get home," said he to Bob. "I promised to be back by five."

"Oh, we'll get back in no time," said Bob. "Remember, Rusher has had a good rest."

They were soon on the road again, Rusher kicking up his heels livelier than before, for the run down to the lake had merely enabled him to get the stiffness out of his limbs.

Sleighs were on all sides and, as the two boys drove along, two different sleighing parties passed them.

"Hullo, Ramdell!" shouted a young man in a cutter. "Got out old Rusher, I see. Want a race?"

"I think I can beat you!" shouted back Bob, and in a moment more the two cutters were side by side, and each horse and driver doing his best to win.

"Oh, Bob, can you hold him?" cried Bert.

"To be sure I can!" answered Bob. "Just you let me alone and see."

"Come on!" yelled the stranger. "Come on, or I'll leave you behind in no time!"

"You'll not leave me behind so quickly," answered Bob. "Go it, Rusher, go it!" he added to his horse, and the steed flew over the smooth road at a rate of speed that filled Bert with astonishment.

Chapter XVII

THE RACE AND THE RUNAWAY

Bert loved to ride and drive, but it must be confessed that he did not enjoy racing.

The road was rather uneven, and he could not help but think what the consequences might be if the cutter should strike a deep hollow or a big stone.

"Don't let Rusher run away," he said to his friend. "Be careful."

Bob was by this time having his hands so full that he could not answer.

"Steady, Rusher, steady!" he called out to the steed. "Steady, old boy!"

But the old race horse was now warmed up to his work and paid no attention to what was said. On and on he sped, until the young man in the other cutter was gradually outdistanced.

"Told you I could beat you!" flung back Bob.

"The race is yours," answered the young man, in much disappointment, and then he dropped further back than ever.

"Better slacken up, Bob," said Bert. "There is no use in driving so hard now."

"I—I can't slacken up," answered Bob. "Steady, Rusher," he called out. "Whoa, old fellow, whoa!"

But the old race horse did not intend to whoa, and on he flew as fast as his legs would carry him, up the first hill and then onward toward the turn before mentioned.

"Be careful at the turn, Bob!" screamed Bert. "Be careful, or we'll go over!"

"Whoa, Rusher!" repeated Bob, and pulled in on the reins with all of his might.

The turn where the sand pit had been was now close at hand. Here the road was rather narrow, so they had to drive close to the opening, now more than half filled with drifted snow. Bert clung to the cutter while Bob continued to haul in on the reins. Then came a crash, as the cutter hit a hidden stone and drove straight for the sand pit.

"Hold on!" cried Bob, and the next instant Bert found himself flying out of the cutter and over the edge of the road. He tried to save himself by clutching at the ice and snow, but it was useless, and in a twinkling he disappeared into the sand pit! Bob followed, while Rusher went on more gayly than ever, hauling the overturned cutter after him.

Down and down went poor Bert into the deep snow, until he thought he was never going to stop. Bob was beside him, and both floundered around wildly until almost the bottom of the pit was reached.

"Oh, Bob!"

"Oh, Bert! Are you hurt?"

"Don't know as I am. But what a tumble!"

"Rusher has run away!"

"I was afraid he'd do that."

For a minute the two boys knew not what to do. The deep snow lay all around them and how to get out of the pit was a serious question.

"It's a wonder we weren't smothered," said Bob. "Are you quite sure no bones have been broken?"

"Bones broken? Why, Bob, it was like coming down on a big feather bed. I only hope Rusher doesn't do any damage."

"So do I."

When the boys finally floundered out of the hollow into which they had fallen, they found themselves in snow up to their waists. On all sides of them were the walls of the sand pit, ten to fifteen feet high.

"I don't see how we are going to get out of this," said Bert dolefully. "We can't climb out."

"We'll have to do it," answered Bob. "Come, follow me."

He led the way through the deep snow to where the walls did not seem to be so high. At one spot the rain had washed down part of the soil.

"Let us try to climb up that slope," said the larger boy and led the way, and Bert followed.

It was hard work and it made Bert pant for breath, for the snow was still up to his waist. But both kept on, and in the end they stood on the edge of the sand pit, opposite to the side which ran along the road.

"Now we have got to walk around," said Bob. "But that will be easy, if we keep to the places where the wind has swept the snow away."

At last they stood on the road, and this reached both struck out for Dalton, less than a mile away.

"I'm afraid I'll catch it, if Rusher has smashed up the cutter," said Bob as they hurried along.

"We did wrong to race," answered Bert.

"Humph! it's no use to cry over spilt milk, Bert."

"I know that, Bob. Was the cutter a new one?"

"No, but I know father won't want it smashed up."

Much downhearted the boys kept on walking. Bert had not wanted to race, yet he felt he was guilty for having taken part. Perhaps his father would have to pay for part of the damage done.

"Maybe old Rusher ran right into town and smashed things right and left," he said to his friend.

"It would be just like him," sighed Bob. "It will make an awful bill to pay, won't it?"

A little further on they came to where a barn and a wagon shed lined the road. Under the shed stood a horse and cutter.

"My gracious me!" burst out Bob.

"Why—why—is it Rusher?" gasped Bert.

"It is!" shouted his friend.

Both boys ran up, and as they did so a farmer came from the barn.

"Oh, Mr. Daly, did you catch our horse?"

"I did, Bob," said the farmer. "Had a runaway, eh?"

"Yes, sir. Rusher threw us both into the old sand pit. I'm ever so glad you caught him. Is the cutter broken?"

"Not that I noticed. I knew you must have had a spill-out. I saw you going to the lake right after dinner."

Both boys inspected the cutter and found it in good condition, outside of a few scratches that did not count. Old Rusher was also all right, for which they were thankful.

"It was nice of you to stop the horse," said Bert to Farmer Daly.

"Oh, I'd do as much for anybody," said the farmer. "That is, if it wasn't too dangerous. Rusher wasn't running very fast when I caught him."

"He was running fast enough when he threw us out," answered Bob.

It did not take the boys long to get into the cutter again.

"Don't let him get away on the road home," sang out Farmer Daly after them.

"No fear of that," answered Bob.

He was very careful how he let Rusher step out. It was growing late, but Bert did not urge him on, so it was half-past five before the Ramdell house was reached.

"You are late after all," said Mr. Bobbsey, rather displeased.

"Oh, we've had such an adventure," cried Bert.

"What happened to you?" questioned Mrs. Bobbsey quickly.

"Rusher threw us into a sand pit," answered Bert, and then told the whole story.

"You can be thankful that you were not hurt," said his mamma.

"I am thankful, mamma."

"Rusher is still full of go," said Mrs. Ramdell. "I have warned my husband not to let Bob drive him."

"Oh, it was the brush with the other cutter that did it," said Bob. "Rusher couldn't stand it to let another horse pass him on the road."

Shortly after this, good-bys were said, and Sam brought around the big family sleigh from the barn. Into this the whole Bobbsey family piled, and off they went, in the gathering gloom of the short winter day.

"I've had a lovely time!" called out Nan.

"So have I had a lovely time," added little Flossie.

"Splendid," came from Freddie. "The baby is awful nice to play with."

"I've had a good time, too," said Bert. "The hockey game was just the best ever, and so was the drive behind Rusher, even if we did get dumped out."

The drive back to Lakeport was enjoyed as much as the drive to Dalton in the morning. On the way the children began to sing, and the voices mingled sweetly with the sounds of the sleigh bells.

"I shall not forget this outing in a hurry," said Nan, as she leaped to the step and ran into the house.

"I shan't forget it either," answered Bert. "But it turned out differently for me from what I thought it would."

Chapter XVIII

A QUARREL IN THE SCHOOLYARD

Three days after the grand sleighing party to Dalton, Nan came down to breakfast looking very pale and worried.

"What is the trouble, Nan?" questioned her mamma. "What has happened?"

"Oh, mamma, I scarcely feel like telling," answered Nan. "I am afraid you'll laugh at me."

"I fancy you had best tell me," went on Mrs. Bobbsey.

"I saw the ghost last night—or rather, early this morning."

"What, the ghost that I saw?" shouted Bert.

"I think it must have been the same. Anyway, it was about that high"—Nan raised her hand to her shoulder—"and all pure white."

"Oh, Nan!" shivered Freddie. "Don't want no ghostses!"

"I don't want to see it," put in Flossie, and edged closer to her mamma as if fearful the ghost might walk into the dining room that minute.

"This is certainly strange," came from Mr. Bobbsey. "Tell us all about it, Nan."

"Oh, papa, you won't laugh?" and Nan's face grew very red. "I—I—didn't think of it then, but it must have been very funny," she continued.

"It's not very funny to see a ghost, Nan," said Mrs. Bobbsey.

"I don't mean that—I mean what I did afterward. You see I was asleep and I woke up all of a sudden, for I thought somebody had passed a hand over my face. When I looked out into the room the ghost was standing right in front of the dresser. I could see into the glass and for the minute I thought there were two ghosts."

"Oh!" came from Flossie. "Two! Wasn't that simply dreadful!" And she crouched closer than ever to her mamma.

"As I was looking, the ghost moved away toward the window and then I saw there was but one. I was so scared I couldn't call anybody."

"I believe you," said Bert. "It's awful, isn't it?"

"This is certainly strange," said Mr. Bobbsey, with a grave look on his face. "What did you do next, Nan."

"You—you won't laugh, papa?"

"No."

"I thought of my umbrella. It was resting against the wall, close to the bed. I turned over and reached for the umbrella, but it slipped down and made a terrible noise as it struck the floor. Then I flung the covers over my head."

"What did you want the umbrella for?" questioned Freddie, in great wonder. "'Twasn't raining."

"I thought I could—could punch the ghost with it," faltered Nan.

At this Bert could hold in no longer, and he set up a shout of laughter, which was instantly repressed by Mr. Bobbsey.

"Oh, Nan, I'm sorry I laughed," said her twin brother, when he could speak. "But the idea of your poking at a ghost with an umbrella!"

"It was more than you tried to do," said Mr. Bobbsey dryly.

"That is so." Bert grew red in the face. "Did you see the ghost after that?" he asked to hide his confusion.

"No."

"Not at all?" asked Mrs. Bobbsey.

"No, mamma. I stayed under the covers for about a minute—just like Bert did—and when I looked the ghost was gone."

"I will have to investigate this," said Mr. Bobbsey seriously. "It is queer that neither I nor your mamma has seen the ghost."

"I ain't seen it," said Flossie.

"Don't want to see it," piped in Freddie.

Dinah, in the kitchen, had heard Nan's story and she was almost scared to death.

"Dat am de strangest t'ing," she said to Sam, when he came for his dinner. "Wot yo' make of it, hey?"

"Dunno," said Sam. "Maybe sumbuddy's gwine to die."

The matter was talked over by the Bobbsey family several times that day, and Mr. Bobbsey remained awake nearly all of that night, on the watch for the ghost. The following night Mrs. Bobbsey watched, and then Dinah took her turn, followed by Sam, who sat in the upper hall in a rocking chair, armed with a club. But the ghost failed to show itself, and after a week the excitement died down once more.

"Perhaps you were dreaming, Nan," said Mrs. Bobbsey.

"No, I wasn't dreaming, mamma, and Bert says he wasn't dreaming either."

"It is strange. I cannot understand it at all."

"Do you believe in ghosts, mamma?"

"No, my dear."

"But I saw something."

"Perhaps it was only a reflection. Sometimes the street lamps throw strange shadows on the walls through the windows."

"It wasn't a shadow," said Nan; and there the talk ended, for Mrs. Bobbsey knew not what to say to comfort her daughter.

In some way the news that a ghost had been seen in the Bobbsey house spread throughout the neighborhood, and many came to ask about it. Even the boys and girls talked about it and asked Nan and Bert all manner of questions, the most of which the twins could not answer.

The "ghost talk," as it was called, gave Danny Rugg a good chance to annoy both Nan and Bert.

"Afraid of a ghost! Afraid of a ghost!" he would cry, whenever he saw them. "Oh, my, but ain't I afraid of a ghost!"

"I think it is perfectly dreadful," said Nan one day, on returning from school. Her eyes were red, showing that she had been crying.

"I'll 'ghost' him, if he yells at us again," said Bert. "I'm not going to stand it, so there!"

"But what will you do, Bert?"

"I'll fight him, that's what I'll do."

"Oh, Bert, you mustn't fight."

"Then he has got to leave you alone—and leave me alone, too."

"If you fight at school, you'll be expelled."

"I don't care, I'm going to make him mind his own business," said Bert recklessly.

Danny Rugg was particularly sore because he had not been invited to Grace Lavine's party. Of all the boys in that neighborhood he was the only one left out, and he fancied it was Nan and Bert's fault.

"They don't like me and they are setting everybody against me," he thought. "I shan't stand it, not me!"

Two days later he followed Bert into the schoolyard, in which a large number of boys were playing.

"Hullo! how's the ghost?" he cried. "Is it still living at your house?"

"You be still about that ghost, Danny Rugg!" cried Bert, with flashing eyes.

"Oh, but wouldn't I like to have a house with a ghost," went on Danny tantalizingly. "And a sister who was afraid of it!"

"Will you be still, or not?"

"Why should I be still? You've got the ghost, haven't you? And Nan is scared to death of it, isn't she?"

"No, she isn't."

"Yes, she is, and so are you and all the rest of the family." And then Danny set up his old shout: "Afraid of a ghost! Afraid of a ghost!"

Some of the other boys followed suit and soon a dozen or more were crying, "Afraid of a ghost!" as loudly as they could.

Bert grew very pale and his breath came thickly. He watched Danny and when he came closer caught him by the arm.

"Let go!" cried the big boy roughly.

"I want you to stop calling like that."

"I shan't stop."

"I say you will!"

Bert had hardly spoken when Danny struck at him and hit him in the arm. Then Bert struck out in return and hit Danny in the chin. A dozen or more blows followed in quick succession. One struck Bert in the eye and blackened that organ, and another reached Danny's nose and made it bleed. Then the two boys clinched and rolled over on the schoolyard pavement.

"A fight! A fight!" came from those looking on, and this was taken up on all sides, while many crowded forward to see what was going on.

The school principal, Mr. Tetlow, was just entering the school at the time. Hearing the cry he ran around into the yard.

"Boys! boys! what does this mean?" he demanded, and forced his way through the crowd to where Bert and Danny lay, still pummeling each other. "Stand up at once and behave yourselves," and reaching down, he caught each by the collar and dragged him to his feet.

Chapter XIX

NAN'S PLEA

Bert's heart sank when he saw that it was the school principal who held him by the collar. He remembered what Nan had said about fighting and being expelled.

"It was Bert Bobbsey's fault," blustered Danny, wiping his bleeding nose on his sleeve.

"No, it wasn't," answered Bert quickly. "It was his fault."

"I say it was your fault!" shouted Danny. "He started the fight, Mr. Tetlow."

"He struck first," went on Bert undauntedly.

"He caught me by the arm and wouldn't let me go," came from Danny.

"I told him to keep still," explained Bert. "He was calling, 'Afraid of a ghost!' at me and I don't like it. And he said my sister Nan was afraid of it, too."

"Both of you march up to my office," said Mr. Tetlow sternly. "And remain there until I come."

"My nose is bleeding," whined Danny.

"You may go and wash your nose first," said the principal.

With a heart that was exceedingly heavy Bert entered the school and made his way to the principal's office. No one was there, and he sank on a chair in a corner. He heard the bells ring and heard the pupils enter the school and go to their various classrooms.

"If I am sent home, what will mamma and papa say?" he thought dismally. He had never yet been sent home for misconduct, and the very idea filled him with nameless dread.

His eye hurt him not a little, but to this he just then paid no attention. He was wondering what Mr. Tetlow would have to say when he came.

Presently the door opened and Danny shuffled in, a wet and bloody handkerchief held to his nose. He sat down on the opposite side of the office, and for several minutes nothing was said by either of the boys.

"I suppose you are going to try to get me into trouble," said Danny at length.

"You're trying to get me into trouble," returned Bert. "I didn't start the quarrel, and you know it."

"I don't know nothing of the kind, Bert Bobbsey! If you say I started the fight—I'll—I'll—tell something more about you."

"Really?"

"Yes, really."

"What can you tell?"

"You know well enough. Mr. Ringley hasn't forgotten about his broken window."

"Well, you broke that, I didn't."

"Humph! maybe I can prove that you broke it."

"Danny Rugg, what do you mean?" exclaimed Bert. "You know I had nothing to do with that broken window."

The big boy was about to say something more in reply when Mr. Tetlow entered the office.

"Boys," said he abruptly, "this is a disgraceful affair. I thought both of you knew better than to fight. It is setting a very bad example to the rest of the scholars. I shall have to punish you both severely."

Mr. Tetlow paused and Bert's heart leaped into his throat. What if he should be expelled? The very thought of it made him shiver.

"I have made a number of inquiries of the other pupils, and I find that you, Danny, started the quarrel. You raised the cry of 'Afraid of a ghost!' when you had no right to do so, and when Bert caught you by the arm and told you to stop you struck him. Is this true?"

"I—I—he hit me in the chin. I told him to let me go."

"He struck me first, Mr. Tetlow," put in Bert. "I am sure all of the boys will say the same."

"Hem! Bert, you can go to your classroom. I will talk to you after school this afternoon."

Somewhat relieved Bert left the office and walked to the classroom, where the other pupils eyed him curiously. It was hard work to put his mind on his lessons, but he did his best, for he did not wish to miss in any of them and thus make matters worse.

"What did the principal do?" whispered the boy who sat next to him.

"Hasn't done anything yet," whispered Bert in return.

"It was Danny's fault," went on the boy. "We'll stick by you."

At noontime Bert walked home with Nan, feeling very much downcast.

"Oh, Bert, what made you fight?" said his twin sister. "I told you not to."

"I couldn't help it, Nan. He told everybody that you were afraid of the ghost."

"And what is Mr. Tetlow going to do?"

"I don't know. He told me to stay in after school this afternoon, as he wanted to talk with me."

"If he expels you, mamma will never get over it."

"I know that, Nan. But—but—I couldn't stand it to have him yelling out, 'Afraid of a ghost!'"

After that Nan said but little. But her thoughts were busy, and by the time they were returning to the school her mind was fully made up.

To all of the school children the principal's office was a place that usually filled them with awe. Rarely did anybody go there excepting when sent by a teacher because of some infringements of the rules.

Nan went to school early that afternoon, and as soon as she had left Bert and the two younger twins, she marched bravely to Mr. Tetlow's office and knocked on the door.

"Come in," said the principal, who was at his desk looking over some school reports.

"If you please, Mr. Tetlow, I came to see you about my brother, Bert Bobbsey," began Nan.

Mr. Tetlow looked at her kindly, for he half expected what was coming.

"What is it, Nan?" he asked.

"I—I—oh, Mr. Tetlow, won't you please let Bert off this time? He only did it because Danny said such things about me; said I was afraid of the ghost, and made all the boys call out that we had a ghost at our house. I—I—think, somehow, that I ought to be punished if he is."

There, it was out, and Nan felt the better for it. Her deep brown eyes looked squarely into the eyes of the principal.

In spite of himself Mr. Tetlow was compelled to smile. He knew something of how the Bobbsey twins were devoted to each other.

"So you think you ought to be punished," he said slowly.

"Yes, if Bert is, for you see, he did it mostly for me."

"You are a brave sister to come in his behalf, Nan. I shall not punish him very severely."

"Oh, thank you for saying that, Mr. Tetlow."

"It was very wrong for him to fight——"

"Yes, I told him that."

"But Danny Rugg did wrong to provoke him. I sincerely trust that both boys forgive each other for what was done. Now you can go."

With a lighter heart Nan left the office. She felt that Bert would not be expelled. And he was not. Instead, Mr. Tetlow made him stay in an hour after school each day that week and write on his slate the sentence, "Fighting is wrong," a hundred times. Danny was also kept in and was made to write the sentence just twice as many times. Then Mr. Tetlow made the two boys shake hands and promise to do better in the future.

The punishment was nothing to what Bert had expected, and he stayed in after school willingly. But Danny was very sulky and plotted all manner of evil things against the Bobbseys.

"He is a very bad boy," said Nan. "If I were you, Bert, I'd have nothing more to do with him."

"I don't intend to have anything to do with him," answered her twin brother. "But, Nan, what do you think he meant when he said he'd make trouble about Mr. Ringley's broken window? Do you imagine he'll tell Mr. Ringley I broke it?"

"How would he dare, when he broke it himself?" burst out Nan.

"I'm sure I don't know. But if he did, what do you suppose Mr. Ringley would do?"

"I'm sure I don't know," came helplessly from Nan. "You can't prove that Danny did it, can you?"

"No."

"It's too bad. I wish the window hadn't been broken."

"So do I," said Bert; and there the talk came to an end, for there seemed nothing more to say.

Chapter XX

St. Valentine's Day

St. Valentine's Day was now close at hand, and all of the children of the neighborhood were saving their money with which to buy valentines.

"I know just the ones I am going to get," said Nan.

"I want some big red hearts," put in Freddie. "Just love hearts, I do!"

"I want the kind you can look into," came from Flossie. "Don't you know, the kind that fold up?"

Two days before St. Valentine's Day the children gathered around the sitting-room table and began to make valentines. They had paper of various colors and pictures cut from old magazines. They worked very hard, and some of the valentines thus manufactured were as good as many that could be bought.

"Oh, I saw just the valentine for Freddie," whispered Nan to Bert. "It had a fireman running to a fire on it."

There were a great many mysterious little packages brought into the house on the afternoon before St. Valentine's Day, and Mr. Bobbsey had to supply quite a few postage stamps.

"My, my, but the postman will have a lot to do to-morrow," said Mr. Bobbsey. "If this keeps on he'll want his wages increased, I am afraid."

The fun began early in the morning. On coming down to breakfast each of the children found a valentine under his or her plate. They were all very pretty.

"Where in the world did they come from?" cried Nan. "Oh, mamma, did you put them there?"

"No, Nan," said Mrs. Bobbsey.

"Then it must have been Dinah!" said Nan, and rushed into the kitchen. "Oh, Dinah, how good of you!"

"'Spect da is from St. Valentine," said the cook, smiling broadly.

"Oh, I know you!" said Nan.

"It's just lubby!" cried Freddie, breaking out into his baby talk. "Just lubby, Dinah! Such a big red heart, too!"

The postman came just before it was time to start for school. He brought six valentines, three for Flossie, two for Freddie and one for Bert.

"Oh, Nan, where is yours?" cried Bert.

"I—I guess he forgot me," said Nan rather soberly.

"Oh, he has made some mistake," said Bert and ran after the letter man. But it was of no use—all the mail for the Bobbseys had been delivered.

"Never mind, he'll come again this afternoon," said Mrs. Bobbsey, who saw how keenly Nan was disappointed.

On her desk in school Nan found two valentines from her schoolmates. One was very pretty, but the other was home-made and represented a girl running away from a figure labeled ghost. Nan put this out of sight as soon as she saw it.

All that day valentines were being delivered in various ways. Freddie found one in his cap, and Bert one between the leaves of his geography. Flossie found one pinned to her cloak, and Nan received another in a pasteboard box labeled Breakfast Food. This last was made of paper roses and was very pretty.

The letter man came that afternoon just as they arrived home from school. This time he had three valentines for Nan and several for the others. Some were comical, but the most of them were beautiful and contained very tender verses. There was much guessing as to who had sent each.

"I have received just as many as I sent out," said Nan, counting them over.

"I sent out two more than I received," said Bert.

"Never mind, Bert; boys don't expect so many as girls," answered Nan.

"I'd like to know who sent that mean thing that was marked ghost," went on her twin brother.

"It must have come from Danny Rugg," said Bert, and he was right. It had come from Danny, but Nan never let him know that she had received it, so his hoped-for fun over it was spoilt.

In the evening there was more fun than ever. All of the children went out and dropped valentines on the front piazzas of their friends' houses. As soon as a valentine was dropped the door bell would be given a sharp ring, and then everybody would run and hide and watch to see who came to the door.

When the Bobbsey children went home they saw somebody on their own front piazza. It was a boy and he was on his knees, placing something under the door mat.

"I really believe it is Danny Rugg!" cried Nan.

"Wait, I'll go and catch him," said Bert, and started forward.

But Danny saw him coming, and leaping over the side rail of the piazza, he ran to the back garden.

"Stop," called Bert. "I know you, Danny Rugg!"

"I ain't Danny Rugg!" shouted Danny in a rough voice. "I'm somebody else."

He continued to run and Bert made after him. At last Danny reached the back fence. There was a gate there, but this was kept locked by Sam, so that tramps might be kept out.

For the moment Danny did not know what to do. Then he caught hold of the top of the fence and tried to scramble over. But there was a sharp nail there and on this his jacket caught.

"I've got you now!" exclaimed Bert, and made a clutch for him. But there followed the sound of ripping cloth and Danny disappeared into the darkness, wearing a jacket that had a big hole torn in it.

"Was it really Danny?" questioned Nan, when Bert came back to the front piazza.

"Yes, and he tore his coat—I heard it rip."

"What do you think of that?"

Nan pointed to an object on the piazza, half under the door mat. There lay a dead rat, and around its neck was a string to which was attached a card reading, "Nan and Bert Bobbsey's Ghost."

"This is certainly awful," said Bert.

The noise on the piazza had brought Mrs. Bobbsey to the door. At the sight of the dead rat, which Freddie had picked up by the tail, she gave a slight scream.

"Oh, Freddie, leave it go!" she said.

"It won't hurt you, mamma," said the little boy. "The real is gone out of it."

"But—but—how did it get here?"

"Danny Rugg brought it," said Bert. "Look at the tag."

He cut the tag off with his pocket-knife and flung the rat into the garbage can. All went into the house, and Mrs. Bobbsey and her husband both read what Danny Rugg had written on the card.

"This is going too far," said Mr. Bobbsey. "I must speak to Mr. Rugg about this." And he did the very next day. As a result, and for having torn his jacket, Danny received the hardest thrashing he had got in a year. This made him more angry than ever against Bert, and also angry at the whole Bobbsey family. But he did not dare to do anything to hurt them at once, for fear of getting caught.

THE KITE WENT UP INTO THE AIR AND SNOOP WITH IT.

Winter was now going fast, and before long the signs of spring began to show on every hand.

Spring made Freddie think of a big kite that he had stored away, in the garret, and one Saturday he and Bert brought the kite forth and fixed the string and the tail.

"There is a good breeze blowing," said Bert. "Let us go and fly it on Roscoe's common."

"I want to see you fly the kite," said Flossie. "Can I go along?"

"Yes, come on," said Bert.

Flossie had been playing with the kitten and hated to leave it. So she went down to the common with Snoop in her arms.

"Don't let Snoop run away from you," said Bert. "He might not find his way back home."

The common was a large one with an old disused barn at one end. Freddie and Bert took the kite to one end and Freddie held it up while Bert prepared to let out the string and "run it up," as he called it.

Now, as it happened, the eyes of Snoop were fixed on the long tail of the kite, and when it went trailing over the ground Snoop leaped from Flossie's arms and made a dash for it. The kitten's claws caught fast in the tail, and in a moment more the kite went up into the air and Snoop with it.

"Oh, my kitten!" called out Freddie. "Snoop has gone up with the kite!"

Chapter XXI

The Rescue of Snoop, the Kitten

It was certainly something that nobody had been expecting, and as the kite went higher and higher, and Snoop with it, both Flossie and Freddie set up a loud cry of fear.

"Snoop will be killed!" exclaimed the little girl. "Oh, poor dear Snoop!" and she wrung her hands in despair.

"Let him down!" shrieked Freddie. "Oh, Bert, please let my dear kitten down, won't you?"

Bert did not hear, for he was running over the common just as hard as he could, in his endeavor to raise the kite. Up and up it still went, with poor Snoop dangling helplessly at the end of the swaying tail.

At last Bert ran past the old barn which I have already mentioned. Just as he did this he happened to look up at the kite.

"Hullo, what's on the tail?" he yelled. "Is that a cat?"

"It's Snoop!" called out Freddie, who was rushing after his big brother. "Oh, Bert, do let him down. If he falls, he'll be killed."

"Well, I never!" ejaculated Bert.

He stopped running and gradually the kite began to settle close to the top of the barn. Poor Snoop was swinging violently at the end of the ragged tail. The swinging brought the frightened creature closer still to the barn, and all of a sudden Snoop let go of the kite tail and landed on the shingles.

"Snoop is on the barn!" cried Bert, as the kite settled on the grass a few yards away.

"Oh, Snoop! Snoop! are you hurt?" cried Freddie, running back a distance, so that he might get a view of the barn top.

Evidently Snoop was not hurt. But he was still scared, for he stood on the edge of the roof, with his tail standing straight up.

"Meow! meow! meow!" he said plaintively.

"He is asking for somebody to take him down," said Freddie. "Aren't you, Snoop?"

"Meow!" answered the black kitten.

"Oh, dear me, what will you do now?" cried Flossie, as she came chasing up.

"Perhaps I can get to the roof from the inside," said Bert, and he darted quickly into the barn.

There were a rickety pair of stairs leading to the barn loft and these he mounted. In the loft all was dark and full of cobwebs. Here and there were small holes through the roof, through which the water came every time it rained.

"Snoop! Snoop!" he called, putting his mouth close to one of the holes.

The kitten turned around in surprise. He hardly knew from whence the voice came, but he evidently knew Bert was calling, for he soon came in that direction.

As the barn was an old one and not fit to use, Bert felt it would do no harm to knock a shingle or two from the roof. Looking around, he espied a stout stick of wood lying on the floor and with this he began an attack on the shingles and soon had two of them broken away.

"Come, Snoop!" he called, looking out of the hole. "Come here!"

But the sound of the blows had frightened the kitten, and Snoop had fled to the slope of the roof on the opposite side of the barn.

"Where is he?" called the boy, to the twins below.

"Gone to the other side," said Freddie. "Don't like the noise, I guess."

"Chase him over here," returned Bert.

Both Freddie and Flossie tried to do so. But Snoop would not budge, but stood on the very edge of the roof, as if meditating a spring to the ground.

"Don't jump, please don't jump, Snoop!" pleaded Flossie. "If you jump you'll surely break a leg, or maybe your back!"

Whether Snoop understood this or not, it would be hard to say. But he did not jump, only stayed where he was and meowed louder than ever.

"Can't you drive him over?" asked Bert, after a long wait.

"Won't come," said Freddie. "Wants to jump down, I guess."

Hearing this, Bert ran down to the lower floor and outside.

"Can't you get a ladder?" asked Flossie. "Perhaps Mr. Roscoe will lend you one."

Mr. Roscoe lived at the other end of the common. He was a very old and very quiet man, and the majority of the girls and boys in Lakeport were afraid of him. He lived all alone and was thought to be queer.

"I—I can see," said Bert hesitatingly.

He ran across the common to Mr. Roscoe's house and rapped on the door. Nobody came and he rapped again, and then a third time.

"Who's there?" asked a voice from within.

"Please, Mr. Roscoe, is that you?" asked Bert.

"Yes."

"Well, our kitten is on the top of your old barn and can't get down. Can you lend me a ladder to get him down with?"

"Kitten on my barn? How did he get there?" and now the old man opened the door slowly and cautiously. He was bent with age and had white hair and a long white beard.

"He went up with a kite," said Bert, and explained the case, to which the old man listened with interest.

"Well! well! well!" exclaimed Mr. Roscoe, in a high piping voice. "Going to take a sail through the air, was he? You'll have to build him a balloon, eh?"

"I think he had better stay on the ground after this."

"He must be a high-flyer of a cat," and the old man chuckled over his joke.

"Will you lend me a ladder?" went on Bert.

"Certainly, my lad. The ladder is in the cow-shed yonder. But you'll have to raise it yourself, or get somebody to raise it for you. My back is too old and stiff for such work."

"I'll try it alone first," answered the boy.

He soon had the long ladder out and was dragging it across the common. It was very heavy and he wondered who he could get to help him raise it. Just then Danny Rugg came along.

"What are you doing with old Roscoe's ladder?" he asked.

Bert was on the point of telling Danny it was none of his business, but he paused and reflected. He wanted no more quarrels with the big boy.

"I am going to get our cat down from the barn roof," he answered.

"Humph!"

"Do you want to help me raise the ladder, Danny?"

"Me? Not much! You can raise your own ladder."

"All right, I will, if you don't want to help me," said Bert, the blood rushing to his face.

"So that's your cat, is it?" cried Danny, looking toward the barn. "I wouldn't have such a black beast as that! We've got a real Maltese at our house."

"We like Snoop very much," answered Bert, and went on with his ladder.

Danny hunted for a stone, and watching his chance threw it at Snoop. It landed close to the kitten's side and made Snoop run to the other side of the barn roof.

"Stop that, Danny Rugg!" cried a voice from the other end of the common, and Nan appeared. She had just heard about the happening to Snoop and was hurrying to the spot to see if she could be of assistance.

"Oh, go on with your old cat!" sneered Danny, and shuffled off past Mr. Roscoe's house.

The old man had come out to see what Bert was going to do with the ladder, and now he came face to face with Danny Rugg.

"Well, is it possible!" murmured the old man to himself. "That boy must belong around here after all!"

When Bert reached the barn he found a dozen boys collected, and several volunteered to assist him in raising the long ladder. It was hard work, and once the ladder slipped, but in the end it rested against the barn roof and then Bert went up in a hurry.

"Come, Snoop!" he called, and the kitten came and perched himself on Bert's shoulder.

When Bert came down the ladder those standing around set up a cheer, and Freddie and Flossie clapped their hands in delight.

"Oh, I'm so glad you got him back!" said Freddie and hugged the kitten almost to death.

"What boy was that who threw the stone?" asked Mr. Roscoe of Nan, while Bert was returning the ladder to the cow-shed.

"That was Danny Rugg," answered Nan. "He is a bad boy."

"I know he is a bad boy," said Mr. Roscoe. "A very bad boy indeed." And then the old man hurried off without another word. What he said meant a good deal, as we shall soon see.

Chapter XXII

THE LAST OF THE GHOST—GOOD-NIGHT

The rescue of the kitten was the main subject of conversation that evening in the Bobbsey household.

"I never dreamed he would go up with the kite," said Flossie. "After this we'll have to keep him in the house when Bert and Freddie do their kite-flying."

Bert had seen Danny Rugg throw the stone at the kitten and was very angry over it. He had also seen Danny talk to Nan.

"I think he's an awful boy," declared Nan. "And Mr. Roscoe thinks he is bad, too."

"He had better stop throwing things or he'll get himself into trouble before long," said Bert.

"It's queer Mr. Ringley never heard about the window," whispered his twin sister.

"So it is. But it may come out yet," replied the brother.

That evening the Bobbseys had their first strawberry shortcake of the season. It was a beautiful cake—one of Dinah's best—and the strawberries were large and luscious.

"Want another piece," said Freddie, smacking his lips. "It's so good, mamma!"

"Freddie, I think you have had enough," said Mrs. Bobbsey.

"Oh, mamma, just a little piece more!" pleaded Freddie, and received the piece, much to his satisfaction.

"Strawberries is beautiful," he declared. "I'm going to raise a whole lot on the farm this summer."

"Oh, mamma, are we going to Uncle Dan's farm this summer?" burst out Nan eagerly.

"Perhaps, Nan," was the reply. "I expect a letter very shortly."

"Meadow Brook is a dandy place," said Bert. "Such a fine swimming hole in the brook!"

"Oh, I love the flowers, and the chickens and cows!" said Flossie.

"I like the rides on the loads of hay," said Nan.

The children talked the subject over until it was time to go to bed. Their Uncle Dan and Aunt Sarah lived at Meadow Brook, and so did their cousin Harry, a boy a little older than Bert, and one who was full of fun and very good-natured in the bargain.

Bert went to bed with his head full of plans for the summer. What glorious times they could have after school closed if they went to their uncle's farm!

It was a full hour before Bert got to sleep. The room was quite bright, for the moon was shining in the corner window. The moon made him think of the ghost he had once seen and he gave a little shudder. He never wanted to see that ghost again.

Bert had been asleep less than an hour when he awoke with a start. He felt sure somebody had touched him on the foot. He opened his eyes at once and looked toward the end of his bed.

The ghost was standing there!

At first Bert could scarcely believe that he saw aright. But it was true and he promptly dove under the covers.

Then he thought of Danny Rugg's cry, "Afraid of a ghost!" and he felt that he ought to have more courage.

"I'm going to see what that is," he said to himself, and shoved back the covers once more.

The figure in white had moved toward the corner of the room. It made no noise and Bert wondered how it would turn next.

"Wonder what will happen if I grab it, or yell?" he asked himself.

With equal silence Bert crawled out of bed. Close at hand stood his base-ball bat, which he had used a few days before. It made a formidable club, and he took hold of it with a good deal of satisfaction.

"Want another piece of strawberry shortcake," came to his ears. "Please give me another piece of strawberry shortcake."

Bert could hardly believe his ears. It was the ghost that was speaking! It wanted strawberry shortcake!

"Freddie!" he almost shouted. "Freddie, is it you?"

The ghost did not answer, but turned towards the door leading into the hallway. Bert ran after the figure in white and caught it by the arm.

The ghost was really Freddie, and he was walking in his sleep, with his eyes tightly closed.

"Well, I declare!" murmured Bert. "Why didn't we think of this before?"

"Please let me have another piece of strawberry shortcake, mamma," pleaded the sleep-walker. "Just a tiny little piece."

Bert had heard that it was a bad thing to awaken a sleep-walker too suddenly, so he took Freddie's arm very gently and walked the little fellow back to his bedroom and placed him on his bed. Then he shook him very gently.

"Oh!" cried Freddie. "Oh! Wha—what do you want? Let me sleep! It isn't time to get up yet."

"Freddie, I want you to wake up," said Bert.

"Who is talking?" came from across the hallway, in Mr. Bobbsey's voice.

"I'm talking, papa," answered Bert. He ran to the doorway of his parents' bedchamber. "I've just found out who the ghost is," he continued.

"The ghost?" Mr. Bobbsey leaped up. "Where is it?"

"In bed now. It was Freddie, walking in his sleep. He was asking for another piece of strawberry shortcake."

By this time the whole household was wide awake.

"Oh, Freddie, was it really you?" cried Nan, going to the little fellow.

"Wasn't walking in my sleep," said Freddie. "Was dreaming 'bout shortcake, that's all. Want to go to sleep again," and he turned over on his pillow.

"Let him sleep," said Mrs. Bobbsey. "We'll have to consult the doctor about this. He will have to have something for his digestion and eat less before going to bed in the future." And the next day the doctor was called in and gave Freddie something which broke up the sleep-walking to a very large extent.

"I am glad you caught Freddie," said Nan, to her twin brother. "If you hadn't, I should always have believed that we had seen a ghost."

"Glad I don't walk in my sleep," said Flossie. "I might tumble downstairs and break my nose."

"I shall watch Freddie in the future," said Mrs. Bobbsey, and she did.

When Bert went to school the next day he met Danny Rugg and the tall boy glared at him very angrily.

"Think you are smart, don't you?" said Danny. "I'm not going to stand it, Bert Bobbsey."

"Oh, Bert, come along and don't speak to him," whispered Nan, who was with her twin brother.

"Went and saw Ringley, didn't you?" went on Danny, edging closer.

"Keep away, Danny Rugg," answered Bert. "I want nothing to do with you, and I haven't been to see Mr. Ringley."

"Yes, you did go and see him," insisted Danny. "Wasn't he to see my father last night?"

"Did Mr. Ringley come to see your father?" asked Bert curiously.

"Yes, he did. And my father—but never mind that now," broke off the tall boy. He had been on the point of saying that his father had given him a severe thrashing. "I'm going to fix you, Bert Bobbsey."

"Don't you dare to strike my brother, Danny Rugg!" put in Nan, stepping in between them.

How much further the quarrel might have gone, it is impossible to say, for just then Mr. Tetlow put in an appearance, and Danny sneaked off in great haste.

When the children came from school they learned that Mrs. Bobbsey had been down-town, buying some shoes for herself and Flossie.

"Mr. Ringley was telling me about his broken window," said she to her husband. "He found out that Danny Rugg broke it. Old Mr. Roscoe saw Danny do it. He didn't know Danny at the time, but he has found out since who Danny was."

"That Rugg boy is a bad one," answered Mr. Bobbsey. "I suppose Mr. Ringley made the Ruggs pay for the window."

"Oh, yes, and Mr. Rugg said he was going to correct Danny, too."

The children heard this talk, but said nothing at the time. But later Nan called Bert out into the garden.

"I see it all," she whispered to her twin brother. "That's why Mr. Roscoe asked me who Danny was, and that's why he said Danny was such a bad boy."

"I'm glad in one way that Danny has been found out," answered Bert, "for that clears me." And he was right, for he never heard of the broken window again.

The children were still waiting anxiously for a letter from their Uncle Dan or their Aunt Sarah. At last a letter came and they listened to it with great delight.

"Oh, what do you think?" cried Nan, dancing up to Bert. "We are to go to Meadow Brook as soon as vacation begins!"

"Good!" shouted Bert, throwing his cap into the air. "Won't we have the best times ever was!" And this proved to be a fact. What happened to the Bobbsey twins at Meadow Brook will be told in another book, which I shall call, "*The Bobbsey Twins in the Country*." The country is a lovely place, especially in the summer time, and all of my young readers can rest assured that the twins enjoyed themselves at Meadow Brook to the utmost.

"I'll be so glad to see Cousin Harry again," said Bert.

"And I'll be glad to see Aunt Sarah," piped in Freddie. "She makes such *beautiful* pies!"

"Think of the lovely big barn," put in Flossie. "It's just like a—a palace to play in on wet days!"

"Oh, Flossie, to compare a barn to a palace!" exclaimed Nan. "But it is a nice place after all," she added, after a moment's thought.

That evening, to celebrate the good news, the twins gave a little party to half a dozen of their most intimate friends. There were music and singing, and all sorts of games, and a magic-lantern exhibition by one of the boys. All enjoyed it greatly and voted the little party a great success.

"Good-night! Good-night!" said the young folks to each other, when the party broke up. And here let us say good-night, too, for my little story has reached its end.

END OF

"The Bobbsey Twins,
Merry Days Indoors and Out"

BY LAURA LEE HOPE

THE BOBBSEY TWINS

IN THE COUNTRY

Chapter I

THE INVITATION

"There goes the bell! It's the letter carrier! Let me answer!" Freddie exclaimed.

"Oh, let me! It's my turn this week!" cried Flossie.

"But I see a blue envelope. That's from Aunt Sarah!" the brother cried.

Meanwhile both children, Freddie and Flossie, were making all possible efforts to reach the front door, which Freddie finally did by jumping over the little divan that stood in the way, it being sweeping day.

"I beat you," laughed the boy, while his sister stood back, acknowledging defeat.

"Well, Dinah had everything in the way and anyhow, maybe it was your turn. Mother is in the sewing room, I guess!" Flossie concluded, and so the two started in search of the mother, with the welcome letter from Aunt Sarah tight in Freddie's chubby fist.

Freddie and Flossie were the younger of the two pairs of twins that belonged to the Bobbsey family. The little ones were four years old, both with light curls framing pretty dimpled faces, and both being just fat enough to be good-natured. The other twins, Nan and Bert, were eight years old, dark and handsome, and as like as "two peas" the neighbors used to say. Some people thought it strange there should be two pairs of twins in one house, but Nan said it was just like four-leaf clovers, that always grow in little patches by themselves.

This morning the letter from Aunt Sarah, always a welcome happening, was especially joyous.

"Do read it out loud," pleaded Flossie, when the blue envelope had been opened in the sewing room by Mrs. Bobbsey.

"When can we go?" broke in Freddie, at a single hint that the missive contained an invitation to visit Meadow Brook, the home of Aunt Sarah in the country.

"Now be patient, children," the mother told them. "I'll read the invitation in just a minute," and she kept her eyes fastened on the blue paper in a way that even to Freddie and Flossie meant something very interesting.

"Aunt Sarah wants to know first how we all are."

"Oh, we're all well," Freddie interrupted, showing some impatience.

"Do listen, Freddie, or we won't hear," Flossie begged him, tugging at his elbow.

"Then she says," continued the mother, "that this is a beautiful summer at Meadow Brook."

"Course it is. We know that!" broke in Freddie again.

"Freddie!" pleaded Flossie.

"And she asks how we would like to visit them this summer."

"Fine, like it—lovely!" the little boy almost shouted, losing track of words in his delight.

"Tell her we'll come, mamma," went on Freddie. "Do send a letter quick won't you, mamma?"

"Freddie Bobbsey!" spoke up Flossie, in a little girl's way of showing indignation. "If you would only keep quiet we could hear about going, but—you always stop mamma. Please, mamma, read the rest," and the golden head was pressed against the mother's shoulder from the arm of the big rocking chair.

"Well, I was only just saying—" pouted Freddie.

"Now listen, dear." The mother went on once more reading from the letter: "Aunt Sarah says Cousin Harry can hardly wait until vacation time to see Bert, and she also says, 'For myself I cannot wait to see the babies. I want to hear Freddie laugh, and I want to hear Flossie "say her piece," as she did last Christmas, then I just want to hug them both to death, and so does their Uncle Daniel.'"

"Good!—goody!" broke in the irrepressible Freddie again. "I'll just hug Aunt Sarah this way," and he fell on his mother's neck and squeezed until she cried for him to stop.

"I guess she'll like that," Freddie wound up, in real satisfaction at his hugging ability.

"Not if you spoil her hair," Flossie insisted, while the overcome mother tried to adjust herself generally.

"Is that all?" Flossie asked.

"No, there is a message for Bert and Nan too, but I must keep that for lunch time. Nobody likes stale news," the mother replied.

"But can't we hear it when Bert and Nan come from school?" coaxed Flossie.

"Of course," the mother assured her. "But you must run out in the air now. We have taken such a long time to read the letter."

"Oh, aren't you glad!" exclaimed Flossie to her brother, as they ran along the stone wall that edged the pretty terrace in front of their home.

"Glad! I'm just—so glad—so glad—I could almost fly up in the air!" the boy managed to say in chunks, for he had never had much experience with words, a very few answering for all his needs.

The morning passed quickly to the little ones, for they had so much to think about now, and when the school children appeared around the corner Flossie and Freddie hurried to meet Nan and Bert, to tell them the news.

"We're going! we're going!" was about all Freddie could say.

"Oh, the letter came—from Aunt Sarah!" was Flossie's way of telling the news. But it was at the lunch table that Mrs. Bobbsey finished the letter.

"'Tell Nan,'" she read, "'that Aunt Sarah has a lot of new patches and tidies to show her, and tell her I have found a new kind of jumble chocolate that I am going to teach her to make.' There, daughter, you see," commented Mrs. Bobbsey, "Aunt Sarah has not forgotten what a good little baker you are."

"Chocolate jumble," remarked Bert, and smacked his lips. "Say, Nan, be sure to learn that. It sounds good," the brother declared.

Just then Dinah, the maid, brought in the chocolate, and the children tried to tell her about going to the country, but so many were talking at once that the good-natured colored girl interrupted the confusion with a hearty laugh.

"Ha! ha! ha! And all you-uns be goin' to de country!"

"Yes, Dinah," Mrs. Bobbsey told her, "and just listen to what Aunt Sarah says about you," and once more the blue letter came out, while Mrs. Bobbsey read:

"'And be sure to bring dear old Dinah! We have plenty of room, and she will so enjoy seeing the farming.'"

"Farming! Ha! ha! Dat I do like. Used to farm all time home in Virginie!" the maid declared. "And I likes it fuss-rate! Yes, Dinah'll go and hoe de corn and" (aside to Bert) "steal de watermelons!"

The prospects were indeed bright for a happy time in the country, and the Bobbseys never disappointed themselves when fun was within their reach.

Chapter II

THE START

With so much to think about, the few weeks that were left between vacation and the country passed quickly for the Bobbseys. As told in any first book, "The Bobbsey Twins," this little family had a splendid home in Lakeport, where Mr. Bobbsey was a lumber merchant. The mother and father were both young themselves, and always took part in their children's joys and sorrows, for there were sorrows sometimes. Think of poor little Freddie getting shut up all alone in a big store with only a little black kitten, "Snoop," to keep him from being scared to death; that was told of in the first book, for Freddie went shopping one day with his mamma, and wandered off a little bit. Presently he found himself in the basement of the store; there he had so much trouble in getting out he fell asleep in the meantime. Then, when he awoke and it was all dark, and the great big janitor came to rescue him—oh!—Freddie thought the man might even be a giant when he first heard the janitor's voice in the dark store.

Freddie often got in trouble, but like most good little boys he was always saved just at the right time, for they say good children have real angels watching over them. Nan, Bert, and Flossie all had plenty of exciting experiences too, as told in "The Bobbsey Twins," for among other neighbors there was Danny Rugg, a boy who always tried to make trouble for Bert, and sometimes almost succeeded in getting Bert into "hot water," as Dinah expressed it.

Of course Nan had her friends, as all big girls have, but Bert, her twin brother, was her dearest chum, just as Freddie was Flossie's.

"When we get to the country we will plant trees, go fishing, and pick blackberries," Nan said one day.

"Yes, and I'm going with Harry out exploring," Bert announced.

"I'm just going to plant things," prim little Flossie lisped. "I just love melons and ice cream and—"

"Ice cream! Can you really plant ice cream?" Freddie asked innocently, which made the others all laugh at Flossie's funny plans.

"I'm going to have chickens," Freddie told them. "I'm going to have one of those queer chicken coops that you shut up tight and when you open it it's just full of little 'kippies.'"

"Oh, an incubator, you mean," Nan explained. "That's a machine for raising chickens without any mother."

"But mine are going to have a mother," Freddie corrected, thinking how sad little chickens would be without a kind mamma like his own.

"But how can they have a mother where there isn't any for them?" Flossie asked, with a girl's queer way of reasoning.

"I'll get them one," Freddie protested. "I'll let Snoop be their mamma."

"A cat! the idea! why, he would eat 'em all up," Flossie argued.

"Not if I whipped him once for doing it," the brother insisted. Then Nan and Bert began to tease him for whipping the kitten after the chickens had been "all eaten up."

So the merry days went on until at last vacation came!

"Just one more night," Nan told Flossie and Freddie when she prepared them for bed, to help her very busy mother. Bert assisted his father with the packing up, for the taking of a whole family to the country meant lots of clothes, besides some books and just a few toys. Then there was Bert's tool box—he knew he would need that at Meadow Brook.

The morning came at last, a beautiful bright day, a rare one for traveling, for a fine shower the evening before had washed and cooled things off splendidly.

"Now come, children," Mr. Bobbsey told the excited youngsters. "Keep track of your things. Sam will be ready in a few minutes, and then we must be off."

Promptly Sam pulled up to the door with the family carriage, and all hurried to get in.

"Oh, Snoop, Snoop!" cried Freddie. "He's in the library in the box! Dinah, get him quick, get him!" and Dinah ran back after the little kitten.

"Here you is, Freddie!" she gasped, out of breath from hurrying. "You don't go and forget poor Snoopy!" and she climbed in beside Sam.

Then they started.

"Oh, my lan' a-massy!" yelled Dinah presently in distress. "Sam Johnson, you jest turn dat hoss around quick," and she jerked at the reins herself. "You heah, Sam? Quick, I tells you. Get back to dat house. I'se forgot to bring—to bring my lunch basket!"

"Oh, never mind, Dinah," Mrs. Bobbsey interrupted. "We will have lunch on the train."

"But I couldn't leab dat nice lunch I got ready fo' de chillen in between, missus," the colored woman urged. "I'll get it quick as a wink. Now, Sam, you rush in dar quick, and fetch dat red and white basket dat smells like chicken!"

So the good-natured maid had her way, much to the delight of Bert and Freddie, who liked nothing so well as one of Dinah's home-made lunches.

The railroad station was reached without mishap, and while Mr. Bobbsey attended to getting the baskets checked at the little window in the big round office, the children sat about "exploring." Freddie hung back a little when a locomotive steamed up. He clung to his mother's skirt, yet wanted to see how the machine worked.

"That's the fireman," Bert told him, pointing to the man in the cab of the engine.

"Fireman!" Freddie repeated. "Not like our firemen. I wouldn't be that kind," He had always wanted to be a fireman who helps to put out fires.

"Oh, this is another kind," his father explained, just then coming up in readiness for the start.

"I guess Snoop's afraid," Freddie whispered to his mother, while he peeped into the little box where Snoop was peacefully purring. Glad of the excuse to get a little further away, Freddie ran back to where Dinah sat on a long shiny bench.

"Say, chile," she began, "you hear dat music ober dar? Well, a big fat lady jest jumped up and down on dat machine and it starts up and plays Swanee Ribber."

"That's a weighing machine," Nan said with a laugh. "You just put a penny in it and it tells you how much you weigh besides playing a tune."

"Lan' o' massy! does it? Wonder has I time to try it?"

"Yes, come on," called Bert. "Father said we have plenty of time," and at the word Dinah set out to get weighed. She looked a little scared, as if it might "go off" first, but when she heard the soft strain of an old melody coming out she almost wanted to dance.

"Now, ain't dat fine!" she exclaimed. "Wouldn't dat be splendid in de kitchen to weigh de flour, Freddie?"

But even the interesting sights in the railroad station had to be given up now, for the porter swung open a big gate and called: "All aboard for Meadow Brook!" and the Bobbseys hurried off.

Chapter III

SNOOP ON THE TRAIN

"I'm glad Dinah looks nice," Flossie whispered to her mother, when she saw how beautiful the parlor car was. "And isn't Freddie good?" the little girl remarked anxiously, as if fearing her brother might forget his best manners in such a grand place.

Freddie and Bert sat near their father on the big soft revolving chairs in the Pullman car, while Nan and Flossie occupied the sofa at the end near their mother. Dinah sat up straight and dignified, and, as Flossie said, really looked nice, in her very clean white waist and her soft black skirt. On her carefully parted hair she wore a neat little black turban. Bert always laughed at the number of "parts" Dinah made in her kinky hair, and declared that she ought to be a civil engineer, she could draw such splendid maps even on the back of her head.

The grandeur of the parlor car almost overcame Freddie, but he clung to Snoop in the pasteboard box and positively refused to let the kitten go into the baggage car. Dinah's lunch basket was so neatly done up the porter carried it very carefully to her seat when she entered the train, although lunch baskets are not often taken in as "Pullman car baggage."

"I'm going to let Snoop out!" whispered Freddie suddenly, and before anyone had a chance to stop him, the little black kitten jumped out of the box, and perched himself on the window sill to look out at the fine scenery.

"Oh!" exclaimed Mrs. Bobbsey, "the porter will put him off the train!" and she tried to catch the now happy little Snoop.

"No, he won't," Mr. Bobbsey assured her. "I will watch out for that."

"Here, Snoop," coaxed Nan, also alarmed. "Come, Snoop!"

But the kitten had been captive long enough to appreciate his liberty now, and so refused to be coaxed. Flossie came down between the velvet chairs very cautiously, but as soon as Snoop saw her arm stretch out for him, he just walked over the back of the highest seat and down into the lap of a sleeping lady!

"Oh, mercy me!" screamed the lady, as she awoke with Snoop's tail whisking over her face. "Goodness, gracious! what is that?" and before she had fully recovered from the shock she actually jumped up on the chair, like the funny pictures of a woman and a mouse.

The people around could not help laughing, but Freddie and the other Bobbseys were frightened.

"Oh, will they kill Snoop now?" Freddie almost cried. "Dinah, please help me get him!"

By this time the much scared lady had found out it was only a little kitten, and feeling very foolish she sat down and coaxed Snoop into her lap again. Mr. Bobbsey hurried to apologize.

"We'll have to put him back in the box," Mr. Bobbsey declared, but that was easier said than done, for no sooner would one of the Bobbseys approach the cat than Snoop would walk himself off. And not on the floor either, but up and down the velvet chairs, and in and out under the passengers' arms. Strange to say, not one of the people minded it, but all petted Snoop until, as Bert said, "He owned the car."

"Dat cat am de worst!" Dinah exclaimed. "'Pears like it was so stuck up an' fine dar ain't no place in dis 'yere Pullin' car good 'nough fer him."

"Oh, the porter! the porter!" Bert cried. "He'll surely throw Snoop out of the window."

"Snoop! Snoop!" the whole family called in chorus, but Snoop saw the porter himself and made up his mind the right thing to do under the circumstances would be to make friends.

"Cat?" exclaimed the good-looking colored man. "Scat! Well, I declare! What you think of that?"

Freddie felt as if he were going to die, he was so scared, and Flossie's tears ran down her cheeks.

"Will he eat him?" Freddie blubbered, thinking of some queer stories he had heard like that. Mr. Bobbsey, too, was a little alarmed and hurried to reach Snoop.

The porter stooped to catch the offending kitten, while Snoop walked right up to him, sniffed his uniform, and stepped upon the outstretched black hand.

"Well, you is a nice little kitten," the porter admitted, fondling Snoop in spite of orders.

"Oh, please, Mr. Porter, give me my cat!" cried Freddie, breaking away from all restraint and reaching Snoop.

"Yours, is it? Well, I don't blame you, boy, for bringing dat cat along. An' say," and the porter leaned down to the frightened Freddie, "it's against orders, but I'd jest like to take dis yer kitten back in de kitchen and treat him, for he's—he's a star!" and he fondled Snoop closer.

"But I didn't know it was wrong, and I'll put him right back in the box," Freddie whimpered, not quite understanding the porter's intention.

"Well, say, son!" the porter exclaimed as Mr. Bobbsey came up. "What do you say if you papa let you come back in de kitchen wid me? Den you can jest see how I treat de kitty-cat!"

So Freddie started off after the porter, who proudly carried Snoop, while Mr. Bobbsey brought up the rear. Everybody along the aisle wanted to pet Snoop, who, from being a little stowaway was now the hero of the occasion. More than once Freddie stumbled against the side of the big seats as the cars swung along like a reckless automobile, but each time his father caught him by the blouse and set him on his feet again, until at last, after passing through the big dining car, the kitchen was reached.

"What you got dar? Somethin' fer soup?" laughed the good-natured cook, who was really fond of cats and wouldn't harm one for the world.

Soon the situation was explained, and as the porters and others gathered around in admiration, Snoop drank soup like a gentleman, and then took two courses, one of fish and one of meat, in splendid traveler fashion.

"Dat's de way to drink soup on a fast train," laughed the porter. "You makes sure of it dat way, and saves your clothes. Ha! ha! ha!" he laughed, remembering how many men have to have their good clothes cleaned of soup after a dinner on a fast train. Reluctantly the men gave Snoop back to Freddie, who, this time, to make sure of no further adventures, put the popular black kitten in his box in spite of protests from the admiring passengers.

"You have missed so much of the beautiful scenery," Nan told Freddie and her father when they joined the party again. "Just see those mountains over there," and then they sat at the broad windows gazing for a long time at the grand scenery as it seemed to rush by.

Chapter IV

A LONG RIDE

The train was speeding along with that regular motion that puts many travelers to sleep, when Freddie curled himself on the sofa and went to sleep.

"Poor little chap!" Mr. Bobbsey remarked. "He is tired out, and he was so worried about Snoop!"

"I'm glad we were able to get this sofa, so many other people like a rest and there are only four sofas on each car," Mrs. Bobbsey explained to Dinah, who was now tucking Freddie in as if he were at home in his own cozy bed. The air cushion was blown up, and put under the yellow head and a shawl was carefully placed over him.

Flossie's pretty dimpled face was pressed close to the window pane, admiring the big world that seemed to be running away from the train, and Bert found the observation end of the train very interesting.

"What a beautiful grove of white birch trees!" Nan exclaimed, as the train swung into a ravine. "And see the soft ferns clinging about them. Mother, the ferns around the birch tree make me think of the fine lace about your throat!"

"Why, daughter, you seem to be quite poetical!" and the mother smiled, for indeed Nan had a very promising mind.

"What time will we get there, papa?" Bert asked, returning from the vestibule.

"In time for dinner Aunt Sarah said, that is if they keep dinner for us until one o'clock," answered the parent, as he consulted his watch.

"It seems as if we had been on the train all night," Flossie remarked.

"Well, we started early, dear," the mother assured the tired little girl. "Perhaps you would like one of Dinah's dainty sandwiches now?"

A light lunch was quickly decided on, and Dinah took Flossie and Nan to a little private room at one end of the train, Bert went with his father to the smoking room on the other end, while the mother remained to watch Freddie. The lunch was put up so that each small sandwich could be eaten without a crumb spilling, as the little squares were each wrapped separately in waxed paper.

There was a queer alcohol lamp in the ladies room, and other handy contrivances for travelers, which amused Flossie and Nan.

"Dat's to heat milk fo' babies," Dinah told the girls, as she put the paper napkins carefully on their laps, and got each a nice drink of icewater out of the cooler.

Meanwhile Bert was enjoying his lunch at the other end of the car, for children always get hungry when traveling, and meals on the train are only served at certain hours. Two other little girls came into the compartment while Flossie and Nan were at lunch. The strange girls wore gingham aprons over their fine white dresses, to keep the car dust off their clothes, and they had paper caps on their heads like the favors worn at children's parties. Seeing there was no stool vacant the strangers darted out again in rather a rude way, Nan thought.

"Take you time, honeys," Dinah told her charges. "If dey is very hungry dey can get ice cream outside."

"But mother never lets us eat strange ice cream," Flossie reminded the maid. "And maybe they can't either."

Soon the lunch was finished, and the Bobbseys felt much refreshed by it. Freddie still slept with Snoop's box close beside him, and Mrs. Bobbsey was reading a magazine.

"One hour more!" Bert announced, beginning to pick things up even that early.

"Now we better all close our eyes and rest, so that we will feel good when we get to Meadow Brook," Mrs. Bobbsey told them. It was no task to obey this suggestion, and the next thing the children knew, mother and father and Dinah were waking them up to get them ready to leave the train.

"Now, don't forget anything," Mr. Bobbsey cautioned the party, as hats and wraps were donned and parcels picked up.

Freddie was still very sleepy and his papa had to carry him off, while the others, with some excitement, hurried after.

"Oh, Snoop, Snoop!" cried Freddie as, having reached the platform, they now saw the train start off. "I forgot Snoop! Get him quick!"

"Dat kitten again!" Dinah exclaimed, with some indignation. "He's more trouble den—den de whole family!"

In an instant the train had gotten up speed, and it seemed Snoop was gone this time sure.

"Snoop!" cried Freddie, in dismay.

Just then the kind porter who had befriended the cat before, appeared on the platform with the perforated box in his hand.

"I wanted to keep him," stammered the porter, "but I knows de little boy 'ud break his heart after him." And he threw the box to Mr. Bobbsey.

There was no time for words, but Mr. Bobbsey thrust a coin in the man's hand and all the members of the Bobbsey family looked their thanks.

"Well, I declare, you can't see anybody," called out a good-natured little lady, trying to surround them all at once.

"Aunt Sarah!" exclaimed the Bobbseys.

"And Uncle Dan!"

"And Harry!"

"Hello! How do? How are you? How be you?" and such kissing and handshaking had not for some time entertained the old agent at the Meadow Brook station.

"Here at last!" Uncle Daniel declared, grabbing up Freddie and giving him the kind of hug Freddie had intended giving Aunt Sarah.

The big wagon from the Bobbsey farm, with the seats running along each side, stood at the other side of the platform, and into this the Bobbseys were gathered, bag and baggage, not forgetting the little black cat.

"All aboard for Meadow Brook farm!" called Bert, as the wagon started off along the shady country road.

Chapter V

MEADOW BROOK

"Oh, how cool the trees are out here!" Flossie exclaimed, as the wagon rumbled along so close to the low trees that Bert could reach out and pick horse-chestnut blossoms.

"My, how sweet it is!" said Dinah, as she sniffed audibly, enjoying the freshness of the country.

Freddie was on the seat with Uncle Dan and had Snoop's box safe in his arms. He wanted to let the cat see along the road, but everybody protested.

"No more Snoop in this trip," laughed Mr. Bobbsey. "He has had all the fun he needs for to-day." So Freddie had to be content.

"Oh, do let me get out?" pleaded Nan presently. "See that field of orange lilies."

"Not now, dear," Aunt Sarah told her. "Dinner is spoiling for us, and we can often walk down here to get flowers."

"Oh, the cute little calf! Look!" Bert exclaimed from his seat next to Harry, who had been telling his cousin of all the plans he had made for a jolly vacation.

"Look at the billy-goat!" called Freddie.

"See, see, that big black chicken flying!" Flossie cried out excitedly.

"That's a hawk!" laughed Bert; "maybe it's a chicken hawk."

"A children hawk!" Flossie exclaimed, missing the word. Then everybody laughed, and Flossie said maybe there were children hawks for bad girls and boys, anyway.

Aunt Sarah and Mrs. Bobbsey were chatting away like two school-girls, while Dinah and the children saw something new and interesting at every few paces old Billy, the horse, took.

"Hello there, neighbor," called a voice from the field at the side of the road. "My horse has fallen in the ditch, and I'll have to trouble you to help me."

"Certainly, certainly, Peter," answered Uncle Daniel, promptly jumping down, with Mr. Bobbsey, Bert, and Harry following. Aunt Sarah leaned over the seat and took the reins, but when she saw in what ditch the other horse had fallen she pulled Billy into the gutter.

"Poor Peter!" she exclaimed. "That's the second horse that fell in that ditch this week. And it's an awful job to get them out. I'll just wait to see if they need our Billy, and if not, we can drive on home, for Martha will be most crazy waiting with dinner."

Uncle Daniel, Mr. Bobbsey, and the boys hurried to where Peter Burns stood at the brink of one of those ditches that look like mud and turn out to be water.

"And that horse is a boarder too!" Peter told them. "Last night we said he looked awful sad, but we didn't think he would commit suicide."

"Got plenty of blankets?" Uncle Daniel asked, pulling his coat off and preparing to help his neighbor, as all good people do in the country.

"Four of them, and these planks. But I couldn't get a man around. Lucky you happened by," Peter Burns answered.

All this time the horse in the ditch moaned as if in pain, but Peter said it was only because he couldn't get on his feet. Harry, being light in weight, slipped a halter over the poor beast's head.

"I could get a strap around him!" Harry suggested, moving out cautiously on the plank.

"All right, my lad, go ahead," Peter told him, passing the big strap over to Bert, who in turn passed it on to Harry.

It was no easy matter to get the strap in place, but with much tugging and splashing of mud Harry succeeded. Then the ropes were attached and everybody pulled vigorously.

"Get up, Ginger! Get up, Ginger!" Peter called lustily, but Ginger only seemed to flop in deeper, through his efforts to raise himself.

"Guess we'll have to get Billy to pull," Uncle Daniel suggested, and Mr. Bobbsey hurried back to the road to unhitch the other horse.

"Don't let Billy fall in!" exclaimed Nan, who was much excited over the accident.

"Can't I go, papa?" Freddie pleaded. "I'll stay away from the edge!"

"You better stay in the wagon; the horse might cut up when he gets out," the father warned Freddie, who reluctantly gave in.

Soon Billy was hitched to the ropes, and with a few kind words from Uncle Daniel the big white horse strained forward, pulling Ginger to his feet as he did so.

"Hurrah!" shouted Freddie from the wagon. "Billy is a circus horse, isn't he, Uncle Dan?"

"He's a good boy," the uncle called back patting Billy affectionately, while Mr. Bobbsey and the boys loosened the straps. The other horse lay on the blankets, and Peter rubbed him with all his might, to save a chill as he told the boys.

Then, after receiving many thanks for the help given, the Bobbseys once more started off toward the farm.

"Hot work," Uncle Daniel remarked to the ladies, as he mopped his forehead.

"I'm so glad you could help Peter," Aunt Sarah told him, "for he does seem to have so much trouble."

"All kinds of things happen in the country," Harry remarked, as Billy headed off for home.

At each house along the way boys would call out to Harry, asking him about going fishing, or berrying, or some other sport, so that Bert felt a good time was in store for him, as the boys were about his own age and seemed so agreeable.

"Nice fellows," Harry remarked by way of introducing Bert.

"They seem so," Bert replied, cordially.

"We've made up a lot of sports," Harry went on, "and we were only waiting for you to come to start out. We've planned a picnic for to-morrow."

"Here we are," called Uncle Daniel as Billy turned into the pretty driveway in front of the Bobbseys' country home. On each side of the drive grew straight lines of boxwood, and back of this hedge were beautiful flowers, shining out grandly now in the July sun.

"Hello, Martha!" called the visitors, as the faithful old servant appeared on the broad white veranda. She was not black like Dinah, but looked as if she was just as merry and full of fun as anyone could be.

"Got here at last!" she exclaimed, taking Dinah's lunch basket.

"Glad to see you, Martha," Dinah told her. "You see, I had to come along. And Snoop too, our kitty. We fetched him."

"The more the merrier," replied the other, "and there's lots of room for all."

"Starved to death!" Harry laughed, as the odor of a fine dinner reached him.

"We'll wash up a bit and join you in a few minutes, ladies," Uncle Daniel said, in his polite way. The horse accident had given plenty of need for a washing up.

"Got Snoop dis time," Freddie lisped, knocking the cover off the box and petting the frightened little black cat. "Hungry, Snoopy?" he asked, pressing his baby cheek to the soft fur.

"Bring the poor kitty out to the kitchen," Martha told him. "I'll get him a nice saucer of fresh milk." And so it happened, as usual, Snoop had his meal first, just as he had had on the Pullman car. Soon after this Martha went outside and rang a big dinner bell that all the men and boys could hear. And then the first vacation dinner was served in the long old-fashioned dining room.

Chapter VI

FRISKY

Although they were tired from their journey, the children had no idea of resting on that beautiful afternoon, so promptly after dinner the baggage was opened, and vacation clothes were put on. Bert, of course, was ready first; and soon he and Harry were running down the road to meet the other boys and perfect their plans for the picnic.

Nan began her pleasures by exploring the flower gardens with Uncle Daniel.

"I pride myself on those zinnias," the uncle told Nan, "just see those yellows, and those pinks. Some are as big as dahlias, aren't they?"

"They are just beautiful, uncle," Nan replied, in real admiration. "I have always loved zinnias. And they last so long?"

"All summer. Then, what do you think of my sweet peas?"

So they went from one flower bed to another, and Nan thought she had never before seen so many pretty plants together.

Flossie and Freddie were out in the barnyard with Aunt Sarah.

"Oh, auntie, what queer little chickens!" Flossie exclaimed, pointing to a lot of pigeons that were eagerly eating corn with the chickens.

"Those are Harry's homer pigeons," the aunt explained. "Some day we must go off to the woods and let the birds fly home with a letter to Dinah and Martha."

"Oh, please do it now," Freddie urged, always in a hurry for things.

"We couldn't to-day, dear," Aunt Sarah told him. "Come, let me show you our new little calf."

"WHOA, FRISKY! WHOA!"

"Let me ride her?" Freddie asked, as they reached the animal.

"Calfs aren't for riding, they're for milk," Flossie spoke up.

"Yes, this one drinks plenty of milk," Aunt Sarah said, while Frisky, the calf, rubbed her head kindly against Aunt Sarah's skirts.

"Then let me take her for a walk," Freddie pleaded, much in love with the pretty creature.

"And they don't walk either," Flossie persisted. "They mostly run."

"I could just hold the rope, couldn't I, Aunt Sarah?"

"If you keep away from the barnyard gate, and hold her very tight," was the consent given finally, much to Freddie's delight.

"Nice Frisky," he told the calf, petting her fondly. "Pretty calf, will you let Snoop play with you?" Frisky was sniffing suspiciously all the time, and Aunt Sarah had taken Flossie in the barn to see the chickens' nests.

"Come, Frisky, take a walk," suggested Freddie, and quite obediently the little cow walked along. But suddenly Frisky spied the open gate and the lovely green grass outside.

Without a moment's warning the calf threw her hind legs up in the air, then bolted straight for the gate, dragging Freddie along after her.

"Whoa, Frisky! whoa!" yelled Freddie, but the calf ran right along.

"Hold tight, Freddie!" called Flossie, as she and Aunt Sarah appeared on the scene.

"Whoa, whoa!" yelled the little boy constantly, but he might as well have called "Get app," for Frisky was going so fast now that poor little Freddie's hands were all but bleeding from the rough rope.

"Look out, Freddie! Let go!" called Aunt Sarah as she saw Frisky heading for the apple tree.

The next minute Frisky made a dash around the tree, once, then again, winding the rope as she went, and throwing Freddie out with force against the side of the terrace.

"Oh," Freddie moaned feebly.

"Are you dead?" cried Flossie, running up with tears in her eyes.

"Oh," moaned the boy again, turning over with much trouble as Aunt Sarah lifted him.

"Oh," he murmured once more, "oh—catch—Frisky!"

"Never mind her," Aunt Sarah said, anxiously. "Are you hurt, dear!"

"No—not—a bit. But look! There goes Frisky! Catch her!"

"Your poor little hands!" Flossie almost cried, kissing the red blisters. "See, they're cut!"

"Firemen have to slide on ropes!" Freddie spoke up, recovering himself, "and I'm going to be a fireman. I was one that time, because I tried to save somebody and didn't care if I got hurted!"

"You are a brave little boy," Aunt Sarah assured him. "You just sit here with sister while I try to get that naughty Frisky before she spoils the garden."

By this time the calf was almost lost to them, as she plunged in and out of the pretty hedges. Fortunately Bert and Harry just turned in the gate.

"Runaway calf! Runaway calf!" called the boys. "Stop the runaway!" and instantly a half-dozen other boys appeared, and all started in pursuit.

But Frisky knew how to run, besides she had the advantage of a good start, and now she just dashed along as if the affair was the biggest joke of her life.

"The river! The river!" called the boys

"She'll jump in!" and indeed the pretty Meadow Brook, or river, that ran along some feet lower than the Bobbseys' house, on the other side of the highway, was now dangerously near the runaway calf.

There was a heavy thicket a few feet further up, and as the boys squeezed in and out of the bushes Frisky plunged into this piece of wood.

"Oh, she's gone now, sure!" called Harry "Listen!"

Sure enough there was a splash!

Frisky must be in the river!

It took some time to reach the spot where the fall might have sounded from, and the boys made their way heavy-hearted, for all loved the pretty little Frisky.

"There's footprints!" Bert discovered emerging from the thick bush.

"And they end here!" Harry finished, indicating the very brink of the river.

"She's gone!"

"But how could she drown so quickly?" Bert asked.

"Guess that's the channel," Tom Mason, one of the neighbors' boys, answered.

"Listen! Thought I heard something in the bushes!" Bert whispered.

But no welcome sound came to tell that poor Frisky was hiding in the brushwood. With heavy hearts the boys turned away. They didn't even feel like talking, somehow. They had counted on bringing the calf back in triumph.

When Flossie and Freddie saw them coming back without Frisky they just had to cry and no one could stop them.

"I tried to be a fireman!" blubbered Freddie. "I didn't care if the rope hurted my hands either!"

"If only I didn't go in to see the chickens nests," Flossie whimpered, "I could have helped Freddie!"

"Never you mind, little 'uns," Dinah told them. "Dinah go and fetch dat Frisky back to-morrer. See if she don't. You jest don't cry no more, but eat you supper and take a good sleep, 'cause we're goin' to have a picnic to-morrer you knows, doesn't youse?"

The others tried to comfort the little ones too, and Uncle Daniel said he knew where he could buy another calf just like Frisky, so after a little while Freddie felt better and even laughed when Martha made the white cat Fluffy and Snoop play ball in the big long kitchen.

"I'm goin' to pray Frisky will come back," Nan told her little brother when she kissed him good-night, "and maybe the dear Lord will find her for you."

"Oh, yes, Nannie, do ask Him," pleaded Freddie, "and tell Him— tell Him if He'll do it this time, I'll be so good I won't never need to bother Him any more."

Freddie meant very well, but it sounded strange, and made Aunt Sarah say, "The Lord bless the little darling!" Then night came and an eventful day closed in on our dear little Bobbseys.

"Seems as if something else ought to happen to-night," Bert remarked to Harry as they prepared to retire. "This was such a full day, wasn't it?"

"It's early yet," Harry answered, "and it's never late here until it's time to get early again."

"Sounds so strange to hear—those—those—"

"Crickets," Harry told him, "and tree toads and katydids. Oh, there's lots to listen to if you shouldn't feel sleepy."

The house was now all quiet, and even the boys had ceased whispering. Suddenly there was a noise in the driveway!

The next minute someone called out in the night!

"Hello there! All asleep! Wake up, somebody!"

Even Freddie did wake up and ran into his mother's room.

"Come down here, Mr. Bobbsey," the voice continued.

"Oh, is that you, Peter? I'll be down directly," called back Uncle Daniel, who very soon after appeared on the front porch.

"Well, I declare!" Uncle Daniel exclaimed, loud enough for all the listeners at the windows to hear. "So you've got her? Well, I'm very glad indeed. Especially on the boys' account."

"Yes," spoke out Peter Burns, "I went in the barn a while ago with the lantern, and there wasn't your calf asleep with mine as cozy as could be. I brought her over to-night for fear you might miss her and get to lookin', otherwise I wouldn't have disturbed you."

By this time the man from the barn was up and out too, and he took Frisky back to her own bed; but not until the little calf had been taken far out on the front lawn so that Freddie could see her from the window "to make sure."

"The Lord did bring her back," Freddie told his mamma as she kissed him good-night again and put him in his bed, happier this time than before. "And I promised to be awful good to pay Him for His trouble," the sleepy boy murmured.

Flossie had been asleep about two hours when she suddenly called to her mother.

"What is it, my dear?" asked Mrs. Bobbsey.

"Somebody is playing the piano," answered the little girl. "Who is it?"

"Nobody is playing. You must be dreaming," answered the mother, and smiled to herself.

"No, I am sure I heard the piano," insisted Flossie.

Mother and daughter listened, but could hear nothing.

"You were surely dreaming," said Mrs. Bobbsey. "Come, I will tuck you in again," and she did so.

But was Flossie dreaming? Let us wait and see.

Chapter VII

A COUNTRY PICNIC

When morning came everyone was astir early, for not only was a happy day promised, but there was Frisky, the runaway, to be looked over. Mr. Richard Bobbsey, Freddie's father, left on an early train for Lakeport, and would not come back to Meadow Brook until Saturday afternoon.

"Let me go out and see Frisky," Freddie insisted, even before his breakfast had been served. "I want to be sure it's her."

"Yes, that's her," Freddie admitted, "'cause there's the rope that cut my hands when I was a real fireman!"

But Frisky didn't seem to care a bit about ropes or firemen, but just chewed and chewed like all cows do, as if there was nothing in this world to do but eat.

"Come on, sonny," called Dinah. "You can help me pick de radishes fo' breakfast," and presently our little boy, with the kind-hearted maid, was up in the garden looking for the best radishes of the early crop.

"See, Freddie," said Dinah. "De red ones show above de ground. And we must only pull de ones wid de big leaves, 'cause dey're ripe."

Freddie bent down so close to find the radishes that a disturbed toad hopped right up at his nose.

"Oh!" he cried, frightened. "Dinah, was that—a—a—a snake?"

"Snake, chile; lan' sakes alive! Dat was a poor little toady—more scare' den you was," and she pointed to the big dock leaf under which the hop-toad was now hiding.

"Let's pick beans," Freddie suggested, liking the garden work.

"Not beans fer breakfast," laughed Dinah.

"That stuff there, then," the boy persisted, pointing to the soft green leaves of early lettuce.

"Well, I dunno. Martha didn't say so, but it sure does look pretty. Yes, I guess we kin pick some fo' salad," and so Dinah showed Freddie how to cut the lettuce heads off and leave the stalks to grow again.

"Out early," laughed Uncle Daniel, seeing the youngest member of the family coming down the garden path with the small basket of vegetables.

"Is it?" Freddie asked, meaning early of course, in his queer way of saying things without words.

"See! see!" called Nan and Flossie, running down the cross path back of the cornfield.

"Such big ones!" Nan exclaimed, referring to the luscious red strawberries in the white dish she held.

"Look at mine," insisted Flossie. "Aren't they bigger?"

"Fine!" ejaculated Dinah.

"But my redishes are-are—redder," argued Freddie, who was not to be outdone by his sisters.

"Ours are sweeter," laughed Nan, trying to tease her little brother.

"Ours are—ours are—"

"Hotter," put in Dinah, which ended the argument.

Bert and Harry had also been out gathering for breakfast, and returned now with a basket of lovely fresh water-cress.

"We can't eat 'em all," Martha told the boys, "But they'll go good in the picnic lunch."

What a pretty breakfast table it was! Such berries, such lettuce, such water-cress, and the radishes!

"Too bad papa had to go so early," Bert remarked. "He just loves green stuff."

"So does Frisky," put in Freddie, and he wondered why everyone laughed.

After breakfast the lunch baskets were put up and while Bert and Harry, Nan and Aunt Sarah, went to invite the neighboring children, Flossie and Freddie were just busy jumping around the kitchen, where Dinah and Martha were making them laugh merrily with funny little stories.

Snoop and Fluffy had become good friends, and now lay close together on the kitchen hearth. Dinah said they were just like two babies, only not so much trouble.

"Put peaches in my basket, Dinah," Freddie ordered.

"And strawberries in mine," added Flossie.

"Now, you-uns jest wait!" Dinah told them; "and when you gets out in de woods if you hasn't 'nough to eat you kin jest climb a tree an' cut down—"

"Wood!" put in Freddie innocently, while Martha said that was about all that could be found in the woods in July.

The boys had come in from inviting the "other fellers," when Uncle Daniel proposed a feature for the picnic.

"How would you like to take two homer pigeons along?" he asked them. "You can send a note back to Martha to say what time you will be home."

"Jolly!" chorused the boys, all instantly making a run for the pigeon house.

"Wait!" Harry told the visitors. "We must be careful not to scare them." Then he went inside the wire cage with a handful of corn.

"See—de—coon; see—de—coon!" called the boys softly, imitating the queer sounds made by the doves cooing.

Harry tossed the corn inside the cage, and as the light and dark homers he wanted tasted the food Harry lowered the little door, and took the birds safely in his arms.

"Now, Bert, you can get the quills," he told his cousin. "Go into the chicken yard and look for two long goose feathers. Tom Mason, you can go in the kitchen and ask Dinah for a piece of tissue paper and a spool of silk thread."

Each boy started off to fulfill his commission, not knowing exactly what for until all came together in the barnyard again.

"Now, Bert," went on Harry, "write very carefully on the slip of paper the message for Martha. Have you a soft pencil?"

Bert found that he had one, and so following his cousin's dictation he wrote on one slip:

"Have dinner ready at five." And on the other he wrote: "John, come for us at four."

"Now," continued Harry, "roll the slips up fine enough to go in the goose quills."

This was done with much difficulty, as the quills were very narrow, but the task was finally finished.

"All ready now," concluded Harry, "to put the letters in the box," and very gently he tied with the silken thread one quill under the wing of each pigeon. Only one feather was used to tie the thread to, and the light quill, the thin paper, and the soft silk made a parcel so very small and light in weight that the pigeons were no way inconvenienced by the messages.

"Now we'll put them in this basket, and they're ready for the picnic," Harry announced to his much interested companions. Then all started for the house with Harry and the basket in the lead.

John, the stableman, was at the door now with the big hay wagon, which had been chosen as the best thing to take the jolly party in.

There was nice fresh hay in the bottom, and seats at the sides for the grown folks, while the little ones nestled in the sweet-smelling hay like live birds.

"It's like a kindergarten party," laughed Nan, as the "birds' nests" reminded her of one of the mother plays.

"No, 'tain't!" Freddie corrected, for he really was not fond of the kindergarten. "It's just like a picnic," he finished.

Besides the Bobbseys there were Tom Mason, Jack Hopkins, and August Stout, friends of Harry. Then, there were Mildred Manners and Mabel Herold, who went as Nan's guests; little Roy Mason was Freddie's company, and Bessie Dimple went with Flossie. The little pigeons kept cooing every now and then, but made no attempt to escape from Harry's basket.

It was a beautiful day, and the long ride through the country was indeed a merry one. Along the way people called out pleasantly from farmhouses, for everybody in Meadow Brook knew the Bobbseys.

"That's their cousins from the city," little boys and girls along the way would say.

"Haven't they pretty clothes!" the girls were sure to add.

"Let's stop for a drink at the spring," suggested August Stout, who was stout by name and nature, and always loved a good drink of water.

The children tumbled out of the wagon safely, and were soon waiting turns at the spring.

There was a round basin built of stones and quite deep. Into this the clear sprinkling water dropped from a little cave in the hill above. On top of the cave a large flat stone was placed. This kept the little waterfall clean and free from the falling leaves.

"Oh, what a cute little pond!" Freddie exclaimed, for he had never seen a real spring before.

"That's a spring," Flossie informed him, although that was all she knew about it.

The big boys were not long dipping their faces in and getting a drink of the cool, clear water, but the girls had to take their hats off, roll up their sleeves, and go through a "regular performance," as Harry said, before they could make up their minds to dip into the water. Mabel brought up her supply with her hands, but when Nan tried it her hands leaked, and the result was her fresh white frock got wet. Flossie's curls tumbled in both sides, and when she had finished she looked as if she had taken a plunge at the seashore.

"Let me! Let me!" cried Freddie impatiently, and without further warning he thrust his yellow head in the spring clear up to his neck!

"Oh, Freddie!" yelled Nan, grabbing him by the heels and thus saving a more serious accident.

"Oh! oh! oh!" spluttered Freddie, nearly choked, "I'm drowned!" and the water really seemed to be running out of his eyes, noses and ears all at once.

"Oh, Freddie!" was all Mrs. Bobbsey could say, as a shower of clean handkerchiefs was sent from the hay wagon to dry the "drowned" boy.

"Just like the flour barrel!" laughed Bert, referring to the funny accident that befell Freddie the winter before, as told in my other book "The Bobbsey Twins, Merry Days Indoors and Out."

"Only that was a dry bath and this a wet one," Nan remarked, as Freddie's curls were shook out in the sun.

"Did you get a drink?" asked August, whose invitation to drink had caused the mishap.

"Yep!" answered Freddie bravely, "and I was a real fireman too, that time, 'cause they always get soaked; don't they, Bert?"

Being assured they did, the party once more started off for the woods. It was getting to be all woods now, only a driveway breaking through the pines, maples, and chestnut trees that abounded in that section.

"Just turn in there, John!" Harry directed, as a particularly thick group of trees appeared. Here were chosen the picnic grounds and all the things taken from the wagon, and before John was out of sight on the return home the children had established their camp and were flying about the woods like little fairies.

"Let's build a furnace," Jack Hopkins suggested.

"Let's," said all the boys, who immediately set out carrying stones and piling them up to build the stove. There was plenty of wood about, and when the fire was built, the raw potatoes that Harry had secretly

"DINNER SERVED IN THE DINING CAR!"

brought along were roasted, finer than any oven could cook them.

Mrs. Bobbsey and Aunt Sarah had spread the tablecloth on the grass, and were now busy opening the baskets and arranging the places. There were so many pretty little nooks to explore in the woods that Mrs. Bobbsey had to warn the children not to get too far away.

"Are there giants?" Freddie asked.

"No, but there are very dark lonely places the woods and little boys might find snakes."

"And bears!" put in Freddie, to which remark his mother said, "perhaps," because there really might be bears in a woods so close to the mountains.

Chapter VIII

FUN IN THE WOODS

"Dinner served in the dining car!" called Bert through the woods, imitating the call of the porter on the Pullman car.

"All ready!" echoed the other boys, banging on an old boiler like the Turks do, instead of ringing a bell.

"Oh, how pretty!" the girls all exclaimed, as they beheld the "feast in the forest," as Nan put it. And indeed it was pretty, for at each place was set a long plume of fern leaves with wood violets at the end, and what could be more beautiful than such a decoration?

"Potatoes first!" Harry announced, "because they may get cold," and at this order everybody broke the freshly roasted potatoes into the paper napkins and touched it up with the extra butter that had come along.

"Simply fine!" declared Nan, with the air of one who knew. Now, my old readers will remember how Nan baked such good cake. So she ought to be an authority on baked potatoes, don't you think?

Next came the sandwiches, with the watercress Harry and Bert had gathered before breakfast, then (and this was a surprise) hot chocolate! This was brought out in Martha's cider jug, and heated in a kettle over the boys' stone furnace.

"It must be fun to camp out," Mabel Herold remarked.

"Yes, just think of the dishes saved," added Mildred Manners, who always had so many dishes to do at home.

"And we really don't need them," Nan argued, passing her tin cup on to Flossie.

"Think how the soldiers get along!" Bert put in.

"And the firemen'" lisped Freddie, who never forgot the heroes of flame and water.

Of course everybody was either sitting on the grass or on a "soft stump." These latter conveniences had been brought by the boys for Aunt Sarah and Mrs. Bobbsey.

"What's that!" exclaimed little Flossie, as something was plainly moving under the tables cloth.

"A snake, a snake!" called everybody at once, for indeed under the white linen was plainly to be seen the creeping form of a reptile.

While the girls made a run for safety the boys carefully lifted the cloth and went for his snakeship.

"There he is! There he is!" shouted Tom Mason, as the thing tried to crawl under the stump lately used as a seat by Mrs. Bobbsey.

"Whack him!" called August Stout, who, armed with a good club, made straight for the stump.

"Look out! He's a big fellow!" Harry declared, as the snake attempted to get upright.

The boys fell back a little now, and as the snake actually stood on the tip of his tail, as they do before striking, Harry sprang forward and dealt him a heavy blow right on the head that laid the intruder flat.

"At him, boys! At him!" called Jack Hopkins, while the snake lay wriggling in the grass; and the boys, making good use of the stunning blow Harry had dealt, piled on as many more blows as their clubs could wield.

All this time the girls and ladies were over on a knoll "high and dry," as Nan said, and now, when assured that the snake was done for they could hardly be induced to come and look at him.

"He's a beauty!" Harry declared, as the boys actually stretched the creature out to measure him. Bert had a rule, and when the snake was measured up he was found to be five feet long!

"He's a black racer!" Jack Hopkins announced, and the others said they guessed he was.

"Lucky we saw him first!" remarked Harry, "Racers are very poisonous!"

"Let's go home; there might be more!", pleaded Flossie, but the boys said the snake hunt was the best fun at the picnic.

"Goodness!" exclaimed Harry suddenly, "we forgot to let the pigeons loose!" and so saying he ran for the basket of birds that hung on the low limb of a pretty maple. First Harry made sure the messages were safe under each bird's wing, then he called:

"All ready!"

Snap! went something that sounded like a shot (but it wasn't), and then away flew the pretty birds to take the messages home to John and Martha. The shot was only a dry stick that Tom Mason snapped to imitate a gun, as they do at bicycle races, but the effect was quite startling and made the girls jump.

"It won't take long for them to get home!" said Bert, watching the birds fly away.

"They'll get lost!" cried Freddie.

"No, they won't. They know which way we came," Nan explained.

"But they was shut up in the basket," argued Freddie.

"Yet they could see," Nan told him.

"Can pigeons see when they're asleep?" inquired the little fellow.

"Maybe," Nan answered.

"Then I'd like to have pigeon eyes," he finished, thinking to himself how fine it would be to see everything going on around and be fast asleep too.

"Oh, mamma, come quick!" called Flossie, running along a path at the edge of the wood. "There's a tree over there pouring water, and it isn't raining a drop!"

Everybody set out now to look at the wonderful tree, which was soon discovered where Flossie had found it.

"There it is!" she exclaimed. "See the water dropping down!"

"A maple tree," Harry informed them, "and that sap is what they make maple sugar out of."

"Oh, catch it!" called Freddie, promptly holding his cap under the drops.

"It would take a good deal to make a sugar cake," Harry said, "but maybe we can get enough of it to make a little cake for Freddie."

At this the country boys began looking around for young maples, and as small limbs of the trees were broken the girls caught the drops in their tin cups. It took quite a while to get a little, but by putting it all together a cupful was finally gathered.

"Now we will put it in a clean milk bottle," Mrs. Bobbsey said, "and maybe we can make maple syrup cake to-morrow."

"Let's have a game of hide-and-seek," Nan suggested.

In a twinkling every boy and girl was hidden behind a tree, and Nan found herself "It." Of course it took a big tree to hide the girls' dresses, and Nan had no trouble in spying Mildred first. Soon the game was going along merrily, and the boys and girls were out of breath trying to get "home free."

"Where's Roy?" exclaimed Tom Mason, the little boy's brother.

"Hiding somewhere," Bessie ventured, for it only seemed a minute before when the little fat boy who was Freddie's companion had been with the others.

"But where is he?" they all soon exclaimed in alarm, as call after call brought no answer.

"Over at the maple tree!" Harry thought.

"Down at the spring," Nan said.

"Looking for flowers," Flossie guessed.

But all these spots were searched, and the little boy was not found.

"Oh, maybe the giants have stoled him!" Freddie cried.

"Or maybe the children's hawk has took him away," Flossie sobbed.

Meanwhile everybody searched and searched, but no Roy could they find.

"The boat!" suddenly exclaimed Tom, making a dash for the pond that ran along at the foot of a steep hill.

"There he is! There he is!" the brother yelled, as getting over the edge of the hill Tom was now in full view of the pond.

"And in the boat," called Harry, close at Tom's heels.

"He's drifting away!" screamed Bert. "Oh, quick, save him!"

Just as the boys said, the little fellow was in the boat and drifting. He did not seem to realize his danger, for as he floated along he ran his little fat hand through the water as happily as if he had been in a steam launch, talking to the captain.

"Can you swim?" the boys asked Bert, who of course had learned that useful art long ago.

"She's quite a long way out," Tom said,

"But we must be careful not to frighten him. See, he has left the oars here. Bert and I can carry one out and swim with one hand. Harry and Jack, can you manage the other?"

The boys said they could, and quickly as the heaviest clothes could be thrown off they were striking out in the little lake toward the baby in the boat. He was only Freddie's age, you know, and perhaps more of a baby than the good-natured Bobbsey boy.

"Sit still, Roy," called the anxious girl from the shore, fearing Roy would upset the boat as the boys neared him. It was hard work to swim and carry oars, but our brave boys managed to do it in time to save Roy. For not a great way down the stream were an old water wheel and a dam. Should the boat drift there what would become of little Roy?

Mrs. Bobbsey and Aunt Sarah were worrying over this as the boys were making their way to the boat.

"Easy now!" called Bert. "Here we are," and at that moment the first pair of swimmers climbed carefully into the boat, one from each side, so as not to tip it over. Jack and Harry were not long in following, and as the boys all sat in the pretty green rowboat with their white under-clothing answering for athletic suits, they looked just like a crew of real oarsmen.

"Hurrah, hurrah!" came shout after shout from the bank. Then as the girls heard the rumble of wheels through the grove they all hurried off to gather up the stuff quickly, and be ready to start as soon as the boys dressed again. The wet under-clothing, of course, was carried home in one of the empty baskets that Freddie ran back over the hill with to save the tired boys the extra walk.

"Here they are! Here they are!" called the girls as the two little fellows, Roy and Freddie, with the basket of wet clothes between them, marched first; then came the two pairs of athletes who proved they were good swimmers by pushing the heavy oars safely to the drifting boat.

"And all the things that happened!" exclaimed Flossie, as John handed her into the hay wagon.

"That made the picnic lively!" declared, John, "and all's well that ends well, you know." So the picnic was over, and all were happy and tired enough to go to bed early that night, as Nan said, seeing the little ones falling asleep in hay wagon on their way home.

Chapter IX

FOURTH OF JULY

The day following the picnic was July third, and as the Meadow Brook children were pretty well tired out from romping in the woods, they were glad of a day's rest before entering upon the festivities of Independence Day.

"How much have you got?" Tom Mason asked the Bobbsey boys.

"Fifty cents together, twenty-five cents each," Harry announced.

"Well, I've got thirty-five, and we had better get our stuff early, for Stimpson sold out before noon last year," concluded Tom.

"I have to get torpedoes for Freddie and Flossie, and Chinese firecrackers for Nan," Bert remarked, as they started for the little country grocery store.

"I guess I'll buy a few snakes, they look so funny coiling out," Tom said.

"I'm going to have sky rockets and Roman candles. Everybody said they were the prettiest last year," said Harry.

"If they have red fire I must get some of it for the girls," thoughtful Bert remarked.

But at the store the boys had to take just what they could get, as Stimpson's supply was very limited.

"Let's make up a parade!" someone suggested, and this being agreed upon the boys started a canvass from house to house, to get all the boys along Meadow Brook road to take part in the procession.

"Can the little ones come too?" August Stout asked, because he always had to look out for his small brother when there was any danger like fireworks around.

"Yes, and we're goin' to let the girls march in a division by themselves," Bert told him. "My sister Nan is going to be captain, and we'll leave all the girls' parts to her."

"Be sure and bring your flag," Harry cautioned Jack Hopkins.

"How would the goat wagons do?" Jack asked.

"Fine; we could let Roy and Freddie ride in them," said Bert. "Tell any of the other fellows who have goat teams to bring them along too."

"Eight o'clock sharp at our lane," Harry told them for the place and time of meeting. Then they went along to finish the arrangements.

"Don't tell the boys," Nan whispered to Mildred, as they too made their way to Stimpson's.

"Won't they be surprised?" exclaimed Mabel.

"Yes, and I am going to carry a real Betsy Ross flag, one with thirteen stars, you know."

"Oh, yes, Betsy Ross made the first flag, didn't she?" remarked Mildred, trying to catch up on history.

"We'll have ten big girls," Nan counted. "Then with Flossie as Liberty we will want Bessie and Nettie for her assistants."

"Attendants," Mabel corrected, for she had seen a city parade like that once.

It was a busy day for everybody, and when Mr. Bobbsey came up on the train from Lakeport that evening he carried boxes and boxes of fireworks for the boys and girls, and even some for the grown folks too.

The girls could hardly sleep that night, they were so excited over their part, but the boys of course were used to that sort of thing, and only slept sounder with the fun in prospect.

"Are you awake, Bert?" called Harry, so early the next morning that the sun was hardly up yet.

"Yep," replied the cousin, jumping out of bed and hastily dressing for the firing of the first gun.

The boys crept through the house very quietly, then ran to the barn for their ammunition. Three big giant fire-crackers were placed in the road directly in front of the house.

"Be careful!" whispered Bert; "they're full of powder."

But Harry was always careful with fireworks, and when he touched the fuses to the "cannons" he made away quickly before they exploded.

Bang! Bang! Bang!

"Hurrah!" shouted Freddie, answering the call from his window, "I'll be right down!"

All the others too were aroused by the first "guns," so that in a very short time there were many boys in the road, firing so many kinds of fire-crackers that Meadow Brook resounded like a real war fort under fire.

"Ouch!" yelled Tom Mason, the first one to burn his fingers. "A sisser caught me right on the thumb."

But such small accidents were not given much attention, and soon Tom was lighting the little red crackers as merrily as before.

"Go on back, girls!" called Bert. "You'll get your dresses burnt if you don't."

The girls were coming too near the battlements then, and Bert did well to warn them off.

Freddie and Flossie were having a great time throwing their little torpedoes at Mr. Bobbsey and Uncle Daniel, who were seated on the piazza watching the sport. Snoop and Fluffy too came in for a scare, for Freddie tossed a couple of torpedoes on the kitchen hearth where the kittens were sleeping.

The boys were having such fun they could hardly be induced to come in for breakfast, but they finally did stop long enough to eat a spare meal.

"It's time to get ready!" whispered Nan to Bert, for the parade had been kept secret from the grown folks.

At the girls' place of meeting, the coach house, Nan found all her company waiting and anxious to dress.

"Just tie your scarfs loose under your left arm," ordered Captain Nan, and the girls quickly obeyed like true cadets. The broad red-white-and-blue bunting was very pretty over the girls' white dresses, and indeed the "cadets" looked as if they would outdo the "regulars" unless the boys too had surprises in store.

"Where's Nettie?" suddenly asked Nan, missing a poor little girl who had been invited.

"She wouldn't come because she had no white dress," Mildred answered.

"Oh, what a shame; she'll be so disappointed! Besides, we need her to make a full line," Nan said. "Just wait a minute. Lock the door after me," and before the others knew what she was going to do, Nan ran off to the house, got one of her own white dresses, rolled it up neatly, and was over the fields to Nettie's house in a few minutes. When Nan came back she brought Nettie with her, and not one of her companions knew it was Nan's dress that Nettie wore.

Soon all the scarfs were tied and the flags arranged. Then Flossie had to be dressed.

She wore a light blue dress with gold stars on it, and on her pretty yellow curls she had a real Liberty crown. Then she had the cleanest, brightest flag, and what a pretty picture she made!

"Oh, isn't she sweet!" all the girls exclaimed in admiration, and indeed she was a little beauty in her Liberty costume.

"There go the drums!" Nan declared. "We must be careful to get down the lane without being seen." This was easily managed, and now the girls and boys met at the end of the lane.

"Hurrah! hurrah!" shouted the boys, beating the drums and blowing their horns to welcome the girls.

"Oh, don't you look fine!" exclaimed Harry, who was captain of the boys.

"And don't you too!" Nan answered, for indeed the boys had such funny big hats on and so many flags and other red-white-and-blue things, that they too made a fine appearance.

"And Freddie!" exclaimed the girls. "Isn't he a lovely Uncle Sam!"

Freddie was dressed in the striped suit Uncle Sam always wears, and had on his yellow curls a tall white hat. He was to ride in Jack Hopkins' goat wagon.

"Fall in!" called Harry, and at the word all the companies fell in line.

"Cadets first," ordered the captain.

Then Flossie walked the very first one. After her came Nan and her company. (No one noticed that Nettie's eyes were a little red from crying. She had been so disappointed at first when she thought she couldn't go in the parade.) After the girls came Freddie as Uncle Sam, in the goat wagon led by Bert (for fear the goat might run away), then fifteen boys, all with drums or fifes or some other things with which to make a noise. Roy was in the second division with his wagon, and last of all came the funniest thing.

A boy dressed up like a bear with a big sign on him:

TEDDY!

He had a gun under his arm and looked too comical for anything.

It was quite warm to wear a big fur robe and false face, but under this was Jack Hopkins, the bear Teddy, and he didn't mind being warm when he made everybody laugh so.

"Right foot, left foot, right foot, forward march!" called Nan, and the procession started up the path straight for the Bobbsey house.

"Goodness gracious, sakes alive! Do come see de childrens! Ha, ha! Dat sure am a parade!" called Dinah, running through the house to the front door to view the procession.

"Oh, isn't it just beautiful!" Martha echoed close at Dinah's heels.

"My!" exclaimed Mrs. Bobbsey; "how did they ever get made up so pretty!"

"And look at Flossie!" exclaimed Aunt Sarah.

"And see Freddie!" put in Uncle Daniel.

"Oh, we must get the camera!" Mr. Bobbsey declared, while the whole household, all excited, stood out on the porch when the parade advanced.

Such drumming and such tooting of fifes and horns!

Freddie's chariot was now in line with the front stoop, and he raised his tall hat to the ladies like a real Uncle Sam.

"Oh, the bear! the bear!" called everybody, as they saw "Teddy" coming up.

"That's great," continued Uncle Daniel.

By this time Mr. Bobbsey had returned with the camera.

"Halt!" called Harry, and the procession stood still.

"Look this way. There now, all ready," said Mr. Bobbsey, and snap went the camera on as pretty a picture as ever covered a plate.

"Right wheel! forward march!" called Nan again, and amid drumming and tooting the procession started off to parade through the center of Meadow Brook.

Chapter X

A GREAT DAY

Never before had such a parade been seen in the little country place, and all along the road cheer after cheer greeted our young friends, for even the few old soldiers who lived in Meadow Brook enjoyed the children's Fourth of July fun.

By lunch time the procession had covered all the ground planned, so from the post office the cadets and regulars started back over the shady country road.

And at home they found a surprise awaiting them!

Ice cream on the lawn for everybody in the parade.

Aunt Sarah and Uncle Daniel had set out all the garden benches, and with the two kinds of ice cream made by Dinah and Martha, besides the cookies and jumbles Aunt Sarah supplied, with ice-cold lemonade that John passed around, surely the tired little soldiers and cadets had splendid refreshment!

"My goat almost runned away!" lisped Freddie. "But I held on tight like a real fireman."

"And mine wanted to stop and eat grass in the middle of the big parade," Roy told them.

"Now eat up your ice cream. Nettie, have some more? Jack, you surely need two plates after carrying that bear skin," said Uncle Daniel.

The youngsters did not have to be urged to eat some more of the good things, and so it took quite a while to "finish up the rations," as Uncle Daniel said.

"They're goin' to shoot the old cannon off, father," Harry told Uncle Daniel, "and we're all going over on the pond bank to see them, at three o'clock."

"They're foolish to put powder in that old cracked gun," remarked Uncle Daniel. "Take care, if you go over, that you all keep at a safe distance."

It was not long until three o'clock, and then when all the red-white-and-blue things had been stored away for another year, the boys hurried off to see Peter Burns fire the old cannon.

Quite a crowd of people had gathered about the pond bank, which was a high green wall like that which surrounds a reservoir.

Peter was busy stuffing the powder in the old gun, and all the others looked on anxiously.

"Let's go up in that big limb of the willow tree," suggested Bert. "We can see it all then, and be out of range of the fire."

So the boys climbed up in the low willow, that leaned over the pond bank.

"They're almost ready," Harry said, seeing the crowd scatter.

"Look out!" yelled Peter, getting hold of the long string that would fire the gun.

Peter gave it a tug, then another.

Everybody held their breath, expecting to hear an awful bang, but the gun didn't go off.

Very cautiously Peter stepped nearer the cannon to see what might be the matter, when the next instant with a terrific report the whole cannon flew up in the air!

Peter fell back! His hat seemed to go up with the gun!

"Oh, he's killed!" yelled the people.

"Poor Peter!" gasped Harry.

"He ought to know better!" said Mr. Mason.

"Father said that cannon was dangerous," Harry added.

By this time the crowd had surrounded Peter, who lay so still and looked so white. The Bobbsey boys climbed down from the tree and joined the others. "He's only unconscious from the shock," spoke up Mr. Mason, who was leaning down very close to Peter. "Stand back, and give him air."

The crowd fell back now, and some of the boys looked around to find the pieces of cannon.

"Don't touch it," said Tom Mason, as a little fellow attempted to pick up a piece of the old gun. "There might be powder in it half lighted."

Mrs. Burns had run over from her home at the report of the accident, and she was now bathing Peter's face with water from the pond.

"He's subject to fainting spells," she told the frightened people, "and I think he'll be all right when he comes to."

Peter looked around, then he sat up and rubbed his eyes.

"Did it go off?" he smiled, remembering the big report.

"Guess it did, and you went off with it," Mr. Mason said. "How do you feel?"

"Oh, I'll be all right when my head clears a bit. I guess I fainted."

"So you did," said Mrs. Burns, "and there's no use scolding you for firing that old gun. Come home now and go to bed; you have had all the fireworks you want for one day."

Quite a crowd followed Peter over to his home, for they could not believe he was not in any way hurt.

"Let us go home," Harry said to his cousin. "We have to get all our fireworks ready before evening."

The boys found all at home enjoying themselves. Freddie's torpedoes still held out, and Flossie had a few more "snakes" left. Nan had company on the lawn, and it indeed was an ideal Fourth of July.

"Look at the balloon!" called John from the carriage house. "It's going to land in the orchard." This announcement caused all the children to hurry up to the orchard, for everybody likes to "catch" a balloon.

"There's a man in it," John exclaimed as the big ball tossed around in the air.

"Yes, that's the balloon that went up from the farmers' picnic," said Harry.

The next minute a parachute shot out from the balloon; and hanging to it the form of a man could be seen.

"Oh, he'll fall!" cried Freddie, all excited. "Let's catch him—in something!"

"He's all right," John assured the little boy. "That umbrella keeps him from coming down too quickly."

"How does it?" Freddie asked.

"Why, you see, sonny, the air gets under the umbrella and holds it up. The man's weight then brings it down gently."

"Oh, maybe he will let us fly up in it," Freddie remarked, much interested.

"Here he comes! here he comes!" the boys called, and sure enough the big parachute, with the man dangling on it, was now coming right down—down—in the harvest-apple tree!

"Hello there!" called the man from above, losing the colored umbrella and quickly dropping himself from the low tree.

"Hello yourself!" answered John. "Did you have a nice ride?"

"First class," replied the man with the stars on his shirt. "But I've got a long walk back to the grove. Could I hire a bicycle around here?"

Harry spoke to his father, and then quickly decided to let the balloon man ride his bicycle down to the picnic grounds.

"You can leave it at the ice-cream stand," Harry told the stranger. "I know the man there, and he will take care of it for me until I call for it."

The children were delighted to talk to a real live man that had been up in a balloon, and the balloonist was indeed very pleasant with the little ones. He took Freddie up in his arms and told him all about how it felt to be up in the sky.

"You're a truly fireman!" Freddie said, after listening to all the dangers there are so far above ground. "I'm a real fireman too!"

Just then the balloon that had been tossing about in the air came down in the other end of the orchard.

"Well, there!" exclaimed the man. "That's good luck. Now, whichever one of you boys gets that balloon first will get ten dollars. That's what we pay for bringing it back!"

With a dash every boy started for the spot where the balloon had landed. There were quite a few others besides the Bobbseys, and they tumbled over each other trying to get there first. Ned Prentice, Nettie's brother, was one of the best runners, and he cut across the orchard to get a clear way out of the crowd.

"Go it, Bert!" called John.

"Keep it up, Harry!" yelled someone else.

"You'd get it, Tom!" came another voice.

But Ned was not in the regular race, and nobody noticed him.

"They've got it," called the excited girls.

"It's Harry!"

"No, it's Bert!"

"'Tisn't either—it's Ned!" called John, as the only poor boy in the crowd proudly touched the big empty gas-bag!

"Three cheers for Ned!" called Uncle Daniel, for he and Mr. Bobbsey had joined in the crowd.

"Hurrah! hurrah! hurrah!" shouted all the boys good-naturedly, for Ned was a favorite companion, besides being one who really needed the money.

"Suppose we drive down," Uncle Daniel suggested. "Then we can bring Ned back with his ten dollars."

This was agreed upon as a good plan, and as quickly as John had hitched up the big wagon ail the boys piled in with the aeronaut and started for the grove.

Chapter XI

THE LITTLE GARDENERS

When little Ned Prentice put the ten-dollar bill in his mother's hand, on that pleasant Fourth of July evening, he felt like a man. His mother could hardly believe the story of Ned's getting the money just for finding a balloon, but when it was explained how valuable the balloon was, and how it sometimes takes days of searching in the woods to find one after the balloonist lets go and drops down with his parachute, she was finally convinced that the money rightfully belonged to Ned.

"No one needs it more than I do," Mrs. Prentice told Mr. Bobbsey, who had brought Ned home in the wagon, "for since the baby was sick we have hardly been able to meet our bills, it cost so much for medicine."

"We were all glad when Ned got there first," Harry said politely, "because we knew he deserved the reward most."

As Ned was a poor boy, and had to work on farms during vacation, his father being dead and only one brother being old enough to go to work, the reward turned out a great blessing, for ten dollars is a good deal of money for a little boy to earn at one time.

"Be sure to come up to our fireworks tonight," Harry called, as they drove away, and Ned promptly accepted the invitation.

"It has certainly been a great Fourth of July!" Uncle Daniel exclaimed, later in the evening when the children fired off their Roman candles and sky rockets and burned the red fire. The little children had beautiful pinwheels and "nigger chasers" that they put off on the porch. Then Nan had a big fire balloon that she sent up, and they watched it until it was out of sight, away over the pond and clear out of Meadow Brook.

It was a very tired lot of children that rolled off to sleep that night, for indeed it had been a great day for them all.

For a few days after the Fourth it rained, as it always does, on account of all the noise that goes up in the air to shake the clouds.

"You can play in the coach house," Aunt Sarah told the children, "but be careful not to run in and out and get wet." The children promised to remember, and soon they were all out in the big wagon house playing merrily. Freddie climbed in the wagon and made believe it was a "big fire engine." Bert attached a bell on the side for him, and when he pulled a rope this bell would clang like a chemical apparatus. Nan and Flossie had all their dolls in the pretty new carriage with the soft gray cushions, and in this the little girls made believe driving to New York and doing some wonderful shopping.

"Freddie, you be coachman," coaxed Flossie, "because we are inside and have to have someone drive us."

"But who will put out all the fires?" Freddie asked, as he clanged the bell vigorously.

"Make b'lieve they are all out," Flossie told him.

"But you can't make b'lieve about fires," argued the little fellow, "'cause they're really."

"I tell you," Nan suggested. "We will suppose this is a great big high tally-ho party, and the ladies always drive them. I'll be away up high on the box, but we ought to have someone blow a horn!"

"I'll blow the horn," Freddie finally gave in, "'cause I got that big fire out now."

So Freddie climbed up on the high coach with his sisters, and blew the horn until Nan told them they had reached New York and were going to stop for dinner.

There were so many splendid things to play with in the coach house, tables, chairs, and everything, that the Bobbseys hardly knew it before it was lunch time, the morning passed so quickly.

It cleared up in the afternoon and John asked the children if they wanted to help him do some transplanting.

"Oh! we would love to," Nan answered, for she did love gardening.

The ground was just right for transplanting, after the rain, and the tender little lettuce plants were as easy to take up as they were to put down again.

"I say, Nan," John told her, "you can have that little patch over there for your garden. I'll give you a couple of dozen plants, and we will see what kind of a farmer you will make."

"Oh, thank you, John," Nan answered. "I'll do just as I have seen you doing," and she began to take the little plants in the pasteboard box from one bed to the other.

"Be careful not to shake the dirt off the roots," said John, "and be sure to put one plant in each place. Put them as far apart here as the length of this little stick, and when you put them in the ground press the earth firmly around the roots."

Flossie was delighted to help her sister, and the two girls made a very nice garden indeed.

"Let's put little stones around the path," Flossie suggested, and John said they could do this if they would be careful not to let the stones get on the garden.

"I want to be a planter too," called Freddie, running up the path to John. "But I want to plant radishes," he continued, "'cause they're the reddist."

"Well, you just wait a few minutes, sonny," said John, "and I'll show you how to plant radishes. I'll be through with this lettuce in a few minutes."

Freddie waited with some impatience, running first to Nan's garden then back to John's. Finally John was ready to put in a late crop of radishes.

"Now, you see, we make a long drill like this," John explained as he took the drill and made a furrow in the soft ground.

"If it rains again that will be a river," said Freddie, for he had often played river at home after a rain.

"Now, you see this seed is very fine," continued John. "But I am going to let you plant it if you're careful."

"That ain't redishes!" exclaimed Freddie "I want to plant redishes."

"But this is the seed, and that's what makes the radishes," John explained.

"Nope, that's black and it can't make it red?" argued Freddie.

"Wait and see," the gardener told him. "You just take this little paper of seeds and scatter them in the drill. See, I have mixed them with sand so they will not grow too thick."

Freddie took the small package, and kneeling down on the board that John used, he dropped the little shower of seeds in the line.

"They're all gone!" he told John presently; "get some more."

"No, that's enough. Now we will see how your crop grows. See, I just cover the seed very lightly like mamma covers Freddie when he sleeps in the summer time."

"Do you cover them more in the winter time too, like mamma does?" Freddie asked.

"Yes, indeed I do," said the gardener, "for seeds are just like babies, they must be kept warm to grow."

Freddie stood watching the line he had planted the seed in.

"They ain't growing yet," he said at last. "Why don't they come up, John?"

"Oh!" laughed the gardener, "they won't come up right away. They have to wake up first. You will see them above the ground in about a week, I guess."

This was rather a disappointment to the little fellow, who never believed in waiting for anything, but he finally consented to let the seeds grow and come back again later to pick the radishes.

"Look at our garden!" called Nan proudly, from across the path. "Doesn't it look straight and pretty?"

"You did very well indeed," said John, inspecting the new lettuce patch. "Now, you'll have to keep it clear of weeds, and if a dry spell should come you must use the watering can."

"I'll come up and tend to it every morning," Nan declared. "I am going to see what kind of lettuce I can raise."

Nan had brought with her a beautiful string of pearl beads set in gold, the gift of one of her aunts. She was very proud of the pearls and loved to wear them whenever her mother would let her.

One afternoon she came to her mother in bitter tears.

"Oh, mamma!" she sobbed. "The—the pearls are gone,"

"Gone! Did you lose them?" questioned Mrs. Bobbsey quickly.

"Yes."

"Where?"

"I—I don't know," and now Nan cried harder than ever.

The news soon spread that the string of pearls were lost, and everybody set to work hunting for them.

"Where do you think you lost 'em?" asked Bert.

"I—I don't know. I was down in the garden, and up the lane, and at the well, and out in the barn, and over to the apple orchard, and feeding the chickens, and over in the hayfield,—and lots of places."

"Then it will be like looking for a needle in a haystack," declared Aunt Sarah.

All the next day the boys and girls hunted for the string of pearls, and the older folks helped. But the string could not be found. Nan felt very bad over her loss, and her mother could do little to console her.

"I—I sup—suppose I'll never see them again," sobbed the girl.

"Oh, I guess they'll turn up some time," said Bert hopefully.

"They can't be lost so very, very bad," lisped Flossie. "'Cause they are somewhere on this farm, ain't they?"

"Yes, but the farm is so very big!" sighed poor Nan.

For a few days Freddie went up to the garden every morning to look for radishes. Then he gave up and declared he knew John had made a mistake and that he didn't plant radishes at all. Nan and Flossie were very faithful attending to their garden, and the beautiful light green lettuce grew splendidly, being grateful for the good care given it.

"When can we pick it?" Nan asked John, as the leaves were getting quite thick.

"In another week!" he told the girls, and so they continued to watch for weeds and kept the ground soft around the plants as John had told them.

Freddie's radishes were above ground now, and growing nicely, but they thought it best not to tell him, as he might pull them up too soon. Nan and Flossie weeded his garden as well as their own and showed they loved to see things grow, for they did not mind the work of attending to them.

"Papa will come up from Lakeport to-night," Nan told Flossie; "and won't he be pleased to see our gardens!"

That evening when Mr. Bobbsey arrived the first thing he had to do was to visit the garden.

"Why, I declare!" he exclaimed in real surprise. "You have done splendidly. This is a fine lettuce patch."

Mrs. Bobbsey and Aunt Sarah had also come up to see the girls' garden, and they too were much surprised at the result of Nan's and Flossie's work.

"Oh!" screamed Freddie from the other side of the garden. "See my redishes! They growed!" and before anyone could stop him he pulled up a whole handful of the little green leaves with the tiny red balls on the roots.

"They growed! They growed!" he shouted, dancing around in delight.

"But you must only pick the ripe ones," his father told him. "And did you really plant them?" Mr. Bobbsey asked in surprise.

"Yep! John showed me," he declared, and the girls said that was really Freddie's garden.

"Now I'll tell you," Aunt Sarah remarked. "We will let our little farmers pick their vegetables for dinner, and then we will be able to say just how good they are."

At this the girls started in to pick the very biggest heads of lettuce, and Freddie looked carefully to get the very reddest radishes in his patch. Finally enough were gathered, and down to the kitchen the vegetables were carried.

"You will have to prepare them for the table," Mrs. Bobbsey said. "Let us see, girls, what a pretty dish you can make."

This was a pleasant task to Nan and Flossie, who both always loved to play at housekeeping, and when at last Nan brought the dish in to the dinner table everybody said how pretty it looked.

"Them's my redishes!" exclaimed Freddie, as he saw the pretty bright red buttons peeping out from between the lettuce leaves.

"But we can all have some, can't we, Freddie?" his father asked.

"Yes, 'course you can. But I don't want all my good redishes smothered in that big dish of green stuff," he pouted.

"Now, Nan, you can serve your vegetables," Aunt Sarah said, and then Nan very neatly put a few crisp lettuce leaves on each small plate, and at the side she placed a few of Freddie's radishes, "with handles on" as Dinah said, meaning the little green stalks.

"Just think, we've done it all from the garden to the table!" Nan exclaimed, justly proud of her success at gardening.

"I done the radishes," put in Freddie, gulping down a drink of water to wash the bite off his tongue, for his radishes were quite hot.

"Well, you have certainly all done very nicely," Mrs. Bobbsey said. "And that kind of play is like going to school, for it teaches you important lessons in nature."

The girls declared they were going to keep a garden all summer, and so they did.

It was an unusually warm night, and so nearly all the doors were left open when the folks went to bed. Freddie was so worked up over his success as a gardener he could not go to sleep.

At last he dozed off, but presently he awoke with a start. What was that strange sound ringing in his ears? He sat up and listened.

Yes, somebody must surely be playing the piano. But what funny music! It seemed to come in funny runs and curious thumps. He called out sharply, and his mother came at once to his side.

"I heard piano-playing," said Freddie, and Mrs. Bobbsey started, for she remembered how Flossie had once told her the same thing.

"Oh, Freddie, are you sure?" she asked.

"Sure," repeated the little fellow. "But it wasn't very good playing."

Mrs. Bobbsey called Uncle Daniel, and the latter lit a lamp and went below into the parlor. Nobody was at the piano or in the room.

"I've made a careful examination," he said, on coming back. "I can see nothing unusual. Some of the children left a piece of cake on the keys of the piano, that's all."

"Well, cake can't play," put in Freddie. "Maybe it was a ghost."

"No, you must have been dreaming," said his mother. "Come, go to sleep," and presently Freddie dropped off. Mrs. Bobbsey was much worried, and the next day the older folks talked the matter over; but nothing came of it.

Chapter XII

Tom's Runaway

"Tom Mason is going to bring his colt out this afternoon," said Harry to Bert, "and we can all take turns trying him."

"Oh, is it that pretty little brown horse I saw in the field back of Tom's home?" asked Bert.

"That's him," Harry replied. "Isn't he a beauty!"

"Yes, I would like first-rate to ride him, but young horses are awful skittish, aren't they?"

"Sometimes, but this one is partly broken. At any rate, we wouldn't have far to fall, for he is a little fellow," said Harry.

So the boys went down to Tom's home at the appointed time, and there they met Jack Hopkins.

"We've made a track around the fields," Tom told his companions, "and we will train him to run around the ring, for father thinks he may be a race-horse some day, he's so swift."

"You may go first," the boys told him, "as he's your horse."

"All right!" Tom replied, making for the stake where Sable, the pony, was tied. Sable marched along quietly enough and made no objections to Tom getting on his back. There was no saddle, but just the bit in the horse's mouth and attached to it a short piece of rein.

"Get app, Sable!" called Tom, snapping a small whip at the pony's side.

But instead of going forward the little horse tried to sit down!

"Whoa! whoa!" called the boys, but Tom clung to Sable's neck and held on in spite of the pony's back being like a toboggan slide.

"Get off there, get off there!" urged Tom, yet the funny little animal only backed down more.

"Light a match and set it under his nose," Harry suggested. "That's the way to make a balky horse go!"

Someone had a match, which was lighted and put where Sable could sniff the sulphur.

"Look out! Hold on, Tom!" yelled the boys all at once, for at that instant Sable bolted off like a deer.

"He's running away!" called Bert, which was plain to be seen, for Tom could neither turn him this way or that, but had all he could do to hold on the frightened animal's neck.

"If he throws him Tom will surely be hurt!" Harry exclaimed, and the boys ran as fast as they could across the field after the runaway.

"Whoa! whoa! whoa!" called everybody after the horse, but that made not the slightest difference to Sable, who just went as if the woods were afire. Suddenly he turned and dashed straight up a big hill and over into a neighbor's cornfield.

"Oh, mercy!" cried Harry, "those people are so mean about their garden, they'll have Tom arrested if there's any corn broken."

Of course it was impossible for a runaway horse to go through a field of corn and do no damage, and Tom realized this too. By this time the dogs were out barking furiously, and altogether there was wild excitement. At one end of the field there was a high board fence.

"If I could only get him there he would have to stop," thought Tom, and suddenly he gave Sable a jerk in that direction.

"Drop off, Tom, drop off!" yelled the boys. "He'll throw you against the fence!"

But at that minute the little horse threw himself against the boards in such a way that Tom slid off, yet held tightly to the reins.

The horse fell, quite exhausted.

As quickly as they could get there the boys came up to help Tom.

"Hurry!" said Harry, "there is scarcely any corn broken, and we can get away before the Trimbles see us. They're away back in the fields planting late cabbage."

Tom felt hardly able to walk, but he limped along while Harry led Sable carefully between the cornhills. It was only a few feet to the edge of the field, and then they were all safe on the road again.

"Are you hurt?" the boys asked Tom, when finally they had a chance to speak about the runaway.

"I feel as if I had dropped from a balloon onto a lot of cobblestones," Tom answered, "but I guess that's only the shaking up I got. That pony certainly can go."

"Yes indeed," Harry admitted; "I guess he doesn't like the smell of sulphur matches. Lucky he was not injured with that fall against the fence."

"I found I had to throw him," Tom said, "and I thought the fence was softer than a tree."

"I suppose we ought to make him run until he is played out," said Bert, "That's the way to cure a horse of running away."

But none of the boys felt like risking their bones even to cure Sable, so the panting animal was led to the stable and for the rest of the day allowed to think over his bad conduct.

But that was not the last of the runaway, for in the evening just after supper old Mr. Trimble paid a visit to Tom's father.

"I came over to tell you what a scallywag of a boy you've got," began the cross old man. "He and a lot of young loafers took a horse and drove him all through my cornfield to-day, and now you've got to pay the damages."

"My son is not a scallywag," Mr. Mason declared, "and if you call him names like loafer and scallywag I'll make you pay damages."

"Oh! you will, eh?" the other sneered. "Think I'm afraid of an old constable up here, do you?"

"Well now, see here," Mr. Mason said, "Be reasonable and do not quarrel over an accident. If any corn is knocked down I'll get Tom to fix it up, if it's broken down we will see what it would cost to replace it. But the boys did not do it purposely, and it was worse for Tom than anyone else, for he's all black and blue from the hard knocks he got."

At this the cross man quieted down and said, Well, he would see about it. Mr. Trimble was one of those queer people who believe all a boy is good for is doing mischief and all a boy deserves is scolding or beating. Perhaps this was because he had no sons of his own and therefore had no regard for the sons of other people.

Mr. Mason went directly to the cornfield with his neighbor. He looked carefully over every hill, and with a spade and hoe he was able to put back into place the few stalks that had been knocked down in Sable's flight.

"There now," said Mr. Mason, "I guess that corn is as good as ever. If it wants any more hoeing Tom will come around in the morning and do it. He is too stiff to move to-night."

So that ended the runaway, except for a very lame boy, Tom Mason, who had to limp around for a day or two from stiffness.

"How would you like to be a jockey!" laughed his companions. "You held on like a champion, but you were not in training for the banging you got."

"Well, I guess Sable will make a fine racehorse," said Tom, "when he's broken. But it will take someone stronger than I am to break him in."

The next afternoon all the boys went fishing. They had been out quite late the night before to find the "night walkers" for bait, as those little worms only come out of the ground after dark. Bert had a new line his father brought from Lakeport, and the others boys had nets and hooks, as most country boys who live near streams are always fond of fishing.

"Let's go over to the cove," Harry said when they all started off. "There's lots of good fish in that dark corner."

So the cove was chosen as a good spot to fish from, and soon the Bobbsey boys and their friends were lying around the edge of the deep clear stream, waiting for a bite.

Bert was the first to jerk his line, and he brought it up with such force that the chubfish on his hook slapped Harry right in the face!

"Look out!" called Harry, trying to dodge the flapping fish. "Put your catch down. He's a good one, but I don't care about having him kiss me that way again."

All the boys laughed at Bert, who was a green fisherman they said. The fish was really a very nice plump chub and weighed more than a pound. He floundered around in the basket and flapped his tail wildly trying to get away from them.

"I've got one," called Tom next, at the same moment pulling his line and bringing up a pretty little sunfish. Now "sunnies" are not considered good eating, so Tom's catch did not come up to Bert's, but it was put in the basket just the same.

"I'm going out on the springboard," August Stout announced, stepping cautiously out on the board from which good swimmers dived.

"You know you can't swim, August," said Harry, "and if you get a catch and jerk it you'll tumble in."

"Oh! I'll be all right," August answered, lying down flat on the narrow springboard and dropping his line.

For a time all the boys lay watching for a bite. No one spoke, for sometimes they say fish are very sensitive to sound and go in another direction if they hear a voice.

It was a beautiful July day, and perhaps the boys were a little lazy. At any rate, they all became so quiet the little woodpeckers on the trees went on with their work pecking at the tree bark as if no human being was in sight.

Suddenly there was a big splash!

"August!" yelled all the boys at once, for indeed August was gone from the springboard.

"Quick!" called Harry to his companions. "He can't swim!"

The next minute the boy in the water came to the top and threw up his arm. But no one was near enough to reach it.

"Strike out, August!" yelled Bert. "We're coming," and one boy after the other dropped in the water now, having thrown off their heavy clothing.

"Oh, where is he?" screamed Bert in terror, for no movement on the water's surface showed them where August was.

"Here!" cried Tom Mason, who was quite a distance out. "Here he is! Help! come quick!"

No need to urge the boys to hasten, for all realized the danger their companion was in.

"Don't pull down, August," went on Tom. "Try to help yourself, or you'll pull me under." Harry had around his neck a strong piece of rope he picked up as he made a dive into the water.

"Take hold of this," he called to August, "and we can all pull."

As the rope was put in August's hand the other boys all took hold and soon towed the unfortunate boy in.

"He's very weak," said Harry when they pulled August up on the shore. "I guess he has swallowed a lot of water. We better roll him on the grass and work his arms up and down. That will revive him."

August was indeed very weak, and had had a narrow escape. For some time his companions worked over him before he opened his eyes and spoke.

"Oh!" he murmured at last, "I'm so sick!"

"I guess you are, August," said Tom, "but you'll be all right soon." They lifted him carefully under a shady tree and removed his wet clothing.

"I'll run over to Smith's and get him something to wear home," said Harry, who hurried across lots and presently returned with an old suit of clothes. August was able to dress himself now, and as soon as he felt strong enough the boys helped him home.

"You can have my fish, August," said Bert nobly.

"And mine too," Tom added. August did not want to accept the boys' offers at first, but at last they prevailed upon him to do so.

"I think I fell asleep," said he, referring to the accident.

"Guess we all did!" added Harry, "for we only woke up when we heard the splash."

It seems the number of accidents country boys have only make them truer friends, for all the things that happened in Meadow Brook made each boy think more of his companions both in being grateful for the help given and being glad no dear friend's life was lost.

Chapter XIII

PICKING PEAS

"Mother," said Harry, using that loved name to show that what he was about to say was something important, "Peter Burns is sick. He has not been able to work since the cannon exploded and gave him the shock, and all his peas are spoiling because there's no one to pick them. Mrs. Burns hired some boys yesterday, but they broke down so many vines she had to stop them; and, mother, would you mind if Bert and I picked some to-day? The sun is not hot."

"Why, my dear," replied Aunt Sarah, "it would be very nice of you to help Peter; he has always been a kind neighbor. I don't think it would do you any harm to pick peas on a cool day like this. Bert can ask his mother, and if she is satisfied you can put on your play overalls and go right along."

Both boys were given the desired permission, and when Tom and Jack heard where the Bobbseys were going they said at once they would go along.

"Are you sure your mother won't mind?" Mrs. Burns asked the boys, knowing Harry's folks did not need the money paid to pick the peas. "Of course I'm very glad to have you if your mothers are satisfied."

Soon each boy had a big basket under his arm, and was off for the beautiful field of soft green peas, that stretched along the pond bank at the side of Mrs. Burns' home. Now, peas are quite an expensive vegetable when they come in first, and farmers who have big fields of them depend upon the return from the crop as an important part of the summer's income. But the peas must be picked just as soon as they are ripe, or else they will spoil. This was why Harry got his friends to turn in to help poor Peter Burns.

"I'll go down this row and you take that." suggested Bert to Harry. "Then we can talk to each other without hollering."

"All right," Harry replied, snapping the peas off the vines and dropping them into his basket like a real farmer.

"Let's have a race," called Tom. "See who gets his basket full first."

"But no skipping for big ones," put in Jack. "You have to pick every ripe one."

The boys all started in at the top of the hill, each working two rows at a time. They were so interested in the race that scarcely a word was spoken. The peas were plentiful and ripe too, so that the baskets were filling up quickly. Mrs. Burns herself was picking, in fact she had been in the field since the very first peep of dawn, and she would be sure to stay out until the darkness would drive her in.

"You are fine pickers," she told the boys, seeing how quickly they worked. "I pay ten cents a basket, you know."

"I guess we can earn a dollar a day at this rate," laughed Tom, whose basket was almost full.

"I'm done," called Jack from his row.

"No, you're not," said Harry, "you have to cover the rim."

"Oh!" exclaimed Jack, who had just slipped between the rows. "Oh! there goes my basket."

And sure enough the big basket had been upset in Jack's fall, and most of the peas were scattered on the ground.

"Ha! ha!" laughed Bert. "I'm first. My basket is full."

"I'm next!" called Tom, picking his basket up in his arms.

"Well, I'll be last I guess," laughed Tom, trying hard to pick up the scattered peas.

"There's mine!" called Harry, and now all the boys carried their baskets to the big bag at the end of the field and dumped them in.

"It won't take long to fill the bag," said Harry, "and it will be so good for Peter to have them ready, for to-morrow is market day."

So the boys worked on right along until lunch time, each having picked four big baskets full. August Stout came along and helped some too, but he could not stay long, as he had to cut some clothes poles for his mother.

"Well, I declare!" said Mrs. Burns, looking at the three full bags the boys had picked. "Isn't that splendid! But I can't pay until Peter comes from market."

"We just did it for fun," answered Harry. "We don't want any pay."

"Indeed you must have forty cents apiece, ten cents a basket," she insisted. "See what a good load you have picked!"

"No, really, Mrs. Burns; mother wouldn't like us to take the money," Harry declared. "We are glad to have helped you, and it was only fun."

Poor Mrs. Burns was so grateful she had to wipe her eyes with her gingham apron.

"Well," she said finally, "There are some people in this world who talk about charity, but a good boy is a gift from heaven," and she said this just like a prayer of blessing on the boys who had helped her.

"The crop would have been spoiled to-morrow," remarked Tom, as he and his companions started up the road. "I'm awfully glad you thought of helping her, Harry."

It seemed all that day everything went right for the boys; they did not have even a single mishap in their games or wanderings. Perhaps it was because they felt so happy over having done a good turn for a poor neighbor.

"Say, fellows," Tom said later, while they sat on the pond bank trying to see something interesting in the cool, clear water, "what do you say if we make up a circus!"

"Fine," the others answered, "but what will be the show?"

"Animals of course," continued Tom; "we've got plenty around here, haven't we?"

"Well, some," Harry admitted. "There's Sable, for instance."

At this the boys all laughed at Tom, remembering the runaway.

"Well, I could be a cowboy, and ride him just the same," spoke up Tom. "I rode him around the track yesterday, and he went all right. He was only scared with that sulphur match when he ran away."

"A circus would be fine," Bert put in. "We could have Frisky as the Sacred Calf."

"And Snoopy as the Wild Cat," said Harry.

"And two trained goats," August added.

"And a real human bear, 'Teddy'?" suggested Jack.

"Then a cage of pigeons," went on Harry.

"Let's get them all in training," said Tom, jumping up suddenly, anxious to begin the sport.

"I tell you!" Harry planned. "We can each train our own animals and then we can bring them together in a well-organized circus."

"When will we have it?" August asked impatiently.

"About next week," Harry thought, and this was decided upon.

During the interval the boys were so busy training that they had little time for other sports, but the girls found out-door life quite as interesting as their brothers did, and now made many discoveries in and about the pretty woodlands.

"Oh, we saw the prettiest little rabbits today," Nan told her mother, after a trip in the woods. "Flossie and Freddie were sitting on an old stump when two rabbits ran right across the road in front of them. Freddie ran after them as far as he could go in the brushwood, but of course no one can go as fast as a rabbit."

"And the squirrels," Flossie told them. "I think the squirrels are the prettiest things that live in the woods. They have tails just like mamma's feather boa and they walk sitting up so cute."

"Oh, I think the rabbits are the nicest," lisped Freddie, "'cause they are Bunnies, and Bunnies bring Easter eggs."

"And we have made the loveliest fern garden up back of the swing," said Flossie. "We got a whole basket of ferns in the woods and transplanted them."

"In the center we have some lovely Jack-in the-pulpits," Nan added. "Some are light green striped, and the largest are purple with gold stripes. The Jacks stand up straight, just like real live boys preaching in a pulpit."

"Don't you think, mamma," asked Flossie, "that daisies and violets make a lovely garden? I have a round place in the middle of our wild flower bed just full of light blue violets and white daisies."

"All flowers are beautiful," their mamma told them, "but I do think with Flossie that daisies and violets are very sweet."

"And, mamma, we got a big piece of the loveliest green moss! It is just like real velvet," said Flossie. "We found a place all covered with it down by the pond, under the dark cedar trees. Nan said it wouldn't grow in our garden, but I brought some home to try. I put it in a cool dark place, and I'm going to put lots of water on it every day."

"Moss must be very cool and damp to grow," Mrs. Bobbsey replied. "I remember how disappointed I used to be when I was a little girl and tried to make it grow around my geraniums. It would always dry up and turn brown in a few days."

"Oh," called Freddie from his garden under the cherry tree, "come quick! Look at the funny bugs!"

Nan and Flossie hurried to where their little brother had dug a hole in the earth.

"They're mice!" exclaimed Nan. "Oh, aren't they cute! Let's catch them. Call Bert or Harry."

While Flossie ran to tell Bert, Nan watched the tiny mice so that they would not get away.

"It's a nest of field mice," Harry told them.

"We'll put them in a cage and have them in our circus."

"But they're my mice," cried Freddie, "and I won't let anybody have them!"

"We're only going to help you take care of them in a little box. Oh, there's the mother—catch her, Harry," called Bert.

The mother mouse was not so easy to catch, however, and the boys had quite a chase after her. At last she ran into a tin box the boys had sunk in the ground when playing golf. Here Harry caught the frightened little creature.

"I've got a queer kind of a trap," Harry said. "It's just like a cage. We can put them in this until we build a larger one. We can make one out of a box with a wire door."

The mice were the smallest, cutest things, not larger than Freddie's thumb. They hardly looked like mice at all, but like some queer little bugs. They were put in the cage trap, mother and all, and then Bert got them a bit of cheese from the kitchen.

"What! Feed mice!" exclaimed Dinah "Sakes alive, chile! you go bringing dem mice in de house to eat all our cake and pie. You just better drown dem in de brook before dey bring a whole lot more mices around here."

"We'll keep them away from the house," Bert told Dinah. "We're going to have a circus, you know, and these will be our trained mice."

Freddie, of course, was delighted with the little things, and wanted to dig for more.

"I tell you!" said Bert. "We might catch butterflies and have them under a big glass on the table with all the small animals."

"That would be good," Harry agreed. "We could catch some big brown ones and some little fancy ones. Then after dark we could get some big moths down by the post office electric light."

The girls, too, went catching butterflies. Nan was able to secure four or five yellow ones in the flower garden near the porch, and Flossie got two of the small brown variety in the nasturtium bed. Harry and Bert searched in the close syringa bushes where the nests are usually found.

"Oh! look at this one!" called Freddie, coming up with a great green butterfly. "Is it bird?" he asked. "See how big it is!"

It really was very large, and had such beautiful wings it might easily be mistaken for some strange bird.

"We will try to keep them alive," said Harry, "and perhaps we can get ma's big glass globe to put them in. She has one she used to put wax flowers under."

"And, oh say!" exclaimed Bert, "couldn't we have an aquarium with snakes and turtles and toads in?"

"Fine!" declared Harry. "We've got a big glass tank I used to have gold fish in. We'll get the other fellows to help catch some snakes, fish, and turtles and toads, and—and anything else that will stand water!"

Then what a time they had hunting for reptiles! It seemed each boy had a different variety on his premises. August Stout brought three turtles and Jack Hopkins caught two snakes under a big stone in his back yard. Tom Mason supplied four lovely gold fish, while Ned Prentice brought three bright green frogs.

"I can catch hop-toads," declared Freddie, and sure enough the little fellow brought two big ones and a baby toad in his hat down to the boys, who had their collection in a glass tank in the barn.

"We can't put the snakes in with the others or they'll eat them up," said Jack. "I'll get a big glass jar for the snakes."

"And say!" said Harry. "Will we charge admission to the show?"

"Sure—five cents each," said Tom, "and give the money to the fresh-air camp over on the mountain."

This was considered a good plan, and now it was only a few days more until Wednesday—the day of the circus!

Chapter XIV

THE CIRCUS

News of the circus had spread from one end of Meadow Brook to the other. Every boy and girl in the place expected to get in to see the sights, and even some grown folks had made up their minds, from what they heard, there would be something interesting for them to see, and so they decided to go too.

Mrs. Bobbsey, Aunt Sarah, Dinah, and Martha had bought tickets for reserved seats (these cost ten cents each). Then Mildred Manners was going to bring her mother and her big sister, and Mabel Herold expected to have her mother with her also. Mr. Bobbsey was coming up from Lakeport purposely to see the circus, and Uncle Daniel had helped the boys put up the seats and fix things generally. A big tent had been borrowed from the Herolds; they were only out at Meadow Brook for the summer, and this tent was erected in the open field between the Bobbsey and the Mason farms, alongside the track where Tom had tried Sable.

The tent had large flaps that opened up the entire front, so that all the exhibits could be shown nicely to the people on the seats out side.

The seats were made of boards set on most anything that would hold them, with a few garden benches for reserved seats at the front.

Everything was ready, and the circus day came at last.

"Lucky it isn't raining," the boys declared as they rushed around putting the final touches to everything.

August Stout was appointed to collect the tickets, and Ned Prentice was to show the people to their seats.

Two o'clock!

Only one hour more!

Lots of children came early to get good seats. Roy Mason sat right in the front row alongside of Freddie. Nettie Prentice was on the very first bench back of the reserved seats. The Herolds came next, and had Aunt Sarah's front garden bench, the red one. Mildred Manners' folks paid ten cents each too, and they had the big green bench from the side porch.

"Give Mrs. Burns a front seat," Harry whispered to Ned, as the busy farmer's wife actually stopped her work to see what all the excitement was about.

The Bobbseys had come—Mr. Bobbsey and all,—and Dinah wore her best black bonnet.

"When will it begin?" Flossie asked, just trembling with excitement.

"I saw Harry and Bert go in the tent some time ago," whispered Nan; "and see, they are loosing the tent flap."

There was a shout of applause when Harry appeared. He actually wore a swallowtail coat and had on a choker—a very high collar—and a bright green tie. He wore long trousers too, and looked so queer even Aunt Sarah had to laugh when she saw him.

"Oh!" exclaimed all the children when they looked inside the tent.

"Isn't it grand!" whispered Flossie.

Then Bert stepped up on the soap box in the middle of the ring.

"Ladies and gentlemen," he began, making a profound bow, "ladies and gentlemen."

Then everybody roared laughing.

Bert had to wait until they got through laughing at his funny costume, which was a good deal like Harry's, only the latter wore a red tie.

In a few moments Bert went on again.

"Ladies and gentlemen! Our first number is Frisky, the Sacred Calf of India!" he exclaimed, imitating that queer-voiced man called a "Barker" and used at circuses.

Snap! snap! went Bert's whip, and out from a side place, back of a big screen, came Jack Hopkins dressed like a real clown, leading our old friend Frisky, the runaway calf.

How awfully funny it was!

The calf had over him a plush portiere that reached clear down to the ground, and over each ear was tied a long-handled feather duster!

Such laughing and clapping as greeted this "first number"!

Frisky just turned around square in front and looked the people straight in the face. This funny move made Mr. Bobbsey "die laughing," as Flossie said, and Uncle Daniel too was hilarious.

"The sacred calf is too sacred to smile," laughed Uncle Daniel, while Dinah and Martha just roared.

The children didn't think they ought to laugh out loud and spoil the show; even Freddie raised his finger to Dinah.

Suddenly the clown jumped on the calf's back. He tried to stand on his head. Then he turned a somersault on to the sawdust.

Everybody clapped hard now, and the children began to shout.

But Bert snapped his whip and the clown went down on his hands and knees to apologize. Of course clowns are not supposed to speak, so Jack did everything by pantomime.

Next he came around and kissed Frisky. This made everybody roar again, and no matter what the clown did it certainly looked very funny.

Finally Bert snapped his whip three times, and the clown jumped on Frisky's back, over the plush curtain and all, and rode off.

"Wasn't that splendid!" everybody exclaimed.

"I really never enjoyed a big circus more than this!" remarked Mrs. Bobbsey to Mrs. Burns. The others all said nice things too; and then Bert announced the next turn.

"Ladies and gentlemen," he began again, "our next number will introduce to you the famous wildcats, Snoop and Fluffy. Real wildcats from the jungle, and this is the first—time—they—have ever been exhibited in—this country!"

Snap went the whip, and out came Harry with our little kitten friends one on each arm.

He whistled, and Snoop climbed on his shoulder!

He whistled again, and Fluffy climbed on the other shoulder.

This "brought the house down," as Uncle Daniel said, and there was so much noise the kittens looked frightened.

Next Harry stretched out both arms straight and the kittens carefully walked over into his hands.

"Well, I declare!" exclaimed Dinah. "Jest see dat Snoopy kitty-cat! If he can't do real reg'lar circus tricks! And jest to think how he cut up on de cars! 'Pears like as if he was doin' it fer jokes den too!"

"And look at Fluffy!" exclaimed Martha; "as white as Snoop is black!" Harry stooped down and let the kittens jump through his hands, which is an old but none the less a very pretty trick.

With the air of a real master, Bert snapped his whip and placed on the table a little piece of board. He rubbed something on each end (it was a bit of dried herring, but the people didn't know that), then Harry put Snoop on one end and Fluffy on the other.

"Oh, a teeter-tauter!" called Freddie, unable to restrain his joy any longer. "I bet on Snoop. He's the heaviest."

At the sound of Freddie's voice Snoop turned around and the move sent Fluffy up the air.

"Oh! oh! oh!" came a chorus from the children, but before anybody in the circus had time to interfere off went Fluffy, as hard as she could run, over the lots, home.

The next minute Snoop was after her, and Harry stood alone in the ring bowing to the "tremendous applause."

When the laughing had ceased Bert made the next announcement.

"Ladies and gentlemen," he said, "we will now introduce our famous menagerie. First we have the singing mice."

"They're mine!" called Freddie, but Nan insisted on him keeping quiet.

"Now you will hear the mice sing," said Bert, and as he held up the cage of little mice somebody whistled a funny tune back of the scenes.

"Good! good!" called Mr. Bobbsey. "We've got real talent here," he added, for indeed the boys had put together a fine show.

"Now you see our aquarium," went on Bert as Harry helped him bring forward the table that held the glass tank.

"Here we have a real sea serpent," he said, pointing to a good fat chub that flopped around in the water.

"Let the little ones walk right up and see them," Bert said. "Form in line and pass in this way."

Not only the children went up, but grown folks too, for they wanted a look into the tank.

"Now here are our alligators and crocodiles," announced Bert, pointing his whip at the turtles.

"And these are sea-lions," he said, pointing out Freddie's hop-toads.

At each announcement everybody laughed, but Bert went on as seriously as if he were deaf.

"In this separate tank," he declared, "we have our boa-constrictors, the largest and fiercest in the world. This is the first time one of this specimen has ever been captured alive. Note the dangerous stripe on his back!"

It was Jack's snakes that came in for this description, and the girls were quite afraid of them, although they were in a glass jar.

"Well, I declare!" said Mrs. Burns. "If this isn't a sure-enough circus. I often paid a half-dollar when I went to see things no better than these!"

Everybody thought everything was splendid, and the boys were well paid for their efforts.

"Now," said Bert, "here are our crystal fish from the deep sea!" (These were Tom's goldfish.) "You will notice how bespangled they are. They say this comes from the fish eating the diamonds lost in shipwrecks."

"What a whopper!" called someone back of the scenes whose voice sounded like Tom Mason's.

Snap! went Bert's whip, and the boys did not interrupt him again.

"The last part of our menagerie is the cage of prize butterflies," said Bert. "These butterflies are rare and scarce and—"

"Hard to catch!" remarked someone not on the programme.

"Now there will be ten minutes' intermission," the announcer said, "so all may have time to see everything in the menagerie.

"After that we will give you the best number of the programme, our chariot race."

"Oh, that's going to be Tom!" exclaimed Roy.

"No, it's Bert," said Flossie.

"Well, Jack has our goat-wagon," said Mildred.

"I guess there'll be a whole lot in the race," said Freddie, "and maybe they'll have firemen."

During the intermission August sold a whole big basket of peanuts, and the people wanted more. They knew all the money was to go to the fresh-air camp, which was probably the reason they bought so generously.

"I don't know when I have enjoyed myself so much," declared Mrs. Manners, fanning herself. "I had no idea boys could be so clever."

"That's because you only have girls," laughed Mrs. Bobbsey.

"Don't you think we ought to give them a treat for working so hard?" whispered Mrs. Herold to Aunt Sarah. "I would be delighted to have them all to dinner," she added, in her society way, for the Herolds were quite rich.

"That would be very nice, I'm sure," Aunt Sarah replied; "boys always have good appetites after having a lot of fun."

All this time there was plenty of noise back of the scenes, and it was evident something big was being prepared.

Presently Bert and Harry came out and lowered the tent flap, first making sure all the little sightseers were outside.

"They're comin'!" exclaimed Freddie, clapping his fat hands.

"Oh, I'm just so nervous!" whispered Flossie! "I hope none of the animals will get loose."

"Now, ladies and gentlemen," called Tom Mason, appearing at the tent, "if you will just turn round the other way in your seats and face that ring we will give you an exhibition of cowboy life on the plains!"

Chapter XV

THE CHARIOT RACE

Tom's costume was a splendid imitation of a cowboy. He wore tan-colored overalls and a jumper, the jumper being slashed up at the sides like an Indian's coat. On his head was a very broad sombrero, this hat having really come from the plains, as it belonged to a West-

"HURRAH! HURRAH!" SHOUTED EVERYBODY.

ern farmer who had lately moved to Meadow Brook.

Presently Tom appeared again, this time riding the fiery Sable.

"Hurrah! hurrah!" shouted the boys, as Tom drove into the ring like a major.

Bert now stepped into the middle of the ring alongside of some soap boxes that were piled up there.

"Now you see ladies and gentlemen," began Bert, laughing a little at the show in broad daylight, "you see this (the soap boxes) is a mail coach. Our cowboy will rob the mail coach from his horse just as they used to do in the mountains of Arizona."

Snap went the whip, and away went Sable around the ring at a nice even canter. After a few turns around Tom urged his horse on a little until he was going on a steady run. Every one kept quiet, for most of Meadow Brook people had heard how Sable had run away some days before.

"There ought to be music," whispered Jack to Harry, for indeed the circus was so real it only lacked a brass band.

Now Bert put on top of the soap boxes Harry's canvas schoolbag stuffed full of papers.

"This is the United States mail," he said. "We will understand that the coach has stopped for a few minutes."

Sable was going along splendidly by this time, and everybody said what a pretty little horse he was.

"He's goin' to steal the mail box now!" whispered Flossie to Freddie. "I hope Sable won't fall or anything."

Snap! snap! went the whip as the horse ran faster and faster.

All of a sudden Tom got a good tight hold on the reins, then he pulled up alongside of the mail coach, leaned over, grabbed the mail bag, and spurred his horse at full speed around the ring.

"Hurrah! hurrah!" shouted everybody.

"Well done!" called Uncle Daniel.

"Couldn't be better!" exclaimed Mr. Bobbsey.

Tom waved his hat now and patted Sable affectionately, as all good riders do when their horses have done well in the ring.

The men admired the little horse so much they came up and asked the "cowboy" a lot of questions about him, how old he was and who broke him in.

"One more number," called Bert. "The chariot race."

At this all took their seats again, and out trotted two clowns, Jack and August, each riding in a little goat wagon.

The goats were decorated with the Fourth of July buntings and the wagons had the tailboards out and were tipped up like circus chariots.

The clowns pulled up in line.

"One, two, three!" called Bert, with a really big revolver up in the air.

"Ready! Set! Go!" Bang! went the revolver (a blank cartridge, of course) and away started the chariots.

Jack wore a broad green belt and August had yellow. Jack darted ahead!

"Go it, green!" shouted one group of boys.

"Pass him, orange!" called another crowd.

Now August passed Jack just as they crossed the line.

"One!" called Bert. "We will have ten rounds."

In the next the wagons kept almost even until just within a few feet of the line, then Jack crossed first.

"Two!" called Bert, while all the boys shouted for their favorite.

In the next three or four turns the riders divided even. Finally the last round was reached and the boys had tied; that is, both were even when the round started. This of course made the race very interesting, as both had equal chances of winning.

"I'll put a dollar on green," called Mr. Bobbsey. "For the fresh-air fund."

"I'll put one on orange," called Uncle Daniel, "for the same charity."

Then the ladies all wanted to bet, but Bert said it was against the rules to allow betting.

"We will take all the money you want to give us," said Bert, "but we cannot allow betting on the races."

"All ready!" called the ringmaster, holding his revolver high in the air again.

Bang went the gun!

Off went the chariots!

My, how those little goats did run!

"Go it, green!"

"Go it, orange!"

Shout after shout greeted the riders as they urged their steeds around the ring.

Suddenly Jack's chariot crossed in front of August.

"Foul!" called Bert, while Jack tried his best to get on his own side again.

"Back! back!" yelled Jack to his horse (goat), but the little animal was too excited to obey.

Finally fat August Stout, the funniest clown: dashed home first and won the race!

"Hurrah for Nero!" called everybody. "Hurrah! hurrah! hurrah!" shouted the boys long and loud.

The circus was over!

The money was counted, and there was exactly twenty-three dollars to be given the poor children in the Meadow Brook Fresh-Air Camp.

Wasn't that splendid? And to think everybody had such a good time too!

Freddie and Roy were allowed to ride home in the goat wagons, and they tried to race along the way.

A committee of five boys, Bert, Harry, Jack, Tom, and August, took the money over to the fresh-air camp the next day, and the managers said it was a very welcome gift, for new coats were needed for some sick children that were expected to come out from the city as soon as provision could be made for them.

"Somebody dropped a two-dollar bill in the ticket box," August told his companions. "Then there were the other two dollars from the race, besides some fifty-cent pieces I don't know who gave. Of course we couldn't make all that just on five-and ten-cent seats. And I took in two dollars on the peanuts besides."

"Well, we're all satisfied," said Harry. "And I guess everybody had a good time."

"Sure they did," spoke up Tom, "and I hope Bert will come out here next year to help us with another big circus. They're the best fun we ever had."

For some days every boy and girl in Meadow Brook talked about the circus, which had really been a greater success than even the boys themselves had expected.

It was a warm afternoon quite late in July—one of those days that make a boy feel lazy and inclined to stretch himself.

Bert and Harry were down back of the barn sitting on the fresh stack of hay that had just been piled up by John the stableman.

"Did you ever try smoking?" Harry asked Bert suddenly, as if he had discovered something new and interesting.

"No!" answered Bert in surprise. "Father wouldn't let me smoke."

"Neither would pa," said Harry, "but I suppose every fellow has to try it some time. I've seen them make cigarettes out of corn silk."

"I suppose that is not as bad as tobacco," replied Bert.

"No," answered Harry, "there's no harm in corn silk. Guess I'll try to roll a cigarette."

At this Harry slid down off the hay and pulled from the fast withering corn some dry silk.

With a good handful he went back to Bert.

"I've got some soft paper," he said, sitting down again and beginning the task.

Bert watched with interest, but really had no idea of doing wrong.

"There!" exclaimed Harry, giving the ends of the cigarette a twist. "How is that?"

"Pretty good," answered Bert; "looks like a real one."

"Let's try it!" went on Harry.

"Not in the hay," exclaimed Bert; "you might drop the match."

At this Harry slid down along the side of the stack, and Bert followed.

It did seem wrong as soon as Harry struck the match, but the cigarette being only corn silk made the boys forget all the warnings never to smoke.

Harry gave a puff or two. Then he choked a little.

"Kinder strong," he spluttered. "You try it!"

Bert put the cigarette in his mouth. He drew it once or twice, then quickly tossed it aside.

"Ouch!" he exclaimed. "Tastes like old shoes!"

At that time John came up and piled on some more hay. The boys of course had to act as if nothing had happened, and dared not look around to find the lighted cigarette even though they wanted to very much.

"I hope it went out," Bert said, as John walked away again.

"If it didn't it's under the hay," said Harry, somewhat alarmed. "But I guess it's out."

"My, look at the storm coming!" Bert exclaimed suddenly. "We ought to help John with that load of hay."

"All right," said Harry, "come along!" and with this the two boys started on a run down through the fields into the open meadow, where the dry hay was being packed up ready to put on the hay rick.

John, of course, was very glad of the help, for it spoils hay to get it wet, so all three worked hard to load up before the heavy shower should come up.

"All ready!" called John, "and no time to lose."

At this the boys jumped up and all started for the barn.

"There's smoke!" exclaimed Harry in terror as they neared the barn.

"The barn is afire!" screamed John the next minute, almost falling from his seat on the wagon in his haste to get down.

"Quick! quick!" yelled the boys, so frightened they could hardly move.

"The hose!" called John, seeing flames now shoot out of the barn windows, "Get the hose, Harry; it's in the coach house. I'll get a bucket while you attach the hose."

By this time everybody was out from the house.

"Oh, mercy!" cried Aunt Sarah. "Our whole barn will be burned."

Uncle Daniel was with John now, pouring water on the flames, that were gaining in spite of all efforts to put them out.

"Where's the firemen!" cried little Freddie, in real tears this time, for he, like all the others, was awfully frightened.

The boys had a stream from the hose now, but this too was of no account, for the flames had shot up from the big pile of dry hay!

"The firemen!" called Freddie again.

"There are no firemen in the country, Freddie," Nan told him. "We have to put the fire out ourselves."

"We can't then," he went on, "and all the other barns will burn too."

There was indeed great danger, for the flames were getting ahead rapidly.

All this time the terrific thunderstorm was coming up.

Clap after clap of thunder rolled over the hills and made the fire look more terrible against the black sky.

"The rain!" exclaimed Uncle Daniel at last, "The rain may put it out; we can't."

At this one terrific clap of thunder came. Then the downpour of rain. It came like a very deluge, and as it fell on the flames it sent out steam and smoke but quickly subdued the cracking and flashing of the fire.

Everybody ran to the back porch now but John and Uncle Daniel. They went in the coach house at the side of the barn.

"How could it have caught fire?" Aunt Sarah said. But Harry and Bert were both very pale, and never said a word.

How heavily the rain did pour down, just like a cloudburst! And as it struck the fire even the smoke began to die out.

"It's going out!" exclaimed Harry. "Oh, I hope it keeps on raining!" Soon there was even no more smoke!

"It's out!" called John, a little later. "That was a lucky storm for us."

Chapter XVI

THE FLOOD

The heavy downpour of rain had ceased now, and everybody ran to the barn to see what damage the fire had done.

"It almost caught my pigeon coop!" said Harry, as he examined the blackened beams in the barn near the wire cage his birds lived in.

"The entire back of this barn will have to be rebuilt," said Uncle Daniel. "John, are you sure you didn't drop a match in the hay?"

"Positive, sir!" answered John. "I never use a match while I'm working. Didn't even have one in my clothes."

Bert whispered something to Harry. It was too much to have John blamed for their wrongdoing.

"Father!" said Harry bravely, but with tears in his eyes. "It was our fault; we set the barn afire!"

"What!" exclaimed Uncle Daniel in surprise. "You boys set the barn afire!"

"Yes," spoke up Bert. "It was mostly my fault. I threw the cigarette away and we couldn't find it."

"Cigarette!" exclaimed Uncle Daniel. "What!—you boys smoking!"

Both Bert and Harry started to cry. They were not used to being spoken to like that, and of course they realized how much it cost to

put that nasty old cigarette in their mouths. Besides there might have
been a great deal more damage if it hadn't been for the rain.

"Come with me!" Uncle Daniel said; "we must find out how all
this happened," and he led the unhappy boys into the coach house,
where they all sat down on a bench.

"Now, Harry, stop your crying, and tell me about it," the father
commanded.

Harry tried to obey, but his tears choked him. Bert was the first
able to speak.

"Oh, Uncle Daniel," he cried, "we really didn't mean to smoke.
We only rolled up some corn silk in a piece of paper and—"

His tears choked back his words now, and Harry said:

"It was I who rolled the cigarette, father, and it was awful, it almost
made us sick. Then when Bert put it in his mouth—"

"I threw it away and it must have fallen in the hay!" said Bert.

"Why didn't you come and tell me?" questioned Uncle Daniel severely. "It was bad enough to do all that, but worse to take the risk of fire!"

"Well, the storm was coming," Harry answered, "and we went to
help John with the hay!"

"Now, boys," said Uncle Daniel, "this has been a very serious
lesson to you and one which you will remember all your lives. I need
not punish you any more; you have suffered enough from the fright of
that awful fire. And if it hadn't been that you were always pretty good
boys the Lord would not have sent that shower to save us as He did."

"I bet I'll never smoke again as long as I live," said Harry deter-
minedly through his tears.

"Neither will I," Bert said firmly, "and I'll try to make other fellows
stop if I can."

"All right," answered Uncle Daniel, "I'm sure you mean that, and
don't forget to thank the Lord to-night for helping us as He did. And
you must ask His pardon too for doing wrong, remember."

This ended the boys' confession, but they could not stop crying
for a long time, and Bert felt so sick and nervous he went to bed
without eating any supper. Uncle Daniel gave orders that no one
should refer to the fire or cause the boys any more worry, as they were
both really very nervous from the shock, so that beyond helping John
clear things up in the burned end of the barn, there was no further

reference to the boys' accident.

Next day it rained very hard—in fact, it was one of those storms that come every summer and do not seem to know when to go away.

"The gate at the sawmill dam is closed," Harry told Bert, "and if the pond gets any higher they won't be able to cross the plank to open up the gate and let the water out."

"That would be dangerous, wouldn't it?" Bert asked.

"Very," replied Harry. "Peter Burns' house is right in line with the dam at the other side of the plank, and if the dam should ever burst that house would be swept away."

"And the barn and henhouse are nearer the pond than the house even!" Bert remarked. "It would be an awful loss for a poor man."

"Let's go up in the attic and see how high the pond is," Harry suggested.

From the top of the house the boys could see across the high pond bank into the water.

"My!" Bert exclaimed; "isn't it awful!"

"Yes, it is," Harry replied. "You see, all the streams from the mountains wash into this pond, and in a big storm like this it gets very dangerous."

"Why do they build houses in such dangerous places?" asked Bert.

"Oh, you see, that house of Burns' has stood there maybe one hundred years—long before any dam was put in the pond to work the sawmill," said Harry.

"Oh, that's it—is it?" Bert replied. "I thought it was queer to put houses right in line with a dam."

"See how strong the water is getting," went on Harry. "Look at that big log floating down."

"It will be fun when it stops raining," remarked Bert. "We can sail things almost anywhere."

"Yes, I've seen the pond come right up across the road down at Hopkins' once," Harry told his cousins. "That was when it had rained a whole week without stopping."

"Say," called Dinah from the foot of the stairs. "You boys up there better get your boots on and look after that Frisky cow. John's gone off somewhere, and dat calf am crying herself sick out in de barn. Maybe she a-gettin' drownded."

It did not take long to get their boots and overcoats on and hurry out to the barn.

"Sure enough, she is getting drownded!" exclaimed Harry, as they saw the poor little calf standing in water up to her knees.

"Where is all the water coming from?" asked Bert.

"I don't know," Harry answered, "unless the tank upstairs has overflowed."

The boys ran up the stairs and found, just as Harry thought, the tank that supplied all the barns with water, and which also gave a supply for the house to be used on the lawn, was flowing over.

"Is there any way of letting it out?" asked Bert, quite frightened.

"We can open all the faucets, besides dipping out pailfuls," said Harry. "But I wish John would get back."

Harry ran to get the big water pail, while Bert turned on the faucet at the outside of the barn, the one in the horse stable, another that supplied water for the chickens and ducks, and the one John used for carriage washing. Frisky, of course, had been moved to a dry corner and now stopped crying.

Harry gathered all the large water pails he could carry, and hurried up to the tank followed by Bert.

"It has gone down already," said Harry, as they looked into the tank again. "But we had better dip out all we can, to make sure. Lucky we found it as soon as we did, for there are all father's tools on the bench right under the tank, besides all those new paints that have just been opened."

"Here comes John now," said Bert, as he heard the barn door open and shut again.

"Come up here, John!" called Harry; "we're almost flooded out. The tank overflowed."

"It did!" exclaimed John. "Gracious! I hope nothing is spoiled."

"Oh, we just caught it in tine," Harry told him, "and we opened up the faucets as soon as we could. Then we began dipping out, to make sure."

"You were smart boys this time," John told him, "and saved a lot of trouble by being so prompt to act. There is going to be a flood sure. The dam is roaring like Niagara, and they haven't opened the gates yet."

"I'm glad we are up high," Bert remarked, for he had never seen a country flood before, and was a good deal frightened at the prospect.

"Hey, John!" called Freddie from the back porch. "Hey, bring me some more nails, will you? I need them for my ark."

"He's building an ark!" laughed Bert. "Guess we'll need it all right if this keeps on."

Harry got some nails from his toolbox in the carriage house, and the boys went up to the house.

There they found Freddie on the hard cement cellar floor, nailing boards together as fast as his little hammer could drive the nails in.

"How's that?" asked the little fellow, standing up the raft.

"I guess that will float," said Bert, "and when it stops raining we can try it."

"I'm going to make a regular ark like the play one I've got home," said Freddie, "only mine will be a big one with room for us all, besides Frisky, Snoop, Fluffy, and—"

"Old Bill. We'll need a horse to tow us back when the water goes down," laughed Harry.

Freddie went on working as seriously as if he really expected to be a little Noah and save all the people from the flood.

"My, but it does rain!" exclaimed somebody on the front porch.

It was Uncle Daniel, who had just returned from the village, soaking wet.

"They can't open the gates," Uncle Daniel told Aunt Sarah. "They let the water get so high the planks sailed away and now they can't get near the dam."

"That is bad for the poor Burns family!" exclaimed Aunt Sarah. "I had better have John drive me down and see if they need anything."

"I stopped in on my way up," Uncle Daniel told her, "and they were about ready to move out. We'll bring them up here if it gets any worse."

"Why don't they go to the gates in a boat?" asked Bert.

"Why, my dear boy," said Uncle Daniel, "anybody who would go near that torrent in a boat might as well jump off the bridge. The falls are twenty-five feet high, and the water seems to have built them up twice that. If one went within two hundred feet of the dam the surging water would carry him over."

"You see," said Harry, explaining it further, "there is like a window in the falls, a long low door. When this is opened the water is drawn down under and does not all have to go over the falls."

"And if there is too much pressure against the stone wall that makes the dam, the wall may be carried away. That's what we call the dam bursting," finished Uncle Daniel.

All this was very interesting to Bert, who could not help being frightened at the situation.

The boys told Uncle Daniel how the tank in the barn had overflowed, and he said they had done good work to prevent any damage.

"Oh, Uncle Daniel!" exclaimed Freddie, just then running up from the cellar. "Come and see my ark! It's most done, and I'm going to put all the animals and things in it to save them from the flood."

"An ark!" exclaimed his uncle, laughing. "Well, you're a sensible little fellow to build an ark to-day, Freddie, for we will surely need one if this keeps up," and away they went to examine the raft Freddie had actually nailed together in the cellar.

That was an awful night in Meadow Brook, and few people went to bed, staying up instead to watch the danger of the flood. The men took turns walking along the pond bank all night long, and their low call each hour seemed to strike terror in the hearts of those who were in danger.

The men carried lanterns, and the little specks of light were all that could be seen through the darkness.

Mrs. Burns had refused to leave her home.

"I will stay as long as I can," she told Uncle Daniel. "I have lived here many a year, and that dam has not broken yet, so I'm not going to give up hope now!"

"But you could hardly get out in time should it break," insisted Uncle Daniel, "and you know we have plenty of room and you are welcome with us."

Still she insisted on staying, and each hour when the watchman would call from the pond bank, just like they used to do in old wartimes: "Two o'clock-and—all is—well!" Mrs. Burns would look up and say, "Dear Lord, I thank Thee!"

Peter, of course, was out with the men. He could not move his barns and chicken house, but he had taken his cow and horse to places of safety.

There were other families along the road in danger as well as the

Burnses, but they were not so near the dam, and would get some warning to escape before the flood could reach them should the dam burst.

How the water roared! And how awfully dark it was! Would morning ever come?

"Four o'clock—the water rises!" shouted the men from the bank.

"Here, Mary!" called Peter Burns at the door of their little home, "you put your shawl on and run up the road as fast as you can! Don't wait to take anything, but go!"

"Oh, my babies' pictures!" she cried. "My dear babies! I must have them."

The poor frightened little woman rushed about the house looking for the much-prized pictures of her babies that were in heaven.

"It's a good thing they all have a safe home to-night," she thought, "for their mother could not give them safety if they were here."

"Come, Mary!" called Peter, outside. "That dam is swaying like a tree-top, and it will go over any minute." With one last look at the little home Mrs. Burns went out and closed the door.

Outside there were people from all along the road. Some driven out of their homes in alarm, others having turned out to help their neighbors.

The watchmen had left the bank. A torrent from the dam would surely wash that away, and brave as the men were they could not watch the flood any longer.

"Get past the willows quick!" called the men. "Let everybody who is not needed hurry up the road!"

Mr. Mason, Mr. Hopkins, Uncle Daniel, and John, besides Peter Burns, were the men most active in the life-saving work. There were not many boats to be had, but what there were had been brought inland early in the day, for otherwise they would have been washed away long before down the stream into the river.

"What's that?" called Uncle Daniel, as there was a heavy crash over near the gates.

Then everybody listened breathless.

It was just coming daylight, and the first streak of dawn saw the end of the awful rain.

Not one man in the crowd dared to run up that pond bank and look over the gates!

"It's pretty strong!" said the watchman. "I expected to hear it crash an hour ago!"

There was another crash!

"There she goes!" said Mr. Burns, and then nobody spoke.

Chapter XVII

A Town Afloat

"Is she going?" asked Uncle Daniel at last, after a wait of several minutes.

Daylight was there now; and was ever dawn more welcome in Meadow Brook!

"I'll go up to the pipes," volunteered John. "And I can see from there."

Now, the pipes were great water conduits, the immense black iron kind that are used for carrying water into cities from reservoirs. They were situated quite a way from the dam, but as it was daylight John could see the gates as he stood on the pipes that crossed above the pond.

Usually boys could walk across these pipes in safety, as they were far above the water, but the flood had raised the stream so that the water just reached the pipes, and John had to be careful.

"What's that?" he said, as he looked down the raging stream.

"Something lies across the dam!" he shouted to the anxious listeners.

This was enough. In another minute every man was on the pond bank.

"The big elm!" they shouted. "It has saved the dam!"

What a wonderful thing had happened! The giant elm tree that for so many, many years had stood on the edge of the stream, was in this great flood washed away, and as it crossed the dam it broke the force of the torrent, really making another waterfall.

"It is safe now!" exclaimed Uncle Daniel in surprise. "It was the tree we heard crash against the bank. The storm is broken at last, and that tree will hold where it is stuck until the force goes down. Then we can open the gates."

To think that the houses were safe again! That poor Mrs. Burns could come back to the old mill home once more!

"We must never have this risk again," said Mr. Mason to Uncle Daniel. "When the water goes down we will open the gates, then the next dry spell that comes when there is little water in the pond we will break that dam and let the water run through in a stream. If the mill people want water power they will have to get it some place where it will not endanger lives."

Uncle Daniel agreed with Mr. Mason, and as they were both town officials, it was quite likely what they said would be done in Meadow Brook.

"Hey, Bert and Harry!" called Tom Mason, as he and Jack Hopkins ran past the Bobbsey place on their way to see the dam. "Come on down and see the flood."

The boys did not wait for breakfast, but with a buttered roll in hand Harry and Bert joined the others and hurried off to the flood.

"Did the dam burst?" was the first question everybody asked along the way, and when told how the elm tree had saved it the people were greatly astonished.

"Look at this," called Tom, as they came to a turn in the road where the pond ran level with the fields. That was where it was only stream, and no embankment had been built around it.

"Look!" exclaimed Jack; "the water has come up clear across the road, and we can only pass by walking on the high board fence."

"Or get a boat," said Tom. "Let's go back to the turn and see if there's a boat tied anywhere."

"Here's Herolds'," called Harry, as they found the pretty little row-boat, used for pleasure by the summer cottagers, tied up to a tree.

"We'll just borrow that," said Jack, and then the four boys lifted the boat to that part of the road where the water ran.

"All get in, and I'll push off," said Harry, who had hip-boots on. The other three climbed in, then Harry gave a good push and scrambled over the edge himself.

"Think of rowing a boat in the middle of a street," said Bert. "That's the way they do in Naples," he added, "but I never expected to see such a thing in Meadow Brook."

The boys pushed along quite easily, as the water was deep enough to use oars in, and soon they had rounded the curve of the road and were in sight of the people looking at the dam.

THE BOYS WERE DASHING OUT NOW RIGHT IN THE STREAM.

"What an immense tree!" exclaimed Bert, as they left their boat and mounted the bank.

"That's what saved the dam!" said Harry. "Now Mrs. Burns can come back home again."

"But look there!" called Tom. "There goes Peter Burns' chicken house."

Sure enough, the henhouse had left its foundation and now toppled over into the stream.

It had been built below the falls, near the Burns house, and Peter had some valuable ducks and chickens in it.

"The chickens!" called Jack, as they ran along. "Get the boat, Harry, and we can save some."

The boys were dashing out now right in the stream, Jack and Tom being good oarsmen.

But the poor chickens! What an awful noise they made, as they tried to keep on the dry side of the floating house!

The ducks, of course, didn't mind it, but they added their queer quacking to the noise.

"We can never catch any of the chickens," said Harry. "We ought to have a rope and pull the house in."

"A rope," called Tom to the crowd on the shore. "Throw us a rope!"

Someone ran off and got one, and it was quickly thrown out to the boys in the boat.

"Push up closer," Tom told Harry and Bert, who had the oars now. Tom made a big loop on the rope and threw it toward the house. But it only landed over a chicken, and caused the frightened fowl to fly high up in the air and rest in a tree on the bank.

"Good!" cried the people on the edge. "One is safe, anyhow!"

Tom threw the rope again. This time it caught on a corner of the henhouse, and as he pulled the knot tight they had the floating house secure.

"Hurrah! hurrah!" shouted the people.

By this time Mr. Mason and Uncle Daniel had reached the spot in their boat.

"Don't pull too hard!" called the men to the boys. "You'll upset your boat."

"Throw the line to us," added Uncle Daniel,

This the boys did, and as it was a long stretch of rope the men were able to get all the way in to shore with it before pulling at the house.

"Now we'll have a tug of war," said Mr. Mason.

"Wait for us!" cried the boys in the boat "We want to have a pull at that."

All this time the chickens were cackling and screeching, as the house in the water lunged from one side to the other. It was a large new coop and built of strong material that made it very heavy.

"Now," said Uncle Daniel, as the boys reached the shore and secured their boat, "all take a good hold."

Every inch of the rope that crossed the water's edge was soon covered with somebody's hand.

"All pull now!" called Mr. Mason, and with a jerk in came the floating house, chickens, ducks and all, and down went everybody that had pulled. The force of the jerk, of course, threw them all to the ground, but that was only fun and gave the boys a good chance to laugh.

Just as soon as the chickens reached the shore they scampered for home—some flying, some running, but all making a noise.

"We may as well finish the job," said Mr. Mason. "Tom, go hitch Sable up to the cart and we'll bring the henhouse back where it belongs."

By running across the fields that were on the highest part of the road Tom was able to get to his barn without a boat, and soon he returned with the cart and Sable.

It took all hands to get the henhouse on the cart, but this was finally done, and away went Sable up the road with the queer load after him in the dump cart.

"You had better put it up on the hill this time," Peter told them. "The water isn't gone down yet." So at last the chicken coop was settled, and not a hen was missing.

There were many sights to be seen about Meadow Brook that afternoon, and the boys enjoyed the flood, now that there was no longer any danger to life.

Bert caught a big salmon and a black-spotted lizard that had been flooded out from some dark place in the mountains, Harry found a pretty toy canoe that some small boy had probably been playing with in the stream before the water rose, and Jack was kept busy towing in all kinds of stuff that had broken loose from barns along the pond.

Freddie had boots on, and was happy sailing his "ark" up and down the road. He insisted on Snoop taking a ride, but cats do not fancy water and the black kitten quickly hid himself up in the hay loft, out of Freddie's reach.

Little by little the water fell, until by the next afternoon there was no longer a river running through the roads. But there were plenty of wet places and enough of streams washing down the rain the gutters to give Freddie a fine canal to sail boats in.

Nan and Flossie had boats too which Bert and Harry made for them. In fact, all the girls along Meadow Brook road found something that would sail while the flood days lasted.

As it was still July the hot sun came down and dried things up pretty quickly, but many haymows were completely spoiled, as were summer vegetables that were too near the pond and came in for their share of the washout.

This loss, however, was nothing compared with what had been expected by the farmers, and all were satisfied that a kind Providence had saved the valley houses from complete destruction.

Chapter XVIII

THE FRESH-AIR CAMP

Quiet had settled down once more upon the little village of Meadow Brook. The excitement of the flood had died away, and now when the month of July was almost gone, and a good part of vacation had gone with it, the children turned their attention to a matter of new interest—the fresh-air camp.

"Mildred Manners was over to the camp yesterday," Nan told her mother, "and she says a whole lot of little girls have come out from the city, and they have such poor clothes. There is no sickness there that anyone could catch, she says (for her uncle is the doctor, you know), but Mildred says her mother is going to show her how to make some aprons for the little girls."

"Why, that would be nice for all you little girls to do," said Mrs. Bobbsey. "Suppose you start a sewing school, and all see what you can make!"

"Oh, that would be lovely!" exclaimed Nan. "When can we start?"

"As soon as we get the materials," the mother replied. "We will ask Aunt Sarah to drive over to the camp this afternoon; then we can see what the children need."

"Can I go?" asked Flossie, much interested in the fresh-air work.

"I guess so," said Mrs. Bobbsey. "If we take the depot wagon there will be room for you and Freddie."

So that was how it came about that our little friends became interested in the fresh-air camp. Nan and Mildred, Flossie and Freddie, with Aunt Sarah and Mrs. Bobbsey, visited the camp in the afternoon.

"What a queer place it is!" whispered Flossie, as they drove up to the tents on the mountain-side.

"Hush," said Nan; "they might hear you."

"Oh, these are war-camps!" exclaimed Freddie when he saw the white tents. "They're just like the war-pictures in my story book!"

The matron who had charge of the camp came up, and when Mrs. Bobbsey explained her business, the matron was pleased and glad to show them through the place.

"Oh, it was your boys who brought us all that money from the circus?" said the woman. "That's why we have all the extra children here—the circus money has paid for them, and they are to have two weeks on this beautiful mountain."

"I'm glad the boys were able to help," said Mrs. Bobbsey. "It really was quite a circus."

"It must have been, when they made so much money," the other answered.

"And we are going to help now," spoke up Nan. "We are starting a sewing school."

"Oh, I'm so glad somebody has thought of clothes," said the matron. "We often get gifts of food, but we need clothes so badly."

"There is no sickness?" asked Mrs. Bobbsey, as they started on a tour of the camp.

"No; we cannot take sick children here now," said the matron. "We had some early in the season, but this is such a fine place for romping we decided to keep this camp for the healthy children and have another for those who are sick."

By this time numbers of little girls and boys crowded around the visitors. They were quite different from the children of Meadow Brook or Lakeport. Somehow they were smaller, but looked older. Poor children begin to worry so young that they soon look much older than they really are.

Nan and Mildred spoke kindly to the girls, while Freddie and Flossie soon made friends with the little boys. One small boy, smaller than Freddie, with sandy hair and beautiful blue eyes, was particularly happy with Freddie. He looked better than the others, was almost as fat as Freddie, and he had such lovely clear skin, as if somebody loved to wash it.

"Where do you lib?" he lisped to Freddie.

"At Uncle Daniel's," Freddie answered. "Where do you live?"

"With mamma," replied the little boy. Then he stopped a minute. "Oh, no; I don't live with mamma now," he corrected himself, "'cause she's gone to heaven, so I live with Mrs. Manily."

Mrs. Manily was the matron, and numbers of the children called her mamma.

"Can I come over and play with you?" asked the boy. "What's your name?"

"His name is Freddie and mine is Flossie," said the latter. "What is your name?"

"Mine is Edward Brooks," said the little stranger, "but everybody calls me Sandy. Do you like Sandy better than Edward?"

"No," replied Flossie. "But I suppose that's a pet name because your hair is that color."

"Is it?" said the boy, tossing his sunny curls around. "Maybe that's why!"

"Guess it is," said Freddie. "But will Mrs. Man let you come over to our house?"

"Mrs. Manily, you mean," said Sandy. "I'll just go and ask her."

"Isn't he cute!" exclaimed Flossie, and the pretty little boy ran in search of Mrs. Manily.

"I'm going to ask mamma if we can bring him home," declared Freddie. "He could sleep in my bed."

The others of the party were now walking through the big tents.

"This is where we eat," the matron explained, as the dining room was entered. The tent was filled with long narrow tables and had benches at the sides. The tables were covered with oilcloth, and in the center of each was a beautiful bunch of fresh wild flowers—the small pretty kind that grow in the woods.

"You ought to see our poor children eat," remarked the matron. "We have just as much as we can do to serve them, they have such good appetites from the country air."

"We must send you some fresh vegetables," said Aunt Sarah, "and some fruit for Sunday."

"We would be very grateful," replied Mrs. Manily, "for of course we cannot afford much of a variety."

Next to the dining room was the dormitory or sleeping tent.

"We have a little boys' brigade," said the matron, "and every pleasant evening they march around with drums and tin fifes. Then, when it is bedtime, we have a boy blow the 'taps' on a tin bugle, just like real soldiers do."

Freddie and Sandy had joined the sightseers now, and Freddie was much interested in the brigade.

"Who is the captain?" he asked of Mrs. Manily.

"Oh, we appoint a new captain each week from the very best boys we have. We only let a very good boy be captain," the matron told him.

In the dormitory were rows and rows of small white cots. They looked very clean and comfortable, and the door of this tent was closed with a big green mosquito netting.

"How old are your babies?" asked Aunt Sarah.

"Sandy is our baby!" replied the matrons patting the little boy fondly, "and he is four years old. We cannot take them any younger without their mothers."

"Freddie is four also," said Mrs. Bobbsey. "What a dear sweet child Sandy is!"

"Yes," said Mrs. Manily, "he has just lost a good mother and his father cannot care for him—that is, he cannot afford to pay his board or hire a housekeeper, so he brought him to the Aid Society. He is the pet of the camp, and you can see he has been well trained."

"No mother and no home!" exclaimed Mrs. Bobbsey. "Dear little fellow! Think of our Freddie being alone in the world like that!"

Mrs. Bobbsey could hardly keep her tears back. She stooped over and kissed Sandy.

"Do you know my mamma?" he asked, looking straight into the lady's kind face.

"Mrs. Manily is your mamma, isn't she?" said Mrs. Bobbsey.

"Yes, she's my number two mamma, but I mean number one that used to sleep with me."

"Come now, Sandy," laughed Mrs. Manily. "Didn't you tell me last night I was the best mamma in the whole world?" and she hugged the little fellow to make him happy again.

"So you are," he laughed, forgetting all his loneliness now. "When I get to be a big man I'm goin' to take you out carriage riding."

"Can't Sandy cone home with us?" asked Freddie. "He can sleep in my bed."

"You are very good," said the matron. "But we cannot let any of our children go visiting without special permission from the Society."

"Well," said Aunt Sarah, "if you get the permission we will be very glad to have Sandy pay us a visit. We have a large place, and would really like to have some good poor child enjoy it. We have company now, but they will leave us soon, and then perhaps we could have a little fresh-air camp of our own."

"The managers have asked us to look for a few private homes that could accommodate some special cases," replied Mrs. Manily, "and I am sure I can arrange it to have Sandy go."

"Oh, let him come now," pleaded Freddie, as Sandy held tight to his hand. "See, we have room in the wagon."

"Well, he might have a ride," consented the matron, and before anyone had a chance to speak again Freddie and Sandy had climbed into the wagon.

Nan and Mildred had been talking to some of the older girls, who were very nice and polite for girls who had no one to teach them at home, and Nan declared that she was coming over to the camp to play with them some whole day.

"We can bring our lunch," said Mildred, "and you can show us all the pleasant play-places you have fixed up in stones over the mountain-side."

One girl, Nellie by name, seemed very smart and bright, and she brought to Mrs. Bobbsey a bunch of ferns and wild flowers she had just gathered while showing Nan and Mildred around.

"You certainly have a lovely place here," said Mrs. Bobbsey, as they got ready to leave, "and you little girls will be quite strong and ready for school again when you go back to the city."

"I don't go to school," said Nellie rather bashfully.

"Why?" asked Aunt Sarah.

"Oh, I go to night school," said the little girl. "But in the daytime I have to work."

"Why, how old are you?" asked Aunt Sarah.

"Twelve," said Nellie shyly.

"Working at twelve years of age!" exclaimed Mrs. Bobbsey in surprise. "What do you do?"

"I'm a cash-girl in a big store," said Nellie with some pride, for many little girls are not smart enough to hold such a position.

"I thought all children had to go to school," Aunt Sarah said to Mrs. Manily.

"So they do," replied the matron, "but in special cases they get permission from the factory inspector. Then they can work during the day and go to school at night."

"I think it's a shame!" said the mother. "That child is not much larger than Nan, and to think of her working in a big store all day, then having to work at night school too!"

"It does not seem right!" admitted the matron; "but, you see, sometimes there is no choice. Either a child must work or go to an institution, and we strain every point to keep them in their homes."

"We will drive back with Sandy," said Aunt Sarah as they got into the wagon.

"Can't Nellie come too?" asked Nan. "There is plenty of room."

The matron said yes, and so the little party started off for a ride along the pretty road.

"I was never in a carriage before in all my life," said Nellie suddenly. "Isn't it grand!"

"Never!" exclaimed the other girls in surprise.

"No," said Nellie. "I've had lots of rides in trolley cars, and we had a ride in a farm wagon the other day, but this is the first time I have ever been in a carriage."

Aunt Sarah was letting Sandy drive, and he, of course, was delighted. Freddie enjoyed it almost as well as Sandy did, and kept telling him which rein to pull on and all that. Old Bill, the horse, knew the road so well he really didn't need any driver, but he went along very nicely with the two little boys talking to him.

"We will stop and have some soda at the post office," said Mrs. Bobbsey. For the post office was also a general store.

This was good news to everybody, and when the man came out for the order Aunt Sarah told him to bring cakes too.

Everybody liked the ice cream soda, but it was plain Nellie and Sandy had not had such a treat in a long time.

"This is the best fun I've had!" declared the little cash-girl, allowing how grateful she was. "And I hope you'll come and see us again," she added politely to Mildred and Nan.

"Oh, we intend to," said Mildred. "You know, we are going to have a sewing school to make aprons for the little ones at the camp."

Old Bill had turned back to the fresh-air quarters again, and soon, too soon, Sandy was handed back to Mrs. Manily, while Nellie jumped down and said what a lovely time she had had.

"Now be sure to come, Sandy," called Freddie, "'cause I'll expect you!"

"I will," said Sandy rather sadly, for he would rather have gone along right then.

"And I'll let you play with Snoop and my playthings," Freddie called again. "Good-bye."

"Good-bye," answered the little fresh children.

Then old Bill took the others home.

Chapter XIX

SEWING SCHOOL

"Let's get Mabel and all the others," said Nan to Mildred. "We ought to take at least six gingham aprons and three nightgowns over to the camp."

Aunt Sarah had turned a big long attic room into a sewing school where Nan and Mildred had full charge. Flossie was to look after the spools of thread, keeping them from tangling up, and the girls agreed to let Freddie cut paper patterns.

This was not a play sewing school but a real one, for Aunt Sarah and Mrs. Bobbsey were to do the operating or machine sewing, while the girls were to sew on tapes, buttons, overhand seams, and do all that.

Mildred and Nan invited Mabel, Nettie, Marie Brenn (she was visiting the Herolds), Bessie, and Anna Thomas, a big girl who lived over Lakeside way.

"Be sure to bring your thimbles and needles," Nan told them. "And come at two o'clock this afternoon."

Every girl came—even Nettie, who was always so busy at home.

Mrs. Bobbsey sat at the machine ready to do stitching while Aunt Sarah was busy "cutting out" on a long table in front of the low window.

"Now, young ladies," said Mrs. Bobbsey, "we have ready some blue gingham aprons. You see how they are cut out; two seams, one at each side, then they are to be closed down the back. There will be a pair of strings on each apron, and you may begin by pressing down a narrow hem on these strings. We will not need to baste them, just press them down with the finger this way."

Mrs. Bobbsey then took up a pair of the sashes and turned in the edges. Immediately the girls followed her instructions, and very soon all of the strings were ready for the machine.

Nan handed them to her mother, and then Aunt Sarah gave out the work.

"Now these are the sleeves," said Aunt Sarah, "and they must each have little gathers brought in at the elbow here between these notches. Next you place the sleeve together notch to notch, and they can be stitched without basting."

"Isn't it lively to work this way?" said Mildred. "It isn't a bit of trouble, and see how quickly we get done."

"Many hands make light work," replied Mrs. Bobbsey. "I guess we will get all the aprons finished this afternoon."

Piece by piece the various parts of the garments were given out, until there remained nothing more to do than to put on buttons and work buttonholes, and overhand the arm holes.

"I'll cut the buttonholes," said Mrs. Bobbsey, "then Nan and Mildred may work the buttonholes by sticking a pin through each hole. The other girls may then sew the buttons on."

It was wonderful how quickly those little pearl buttons went down the backs of the aprons.

"I believe I could make an apron all alone now," said Nan, "if it was cut out."

"So could I," declared Mildred. "It isn't hard at all."

"Well, here's my patterns," spoke up Freddie, who with Flossie had been busy over in the corner cutting "ladies" out of a fashion paper.

"No, they're paper dolls," said Flossie, who was standing them all up in a row, "and we are going to give them to the fresh-air children to play with on rainy days."

It was only half-past four when Nan rang the bell to dismiss the sewing school.

"We have had such a lovely time," said Mabel, "we would like to have sewing to do every week."

"Well, you are welcome to come," said Aunt Sarah. "We will make night dresses for the poor little ones next week, then after that you might all bring your own work, mending, fancywork or tidies, whatever you have to do."

"And we might each pay five cents to sew for the fresh-air children," suggested Mildred.

"Yes, all charity sewing classes have a fund," Mrs. Bobbsey remarked. "That would be a good idea."

"Now let us fold up the aprons," said Nan. "Don't they look pretty?"

And indeed the half-dozen blue-and-white ginghams did look very nice, for they were carefully made and all smooth and even.

"When can we iron them out?" asked Flossie, anxious to deliver the gifts to the needy little ones.

"To-morrow afternoon," replied her mother. "The boys are going to pick vegetables in the morning, and we will drive over in the afternoon."

Uncle Daniel had given the boys permission to pick all the butter-beans and string-beans that were ripe, besides three dozen ears of the choicest corn, called "Country Gentleman."

"Children can only eat very tender corn," said Uncle Daniel, "and as that is sweet and milky they will have no trouble digesting it."

Harry looked over every ear of the green corn by pulling the husks down and any that seemed a bit overripe he discarded.

"We will have to take the long wagon," said Bert, as they began to count up the baskets. There were two of beans, three of corn, one of lettuce, two of sweet apples, besides five bunches of Freddie's radishes.

"Be sure to bring Sandy back with you," called Freddie, who did not go to the camp this time. "Tell him I'll let him be my twin brother."

Nan and Aunt Sarah went with the boys, but how disappointed they were to find a strange matron in charge of the camp, and Sandy's eyes red from crying after Mrs. Manily.

"Oh, I knowed you would come to take me to Freddie," cried he, "'cause my other mamma is gone too, and I'm all alone."

"Mrs. Manily was called away by sickness in her family," explained the new matron, "and I cannot do anything with this little boy."

"He was so fond of Mrs. Manily," said Aunt Sarah, "and besides he remembers how lonely he was when his own mother went away. Maybe we could bring him over to our house for a few days."

"Yes, Mrs. Manily spoke of that," said the matron, "and she had received permission from the Society to let Edward pay a visit to Mrs. Daniel Bobbsey. See, here is the card."

"Oh, that will be lovely!" cried Nan, hugging Sandy as tight as her arms could squeeze.

"Freddie told us to be sure to bring you back with us."

"I am so glad to get these things," the matron said to Aunt Sarah, as she took the aprons, "for everybody has been upset with Mrs. Manily having to leave so suddenly. The aprons are lovely. Did the little girls make them?"

Aunt Sarah told her about the sewing school, and then she said she was going to have a little account printed about it in the year's report of good work done for the Aid Society.

"And Mrs. Manily has written an account of your circus," the matron told Harry and Bert, for she had heard about the boys and their successful charity work.

Some of the girls who knew Nan came up now and told her how Nellie, the little cash-girl, had been taken sick and had had to be removed to the hospital tent over in the other mountain.

This was sad news to Nan, for she loved the little cash-girl, and hoped to see her and perhaps have her pay a visit to Aunt Sarah's.

"Is she very sick?" Aunt Sarah asked the matron.

"Yes indeed," the other replied. "But the doctor will soon cure her, I think."

"The child is too young to work so hard," Aunt Sarah declared. "It is no wonder her health breaks down at the slightest cause, when she has no strength laid away to fight sickness."

By this time a big girl had washed and dressed Sandy, and now what a pretty boy he was! He wore a blue-and-white-striped linen suit and had a jaunty little white cap just like Freddie's.

He was so anxious to go that he jumped in the wagon before the others were ready to start.

"Get app, Bill!" he called, grabbing at the reins, and off the old horse started with no one in the wagon but Sandy!

Sandy had given the reins such a jerk that Bill started to run, and the more the little boy tried to stop him the harder he went!

"Don't slap him with the reins!" called Harry, who was now running down the hill as hard as he could after the wagon. "Pull on the reins!" he called again.

But Sandy was so excited he kept slapping the straps up and down on poor Bill, which to the horse, of course, meant to go faster.

"He'll drive in the brook," called Bert in alarm also rushing after the runaway. "Whoa, Bill! whoa, Bill!" called everybody, the children from the camp having now joined in following the wagon.

The brook was directly in front of Sandy.

"Quick, Harry!" yelled Bert. "You'll get him in a minute."

It was no easy matter, however, to overtake Sandy, for the horse had been on a run from the start. But Sandy kept his seat well, and even seemed to think it good fun now to have everybody running after him and no one able to catch him.

"Oh, I'm so afraid he'll go in the pond!" Nan told Aunt Sarah almost in tears.

"Bill would sit down first," declared Aunt Sarah, who knew her horse to be an intelligent animal.

"Oh! oh! oh!" screamed everybody, for the horse had crossed from the road into the little field that lay next the water.

"Whoa, Bill!" shouted Aunt Sarah at the top of her voice, and instantly the horse stood still.

The next minute both Bert and Harry were in the wagon beside Sandy.

"Can't I drive?" asked the little fellow innocently, while Harry was backing out of the swamp.

"You certainly made Bill go," Harry admitted, all out of breath from running.

"And you gave us a good run too," added Bert, who was red in the face from his violent exercise.

"Bill knew ma meant it when she said whoa!" Harry remarked to Bert. "I tell you, he stopped just in time, for a few feet further would have sunk horse, wagon, and all in the swamp."

Of course it was all an accident, for Sandy had no idea of starting the horse off, so no one blamed him when they got back to the road.

"We'll all get in this time," laughed Aunt Sarah to the matron. "And I'll send the boys over Sunday to let you know how Sandy is."

"Oh, he will be all right with Freddie!" Bert said, patting the little stranger on the shoulders. "We will take good care of him."

It was a pleasant ride back to the Bobbsey farm, and all enjoyed it—especially Sandy, who had gotten the idea he was a first-class driver and knew all about horses, old Bill, in particular.

"Hurrah! hurrah!" shouted Freddie, when the wagon turned in the drive. "I knowed you would come, Sandy!" and the next minute the two little boys were hand in hand running up to the barn to see Frisky, Snoop, the chickens, ducks, pigeons, and everything at once.

Sandy was a little city boy and knew nothing about real live country life, so that everything seemed quite wonderful to him, especially the chickens and ducks. He was rather afraid of anything as big as Frisky.

Snoop and Fluffy were put through their circus tricks for the stranger's benefit, and then Freddie let Sandy turn on his trapeze up under the apple tree and showed him all the different kinds of turns Bert and Harry had taught the younger twin how to perform on the swing.

"How long can you stay?" Freddie asked his little friend, while they were swinging.

"I don't know," Sandy replied vaguely.

"Maybe you could go to the seashore with us," Freddie ventured. "We are only going to stay in the country this month."

"Maybe I could go," lisped Sandy, "'cause nobody ain't got charge of me now. Mrs. Manily has gone away, you know, and I don't b'lieve in the other lady, do you?"

Freddie did not quite understand this but he said "no" just to agree with Sandy.

"And you know the big girl, Nellie, who always curled my hair without pulling it,—she's gone away too, so maybe I'm your brother now," went on the little orphan.

"Course you are!" spoke up Freddie manfully, throwing his arms around the other, "You're my twin brother too, 'cause that's the realest kind. We are all twins, you know—Nan and Bert, and Flossie and me and you!"

By this time the other Bobbseys had come out to welcome Sandy. They thought it best to let Freddie entertain him at first, so that he would not be strange, but now Uncle Daniel just took the little fellow up in his arms and into his heart, for all good men love boys, especially when they are such real little men as Sandy and Freddie happened to be.

"He's my twin brother, Uncle Daniel," Freddie insisted. "Don't you think he's just like me curls and all?"

"He is certainly a fine little chap!" the uncle replied, meaning every word of it, "and he is quite some like you too. Now let us feed the chickens. See how they are around us expecting something to eat?"

The fowls were almost ready to eat the pearl buttons off Sandy's coat, so eager were they for their meal, and it was great fun for the two little boys to toss the corn to them.

"Granny will eat from your hand," exclaimed Uncle Daniel, "You see, she is just like granite-gray stone, but we call her Granny for short."

The Plymouth Rock hen came up to Sandy, and much to his delight ate the corn out of his little white hand.

"Oh, she's a pretty chicken!" he said, stroking Granny as he would a kitten. "I dust love chitens," he added, sitting right down on the sandy ground to let Granny come up on his lap. There was so much to see in the poultry yard that Sandy, Freddie, and Uncle Daniel lingered there until Martha appeared at the back door and rang the big dinner bell in a way that meant, "Hurry up! something will get cold if you don't."

And the something proved to be chicken pot-pie with dumplings that everybody loves. And after that there came apple pudding with hard sauce, just full of sugar.

"Is it a party?" Sandy whispered to Freddie, for he was not accustomed to more than bread and milk at his evening meal.

"Yes, I guess so," ventured Freddie; "it's because you came," and then Dinah brought in little play cups of chocolate with jumbles on the side, and Mrs. Bobbsey said that would be better than the pudding for Freddie and Sandy.

"I guess I'll just live here," solemnly said the little stranger, as if his decision in such a matter should not be questioned.

"I guess you better!" Freddie agreed, "'cause it's nicer than over there, isn't it?"

"Lots," replied Sandy, "only maybe Mrs. Manily will cry for me," and he looked sad as his big blue eyes turned around and blinked to keep back some tears. "I dust love Mrs. Manily, Freddie; don't you?" he asked wistfully.

Then Harry and Bert jumped up to start the phonograph, and that was like a band wagon to the little fellows, who liked to hear the popular tunes called off by the funny man in the big bright horn.

Chapter XX

A Midnight Scare

"Sometimes I'm afraid in the bed tent over there," said Sandy to Freddie. "'Cause there ain't nothing to keep the dark out but a piece of veil in the door."

"Mosquito netting," corrected Freddie. "I would be afraid to sleep outdoors that way too. 'Cause maybe there's snakes."

"There sure is," declared the other little fellow, cuddling up closer to Freddie. "'Cause one of the boys, Tommy his name is, killed two the other day."

"Well, there ain't no snakes around here," declared Freddie, "an' this bed was put in this room, right next to mama's, for me, so you needn't be scared when Aunt Sarah comes and turns out the lights."

Both little boys were very sleepy, and in spite of having so many things to tell each other the sand-man came around and interrupted them, actually making their eyes fall down like porch screens when someone touches the string.

Mrs. Bobbsey came up and looked in at the door.

Two little sunny heads so close together!

"Why should that little darling be left alone over in the dark tent!" she thought. "See how happy he is with our own dear son Freddie."

Then she tucked them a little bit, half closed the door, and turned out the hall light.

Everybody must have been dreaming for hours, it seemed so at any rate, when suddenly all were awake again.

What was it?

What woke up the household with such a start?

"There it is again!" screamed Flossie. "Oh, mamma, mamma, come in my room quick!"

Sandy grabbed hold of Freddie.

"We're all right," whispered the brave little Freddie. "It's only the girls that's hollering."

Then they both put their curls under the bed-quilts.

"Someone's playing the piano," Bert said to Harry; and, sure enough, a nocturnal solo was coming up in queer chunks from the parlor.

"It's a crazy burglar, and he never saw a piano before," Flossie said.

The hall clock just struck midnight. That seemed to make everybody more frightened.

Uncle Daniel was hurrying down the stairs now.

"There it is again," whispered Bert, as another group of wild chords came from the piano.

"It must be cats!" exclaimed Uncle Daniel. "Harry, come down here and help light up, and we'll solve this mystery."

Without a moment's hesitation Bert and Harry were down the stairs and had the hall light burning as quickly as a good match could be struck.

But there was no more music and no cats about.

"Where is Snoop?" asked Uncle Daniel.

The boys opened the hall door into the cellar-way, and found there Snoop on his cushion and Fluffy on hers.

"It wasn't the cats," they declared.

"What could it be?"

Uncle Daniel even lighted the piano lamp, which gave a strong light, but there didn't seem to be any disturbance about.

"It certainly was the piano," he said, much puzzled.

"And sounded like a cat serenade," ventured Harry.

"Well, she isn't around here," laughed Uncle Daniel, "and we never heard of a ghost in Meadow Brook before."

All this time the people upstairs waited anxiously. Flossie held Nan so tightly about the neck that the elder sister could hardly breathe. Freddie and Sandy were still under the bedclothes, while Mrs. Bobbsey and Aunt Sarah listened in the hall.

"Dat sure is a ghost," whispered Dinah to Martha in the hall above. "Ghosts always lub music," and her funny big eyes rolled around in that queer way colored people have of expressing themselves.

"Ghosts nothin'," replied Martha indignantly. "I dusted every key of the piano to-day, and I guess I could smell a ghost about as quick as anybody."

"Well, I don't see that we can do any good by sitting around here," remarked Uncle Dan to the boys, after the lapse of some minutes. "We may as well put out the lights and get into bed again."

"But I cannot see what it could be!" Mrs. Bobbsey insisted, as they all prepared to retire again.

"Neither can we!" agreed Uncle Daniel. "Maybe our piano has one of those self-playing tricks, and somebody wound it up by accident."

But no sooner were the lights out and the house quiet than the piano started again.

"Hush! keep quiet!" whispered Uncle Daniel. "I'll get it this time, whatever it is!"

With matches in one hand and a candle in the other he started downstairs in the dark without making a sound, while the piano kept on playing in "chunks" as Harry said, same as it did before.

Once in the parlor Uncle Daniel struck a match and put it to the candle, and then the music ceased.

"There he is!" he called, and Flossie thought she surely would die. Slam! went the music-book at something, and Sandy almost choked with fear.

Bang! went something else, that brought Bert and Harry downstairs to help catch the burglar.

"There he is in the corner!" called Uncle Daniel to the boys, and then began such a slam banging time that the people upstairs were in terror that the burglar would kill Harry and Bert and Uncle Daniel.

"We've got him' We've got him!" declared Harry, while Bert lighted the lamp.

"Is he dead?" screamed Aunt Sarah from the stairs.

"As a door-nail!" answered Harry.

"What is it?" asked Mrs. Bobbsey, hardly able to speak.

"A big gray rat," replied Uncle Daniel, and everybody had a good laugh.

"I thought it might be that," said Mrs. Bobbsey.

"So did I," declared Nan. "But I wasn't sure."

"I thought it was a big burglar," Flossie said, her voice still shaking from the fright.

"I thought it was a policeman," faltered Sandy. " 'Cause they always bang things like that."

"And I thought, sure's yo' life, it was a real ghost," laughed Dinah. " 'Cause de clock jest struck fer de ghost hour. Ha! ha! dat was such a musicanious rat."

"He must have come in from the fields where John has been plowing. Like a cat in a strange garret, he didn't know what to do in a parlor," said Uncle Daniel.

Harry took the candle and looked carefully over the keys.

"Why, there's something like seeds on the keys!" he said.

"Oh, I have it!" exclaimed Bert. "Nan left her hat on the piano last night, and it has those funny straw flowers on it. See, the rat got some of them off and they dropped on the keys."

"And the other time he came for the cake," said Aunt Sarah.

"That's it," declared Uncle Daniel, "and each time we scared him off he came back again to finish his meal. But I guess he is through now," and so saying he took the dead rodent and raising the side window tossed him out.

It was some time before everybody got quieted down again, but finally the rat scare was over and the Bobbseys turned to dreams of the happy summer-time they were enjoying.

When Uncle Dan came up from the post office the next morning he brought a note from the fresh-air camp.

"Sandy has to go back!" Nan whispered to Bert. "His own father in the city has sent for him, but mamma says not to say anything to

Sandy or Freddie—they might worry. Aunt Sarah will drive over and bring Sandy, then they can fix it. I'm so sorry he has to go away."

"So am I," answered Nan's twin. "I don't see why they can't let the little fellow alone when he is happy with us."

"But it's his own father, you know, and something about a rich aunt. Maybe she is going to adopt Sandy."

"We ought to adopt him; he's all right with us," Bert grumbled. "What did his rich aunt let him cry his eyes out for if she cared anything for him?"

"Maybe she didn't know about him then," Nan considered. "I'm sure everybody would have to love Sandy."

At that Sandy ran along the path with Freddie. He looked like a live buttercup, so fresh and bright, his sunny sandy curls blowing in the soft breeze. Mrs. Bobbsey had just called the children to her.

"We are going over to see Mrs. Manily today, Sandy," she said. "Won't you be awfully glad to see your own dear Mamma Manily again?"

"Yep," he faltered, getting a better hold on Freddie's hand, "but I want to come back here," he finished.

Poor darling! So many changes of home in his life had made him fear another.

"Oh, I am sure you will come to see us again," Mrs. Bobbsey declared. "Maybe you can come to Lakeport when we go home in the fall."

"No, I'm comin' back here," he insisted, "to see Freddie, and auntie, and uncle, and all of them."

"Well, we must get ready now," said Mrs. Bobbsey. "John has gone to bring the wagon."

Freddie insisted upon going to the camp with Sandy, "to make sure he would come down again," he said.

It was only the happiness of seeing Mamma Manily once more that kept Sandy from crying when they told him he was to go on a great big fast train to see his own papa.

"You see," Mrs. Manily explained to Mrs. Bobbsey, "a wealthy aunt of Edward's expects to adopt him, so we will have to give him up, I am afraid."

"I hope you can keep track of him," answered Mrs. Bobbsey, "for we are all so attached to him. I think we would have applied to the

Aid Society to let him share our home if the other claim had not come first and taken him from us."

Then Freddie kissed Sandy good-bye. It was not the kind of a caress that girls give, but the two little fellows said good-bye, kissed each other very quickly, then looked down at the ground in a brave effort not to cry.

Mrs. Bobbsey gave Sandy a real mother's love kiss, and he said:

"Oh, I'm comin' beck—to-morrow. I won't stay in the city. I'll just run away and come back."

So Sandy was gone to another home, and we hope he will grow to be as fine a boy as he has been a loving child.

"How lonely it seems," said Nan that afternoon. "Sandy was so jolly."

Freddie followed John all over the place, and could not find anything worth doing. Even Dinah sniffed a little when she fed the kittens and didn't have "dat little buttercup around to tease dem."

"Well," said Uncle Daniel next day, "we are going to have a very poor crop of apples this year, so I think we had better have some cider made from the early fruit. Harry and Bert, you can help John if you like, and take a load of apples to the cider mill to-day to be ground."

The boys willingly agreed to help John, for they liked that sort of work, especially Bert, to whom it was new.

"We'll take the red astrachans and sheepnoses to-day," John said. "Those trees over there are loaded, you see. Then there are the orange apples in the next row; they make good cider."

The early apples were very plentiful, and it took scarcely any time to make up a load and start off for the cider mill.

"Old Bennett who runs the mill is a queer chap," Harry told Bert going over; "he's a soldier, and he'll be sure to quiz you on history."

"I like old soldiers," Bert declared; "if they do talk a lot, they've got a lot to talk about."

John said that was true, and he agreed that old Ben Bennett was an interesting talker.

"Here we are," said Harry, as they pulled up before a kind of barn. Old Ben sat outside on his wooden bench.

"Hello, Ben," they called out together, "we're bringing you work early this year."

"So much the better," said the old soldier; "There's nothing like work to keep a fellow young."

"Well, you see," went on John, "we can't count on any late apples this year, so, as we must have cider, we thought that we had better make hay while the sun shines."

"How much have you got there?" asked Ben, looking over the load.

"About a barrel, I guess," answered John "Could you run them through for us this morning?"

"Certainly, certainly!" replied the others. "Just haul them on, and we'll set to work as quick as we did that morning at Harper's Ferry. Who is this lad?" he asked, indicating Bert.

"My cousin from the city," said Harry, "Bert's his name."

"Glad to see you, Bert, glad to see you!" and the old soldier shook hands warmly. "When they call you out, son, just tell them you knew Ben Bennett of the Sixth Massachusetts. And they'll give you a good gun," and he clapped Bert on the back as if he actually saw a war coming down the hill back of the cider mill.

It did not take long to unload the apples and get them inside.

"We'll feed them in the hopper," said John, "if you just get the sacks out, Ben."

"All right, all right, my lad; you can fire the first volley if you've a mind to," and Ben opened up the big cask that held the apples to be chopped. When a few bushels had been filled in by the boys John began to grind. He turned the big stick round and round, and this in turn set the wheel in motion that held the knives that chopped the apples.

"Where does the cider come from?" asked Bert, much interested.

"We haven't come to that yet," Harry replied; "they have to go through this hopper first."

"Fine juicy apples," remarked Ben. "Don't know but it's just as well to make cider now when you have a crop like this."

"Father thought so," Harry added, putting in the last scoop of sheepnoses. "If it turns to vinegar we can use it for pickles this fall."

The next part of the process seemed very queer to Bert; the pulp or chopped apples were put in sacks like meal-bags, folded over so as to hold in the pulp. A number of the folded sacks were then placed in another machine "like a big layer cake," Bert said, and by turning a screw a great press was brought down upon the soft apples.

"Now the boys can turn," John suggested, and at this both Bert and Harry grabbed hold of the long handle that turned the press and started on a run around the machine.

"Oh, there she comes!" cried Bert, as the juice began to ooze out in the tub. "That's cider, all right! I smell it."

"Fine and sweet too," declared Ben, seeing to it that the tub was well under the spout.

"But I don't want you young fellows to do all my work."

"Oh, this is fun," spoke up Bert, as the color mounted to his cheeks from the exercise. A strong stream was pouring into the tub now, and the wholesome odor of good sweet cider filled the room.

"I think I'll try to get a horse this fall when my next pension comes due," said old Ben, "I'm a little stiff to run around with that handle like you young lads, and sometimes I'm full of rheumatism too."

"Father said he would sell our Bill very cheap if he wasn't put at hard work," Harry said.

"We have had him so long we don't want to see him put to a plow or anything heavy, but I should think this would be quite easy for him."

"Just the thing for a worn-out war-horse like myself," answered Ben, much interested. "Tell your father not to think of selling Bill till I get a chance to see him. I won't have my pension money for two months yet, but I might make a deposit if any more work comes in."

"Oh, that would be all right," spoke up John. "Mr. Bobbsey would not be afraid to trust you."

"There now!" exclaimed Ben; "I guess you've got all the juice out. John, you can fill it in your keg, I suppose, since you have been so good as to do all the rest. Will you try it, boys?"

"Yes, we would like to, Ben," Harry replied.

"It's a little warm to make cider in July," and he wiped his face to cool off some.

Ben went to his homemade cupboard and brought out a tin cup.

"There's a cup," he said, "that I drank out of at Harper's Ferry. I keep it in everyday use, so as not to lose sight of it."

Bert took the old tin cup and regarded it reverently.

"Think of us drinking out of that cup," reflected Bert. "Why, it's a war relic!"

"How's the cider?" asked the old soldier.

"Couldn't be better," said Harry. "I guess the cup helps the flavor."

This pleased old Ben, for the light of glory that comes to all veterans, whether private or general, shone in his eyes.

"Well, a soldier has two lives," he declared. "The one under fire and the other here," tapping his head and meaning that the memories of battles made the other life.

The cider was ready now, and the Bobbseys prepared to leave.

"I'll tell father about Bill," said Harry. "I'm sure he will save him for you."

"All right, sonny—thank you, thank you! Good-bye, lads; come again, and maybe some day I'll give you the war cup!" called the soldier.

"That would be a relic!" exclaimed Harry. "And I guess father will give him Bill for nothing, for we always do what we can for old soldiers."

"I never saw cider made before," remarked Bert, "and I think it's fun. I had a good time to-day."

"Glad you did," said John, "for vacation is slipping now and you want to enjoy it while it lasts."

That evening at dinner the new cider was sampled, and everybody pronounced it very fine.

Chapter XXI

WHAT THE WELL CONTAINED

The next day everybody was out early.

"The men are going to clean the well," Harry told the others, "and it's lots of fun to see all the stuff they bring up."

"Can we go?" Freddie asked.

"Nan will have to take charge of you and Flossie," said Mrs. Bobbsey, "for wells are very dangerous, you know."

This was arranged, and the little ones promised to do exactly as Nan told them.

The well to be cleaned was the big one at the corner of the road and the lane. From the well a number of families got their supply of water, and it being on the road many passersby also enjoyed from it a good cold drink.

"There they come," called Bert, as two men dressed like divers came up the road.

They wore complete rubber suits, hip-boots, rubber coats, and rubber caps. Then they had some queer-looking machines, a windlass, a force pump, grappling irons, and other tools.

The boys gathered around the men—all interested, of course, in the work.

"Now keep back," ordered Nan to the little ones. "You can see just as well from this big stone, and you will not be in any danger here."

So Freddie and Flossie mounted the rock while the large boys got in closer to the well.

First the men removed the well shelter—the wooden house that covered the well. Then they put over the big hole a platform open in the center. Over this they set up the windlass, and then one of the men got in a big bucket.

"Oh, he'll get drownded!" cried Freddie.

"No, he won't," said Flossie. "He's a diver like's in my picture book."

"Is he, Nan?" asked the other little one.

"Yes, he is one kind of a diver," the sister explained, "only he doesn't have to wear that funny hat with air pipes in it like ocean divers wear."

"But he's away down in the water now," persisted Freddie. "Maybe he's dead."

"See, there he is up again," said Nan, as the man in the bucket stepped out on the platform over the well.

"He just went down to see how deep the water was," Bert called over. "Now they are going to pump it out."

The queer-looking pump, with great long pipes was now sunk into the well, and soon a strong stream of water was flowing from the spout.

"Oh, let's sail boats!" exclaimed Freddie, and then all the bits of clean sticks and boards around were turned into boats by Flossie and Freddie. As the water had a good clear sweep down the hill the boats went along splendidly, and the little folks had a very fine time of it indeed.

"Don't fall in," called Nan. "Freddie, look out for that deep hole in the gutter, where the tree fell down in the big flood."

But for once Freddie managed to save himself, while Flossie took no risk at all, but walked past that part of the "river" without guiding her "steamboat."

Presently the water in the "river" became weaker and weaker, until only the smallest stream made its way along.

"We can't sail boats in mud," declared Freddie with some impatience. "Let's go back and see what they're doing at the well."

Now the big pump had been removed and the man was going down in the bucket again.

"We lost lots of things in there," remarked Tom Mason. "I bet they'll bring up some queer stuff."

It took a few minutes for the other man to send the lanterns down after his companion and then remove the top platform so as to give all the air and light possible to the bottom of the well.

"Now the man in the well can see stars in the sky," said Harry to the other boys.

"But there are no stars in the sky," Bert contradicted, looking up at the clear blue sky of the fine summer day.

"Oh! yes there are," laughed the man at the well, "lots of them too, but you can only see them in the dark, and it's good and dark down in that deep well."

This seemed very strange, but of course it was true; and the well cleaner told them if they didn't believe it, just to look up a chimney some day, and they would see the same strange thing.

At a signal from the man in the well the other raised the first bucket of stuff and dumped it on the ground.

"Hurrah! Our football!" exclaimed Harry, yanking out from the muddy things the big black rubber ball lost the year before.

"And our baseball," called Tom Mason, as another ball was extracted from the pile.

"Peter Burns' dinner pail," laughed Harry, rescuing that article from the heap.

"And somebody's old shoe!" put in Bert, but he didn't bother pulling that out of the mud.

"Oh, there's Nellie Prentice's rubber doll!" exclaimed Harry. "August and Ned were playing ball with it and let it fly in the well."

Harry wiped the mud off the doll and brought it over to Nan.

"I'm sure Nellie will be glad to get this back," said Nan, "for it's a good doll, and she probably never had one since she lost it."

The doll was not injured by its long imprisonment in the well and when washed up was as good as ever. Nan took charge of it, and promised to give it to Nellie just as soon as she could go over to see her.

Another bucket of stuff had been brought up by that time, and the first thing pulled out was a big long pipe, the kind Germans generally use.

"That's old Hans Bruen's," declared Tom "I remember the night he dropped it."

"Foolish Hans—to try to drink with a pipe like that in his mouth!" laughed the well cleaner.

As the pipe had a wooden bowl and a hard porcelain stem it was not broken, so Tom took care of it, knowing how glad Hans would be to get his old friend "Johnnie Smoker" back again.

Besides all kinds of tin cups, pails, and saucepans, the well was found to contain a good number of boys' caps and some girls' too, that had slipped off in attempts made to get a good cool drink out of the bucket.

Finally the man gave a signal that he was ready to come up, and soon the windlass was adjusted again and the man in very muddy boots came to the top.

"Look at this!" he said to the boys' holding a beautiful gold watch. "Ever hear of anyone losing a watch in the well?"

No one had heard of such a loss, and as there was no name anywhere on the watch that might lead to its identification, the well cleaner put it away in his vest pocket under the rubber coat.

"And what do you think of this?" the man continued, and drew from his pocket a beautiful string of pearl beads set in gold.

"My beads! My lost beads!" screamed Nan. "Oh, how glad I am that you found them!"

She took the beads and looked at them carefully. They were a bit dirty, but otherwise as good as ever.

"I thought I should never see these again," said Nan. "I must tell mamma of this!" And she started for the house with flying feet. Mrs. Bobbsey was glad indeed to learn that the strings of pearls had been found, and everybody declared that Nan was certainly lucky.

"I am going to fasten them on good and tight after this," said Nan, and she did.

Down by the well the man was not yet through handing over the things he had found.

"And there's a wedding ring!" he said next, while he turned out in his hand a thin gold band.

"Oh, Mrs. Burns lost that!" chorused a number of the boys. "She felt dreadful over it too. She'll be tickled to get that back all right."

"Well, here," said the man, turning to Harry. "I guess you're the biggest boy; I'll let you take that back to Mrs. Burns with my best wishes," and he handed Harry the long-lost wedding ring.

It was only a short distance to Mrs. Burns' house, and Harry lost no time in getting there.

"She was just delighted," Harry told the man, upon returning to the well. "She says Peter will send you over something for finding it."

"No need," replied the other; "they're welcome to their own."

The last part of the well-cleaning was the actual scrubbing of the big stone in the bottom.

This stone had a hole in the middle through which the water sprang up, and when the flag had been scrubbed the well was clean indeed.

"Now you people will have good water," declared the men, as they gathered all their tools, having first put the top on the well and tried a bucketful of water before starting off.

"And are there really stars in the bottom of the well?" questioned Freddie.

"Not exactly," said the man, "but there are lots of other things in the bottoms of wells. You must get your daddy to show you the sky through a fireplace, and you will then know how the stars look in daylight," he finished, saying good-bye to all and starting off for the big deep well-pump over in the picnic grove, that had not been cleaned since it had been dug there three years before.

Chapter XXII

LITTLE JACK HORNER.—GOOD-BYE

"I've got a special delivery letter for you," called the boy from the post office to Harry.

Now when Jim Dexter rode his wheel with the special delivery mail everybody about Meadow Brook knew the rush letter bore important news.

Jim jumped off his wheel and, opening the little bag, pulled out a letter for Mrs. Richard Bobbsey from Mrs. William Minturn of Ocean Cliff.

"I'll take it upstairs and have your book signed," Harry offered, while Jim sat on the porch to rest.

"That's from Aunt Emily," Bert told Harry when the messenger boy rode off again. "I guess we're going down to Ocean Cliff to visit there."

"I hope you won't go very soon," replied Harry. "We've arranged a lot of ball matches next month. We're going to play the school nine first, then we're to play the boys at Cedarhurst and a picked nine from South Meadow Brook."

"I'd like first-rate to be here for the games," said Bert. "I'm a good batter."

"You're the player we need then, for Jim Smith is a first-rate pitcher and we've got really a fine catcher in Tom Mason, but it's hard to get a fellow to hit the ball far enough to give us runs."

"Oh, Bert!" called Nan, running out of the house. "That was an invitation for us to go to Aunt Emily's at the seashore. And Cousin Dorothy says we will have such a lovely time! But I'm sure we could never have a better time than we had here, Harry," she added to her cousin.

"I'll be awfully sorry to have you go, Nan," replied Harry. "We have had so much fun all month. I'll just be dead lonesome, I'm sure," and Harry sat down in dejection, just as if his loved cousins had gone already.

"There's no boy at Uncle William's," said Bert. "Of course Nan will have Dorothy, but I'll have to look around for a chum, I suppose."

"Oh, you'll find lots of boys at the beach," said Harry. "And to think of the fun at the ocean! Mother says we will go to the shore next summer."

"I wish you were going with us," said Bert politely.

"Maybe you will come down for a day while we are there," sug-

206 THE BOBBSEY TWINS, VOLUME 1

gested Nan. "Aunt Emily isn't just exactly your aunt, because she's mamma's sister, and it's papa who is Uncle Daniel's brother. But the Minturns, Aunt Emily's folks, you know, have been up here and are all like real cousins."

"We're going away!" exclaimed Freddie, joining the others just then. "Mamma says I can stick my toes in the water till the crabs bite me, but I'm going to have a fishhook and catch them first."

"Are you going to take Snoop?" Harry asked his little cousin.

"Yep," replied the youngster. "He knows how to go on trains now."

"Dorothy has a pair of donkeys," Nan told them, "and a cart we can go riding in every day."

"I'll be the driver," announced Freddie. "And I suppose you'll have a sailboat, Bert!" said Harry.

"Not in the ocean," said nervous little Flossie, who had been listening all the time and never said a word until she thought there was some danger coming.

"Certainly not," said Bert; "there is always a little lake of quiet water around ocean places."

Aunt Sarah came out now, all dressed for a drive.

"Well, my dears," she said, "you are going to Ocean Cliff to-morrow, so you can invite all your Meadow Brook friends to a little lawn party to-day. I'm going down now to the village to order some good things for you. I want you all to have a nice time this afternoon."

"I'm going to give some of my books to Nettie," said Flossie, "and some of my paper dolls too."

"Yes. Nettie has not many things to play with," agreed Nan, "and we can get plenty more."

"I'm going to get all my birds' nests together," said Bert, "and that pretty white birch bark to make picture frames for Christmas."

"I've got lovely pressed flowers to put on Christmas post-cards," said Nan. "I'm going to mount them on plain white cards with little verses written for each friend. Won't that be pretty?"

Then what a time there was packing up again! Of course Mrs. Bobbsey had expected to go, and had most of the big things ready but the children had so many souvenirs.

"John gave me this," cried Freddie, pulling a great big pumpkin in his express wagon down to the house. "And I'm going to bring it to Aunt Emily."

"Oh, how could we bring that!" protested Nan.

"In the trunk, of course," Freddie insisted.

"Well, I have to carry a box of ferns," said Flossie; "I'm going to take them for the porch. There are no ferns around the salt water, mamma says."

So each child had his or her own pet remembrances to carry away from Meadow Brook.

"We had better go and invite the girls for this afternoon," Nan said to Flossie.

"And we must look after the boys," Harry told Bert.

A short invitation was not considered unusual in the country, so it was an easy matter to get all the children together in time for the farewell lawn party.

"We all hope you will come again next year," said Mildred Manners. "We have had such a lovely time this summer. And I brought you this little handkerchief to remember me by." The gift was a choice bit of lace, and Nan was much pleased to accept it.

"There is something to remember me by," said Mabel Herold, presenting Nan with a postcard album.

The little girls brought Flossie a gold-striped cup and saucer, a set of doll's patterns, and the dearest little parasol. This last was from Bessie Dimple.

And Nettie brought—what do you think?

A little live duck for Freddie!

It was just like a lump of cotton batting, so soft and fluffy.

"We'll fatten him up for Christmas," laughed Bert, joking.

"No, you won't!" snapped Freddie. "I are going to have a little house for him and a lake, and a boat—"

"Are you going to teach him to row?" teased Harry.

"Well, he can swim better than—than—"

"August Stout," answered Bert, remembering how August had fallen in the pond the day they went fishing.

When the ice cream and cake had been served on the lawn, Mrs. Bobbsey brought out a big round white paper pie. This she placed in the middle of a nice clean spot on the lawn, and all around the pie she drew out long white ribbons. On each ribbon was pinned the name of one of the guests.

"Now this is your Jack Horner pie," said Mrs. Bobbsey, "and when you put in your thumb you will pull out a plum."

Nan read off the names, and each girl or boy took the place assigned. Finally everybody had in hand a ribbon.

"Nettle has number one," said Nan; "you pull first, Nettie."

Nettie jerked her ribbon and pulled out on the end of it the dearest little play piano. It was made of paper, of course, and so very small it could stand on Nettie's hand.

"Give us a tune!" laughed the boys, while Nettie saw it really was a little box of candy.

"Mildred next," announced Nan.

On the end of Mildred's ribbon came an automobile!

This caused a laugh, for Mildred was very fond of automobile rides.

Mabel got a hobby-horse—because she was learning to ride horseback.

Nan received a sewing machine, to remind her of the fresh-air work.

Of course Tom Mason got a horse—a donkey it really was; and Jack Hopkins' gift was a wheelbarrow. Harry pulled out a boat, and Bert got a cider barrel.

They were all souvenirs, full of candy, favors for the party, and they caused no end of fun.

Freddie was the last to pull and he got—

A bunch of real radishes from his own garden!

"But they're not candy," he protested, as he burned his tongue with one.

"Well, we are going to let you and Flossie put your thumbs in the pie," said his mamma, "and whoever gets the prize will be the real Jack Horner."

All but the center of the pie was gone now, and in this Flossie first put her thumb. She could only put in one finger and only fish just one, and she brought out—a little gold ring from Aunt Sarah.

"Oh, isn't it sweet!" the girls all exclaimed.

Then Freddie had his turn.

"Can't I put in two fingers?" he pleaded.

"No; only one!" his mother insisted.

After careful preparation Freddie put in his thumb and pulled out a big candy plum!

"Open it!" called Nan.

The plum was put together in halves, and when Freddie opened it he found a real "going" watch from Uncle Daniel.

"I can tell time!" declared the happy boy, for he had been learning the hours on Martha's clock in the kitchen.

"What time is it, then?" asked Bert.

Freddie looked at his watch and counted around it two or three times.

"Four o'clock!" he said at last, and he was only twenty minutes out of the way. The watch was the kind little boys use first, with very plain figures on it, and it was quite certain before Freddie paid his next visit to Uncle Daniel's he would have learned how to tell time exactly on his first "real" watch.

The party was over, the children said good bye, and besides the play favors each carried away a real gift, that of friendship for the little Bobbseys.

"Maybe you can come down to the seashore on an excursion," said Nan to her friends. "They often have Sunday-school excursions to Sunset Beach."

"We will if we can," answered Mabel, "but if I don't see you there, I may call on you at Lakeport, when we go to the city."

"Oh yes, do!" insisted Nan. "I'll be home all winter I guess, but I might go to boarding school. Anyhow, I'll write to you. Good-bye, girls!"

"Good-bye!" was the answering cry, and then the visitors left in a crowd, waving their hands as they disappeared around a turn of the road.

"What a perfectly lovely time we have had!" declared Nan to Bert.

"Oh, the country can't be beat!" answered her twin brother. "Still, I'll be glad to get to the seashore, won't you?"

"Oh yes; I want to see Cousin Dorothy."

"And I want to see the big ocean," put in Freddie.

"I want to ride on one of the funny donkeys," lisped Flossie. "And I want to make a sand castle."

"Me too!" chimed in Freddie.

"Hurrah for the seashore!" cried Bert, throwing his cap into the air, and then all went into the house, to get ready for a trip they looked forward to with extreme pleasure. And here let us say good-bye, hoping to meet the Bobbsey Twins again.

END OF
"The Bobbsey Twins in the Country"
BY LAURA LEE HOPE

THE BOBBSEY TWINS

AT THE SEASHORE

Chapter I

CHASING THE DUCK

"Suah's yo' lib, we do keep a-movin'!" cried Dinah, as she climbed into the big depot wagon.

"We didn't forget Snoop this time," exclaimed Freddie, following close on Dinah's heels, with the box containing Snoop, his pet cat, who always went traveling with the little fellow.

"I'm glad I covered up the ferns with wet paper," Flossie remarked, "for this sun would surely kill them if it could get at them."

"Bert, you may carry my satchel," said Mrs. Bobbsey, "and be careful, as there are some glasses of jelly in it, you know."

"I wish I had put my hat in my trunk," remarked Nan. "I'm sure someone will sit on this box and smash it before we get there."

"Now, all ready!" called Uncle Daniel, as he prepared to start old Bill, the horse.

"Wait a minute!" Aunt Sarah ordered. "There was another box, I'm sure. Freddie, didn't you fix that blue shoe box to bring along?"

"Oh, yes, that's my little duck, Downy. Get him quick, some-body, he's on the sofa in the bay window!"

Bert climbed out and lost no time in securing the missing box.

"Now we are all ready this time," Mr. Bobbsey declared, while Bill started on his usual trot down the country road to the depot.

The Bobbseys were leaving the country for the seashore. As told in our first volume, "The Bobbsey Twins," the little family consisted of two pairs of twins, Nan and Bert, age eight, dark and handsome, and as like as two peas, and Flossie and Freddie, age four, as light as the others were dark, and "just exactly chums," as Flossie always declared.

The Bobbsey twins lived at Lakeport, where Mr. Richard Bobbsey had large lumber yards. The mother and father were quite young themselves, and so enjoyed the good times that came as naturally as sunshine to the little Bobbseys. Dinah, the colored maid, had been with the family so long the children at Lakeport called her Dinah Bobbsey, although her real name was Mrs. Sam Johnston, and her husband, Sam, was the man of all work about the Bobbsey home.

Our first volume told all about the Lakeport home, and our second book, "*The Bobbsey Twins in the Country*," was the story of the Bobbseys on a visit to Aunt Sarah and Uncle Daniel Bobbsey in their beautiful country home at Meadow Brook. Here Cousin Harry, a boy Bert's age, shared all the sports with the family from Lakeport. Now the Lakeport Bobbseys were leaving Meadow Brook, to spend the month of August with Uncle William and Aunt Emily Minturn at their seashore home, called Ocean Cliff, located near the village of Sunset Beach. There they were also to meet their cousin, Dorothy Minturn, who was just a year older than Nan.

It was a beautiful morning, the very first day of August, that our little party started off. Along the Meadow Brook road everybody called out "Good-by!" for in the small country place all the Bobbseys were well known, and even those from Lakeport had many friends there.

Nettie Prentice, the one poor child in the immediate neighborhood (she only lived two farms away from Aunt Sarah), ran out to the wagon as Uncle Daniel hurried old Bill to the depot.

"Oh, here, Nan!" she called. "Do take these flowers if you can carry them. They are in wet cotton battin at the stems, and they won't fade a bit all day," and Nettie offered to Nan a gorgeous bouquet of lovely pure white, waxy lilies, that grow so many on a stalk and have such a delicious fragrance. Nettie's house was an old homestead, and there delicate blooms crowded around the sitting-room window.

Nan let her hatbox down and took the flowers.

"These are lovely, Nettie," she exclaimed; "I'll take them, no matter how I carry them. Thank you so much, and I hope I'll see you next summer."

"Yes, do come out again!" Nettie faltered, for she would miss Nan, the city girl had always been so kind—even lent her one of her own dresses for the wonderful Fourth of July parade.

"Maybe you will come down to the beach on an excursion," called Nan, as Bill started off again with no time to lose.

"I don't think so," answered Nettie, for she had never been on an excursion—poor people can rarely afford to spend money for such pleasures.

"I've got my duck," called Freddie to the little girl, who had given the little creature to Freddie at the farewell party as a souvenir of Meadow Brook.

"Have you?" laughed Nettie. "Give him plenty of water, Freddie, let him loose in the ocean for a swim!" Then Nettie ran back to her home duties.

"Queer," remarked Nan, as they hurried on. "The two girls I thought the most of in Meadow Brook were poor: Nettie Prentice, and Nellie the little cash girl at the fresh-air camp. Somehow, poor girls seem so real and they talk to you so close—I mean they seem to just speak right out of their eyes and hearts."

"That's what we call sincerity, daughter," said Mrs. Bobbsey. "You see, children who have trials learn to appreciate more keenly than we, who have everything we need. That appreciation shows in their eyes, and so they seem closer to you, as you say."

"Oh! oh! oh!" screamed Freddie, "I think my duck is choked. He's got his head out the hole. Take Snoop, quick, Bert, till I get Downy in again," and the poor little fellow looked as scared as did the duck with his "head out of the hole."

"He can't get it in again," cried Freddie, pushing gently on the little lump of down with the queer yellow bill—the duck's head. "The hole ain't big enough and he'll surely choke in it."

"Tear the cardboard down," said Bert. "That's easy enough," and the older brother, coming to the rescue, put his fingers under the choking neck, gave the paper box a jerk, and freed poor Downy.

"When we get to the depot we will have to paste some paper over the tear," continued Bert, "or Downy will get out further next time."

"Here we are," called Uncle Daniel, pulling up to the old station.

"I'll attend to the baggage," announced Mr. Bobbsey, "while you folks all go to the farther end of the platform. Our car will stop there."

For a little place like Meadow Brook seven people getting on the Express seemed like an excursion, and Dave, the lame old agent, hobbled about with some consequence, as he gave the man in the baggage car instruction about the trunk and valises. During that brief period, Harry, Aunt Sarah, and Uncle Daniel were all busy with "good-byes": Aunt Sarah giving Flossie one kiss more, and Uncle Daniel tossing Freddie up in the air in spite of the danger to Downy, the duck.

"All aboard!" called the conductor.

"Good-by!"

"Good-by!"

"Come and see us at Christmas!" called Bert to Harry.

"I may go down to the beach!" answered Harry while the train brakes flew off.

"We will expect you Thanksgiving," Mrs. Bobbsey nodded out the window to Aunt Sarah.

"I'll come if I can," called back the other.

"Good-by! Good-by!"

"Now, let us all watch out for the last look at dear old Meadow Brook," exclaimed Nan, standing up by the window.

"Let Snoop see!" said Freddie, with his hand on the cover of the kitten's box.

"Oh, no!" called everybody at once. "If you let that cat out we will have just as much trouble as we did coming up. Keep him in his box."

"He would like to see too," pouted Freddie. "Snoop liked Meadow Brook. Didn't you, Snoopy!" putting his nose close to the holes in the box.

"I suppose by the time we come back from the beach Freddie will have a regular menagerie," said Bert, with a laugh. "He had a kitten first, now he has a kitten and a duck, and next he'll have a kitten, a duck, and a—"

"Sea-serpent," put in Freddie, believing that he might get such a monster if he cared to possess one.

"There goes the last of Meadow Brook," sighed Nan, as the train rounded a curve and slowed up on a pretty bridge. "And we did have such a lovely time there!"

"Isn't it going to be just as nice at the ocean?" Freddie inquired, with some concern.

"We hope so," his mother replied, "but sister Nan always likes to be grateful for what she has enjoyed."

"So am I," insisted the little fellow, not really knowing what he meant himself.

"I likes dis yere car de best," spoke up Dinah, looking around at the ordinary day coach, the kind used in short journeys. "De red velvet seats seems de most homey," she went on, throwing her kinky head back, "and I likes to lean back wit'out tumbling ober."

"And there's more to see," agreed Bert. "In the Pullman cars there are so few people and they're always—"

"Proud," put in Flossie.

"Yes, they seem so," declared her brother, "but see all the people in this car, just eating and sleeping and enjoying themselves."

Now in our last book, "*The Bobbsey Twins in the Country*," we told about the trip to Meadow Brook in the Pullman car, and how Snoop, the kitten, got out of his box, and had some queer experiences. This time our friends were traveling in the car with the ordinary passengers, and, of course, as Bert said, there was more to be seen and the sights were different.

"It is splendid to have so much room," declared Mrs. Bobbsey, for Nan and Flossie had a big seat turned towards Bert and Freddie's, while Dinah had a seat all to herself (with some boxes of course), and Mr. and Mrs. Bobbsey had another seat. The high-back, broad plush seats gave more room than the narrow, revolving chairs, besides, the day coach afforded so much more freedom for children.

"What a cute little baby!" exclaimed Nan, referring to a tiny tot sleeping under a big white netting, across the aisle.

"We must be quiet," said Mrs. Bobbsey, "and let the little baby sleep. It is hard to travel in hot weather."

"Don't you think the duck should have a drink?" suggested Mr. Bobbsey. "You have a little cup for him, haven't you, Freddie?"

"Yep!" answered Freddie, promptly, pulling the cover off Downy's box.

Instantly the duck flew out!

"Oh ! oh! oh!" yelled everybody, as the little white bird went flying out through the car. First he rested on the seat, then he tried to get through the window. Somebody near by thought he had him, but the duck dodged, and made straight for the looking glass at the end of the car.

"Oh, do get him, somebody!" cried Freddie, while the other strange children in the car yelled in delight at the fun.

"He's kissing himself in the looking glass," declared one youngster, as the frightened little duck flapped his wings helplessly against the mirror.

"He thinks it's another duck," called a boy from the back of the car, clapping his hands in glee.

Mr. Bobbsey had gone up carefully with his soft hat in his hand.

Everybody stopped talking, so the duck would keep in its place.

Nan held Freddie and insisted on him not speaking a word.

Mr. Bobbsey went as cautiously as possible. One step more and he would have had the duck.

He raised his hand with the open hat—and brought it down on the looking glass!

The duck was now gazing down from the chandelier!

"Ha! ha! ha!" the boys laughed, "that's a wild duck, sure!"

"Who's got a gun!" the boy in the back hollered.

"Oh, will they shoot my duck!" cried Freddie, in real tears.

"No, they're only making fun," said Bert. "You keep quiet and we will get him all right."

By this time almost everyone in the car had joined in the duck hunt, while the frightened little bird seemed about ready to surrender. Downy had chosen the highest hanging lamps as his point of vantage, and from there he attempted to ward off all attacks of the enemy. No matter what was thrown at him he simply flew around the lamp.

As it was a warm day, chasing the duck was rather too vigorous exercise to be enjoyable within the close confines of a poorly ventilated car, but that bird had to be caught somehow.

"Oh, the net!" cried Bert, "that mosquito netting over there. We could stretch it up and surely catch him."

This was a happy thought. The baby, of course, was awake and joined in the excitement, so that her big white mosquito netting was readily placed at the disposal of the duck hunters.

A boy named Will offered to help Bert.

"I'll hold one end here," said Will, "and you can stretch yours opposite, so we will screen off half of the car, then when he comes this way we can readily bag him."

Will was somewhat older than Bert, and had been used to hunting, so that the present emergency was sport to him.

The boys now brought the netting straight across the car like a big white screen, for each held his hands up high, besides standing on the arm of the car seats.

"Now drive him this way," called Bert to his father and the men who were helping him.

"Shoo! Shoo! Shoo!" yelled everybody, throwing hats, books, and newspapers at the poor lost duck.

"Shoo!" again called a little old lady, actually letting her black silk bag fly at the lamp.

Of course poor Downy had to shoo, right into the net!

Bert and Will brought up the four ends of the trap and Downy flopped.

"That's the time we bagged our game," laughed Will, while everybody shouted and clapped, for it does not take much to afford real amusement to passengers, who are traveling and can see little but the other people, the conductor, and newspapers.

"We've got him at last," cried Freddie in real glee, for he loved the little duck and feared losing his companionship.

"And he will have to have his meals served in his room for the rest of his trip," laughed Mrs. Bobbsey, as the tired little Downy was once more put in his perforated box, along the side of the tin dipper of water, which surely the poor duck needed by this time.

Chapter II

A TRAVELING MENAGERIE

It took some time for the people to get settled down again, for all had enjoyed the fun with the duck. The boys wanted Freddie to let him out of the box, on the quiet, but Bert overheard the plot and put a stop to it. Then, when the strange youngsters got better acquainted, and learned that the other box contained a little black kitten, they insisted on seeing it.

"We'll hold him tight," declared the boy from the back seat, "and nothing will happen to him."

"But you don't know Snoop," insisted Bert. "We nearly lost him coming up in the train, and he's the biggest member of Freddie's menagerie, so we have to take good care of him."

Mr. Bobbsey, too, insisted that the cat should not be taken out of the box; so the boys reluctantly gave in.

"Now let us look around a little," suggested Mrs. Bobbsey, when quiet had come again, and only the rolling of the train and an occa-

sional shrill whistle broke in on the continuous rumble of the day's
journey.

"Yes, Dinah can watch the things and we can look through the
other cars," agreed Mr. Bobbsey. "We might find someone we know
going down to the shore."

"Be awful careful of Snoop and Downy," cautioned Freddie, as
Dinah took up her picket duty. "Look out the boys don't get 'em,"
with a wise look at the youngsters, who were spoiling for more sport of
some kind.

"Dis yeah circus won't move 'way from Dinah," she laughed. "When
I goes on de police fo'ce I takes good care ob my beat, and you needn't
be a-worryin', Freddie, de Snoopy kitty cat and de Downy duck will
be heah when you comes back," and she nodded her wooly head in
real earnest.

It was an easy matter to go from one car to the other as they were
vestibuled, so that the Bobbsey family made a tour of the entire train,
the boys with their father even going through the smoker into the
baggage car, and having a chance to see what their own trunk looked
like with a couple of railroad men sitting on it.

"Don't you want a job?" the baggagemaster asked Freddie. "We
need a man about your size to lift trunks off the cars for us."

Of course the man was only joking, but Freddie always felt like a
real man and he answered promptly:

"Nope, I'm goin' to be a fireman. I've put lots of fires out already,
besides gettin' awful hurted on the ropes with 'Frisky.'"

"Frisky, who is he?" inquired the men.

"Why, our cow out in Meadow Brook. Don't you know Frisky?"
and Freddie looked very much surprised that two grown-up people
had never met the cow that had given him so much trouble.

"Why didn't you bring him along?" the men asked further.

"Have you got a cow car?" Freddie asked in turn.

"Yes, we have. Would you like to see one?" went on one of the
railroaders. "If your papa will bring you out on the platform at the
next stop, I'll show you how our cows travel."

Mr. Bobbsey promised to do this, and the party moved back to
meet Nan, Flossie, and their mamma. Freddie told them at once about
his promised excursion to the cattle car, and, of course, the others
wanted to see, too.

"If we stop for a few minutes you may all come out," Mr. Bobbsey said. "But it is always risky to get off and have to scramble to get back again. Sometimes they promise us five minutes and give us two, taking the other three to make up for lost time."

The train gave a jerk, and the next minute they drew up to a little way station.

"Here we are, come now," called Mr. Bobbsey, picking Freddie up in his arms, and telling the others to hurry after him.

"Oh, there go the boys from our car!" called Bert, as quite a party of youngsters alighted. "They must be going on a picnic; see their lunch boxes."

"I hope Snoop is all right," Freddie reflected, seeing all the lunch boxes that looked so much like Snoop's cage.

"Come on, little fellow," called the baggage man, "we only have a few minutes."

Then they took Freddie to the rear car and showed him a big cage of cows—it was a cage made of slates, with openings between, and through the openings could be seen the crowded cattle.

"Oh, I would never put Frisky in a place like that," declared Freddie; "he wouldn't have room to move."

"There is not much room, that's a fact," agreed the man. "But you see cows are not first-class passengers."

"But they are good, and know how to play, and they give milk," said Freddie, speaking up bravely for his country friends. "What are you going to do with all of these cows'"

"I don't know," replied the man, not just wanting to talk about beefsteak. "Maybe they're going out to the pasture."

One pretty little cow tried to put her head out through the bars, and Bert managed to give her a couple of crackers from his pocket. She nibbled them up and bobbed her head as if to say:

"Thank you, I was very hungry."

"They are awfully crowded," Nan ventured, "and it must be dreadful to be packed in so. How do they manage to get a drink?"

"They will be watered to-night," replied the man, and then the Bobbseys had to all hurry to get on the train again, for the locomotive whistle had blown and the bell was ringing.

They found Dinah with her face pressed close to the window pane, enjoying the sights on the platform.

"I specked you was clean gone and left me," she laughed. "S'pose you saw lots of circuses, Freddie?"

"A whole carful," he answered, "but, Dinah," he went on, looking scared, "where's Snoop?"

The box was gone!

"Right where you left him," she declared. "I nebber left dis yeah spot, and nobody doan come ter steal de Snoopy kitty cat."

Dinah was crawling around much excited, looking for the missing box. Bert, Nan, and Flossie, of course, all rummaged about, and even Mr. and Mrs. Bobbsey joined in the search. But there was no box to be found.

"Oh, the boys have stoled my cat!" wailed Freddie. "I dust knowed they would!" and he cried outright, for Snoop was a dear companion of the little fellow, and why should he not cry at losing his pet?

"Now wait," commanded his father, "we must not give up so easily. Perhaps the boys hid him some place."

"But suah's you lib I nebber did leab dis yeah seat," insisted Dinah, which was very true. But how could she watch those boys and keep her face so close to the window? Besides, a train makes lots of noise to hide boys' pranks.

"Now, we will begin a systematic search," said Mr. Bobbsey, who had already found out from the conductor and brakeman that they knew nothing about the lost box. "We will look in and under every seat. Then we will go through all the baggage in the hangers" (meaning the overhead wire baskets), "and see if we cannot find Snoop."

The other passengers were very kind and all helped in the hunt. The old lady who had thrown her hand bag at Downy thought she had seen a boy come in the door at the far end of the car, and go out again quickly, but otherwise no one could give any information that would lead to the discovery of the person or parties who had stolen Snoop.

All kinds of traveling necessities were upset in the search. Some jelly got spilled, some fresh country eggs were cracked, but everybody was good-natured and no one complained.

Yet, after a thorough overhauling of the entire car there was no Snoop to be found!

"He's gone!" they all admitted, the children falling into tears, while the older people looked troubled.

"They could hardly have stolen him," Mr. Bobbsey reflected, "and the conductor is sure not one of those boys went in another car, for they all left the train at Ramsley's."

"I don't care!" cried Freddie, aloud, "I'll just have every one of them arrested when we get to Auntie's. I knowed they had Snoop in their boxes."

How Snoop could be "in boxes" and how the boys could be found at Auntie's were two much mixed points, but no one bothered Freddie about such trifles in his present grief.

"Why doan you call dat kitty cat?" suggested Dinah, for all this time no one had thought of that.

"I couldn't," answered Freddie, "'cause he ain't here to call." And he went on crying.

"Snoop! Snoop! Snoop Cat!" called Dinah, but there was no familiar "me-ow" to answer her.

"Now, Freddie boy," she insisted, "if dat cat is alibe he will answer if youse call him, so just you stop a-sniffing and come along. Dere's a good chile," and she patted him in her old way. "Come wit Dinah and we will find Snoop."

With a faint heart the little fellow started to call, beginning at the front door and walking slowly along toward the rear.

"Stoop down now and den," ordered Dinah, "cause he might be hiding, you know."

Freddie had reached the rear door and he stopped.

"Now jist gib one more good call" said Dinah, and Freddie did.

"Snoop! Snoop!" he called.

"Me-ow," came a faint answer.

"Oh, I heard him!" cried Freddie.

"So did I!" declared Dinah.

Instantly all the other Bobbseys were on the scene.

"He's somewhere down here," said Dinah. "Call him, Freddie!"

"Snoop! Snoop!" called the boy again.

"Me-ow—me-ow!" came a distant answer.

"In the stove!" declared Bert, jerking open the door of the stove, which, of course, was not used in summer, and bringing out the poor, frightened, little cat.

Chapter III

RAILROAD TENNIS

"Oh, poor little Snoop!" whispered Freddie, right into his kitten's ear. "I'm so glad I got you back again!"

"So are we all," said a kind lady passenger who had been in the searching party. "You have had quite some trouble for a small boy, with two animals to take care of."

Everybody seemed pleased that the mischievous boys' pranks had not hurt the cat, for Snoop was safe enough in the stove, only, of course, it was very dark and close in there, and Snoop thought he surely was deserted by all his good friends. Perhaps he expected Freddie would find him, at any rate he immediately started in to "purr-rr," in a cat's way of talking, when Freddie took him in his arms, and fondled him.

"We had better have our lunch now," suggested Mrs. Bobbsey, "I'm sure the children are hungry."

"It's just like a picnic," remarked Flossie, when Dinah handed around the paper napkins and Mrs. Bobbsey served out the chicken and cold-tongue sandwiches. There were olives and celery too, besides apples and early peaches from Uncle Daniel's farm.

"Let us look at the timetable, see where we are now, and then see where we will be when we finish," proposed Bert.

"Oh yes," said Nan, "let us see how many miles it takes to eat a sandwich."

Mr. Bobbsey offered one to the conductor, who just came to punch tickets.

"This is not the regular business man's five-minute lunch, but the five-mile article seems more enjoyable," said Mr. Bobbsey.

"Easier digested," agreed the conductor, accepting a sandwich. "You had good chickens out at Meadow Brook," he went on, complimenting the tasty morsel he was chewing with so much relish.

"Yes, and ducks," said Freddie, which remark made everybody laugh, for it brought to mind the funny adventure of little white Downy, the duck.

"They certainly can fly," said the conductor with a smile, as he went along with a polite bow to the sandwich party.

Bert had attended to the wants of the animals, not trusting Freddie to open the boxes. Snoop got a chicken leg and Downy had some of his own soft food, that had been prepared by Aunt Sarah and carried along in a small tin can.

"Well, I'se done," announced Dinah, picking up her crumbs in her napkins. "Bert, how many miles you say it takes me to eat?"

"Let me see! Five, eight, twelve, fourteen: well, I guess Dinah, you had fifteen miles of a chicken sandwich."

"An' you go 'long!" she protested. "'Taint no sech thing. I ain't got sich a long appetite as date. Fifteen miles! Lan'a massa! whot you take me fo?"

Everybody laughed and the children clapped hands at the length of Dinah's appetite, but when the others had finished they found their own were even longer than the maid's, the average being eighteen miles!

"When will we get to Aunt Emily's?" Flossie asked, growing tired over the day's journey.

"Not until night," her father answered. "When we leave the train we will have quite a way to go by stage. We could go all the way by train, but it would be a long distance around, and I think the stage ride in the fresh air will do us good."

"Oh yes, let's go by the stage," pleaded Freddie, to whom the word stage was a stranger, except in the way it had been used at the Meadow Brook circus.

"This stage will be a great, big wagon," Bert told him, "with seats along the sides."

"Can I sit up top and drive?" the little one asked.

"Maybe the man will let you sit by him," answered Mr. Bobbsey, "but you could hardly drive a big horse over those rough roads."

The train came to a standstill, just then, on a switch. There was no station, but the shore train had taken on another section.

"Can Flossie and I walk through that new car?" Nan asked, as the cars had been separated and the new section joined to that directly back of the one which the Bobbseys were in.

"Why, yes, if you are very careful," the mother replied, and so the two little girls started off.

Dinah took Freddie on her lap and told him his favorite story about "Pickin' cotton in de Souf," and soon the tired little yellow head fell off in the land of Nod.

Bert and his father were enjoying their magazines, while Mrs. Bobbsey busied herself with some fancy work, so a half-hour passed without any more excitement. At the end of that time the girls returned.

"Oh, mother!" exclaimed Nan, "we found Mrs. Manily, the matron of the Meadow Brook Fresh Air Camp, and she told us Nellie, the little cash girl, was so run down the doctors think she will have to go to the seashore. Mother, couldn't we have her down with us awhile?"

"We are only going to visit, you know, daughter, and how can we invite more company? But where is Mrs. Manily? I would like to talk to her," said Mrs. Bobbsey, who was always interested in those who worked to help the poor.

Nan and Flossie brought their mother into the next car to see the matron. We told in our book, "The Bobbsey Twins in the Country," how good a matron this Mrs. Manily was, and how little Nellie, the cash girl, one of the visitors at the Fresh Air Camp, was taken sick while there, and had to go to the hospital tent. It was this little girl that Nan wanted to have enjoy the seashore, and perhaps visit Aunt Emily.

Mrs. Manily was very glad to see Mrs. Bobbsey, for the latter had helped with money and clothing to care for the poor children at the Meadow Brook Camp.

"Why, how pleasant to meet a friend in traveling!" said the matron as she shook hands with Mrs. Bobbsey. "You are all off for the seashore, the girls tell me."

"Yes," replied Mrs. Bobbsey. "One month at the beach, and we must then hurry home to Lakeport for the school days. But Nan tells me little Nellie is not well yet?"

"No, I am afraid she will need another change of air to undo the trouble made by her close confinement in a city store. She is not seriously sick, but so run down that it will take some time for her to get strong again," said the matron.

"Have you a camp at the seashore?" asked Mrs. Bobbsey.

"No; indeed, I wish we had," answered the matron. "I am just going down now to see if I can't find some place where Nellie can stay for a few weeks."

"I'm going to visit my sister, Mrs. Minturn, at Ocean Cliff, near

Sunset Beach," said Mrs. Bobbsey. "They have a large cottage and are always charitable. If they have no other company I think, perhaps, they would be glad to give poor little Nellie a room."

"That would be splendid!" exclaimed the matron. "I was going to do a line of work I never did before. I was just going to call on some of the well-to-do people, and ask them to take Nellie. We had no funds, and I felt so much depended on the change of air, I simply made up my mind to go and do what I could."

"Then you can look in at my sister's first," said Mrs. Bobbsey. "If she cannot accommodate you, perhaps she can tell who could. Now, won't you come in the other car with us, and we can finish our journey together?"

"Yes, indeed I will. Thank you," said the matron, gathering up her belongings and making her way to the Bobbsey quarters in the other car.

"Won't it be lovely to have Nellie with us!" Nan said to Flossie, as they passed along. "I am sure Aunt Emily will say yes."

"So am I," said little Flossie, whose kind heart always went out when it should. "I know surely they would not let Nellie die in the city while we enjoy the seaside."

Freddie was awake now, and also glad to see Mrs. Manily.

"Where's Sandy?" he inquired at once. Sandy had been his little chum from the Meadow Brook Camp.

"I guess he is having a nice time somewhere," replied Mrs. Manily. "His aunt found him out, you know, and is going to take care of him now."

"Well, I wish he was here too," said Freddie, rubbing his eyes. "We're goin' to have lots of fun fishing in the ocean."

The plan for Nellie was told to Mr. Bobbsey, who, of course agreed it would be very nice if Aunt Emily and Uncle William were satisfied.

"And what do you suppose those boxes contain?" said Mrs. Bobbsey to Mrs. Manily, pointing to the three boxes in the hanger above them.

"Shoes?" ventured the matron.

"Nope," said Freddie. "One hat, and my duck and my cat. Downy is my duck and Snoop is my cat."

Then Nan told about the flight of the duck and the "kidnapping" of Snoop.

"We put them up there out of the way," finished Nan, "so that nothing more can happen to them."

The afternoon was wearing out now, and the strong summer sun shrunk into thin strips through the trees, while the train dashed along. As the ocean air came in the windows, the long line of woodland melted into pretty little streams, that make their way in patches for many miles from the ocean front. "Like 'Baby Waters'" Nan said, "just growing out from the ocean, and getting a little bit bigger every year."

"Won't we soon be there?" asked Freddie, for long journeys are always tiresome, especially to a little boy accustomed to many changes in the day's play.

"One hour more," said Mr. Bobbsey, consulting his watch.

"Let's have a game of ball, Nan?" suggested Bert, who never traveled without a tennis ball in his pocket.

"How could we?" the sister inquired.

"Easily," said Bert. "We'll make up a new kind of game. We will start in the middle of the car, at the two center seats, and each move a seat away at every catch. Then, whoever misses first must go back to center again, and the one that gets to the end first, wins."

"All right," agreed Nan, who always enjoyed her twin brother's games. "We will call it Railroad Tennis."

Just as soon as Nan and Bert took their places, the other passengers became very much interested. There is such a monotony on trains that the sports the Bobbseys introduced were welcome indeed.

We do not like to seem proud, but certainly these twins did look pretty. Nan with her fine back eyes and red cheeks, and Bert just matching her; only his hair curled around, while hers fell down. Their interest in Railroad Tennis made their faces all the prettier, and no wonder the people watched them so closely.

Freddie was made umpire, to keep him out of a more active part, because he might do damage with a ball in a train, his mother said; so, as Nan and Bert passed the ball, he called,—his father prompting him:

"Ball one!"

"Ball two!"

"Ball three "

Bert jerked with a sudden jolt of the train and missed.

"Striker's out!" called the umpire, while everybody laughed because the boy had missed first.

Then Bert had to go all the way back to center, while Nan was four seats down.

Three more balls were passed, then Nan missed.

"I shouldn't have to go all the way back for the miss," protested Nan. "You went three seats back, so I'll go three back."

This was agreed to by the umpire, and the game continued.

A smooth stretch of road gave a good chance for catching, and both sister and brother kept moving toward the doors now, with three points "to the good" for Nan, as a big boy said.

Who would miss now? Everybody waited to see. The train struck a curve! Bert threw a wild ball and Nan missed it.

"Foul ball!" called the umpire, and Bert did not dispute it.

Then Nan delivered the ball.

"Oh, mercy me!" shrieked the old lady, who had thrown the handbag at Downy, the duck, "my glasses!" and there, upon the floor, lay the pieces. Nan's ball had hit the lady right in the glasses, and it was very lucky they did not break until they came in contact with the floor.

"I'm so sorry!" Nan faltered. "The car jerked so I could not keep it."

"Never mind, my dear," answered the nice old lady, "I just enjoyed that game as much as you did, and if I hadn't stuck my eyes out so, they would not have met your ball. So, it's all right. I have another pair in my bag."

So the game ended with the accident, for it was now time to gather up the baggage for the last stop.

Chapter IV

NIGHT IN A BARN

"Beach Junction! All off for the Junction!" called the train men, while the Bobbseys and Mrs. Manily hurried out to the small station, where numbers of carriages waited to take passengers to their cottages on the cliffs or by the sea.

"Sure we haven't forgotten anything?" asked Mrs. Bobbsey, taking a hasty inventory of the hand baggage.

"Bert's got Snoop and I've got Downy," answered Freddie, as if the animals were all that counted.

"And I've got my hatbox and flowers," added Nan.

"And I have my ferns," said little Flossie.

"I guess we're all here this time," Mr. Bobbsey finished, for nothing at all seemed to be missing.

It was almost nightfall, and the beautiful glow of an ocean sunset rested over the place. At the rear of the station an aged stage driver sat nodding on his turnout. The stage coach was an "old timer," and had carried many a merry party of sightseers through the sandy roads of Oceanport and Sunset Beach, while Hank, the driver, called out all spots of interest along the way. And Hank had a way of making things interesting.

"Pike's Peak," he would call out for Cliff Hill.

"The Giant's Causeway," he would announce for Rocky Turn.

And so Hank was a very popular stage driver, and never had to look for trade—it always came to him.

"That's our coach," said Mr. Bobbsey, espying Hank. "Hello there! Going to the beach?" he called to the sleepy driver.

"That's for you to say," replied Hank, straightening up.

"Could we get to Ocean Cliff—Minturn's place—before dark?" asked Mr. Bobbsey, noticing how rickety the old stagecoach was.

"Can't promise," answered Hank, "but you can just pile in and we'll try it."

There was no choice, so the party "piled" into the carryall.

"Isn't this fun?" remarked Mrs. Manily, taking her seat up under the front window. "It's like going on a May ride."

"I'm afraid it will be a moonlight ride at this rate," laughed Mr. Bobbsey, as the stagecoach started to rattle on. Freddie wanted to sit in front with Hank but Mrs. Bobbsey thought it safer inside, for, indeed, the ride was risky enough, inside or out. As they joggled on the noise of the wheels grew louder and louder, until our friends could only make themselves heard by screaming at each other.

"Night is coming," called Mrs. Bobbsey, and Dinah said: "Suah 'nough we be out in de night dis time."

It seemed as if the old horses wanted to stand still, they moved so slowly, and the old wagon creaked and cracked until Hank, himself, turned round, looked in the window, and shouted:

"All right there?"

"Guess so," called back Mr. Bobbsey, "but we don't see the ocean yet."

"Oh, we'll get there," drawled Hank, lazily.

"We should have gone all the way by train," declared Mrs. Bobbsey, in alarm, as the stage gave one squeak louder than the others.

"Haven't you got any lanterns?" shouted Mr. Bobbsey to Hank, for it was pitch-dark now.

"Never use one," answered the driver. "When it's good and dark the moon will come up, but we'll be there 'fore that. Get 'long there, Doll!" he called to one horse. "Go 'long, Kit!" he urged the other.

The horses did move a little faster at that, then suddenly something snapped and the horses turned to one side.

"Whoa! Whoa!" called Hank, jerking on the reins. But it was too late! The stage coach was in a hole! Several screamed.

"Sit still!" called Mr. Bobbsey to the excited party. "It's only a broken shaft and the coach can't upset now."

Flossie began to cry. It was so dark and black in that hole.

Hank looked at the broken wagon.

"Well, we're done now," he announced, with as little concern as if the party had been safely landed on Aunt Emily's piazza, instead of in a hole on the roadside.

"Do you mean to say you can't fix it up?" Mr. Bobbsey almost gasped.

"Not till I get the stage to the blacksmith's," replied Hank.

"Then, what are we going to do?" Mr. Bobbsey asked, impatiently.

"Well, there's an empty barn over there," Hank answered. "The best thing you can do is pitch your tent there till I get back with another wagon."

"Barn!" exclaimed Mrs. Bobbsey.

"How long will it take you to get a wagon?" demanded Mr. Bobbsey.

"Not long," said Hank, sprucing up a trifle. "You just get yourselves comfortable in that there barn. I'll get the coach to one side, and take a horse down to Sterritt's. He'll let me have a horse and a wagon, and I'll be back as soon as I kin make it."

"There seems nothing else to do," Mr. Bobbsey said. "We may as well make the best of it."

"Why, yes," Mrs. Manily spoke up, "we can pretend we are having a barn dance." And she smiled, faintly.

Nevertheless, it was not very jolly to make their way to the barn in the dark. Dinah had to carry Freddie, he was so sleepy; Mrs. Manily took good care of Flossie. But, of course, there was the duck and the cat, that could not be very safely left in the broken-down stagecoach.

"Say, papa!" Bert exclaimed, suddenly, "I saw an old lantern up under the seat in that stagecoach. Maybe it has some oil in it. I'll go back and see."

"All right, son," replied the father, "we won't get far ahead of you." And while Bert made his way back to the wagon, the others bumped up and down through the fields that led to the vacant barn.

There was no house within sight. The barn belonged to a house up the road that the owners had not moved into that season.

"I got one!" called Bert, running up from the road. "This lantern has oil in, I can hear it rattle. Have you a match, pa?"

Mr. Bobbsey had, and when the lantern had been lighted, Bert marched on ahead of the party, swinging it in real signal fashion.

"You ought to be a brakeman," Nan told her twin brother, at which remark Bert swung his light above his head and made all sorts of funny railroad gestures.

The barn door was found unlocked, and excepting for the awful stillness about, it was not really so bad to find refuge in a good, clean place like that, for outside it was very damp—almost wet with the ocean spray. Mr. Bobbsey found seats for all, and with the big carriage doors swung open, the party sat and listened for every sound that might mean the return of the stage driver.

"Come, Freddie chile," said Dinah, "put yer head down on Dinah's lap. She won't let nothin' tech you. An' youse kin jest go to sleep if youse a mind ter. I'se a-watchin' out."

The invitation was welcome to the tired little youngster, and it was not long before he had followed Dinah's invitation.

Next, Flossie cuddled up in Mrs. Manily's arms and stopped thinking for a while.

"It is awfully lonely," whispered Nan, to her mother, "I do wish that man would come back."

"So do I," agreed the mother. "This is not a very comfortable hotel, especially as we are all tired out from a day's journey."

"What was that?" asked Bert, as a strange sound, like a howl, was heard.

"A dog," lightly answered the father.

"I don't think so," said Bert. "Listen!"

"Oh!" cried Flossie, starting up and clinging closer to Mrs. Manily, "I'm just scared to death!"

"Dinah, I want to go home," cried Freddie. "Take me right straight home."

"Hush, children, you are safe," insisted their mother. "The stage driver will be back in a few minutes."

"But what is that funny noise?" asked Freddie. "It ain't no cow, nor no dog."

The queer "Whoo-oo-oo" came louder each time. It went up and down like a scale, and "left a hole in the air," Bert declared.

"It's an owl!" exclaimed Mrs. Bobbsey, and she was right, for up in the abandoned hay loft the queer old birds had found a quiet place, and had not been disturbed before by visitors.

"Let's get after them," proposed Bert, with lantern in hand.

"You would have a queer hunt," his father told him; "I guess you had better not think of it. Hark! there's a wagon! I guess Hank is coming back to us," and the welcome sound of wheels on the road brought the party to their feet again.

"Hello there!" called Hank. "Here you are. Come along now, we'll make it this time."

It did not take the Bobbseys long to reach the roadside and there they found Hank with a big farm wagon. The seats were made of boards, and there was nothing to hold on to but the edge of the boards.

But the prospect of getting to Aunt Emily's at last made up for all their inconveniences, and when finally Hank pulled the reins again, our friends gave a sigh of relief.

Chapter V

A QUEER STAGE DRIVER

"I reckon I'll have to make another trip to get that old coach down to the shop," growled the stage driver, as he tried to hurry the horses, Kit and Doll, along.

"I hardly think it is worth moving," Mr. Bobbsey said, feeling somewhat indignant that a hackman should impose upon his passengers by risking their lives in such a broken-down wagon.

"Not worth it? Wall! I guess Hank don't go back on the old coach like that. Why, a little grease and a few bolts will put that rig in tip-top order." And he never made the slightest excuse for the troubles he had brought upon the Bobbseys.

"Oh, my!" cried Nan, "my hatbox! Bert you have put your foot right into my best hat!"

"Couldn't help it," answered the brother; "I either had to go through your box or go out of the back of this wagon, when that seat slipped," and he tried to adjust the board that had fallen into the wagon.

"Land sakes alive!" exclaimed Dinah. "Say, you driver man there!" she called in real earnest, "ef you doan go a little carefuler wit dis yere wagon you'll be spilling us all out. I just caught dat cat's box a-sliding, and Ian' only knows how dat poor little Downy duck is, way down under dat old board."

"Hold on tight," replied Hank, as if the whole thing were a joke, and his wagon had the privilege of a toboggan slide.

"My!" sighed Mrs. Bobbsey, putting her arms closer about Flossie, "I hope nothing more happens."

"I am sure we are all right now," Mrs. Manily assured her. "The road is broad and smooth here, and it can't be far to the beach."

"Here comes a carriage," said Bert, as two pretty coach lights flashed through the trees.

"Hello there!" called someone from the carriage.

"Uncle William!" Nan almost screamed, and the next minute the carriage drew up alongside the wagon.

"Well, I declare," said Uncle William Minturn, jumping front his seat, and beginning to help the stranded party.

"We are all here," began Mr. Bobbsey, "but it was hard work to keep ourselves together."

"Oh, Uncle William," cried Freddie, "put me in your carriage. This one is breakin' down every minute."

"Come right along, my boy. I'll fix you up first," declared the uncle, giving his little nephew a good hug as he placed him on the comfortable cushions inside the big carriage.

There was not much chance for greetings as everybody was too anxious to get out of the old wagon. So, when all the boxes had been carefully put outside with the driver, and all the passengers had taken their places on the long side seats (it was one of those large side-seated carriages that Uncle William had brought, knowing he would have a big party to carry), then with a sigh of relief Mrs. Bobbsey attempted to tell something of their experiences.

"But how did you know where we were?" Bert asked.

"We had been waiting for you since four o'clock," replied Uncle William. "Then I found out that the train was late, and we waited some more. But when it came to be night and you had not arrived, I set out looking for you. I went to the Junction first, and the agent there told me you had gone in Hank's stage. I happened to be near enough to the livery stable to hear some fellows talking about Hank's breakdown, with a big party aboard. I knew then what had happened, and sent Dorothy home,—she had been out most of the afternoon waiting—got this carryall, and here we are," and Uncle William only had to hint "hurry up" to his horses and away they went.

"Oh, we did have the awfulest time," insisted Freddie.

"I feel as if we hadn't seen a house in a whole year," sighed little Flossie.

"And we only left Meadow Brook this morning," added Nan. "It does seem much longer than a day since we started."

"Well, you will be in Aunt Emily's arms in about two minutes now," declared Uncle William, as through the trees the lights from Ocean Cliff, the Minturn cottage, could now be seen.

"Hello! Hello!" called voices from the veranda.

"Aunt Emily and Dorothy!" exclaimed Bert, and called back to them:

"Here we come! Here we are!" and the wagon turned in to the broad steps at the side of the veranda.

"I've been worried to death," declared Aunt Emily, as she began kissing the girls.

"We have brought company," said Mrs. Bobbsey, introducing Mrs. Manily, "and I don't know what we should have done in all our troubles if she had not been along to cheer us up."

"We are delighted to have you," said Aunt Emily to Mrs. Manily, while they all made their way indoors.

"Oh, Nan!" cried Dorothy, hugging her cousin as tightly as ever she could, "I thought you would never come!"

"We were an awfully long time getting here," Nan answered, returning her cousin's caress, "but we had so many accidents."

"Nothing happened to your appetites, I hope," laughed Uncle William, as the dining-room doors were swung open and a table laden with good things came into sight.

"I think I could eat," said Mrs. Bobbsey, then the mechanical piano player was started, and the party made their way to the dining room.

Uncle William took Mrs. Manily to her place, as she was a stranger; Bert sat between Dorothy and Nan, Mr. Bobbsey looked after Aunt Emily, and Mr. Jack Burnet, a friend of Uncle William, who had been spending the evening at the cottage, escorted Mrs. Bobbsey to her place.

"Come, Flossie, my dear, you see I have gotten a tall chair for you," said Aunt Emily, and Flossie was made comfortable in one of those "between" chairs, higher than the others, and not as high as a baby's.

It was quite a brilliant dinner party, for the Minturns were well-to-do and enjoyed their prosperity as they went along. Mrs. Minturn had been a society belle when she was married. She was now a graceful young hostess, with a handsome husband. She had married earlier than her sister, Mrs. Bobbsey, but kept up her good times in spite of the home cares that followed. During the dinner, Dinah helped the waitress, being perhaps a little jealous that any other maid should look after the wants of Flossie and Freddie.

"Oh, Dinah!" exclaimed Freddie, as she came in with more milk for him, "did you take Snoop out of the box and did you give Downy some water?"

"I suah did, chile," said Dinah, "and you jest ought ter see that Downy duck fly 'round de kitchen. Why, he jest got one of dem fits he had on de train, and we had to shut him in de pantry to get hold ob him."

The waitress, too, told about the flying duck, and everybody enjoyed hearing about the pranks of Freddie's animals.

"We've got a lovely little pond for him, Freddie," said Dorothy. "There is a real little lake out near my donkey barn, and your duck will have a lovely time there."

"But he has to swim in the ocean," insisted Freddie, "'cause we're going to train him to be a circus duck."

"You will have to put him in a bag and tie a rope to him then," Uncle William teased, "because that's the only way a duck can swim in the ocean."

"But you don't know about Downy," argued Freddie. "He's wonderful! He even tried to swim without any water, on the train."

"Through the looking glass!" said Bert, laughing.

"And through the air," added Nan.

"I tell you, Freddie," said Uncle William, quite seriously: "we could get an airship for him maybe; then he could really swim without water."

But Freddie took no notice of the way they tried to make fun of his duck, for he felt Downy was really wonderful, as he said, and would do some wonderful things as soon as it got a chance.

When dinner was over, Dorothy took Nan up to her room. On the dresser, in a cut-glass bowl, were little Nettie Prentice's lilies that Nan had carried all the way from Meadow Brook, and they were freshened up beautifully, thanks to Dorothy's thoughtfulness in giving them a cold spray in the bath tub.

"What a lovely room!" Nan exclaimed, in unconcealed admiration.

"Do you like it?" said Dorothy. "It has a lovely view of the ocean and I chose it for you because I know you like to see pretty sights out of your window. The sun seems to rise just under this window," and she brushed aside the dainty curtains.

The moonlight made a bright path out on the ocean and Nan stood looking out, spellbound.

"I think the ocean is so grand," she said. "It always makes me feel so small and helpless."

"When you are under a big wave," laughed her cousin, who had a way of being jolly. "I felt that way the other day. Just see my arm," and Dorothy pushed up her short sleeve, displaying a black and blue bruise too high up to be seen except in an evening dress or bathing costume.

"How did you do that?" asked Nan, in sympathy.

"Ran into a pier," returned the cousin, with unconcern. "I thought my arm was broken first. But we must go down," said Dorothy, while Nan wanted to see all the things in her pretty room. "We always sit outside before retiring. Mamma says the ocean sings a lullaby that cures all sorts of bad dreams and sleeplessness."

On the veranda Nan and Dorothy joined the others. Freddie was almost asleep in Aunt Emily's arms; Uncle William, Mr. Bobbsey, and Mr. Burnet were talking, with Bert as an interested listener; while Mrs. Manily told Aunt Emily of her mission to the beach. As the children had thought, Aunt Emily readily gave consent to have Nellie, the little cash girl, come to Ocean Cliff, and on the morrow Nan and Dorothy were to write the letter of invitation.

Chapter VI

THE OCEAN

Is there anything more beautiful than sunrise on the ocean?

Nan crept out of bed at the first peep of dawn, and still in her white robe, she sat in the low window seat to see the sun rise "under her window."

"What a beautiful place!" Nan thought, when dawn gave her a chance to see Ocean Cliff. "Dorothy must be awfully happy here. To see the ocean from a bedroom window!" and she watched the streaks of dawn make maps on the waves. "If I were a writer I would always put the ocean in my book," she told herself, "for there are so many children who never have a chance to see the wonderful world of water!"

Nettie's flowers were still on the dresser.

"Poor little Nettie Prentice," thought Nan. "She has never seen the ocean and I wonder if she ever will!"

Nan touched the lilies reverently. There was something in the stillness of daybreak that made the girl's heart go out to poor Nettie, just like the timid little sunbeams went out over the waters, trying to do their small part in lighting up a day.

"I'll just put the lilies out in the dew," Nan went on to herself, raising the window quietly, for the household was yet asleep. "Perhaps I'll find someone sick or lonely to-morrow who will like them, and it will be so much better if they bring joy to someone, for they are so sweet and pretty to die just for me."

"Oh!" screamed Nan the next minute, for someone had crept up behind her and covered her eyes with hands. "It is you, Dorothy!" she declared, getting hold of the small fingers. "Did I wake you with the window?"

"Yes, indeed, I thought someone was getting in from the piazza. They always come near morning," said Dorothy, dropping down on the cushions of the window seat like a goddess of morn, for Dorothy was a beautiful girl, all pink and gold, Bert said, excepting for her eyes, and they were like Meadow Brook violets, deep blue. "Did you have the nightmare?" she asked.

"Nightmare, indeed!" Nan exclaimed. "Why, you told me the sun would rise under my window and I got up to—"

"See it do the rise!" laughed Dorothy, in her jolly way. "Well, if I had my say I'd make Mr. Sol-Sun wear a mask and keep his glare to himself until respectable people felt like crawling out. I lower my awning and close the inside blinds every night. I like sunshine in reasonable doses at reasonable hours, but the moon is good enough for me in the meantime," and she fell over in a pretty lump, feigning sleep in Nan's cushions.

"I hope I did not wake anyone else," said Nan.

"Makes no difference about me, of course," laughed the jolly Dorothy. "Well, I'll pay you back, Nan. Be careful. I am bound to get even," and Nan knew that some trick was in store for her, as Dorothy had the reputation of being full of fun, and always playing tricks.

The sun was up in real earnest now, and the girls raised the window sash to let in the soft morning air.

"I think this would really cure Nellie, my little city friend," said Nan, "and you don't know what a nice girl she is."

"Just bring her down and I'll find out all about her," said Dorothy. "I love city girls. They are so wide awake, and never say silly things like—like some girls I know," she finished, giving her own cousin a good hug that belied the attempt at making fun of her.

"Nellie is sensible," Nan said, "and yet she knows how to laugh, too. She said she had never been in a carriage until she had a ride with us at Meadow Brook. Think of that!"

"Wait till she sees my donkeys!" Dorothy finished, gathering herself up from the cushions and preparing to leave. "Well, Nannie dear, I have had a lovely time," and she made a mock social bow. "Come to see me some time and have some of my dawn, only don't come before eleven A.M. or you might get mixed up, for its awful dark in the blue room until that hour." And like a real fairy Dorothy shook her golden hair and, stooping low in myth fashion, made a "bee-line" across the hall.

"She doesn't need any brother," Nan thought as she saw Dorothy

THEY RODE ALONG THE SANDY DRIVEWAY.

bolt in her door like a squirrel; "she is so jolly and funny!"

But the girls were not the only ones who arose early that morning, for Bert and his father came in to breakfast from a walk on the sands.

"It's better than Meadow Brook," Bert told Nan, as she took her place at the table. "I wish Harry would come down."

"It is so pleasant we want all our friends to enjoy it," said Mrs. Bobbsey. "But I'm sure you have quite a hotel full now, haven't you, Dorothy?"

"Lots more rooms up near the roof," replied Dorothy, "and it's a pity to waste them when there's plenty of ocean to spare. Now, Freddie," went on Dorothy, "when we finish breakfast I am going to show you my donkeys. I called one Doodle and the other Dandy, because papa gave them to me on Decoration Day."

"Why didn't you call one Uncle Sam?" asked Freddie, remembering his part in the Meadow Brook parade.

"Well, I thought Doodle Dandy was near enough red, white, and blue," said Dorothy.

The children finished breakfast rather suddenly and then made their way to the donkey barn.

"Oh, aren't they lovely!" exclaimed Nan, patting the pretty gray animals. "I think they are prettier than horses, they are not so tall."

"I know all about goats and donkeys," declared Freddie.

"I know Nan likes everything early, so we will give her an early ride," proposed Dorothy.

The Bobbseys watched their cousin with interest as she fastened all the bright buckles and put the straps together, harnessing the donkeys. Bert helped so readily that he declared he would do all the harnessing thereafter. The cart was one of those pretty, little basket affairs, with seats at the side, and Bert was very proud of being able to drive a team. There were Dorothy, Nan, Freddie, Flossie, and Bert in the cart when they rode along the sandy driveway, and they made a very pretty party in their bright summer costumes. Freddie had hold of Doodle's reins, and he insisted that his horse went along better than did Dandy, on the other side.

"Oh, won't Nellie enjoy this!" cried Nan, thinking of the little city girl who had only had one carriage ride in all her life.

"Mrs. Manily is going up to the city to bring her to-day," said

Bert. "Aunt Emily sent for the depot wagon just as we came out."

Like many people at the seashore, the Minturns did not keep their own horses, but simply had to telephone from their house to the livery stable when they wanted a carriage.

"Oh, I see the ocean!" called out Freddie, as Bert drove nearer the noise of the waves. "Why didn't we bring Downy for his swim?"

"Too early to bathe yet!" said Dorothy. "We have a bathing house all to ourselves,—papa rented it for the summer,—and about eleven o'clock we will come down and take a dip. Mamma always comes with me or sends Susan, our maid. Mamma cannot believe I really know how to swim."

"And do you?" asked Nan, in surprise.

"Wait until you see!" replied the cousin. "And I am going to teach you, too."

"I'd love to know how, but it must be awfully hard to learn," answered Nan.

"Not a bit," went on Dorothy; "I learned in one week. We have a pool just over there, and lots of girls are learning every day. You can drive right along the beach, Bert; the donkeys are much safer than horses and never attempt to run away."

How delightful it was to ride so close to the great rolling ocean! Even Freddie stopped exclaiming, and just watched the waves, as one after another they tried to get right under Dorothy's cart.

"It makes me almost afraid!" faltered little Flossie, as the great big waves came up so high out on the waters, they seemed like mountains that would surely cover up the donkey cart. But when they "broke" on the sands they were only little splashy puddles for babies to wash their pink toes in.

"There's Blanche Bowden," said Dorothy, as another little cart, a pony cart, came along. "We have lovely times together. I have invited her up to meet us this afternoon, Nan."

The other girl bowed pleasantly from her cart, and even Freddie remembered to raise his cap, something he did not always think necessary for "just girls."

"Some afternoon our dancing class is going to have a matinee," said Dorothy. "Do you like dancing, Bert?"

"Some," replied her cousin in a boy's indifferent way. "Nan is a good dancer."

"Oh, we don't have real dances," protested Nan; "they are mostly drills and exercises. Mamma doesn't believe in young children going right into society. She thinks we will be old soon enough."

"We don't have grown-up dances," said Dorothy, "only the two-step and minuet. I think the minuet is the prettiest of all dances."

"We have had the varsovienne," said Nan, "that is like the minuet. Mother says they are old-time dances, but they are new in our class."

"We may have a costume affair next month," went on Dorothy. "Some of the girls want it, but I don't like wigs and long dresses, especially for dancing. I get all tangled up in a train dress."

"I never wore one," said Nan, "excepting at play, and I can't see how any girl can dance with a lot of long skirts dangling around."

"Oh, they mostly bow and smile," put in Bert, "and a boy has to be awfully careful at one of those affairs. If he should step on a skirt there surely would be trouble," and he snapped his whip at the donkeys with the air of one who had little regard for the graceful art of dancing.

"We had better go back now," said Dorothy, presently. "You haven't had a chance to see our own place yet, but I thought you wanted to get acquainted with the ocean first. Everybody does!"

"I have enjoyed it so much!" declared Nan. "It is pleasanter now than when the sun grows hot."

"But we need the sun for bathing," Dorothy told her. "That is why we 'go in' at the noon hour."

The drive back to the Cliff seemed very short, and when the children drove up to the side porch they found Mrs. Bobbsey and Aunt Emily sitting outside with their fancy work.

Freddie could hardly find words to tell his mother how big the ocean was, and Flossie declared the water ran right into the sky it was so high.

"Now, girls," said Aunt Emily, "Mrs. Manily has gone to bring Nellie down, so you must go and arrange her room. I think the front room over Nan's will be best. Now get out all your pretty things, Dorothy, for little Nellie may be lonely and want some things to look at."

"All right, mother," answered Dorothy, letting Bert put the donkeys away, "we'll make her room look like—like a valentine," she finished, always getting some fun in even where very serious matters were concerned.

The two girls, with Flossie looking on, were soon very busy with Nellie's room.

"We must not make it too fussy," said Dorothy, "or Nellie may not feel at home; and we certainly want her to enjoy herself. Will we put a pink or blue set on the dresser?"

"Blue," said Nan, "for I know she loves blue. She said so when we picked violets at Meadow Brook."

"All right," agreed Dorothy. "And say! Let's fix up something funny! We'll get all the alarm clocks in the house and set them so they will go off one after the other, just when Nellie gets to bed, say about nine o'clock. We'll hide them so she will just about find one when the other starts! She isn't really sick, is she?" Dorothy asked, suddenly remembering that the visitor might not be in as good spirits as she herself was.

"Oh, no, only run down," answered Nan, "and I'm sure she would enjoy the joke."

So the girls went on fixing up the pretty little room. Nan ran downstairs and brought up Nettie Prentice's flowers.

"I thought they would do someone good," she said. "They are so fragrant."

"Aren't they!" Dorothy said, burying her pretty nose in the white lilies. "They smell better than florists' bouquets. I suppose that's from the country air. Now I'll go collect clocks," and without asking anyone's permission Dorothy went from room to room, snatching alarm clocks from every dresser that held one.

"Susan's is a peach," she told Nan, apologizing with a smile, for the slang. "It goes off for fifteen minutes if you don't stop it, and it sounds like a church bell."

"Nellie will think she has gotten into college," Nan said, laughing. "This is like hazing, isn't it?"

"Only we won't really annoy her," said Dorothy. "We just want to make her laugh. College boys, they say, do all sorts of mean things. Make a boy swim in an icy river and all that."

"I hope Bert never goes to a school where they do hazing," said Nan, feeling for her brother's safety. "I think such sport is just wicked!"

"So do I," declared Dorothy, "and if I were a new fellow, and they played such tricks on me, I would just wait for years if I had to, to pay them back."

"I'd put medicine in their coffee, or do something."

"They ought to be arrested," Nan said, "and if the professors can't stop it they should not be allowed to run such schools."

"There," said Dorothy, "I guess everything is all right for Nellie." She put a rose jar on a table in the alcove window. "Now I'll wind the clocks. You mustn't look where I put them," and she insisted that not even Nan should know the mystery of the clocks. "This will be a real surprise party," finished Dorothy, having put each of five clocks in its hiding place, and leaving the tick-ticks to think it over, all by themselves, before going off.

Chapter VII

NELLIE

"Shall I take my cart over to meet Nellie and Mrs. Manily, mother?" Dorothy asked Mrs. Minturn, that afternoon, when the city train was about due.

"Why, yes, daughter, I think that would be very nice," replied the mother. "I intended to send the depot wagon, but the cart would be very enjoyable."

Bert had the donkeys hitched up and at the door for Nan and Dorothy in a very few minutes, and within a half-hour from that time Nan was greeting Nellie at the station, and making her acquainted with Dorothy.

If Dorothy had expected to find in the little cash girl a poor, sickly, ill child, she must have been disappointed, for the girl that came with Mrs. Manily had none of these failings. She was tall and graceful, very pale, but nicely dressed, thanks to Mrs. Manily's attention after she reached the city on the morning train. With a gift from Mrs. Bobbsey, Nellie was "fitted up from head to foot," and now looked quite as refined a little girl as might be met anywhere.

"You were so kind to invite me!" Nellie said to Dorothy, as she took her seat in the cart. "This is such a lovely place!" and she nodded toward the wonderful ocean, without giving a hint that she had never before seen it.

"Yes, you are sure the air is so strong you must swallow strength all the time," and Nellie knew from the remark that Dorothy was a jolly girl, and would not talk sickness, like the people who visit poor children at hospital tents.

Even Mrs. Manily, who knew Nellie to be a capable girl, was surprised at the way she "fell in" with Nan and Dorothy, and Mrs. Manily was quite charmed with her quiet, reserved manner. The fact was that Nellie had met so many strangers in the big department store, she was entirely at ease and accustomed to the little polite sayings of people in the fashionable world.

When Nellie unpacked her bag she brought out something for Freddie. It was a little milk wagon, with real cans, which Freddie could fill up with "milk" and deliver to customers.

"That is to make you think of Meadow Brook," said Nellie, when she gave him the little wagon.

"Yes, and when there's a fire," answered Freddie, "I can fill the cans with water and dump it on the fire like they do in Meadow Brook, too." Freddie always insisted on being a fireman and had a great idea of putting fires out and climbing ladders.

There was still an hour to spare before dinner, and Nan proposed that they take a walk down to the beach. Nellie went along, of course, but when they got to the great stretch of white sand, near the waves, the girls noticed Nellie was about to cry.

"Maybe she is too tired," Nan whispered to Dorothy, as they made some excuse to go back home again. All along the way Nellie was very quiet, almost in tears, and the other girls were disappointed, for they had expected her to enjoy the ocean so much. As soon as they reached home Nellie went to her room, and Nan and Dorothy told Mrs. Minturn about their friend's sudden sadness. Mrs. Minturn of course, went up to see if she could do anything for Nellie.

There she found the little stranger crying as if her heart would break.

"Oh, I can't help it, Mrs. Minturn!" she sobbed. "It was the ocean. Father must be somewhere in that big, wild sea!" and again she cried almost hysterically.

"Tell me about it, dear," said Mrs. Minturn, with her arm around the child. "Was your father drowned at sea?"

"Oh no; that is, we hope he wasn't." said Nellie, through her tears, "but sometimes we feel he must be dead or he would write to poor mother."

"Now dry your tears, dear, or you will have a headache," said Mrs. Minturn, and Nellie soon recovered her composure.

"You see," she began, "we had such a nice home and father was always so good. But a man came and asked him to go to sea. The man said they would make lots of money in a short time. This man was a great friend of father and he said he needed someone he could trust on this voyage. First father said no, but when he talked it over with mother, they, thought it would be best to go, if they could get so much money in a short time, so he went."

Here Nellie stopped again and her dark eyes tried hard to keep back the tears.

"When was that?" Mrs. Minturn asked.

"A year ago," Nellie replied, "and he was only to be away six months at the most."

"And that was why you had to leave school, wasn't it?" Mrs. Minturn questioned further.

"Yes, we had not much money saved, and mother got sick from worrying, so I did not mind going to work. I'm going back to the store again as soon as the doctor says I can," and the little girl showed how anxious she was to help her mother.

"But your father may come back," said Mrs. Minturn; "sailors are often out drifting about for months, and come in finally. I would not be discouraged—you cannot tell what day your father may come back with all the money, and even more than he expected."

"Oh, I know," said Nellie. "I won't feel like that again. It was only because it was the first time I saw the ocean. I'm never homesick or blue. I don't believe in making people pity you all the time." And the brave little girl jumped up, dried her eyes, and looked as if she would never cry again as long as she lived—like one who had cried it out and done with it.

"Yes, you must have a good time with the girls," said Mrs. Minturn. "I guess you need fun more than any medicine."

That evening at dinner Nellie was her bright happy self again, and the three girls chatted merrily about all the good times they would have at the seashore.

There was a ride to the depot after dinner, for Mrs. Manily insisted that she had to leave for the city that evening, and after a game of ball on the lawn, in which everybody, even Flossie and Freddie, had a hand, the children prepared to retire. There was to be a shell hunt very early in the morning (that was a long walk on the beach, looking for choice shells), so the girls wanted to go to bed an hour before the usual time.

"Wait till the clock strikes, Nellie," sang Dorothy, as they went upstairs, and, of course, no one but Nan knew what she meant.

Two hours after this the house was all quiet, when suddenly, there was the buzz of an alarm clock.

"What was that?" asked Mrs. Minturn, coming out in the hall.

"An alarm clock," called Nellie, in whose room the disturbance was. "I found it under my pillow," she added innocently, never suspecting that Dorothy had put it there purposely.

By and by everything was quiet again, when another gong went off.

"Well, I declare!" said Mrs. Minturn. "I do believe Dorothy has been up to some pranks."

"Ding—a-ling—a-long—a-ling!" went the clock, and Nellie was laughing outright, as she searched about the room for the newest alarm. She had a good hunt, too, for the clock was in the shoe box in the farthest corner of the room.

After that there was quite an intermission, as Dorothy expressed it. Even Nellie had stopped laughing and felt very sleepy, when another clock started.

This was the big gong that belonged in Susan's room, and at the sound of it Freddie rushed out in the hall, yelling.

"That's a fire bell! Fire! fire! fire!" he shouted, while everybody else came out this time to investigate the disturbance.

"Now, Dorothy!" said Mrs. Minturn, "I know you have done this. Where did you put those clocks?"

Dorothy only laughed in reply, for the big bell was ringing furiously all the time. Nellie had her dressing robe on, and opened the door to those outside her room.

"I guess it's ghosts," she laughed. "They are all over."

"A serenade," called Bert, from his door.

"What ails dem der clocks?" shouted Dinah. "'Pears like as if dey had a fit, suah. Nebber heard such clockin' since we was in de country," and Susan, who had discovered the loss of her clock, laughed heartily, knowing very well who had taken the alarm away.

When the fifteen minutes were up that clock stopped, and another started. Then there was a regularly cannonading, Bert said, for there was scarcely a moment's quiet until every one of the six clocks had gone off "bing, bang, biff," as Freddie said.

There was no use trying to locate them, for they went off so rapidly that Nellie knew they would go until they were "all done," so she just sat down and waited.

"Think you'll wake up in time?" asked Dorothy, full of mischief as she came into the clock corner.

"I guess so," Nellie answered, laughing. "We surely were alarmed to-night." Then aside to Nan, Nellie whispered: "Wait, we'll get even with her, won't we?" And Nan nodded with a sparkle in her eyes.

Chapter VIII

Exploring—A Race For Pond Lilies

"Now let's explore," Bert said to the girls the next morning. "We haven't had a chance yet to see the lake, the woods, or the island."

"Hal Bingham is coming over to see you this morning," Dorothy told Bert. "He said you must be tired toting girls around, and he knows everything interesting around here to show you."

"Glad of it," said Bert. "You girls are very nice, of course, but a boy needs another fellow in a place like this," and he swung himself over the rail of the veranda, instead of walking down the steps.

It was quite early, for there was so much planned, to be accomplished before the sun got too hot, that all the children kept to their promise to get up early, and be ready for the day's fun by seven o'clock. The girls, with Mrs. Bobbsey, Mrs. Minturn, and Freddie, were to go shell hunting, but as Bert had taken that trip with his father on the first morning after their arrival, he preferred to look over the woods and lake at the back of the Minturn home, where the land slid down from the rough cliff upon which the house stood.

"Here comes Hal now," called Dorothy, as a boy came whistling up the path. He was taller than Bert, but not much older, and he had a very "jolly squint" in his black eyes; that is, Dorothy called it a "jolly squint," but other people said it was merely a twinkle. But all agreed that Hal was a real boy, the greatest compliment that could be paid him.

There was not much need of an introduction, although Dorothy did call down from the porch, "Bert that's Hal; Hal that's Bert," to which announcement the boys called back, "All right, Dorothy. We'll get along."

"Have you been on the lake yet?" Hal asked, as they started down the green stretch that bounded the pretty lake on one side, while a strip of woodland pressed close to the edge across the sheet of water.

"No," Bert answered, "we have had so much coming and going to the depot since we came down, I couldn't get a chance to look around much. It's an awfully pretty lake, isn't it?"

"Yes, and it runs in and out for miles," Hal replied. "I have a canoe down here at our boathouse. Let's take a sail."

The Bingham property, like the Minturn, was on a cliff at the front, and ran back to the lake, where the little boathouse was situated. The house was made of cedars, bound together in rustic fashion, and had comfortable seats inside for ladies to keep out of the sun while waiting for a sail.

"Father and I built this house," Hal told Bert. "We were waiting so long for the carpenters, we finally got a man to bring these cedars in from Oakland. Then we had him cut them, that is, the line of uprights, and we built the boathouse without any trouble at all. It was sport to arrange all the little turns and twists, like building a block house in the nursery."

"You certainly made a good job of it," said Bert, looking critically over the boathouse.

"It's all in the design, of course; the nailing together is the easiest part."

"You might think so," said Hal, "but it's hard to drive a nail in round cedar. But we thought it so interesting, we didn't mind the trouble," finished Hal, as he prepared to untie his canoe.

"What a pretty boat!" exclaimed Bert, in real admiration.

The canoe was green and brown, the body being colored like

bark, while inside, the lining was of pale green. The name, Dorothy, shone in rustic letters just above the water edge.

"And you called it Dorothy," Bert remarked.

"Yes, she's the liveliest girl I know, and a good friend of mine all summer," said Hal. "There are some boys down the avenue, but they don't know as much about good times as Dorothy does. Why, she can swim, row, paddle, climb trees, and goes in for almost any sport that's on. Last week she swam so far in the sun she couldn't touch an oar or paddle for days, her arms were so blistered. But she didn't go around with her hands in a muff at that. Dorothy's all right," finished Hal.

Bert liked to hear his cousin complimented, especially when he had such admiration himself for the girl who never pouted, and he knew that the tribute did not in any way take from Dorothy's other good quality, that of being a refined and cultured girl.

"Girls don't have to be babies to be ladylike," added Bert. "Nan always plays ball with me, and can skate and all that. She's not afraid of a snowball, either."

"Well, I'm all alone," said Hal. "Haven't even got a first cousin. We've been coming down here since I was a youngster, so that's why Dorothy seems like my sister. We used to make mud pies together."

The boys were in the canoe now, and each took a paddle. The water was so smooth that the paddles merely patted it, like "brushing a cat's back," Bert said, and soon the little bark was gliding along down the lake, in and out of the turns, until the "narrows" were reached.

"Here's where we get our pond lilies," said Hal.

"Oh, let's get some!" exclaimed Bert. "Mother is so fond of them."

It was not difficult to gather the beautiful blooms, that nested so cosily on the cool waters, too fond of their cradle to ever want to creep, or walk upon their slender green limbs. They just rocked there, with every tiny ripple of the water, and only woke up to see the warm sunlight bleaching their dainty, yellow heads.

"Aren't they fragrant?" said Bert, as he put one after the other into the bottom of the canoe.

"There's nothing like them," declared Hal. "Some people like roses best, but give me the pretty pond lilies," he finished.

The morning passed quickly, for there was so much to see around the lake. Wild ducks tried to find out how near they could go to the water without touching it, and occasionally one would splash in, by accident.

"What large birds there are around the sea," Bert remarked. "I suppose they have to be big and strong to stand long trips without food when the waves are very rough and they can hardly see fish."

"Yes, and they have such fine plumage," said Hal. "I've seen birds around here just like those in museums, all colors, and with all kinds of feathers—Birds of Paradise, I guess they call them."

"Do you ever go shooting?"

"No, not in summer time," replied Hal. "But sometimes father and I take a run down here about Thanksgiving. That's the time for sea-side sport. Why, last year we fished with rakes; just raked the fish up in piles—'frosties,' they call them."

"That must be fun," reflected Bert.

"Maybe you could come this year," continued Hal. "We might make up a party, if you have school vacation for a week. We could camp out in our house, and get our meals at the hotel."

"That would be fine!" exclaimed Bert. "Maybe Uncle William would come, and perhaps my Cousin Harry, from Meadow Brook. He loves that sort of sport. By the way, we expect him down for a few days; perhaps next week."

"Good!" cried Hal. "The boat carnival is on next week. I'm sure he would enjoy that."

The boys were back at the boathouse now, and Bert gathered up his pond lilies.

"There'll be a scramble for them when the girls see them," he said. "Nellie McLaughlin, next to Dorothy, is out for fun. She is not a bit like a sick girl."

"Perhaps she isn't sick now," said Hal, "but has to be careful. She seems quite thin."

"Mother says she wants fun, more than medicine," went on Bert. "I guess she had to go to work because her father is away at sea. He's been gone a year and he only expected to be away six months."

"So is my Uncle George," remarked Hal. "He went to the West Indies to bring back a valuable cargo of wood. He had only a small vessel, and a few men. Say, did you say her name was McLaughlin?" exclaimed Hal, suddenly.

"Yes; they call him Mack for short, but his name is McLaughlin."

"Why, that was the name of the man who went with Uncle George!" declared Hal. "Maybe it was her father."

"Sounds like it," Bert said. "Tell Uncle William about it sometime. I wouldn't mention it to Nellie, she cut up so, they said, the first time she saw the ocean. Poor thing! I suppose she just imagined her father was tossing about in the waves."

The boys had tied the canoe to its post, and now made their way up over the hill toward the house.

"Here they come," said Bert, as Nan, Nellie, and Dorothy came racing down the hill.

"Oh!" cried Dorothy, "give me some!"

"Oh, you know me, Bert?" pleaded Nellie.

"Hal, I wound up your kite string, didn't I?" insisted Nan, by way of showing that she surely deserved some of Hal's pond lilies.

"And I found your ball in the bushes, Bert," urged Dorothy.

"They're not for little girls," Hal said, waving his hand comically, like a duke in a comic opera. "Run along, little girls, run along," he said, rolling his r's in real stage fashion, and holding the pond lilies against his heart.

"But if we get them, may we have them sir knight?" asked Dorothy, keeping up the joke.

"You surely can!" replied Hal, running short on his stage words.

At this Nellie dashed into the path ahead of Hal, and Dorothy turned toward Bert. Nan crowded in close to Dorothy, and the boys had some dodging to get a start. Finally Hal shot out back of the big bush, and Nellie darted after him. Of course, the boys were better runners than the girls, but somehow, girls always expect something wonderful to happen, when they start on a race like that. Hal had tennis slippers on, and he went like a deer. But just as he was about to call "home free" and as he reached the donkey barn, he turned on his ankle.

Nellie had her hands on the pond lilies instantly, for Hal was obliged to stop and nurse his ankle.

"They're yours," he gave in, handing her the beautiful bunch of blooms.

"Oh, aren't they lovely!" exclaimed the little cash girl, but no one knew that was the first time she ever, in all her life, held a pond lily in her hand.

"I'm going to give them to Mrs. Bobbsey," she decided, starting at once to the house with the fragrant prize in her arms. Neither Dorothy nor Nan had caught Bert, but he handed his flowers to his cousin.

"Give them to Aunt Emily," he said gallantly, while Dorothy took the bouquet and declared she could have caught Bert, anyhow, if she "only had a few more feet," whatever that meant.

Chapter IX

FUN ON THE SANDS

"How many shells did you get in your hunt?" Bert asked the girls, when the excitement over the pond lilies had died away.

"We never went," replied Dorothy. "First, Freddie fell down and had to cry awhile, then he had to stop to see the gutter band, next he had a ride on the five-cent donkey, and by that time there were so many people out, mother said there would not be a pretty shell left, so we decided to go to-morrow morning."

"Then Hal and I will go along," said Bert. "I want to look for nets, to put in my den at home."

"We are going for a swim now," went on Dorothy; "we only came back for our suits."

"There seems so much to do down here, it will take a week to have a try at everything," said Bert. "I've only been in the water once, but I'm going for a good swim now. Come along, Hal."

"Yes, we always go before lunch," said Hal starting off for his suit.

Soon Dorothy, Nan, Nellie, and Flossie appeared with their suits done up in the neat little rubber bags that Aunt Emily had bought at a hospital fair. Then Freddie came with Mrs. Bobbsey, and Dorothy, with her bag on a stick over her shoulder, led the procession to the beach.

As Dorothy told Nan, they had a comfortable bathhouse rented for the season, with plenty of hooks to hang things on, besides a mirror, to see how one's hair looked, after the waves had done it up mermaid fashion.

It did not take the girls long to get ready, and presently all appeared on the beach in pretty blue and white suits, with the large white sailor collars, that always make bathing suits look just right, because real sailors wear that shape of collar.

Flossie wore a white flannel suit, and with her pretty yellow curls, she "looked like a doll," so Nellie said. Freddie's suit was white too, as he always had things as near like his twin sister's as a boy's clothes could be. Altogether the party made a pretty summer picture, as they ran down to the waves, and promptly dipped in.

"Put your head under or you'll take cold," called Dorothy, as she emerged from a big wave that had completely covered her up.

Nellie and Nan "ducked" under, but Flossie was a little timid, and held her mother's right hand even tighter than Freddie clung to her left.

"We must get hold of the ropes," declared Mrs. Bobbsey, seeing a big wave coming.

They just reached the ropes when the wave caught them. Nellie and Nan were out farther, and the billow struck Nellie with such force it actually washed her up on shore.

"Ha! ha!" laughed Dorothy, "Nellie got the first tumble." And then the waves kept dashing in so quickly that there was no more chance for conversation. Freddie ducked under as every wave came, but Flossie was not always quick enough, and it was very hard for her to keep hold of the ropes when a big splasher dashed against her. Dorothy had not permission to swim out as far as she wanted to go, for her mother did not allow her outside the lines, excepting when Mr. Minturn was swimming near her, so she had to be content with floating around near where the other girls bounced up and down, like the bubbles on the billows.

"Look out, Nan!" called Dorothy, suddenly, as Nan stood for a moment fixing her belt. But the warning came too late, for the next minute a wave picked Nan up and tossed her with such force against a pier, that everybody thought she must be hurt. Mrs. Bobbsey was quite frightened, and ran out on the beach, putting Freddie and Flossie at a safe distance from the water, while she made her way to where Nan had been tossed.

For a minute or so, it seemed, Nan disappeared, but presently she bobbed up, out of breath, but laughing, for Hal had her by the hand, and was helping her to shore. The boys had been swimming around by themselves near by, and Hal saw the wave making for Nan just in time to get there first.

HE HAD ONLY GONE A FEW STROKES WHEN BERT APPEARED
WITH NELLIE UNDER HIS ARM.

"I had to swim that time," laughed Nan, "whether I knew how or not."

"You made a pretty good attempt," Hal told her; "and the water is very deep around those piles. You had better not go out so far again, until you've learned a few strokes in the pools. Get Dorothy to teach you."

"Oh, oh, oh, Nellie!" screamed Mrs. Bobbsey. "Where is she? She has gone under that wave!"

Sure enough, Nellie had disappeared. She had only let go the ropes one minute, but she had her back to the ocean watching Nan's rescue, when a big billow struck her, knocked her down, and then where was she?

"Oh," cried Freddie. "She is surely drowned!"

Hal struck out toward where Nellie had been last seen, but he had only gone a few strokes when Bert appeared with Nellie under his arm. She had received just the same kind of toss Nan got, and fortunately Bert was just as near by to save her, as Hal had been to save Nan. Nellie, too, was laughing and out of breath when Bert towed her in.

"I felt like a rubber ball," she said, as soon as she could speak, "and Bert caught me on the first bounce."

"You girls should have ropes around your waists, and get someone to hold the other end," teased Dorothy, coming out with the others on the sands.

"Well, I think we have all had enough of the water for this morning," said Mrs. Bobbsey, too nervous to let the girls go in again.

Boys and girls were willing to take a sun bath on the beach, so, while Hal and Bert started in to build a sand house for Freddie, the four girls capered around, playing tag and enjoying themselves generally. Flossie thought it great fun to dig for the little soft crabs that hide in the deep damp sand. She found a pasteboard box and into this she put all her fish.

"I've got a whole dozen!" she called to Freddie, presently. But Freddie was so busy with his sand castle he didn't have time to bother with baby crabs.

"Look at our fort," called Bert to the girls. "We can shoot right through our battlements," he declared, as he sank down in the sand and looked out through the holes in the sand fort.

"Shoot the Indian and you get a cigar," called Dorothy, taking her place as "Indian" in front of the fort, and playing target for the boys.

First Hal tossed a pebble through a window in the fort, then Bert tried it, but neither stone went anywhere near Dorothy, the "Indian."

"Now, my turn," she claimed, squatting down back of the sand wall and taking aim at Hal, who stood out front.

And if she didn't hit him—just on the foot with a little white pebble!

"Hurrah for our sharpshooter!" cried Bert.

Of course the hard part of the trick was to toss a pebble through the window without knocking down the wall, but Dorothy stood to one side, and swung her arm, so that the stone went straight through and reached Hal, who stood ten feet away.

"I'm next," said Nellie, taking her place behind "the guns."

Nellie swung her arm and down came the fort!

"Oh my!" called Freddie, "you've knocked down the whole gun wall. You'll have to be—"

"Court-martialed," said Hal, helping Freddie out with his war terms.

"She's a prisoner of war," announced Bert, getting hold of Nellie, who dropped her head and acted like someone in real distress. Just as if it were all true, Nan and Dorothy stood by, wringing their hands, in horror, while the boys brought the poor prisoner to the frontier, bound her hands with a piece of cord, and stood her up against an abandoned umbrella pole.

Hal acted as judge.

"Have you anything to say why sentence should not be pronounced upon you?" he asked in a severe voice.

"I have," sighed Nellie. "I did not intend to betray my country. The enemy caused the—the—downfall of Quebec," she stammered, just because the name of that place happened to come to her lips.

"Who is her counsel?" asked the Judge.

"Your honor," spoke up Dorothy, "this soldier has done good service. She has pegged stones at your honor with good effect, she has even captured a company of wild pond lilies in your very ranks, and now, your honor, I plead for mercy."

The play of the children had, by this time, attracted quite a crowd, for the bathing hour was over, and idlers tarried about.

"Fair play!" called a strange boy in the crowd, taking up the spirit of fun. "That soldier has done good service. She took a sassy little crab out of my ear this very day!"

Freddie looked on as if it were all true. Flossie did not laugh a bit, but really seemed quite frightened.

"I move that sentence be pronounced," called Bert, being on the side of the prosecution.

"The prisoner will look this way!" commanded Hal.

Nellie tossed back her wet brown curls and faced the crowd.

"The sentence of the court is that the prisoner be transported for life," announced Hal, while four boys fell in around Nellie, and she silently marched in military fashion toward the bathing pavilion, with Dorothy and Nan at her heels.

Here the war game ended, and everyone was satisfied with that day's fun on the sands.

Chapter X

THE SHELL HUNT

"Now, all ready for the hunting expedition," called Uncle William, very early the next morning, he having taken a day away from his office in the city, to enjoy himself with the Bobbseys at the seashore.

It was to be a long journey, so Aunt Emily thought it wise to take the donkey cart, so that the weary travelers, as they fell by the wayside, might be put in the cart until refreshed. Besides, the shells and things could be brought home in the cart. Freddie expected to capture a real sea serpent, and Dorothy declared she would bring back a whale. Nellie had an idea she would find something valuable, maybe a diamond, that some fish had swallowed in mistake for a lump of sugar at the bottom of the sea. So, with pleasant expectations, the party started off, Bert and Hal acting as guides, and leading the way.

"If you feel like climbing down the rocks here we can walk all along the edge," said Hal. "But be careful!" he cautioned, "the rocks are awfully slippery. Dorothy will have to go on ahead down the road with the donkeys, and we can meet her at the Point."

Freddie and Flossie went along with Dorothy, as the descent was considered too dangerous for the little ones. Dorothy let Freddie drive to make up for the fun the others had sliding down the rocks.

Uncle Daniel started down the cliffs first, and close behind him came Mrs. Bobbsey and Aunt Emily. Nan and Nellie took another path, if a small strip of jagged rock could be called a path, while Hal and Bert scaled down over the very roughest part, it seemed to the girls.

"Oh, mercy!" called Nan, as a rock slipped from under her foot and she promptly slipped after it. "Nellie, give me your hand or I'll slide into the ocean!"

Nellie tried to cross over to Nan, but in doing so she lost her footing and fell, then turned over twice, and only stopped as she came in contact with Uncle William's heels.

"Are you hurt?" everybody asked at once, but Nellie promptly jumped up, showing the toss had not injured her in the least.

"I thought I was going to get an unexpected bath that time," she said, laughing, "only for Mr. Minturn interfering. I saw a star in each heel of his shoe," she declared' "and I was never before glad to bump my nose."

Without further accident the party reached the sands, and saw Dorothy and the little ones a short distance away. Freddie had already filled his cap with little shells, and Flossie was busy selecting some of the finest from a collection she had made.

"Let's dig," said Hal to Bert. "There are all sorts of mussels, crabs, clams, and oysters around here. The fisheries are just above that point."

So the boys began searching in the wet sand, now and then bringing up a "fairy crab" or a baby clam.

"Here's an oyster," called Nellie, coming up with the shellfish in her hand. It was a large oyster and had been washed quite clean by the noisy waves.

"Let's open it," said Hal. "Shall I, Nellie?"

"Yes, if you want to," replied the girl, indifferently, for she did not care about the little morsel. Hal opened it easily with his knife, and then he asked who was hungry.

"Oh, see here!" he called, suddenly. "What this? It looks like a pearl."

"Let me see," said Mr. Minturn, taking the little shell in his hand, and turning out the oyster. "Yes, that surely is a pearl. Now, Nellie, you have a prize. Sometimes these little pearls are quite valuable. At any rate, you can have it set in a ring," declared Mr. Minturn.

"Oh, let me see," pleaded Dorothy. "I've always looked for pearls, and never could find one. How lucky you are, Nellie. It's worth some money."

"Maybe it isn't a pearl at all," objected Nellie, hardly believing that anything of value could be picked up so easily.

"Yes, it is," declared Mr. Minturn. "I've seen that kind before. I'll take care of it for you, and find out what it is worth," and he very carefully sealed the tiny speck in an envelope which he put in his pocketbook.

After that everybody wanted to dig for oysters, but it seemed the one that Nellie found had been washed in somehow, for the oyster beds were out in deeper water. Yet, every time Freddie found a clam or a mussel, he wanted it opened to look for pearls.

"Let us get a box of very small shells and we can string them for necklaces," suggested Nan. "We can keep them for Christmas gifts too, if we string them well."

"Oh, I've got enough for beads and bracelets," declared Flossie, for, indeed, she had lost no time in filling her box with the prettiest shells to be found on the sands.

"Oh, I see a net," called Bert, running toward a lot of driftwood in which an old net was tangled. Bert soon disentangled it and it proved to be a large piece of seine, the kind that is often used to decorate walls in libraries.

"Just what I wanted!" he declared. "And smell the salt. I will always have the ocean in my room now, for I can close my eyes and smell the salt water."

"It is a good piece," declared Hal. "You were lucky to find it. Those sell for a couple of dollars to art dealers."

"Well, I won't sell mine at any price," Bert said. "I've been wishing for a net to put back of my swords and Indian arrows. They make a fine decoration."

The grown folks had come up now, and all agreed the seine was a very pretty one.

"Well, I declare!" said Uncle William, "I have often looked for a piece of net and never could get that kind. You and Nellie were the lucky ones to-day."

"Oh, oh, oh!" screamed Freddie. "What's that?" and before he had a chance to think, he ran down to the edge of the water to meet a big barrel that had been washed in.

"Look out!" screamed Bert, but Freddie was looking in, and at that moment the water washed in right over Freddie's shoes, stockings, and all.

"Oh!" screamed everybody in chorus, for the next instant a stronger wave came in and knocked Freddie down. Quick as a flash Dorothy, who was nearest the edge, jumped in after Freddie, for as the wave receded the little boy fell in again, and might have been washed out into real danger if he had not been promptly rescued.

But as it was he was dripping wet, even his curls had been washed, and his linen suit looked just like one of Dinah's dish towels. Dorothy, too, was wet to the knees, but she did not mind that. The day was warming up and she could get along without shoes or stockings until she reached home.

"Freddie's always fallin' in," gasped Flossie, who was always getting frightened at her twin brother's accidents.

"Well, I get out, don't I?" pouted Freddie, not feeling very happy in his wet clothing.

"Now we must hurry home," insisted Mrs. Bobbsey, as she put Freddie in the donkey cart, while Dorothy, after pulling off her wet shoes and stockings, put a robe over her feet, whipped up the donkeys, Doodle and Dandy, and with Freddie and Flossie in the seat of the cart, the shells and net in the bottom, started off towards the cliffs, there to fix Freddie up in dry clothing. Of course he was not "wet to the skin," as he said, but his shoes and stockings were soaked, and his waist was wet, and that was enough. Five minutes later Dorothy pulled up the donkeys at the kitchen door, where Dinah took Freddie in her arms, and soon after fixed him up.

"You is de greatest boy for fallin' in," she declared. "Nebber saw sech a faller. But all de same you'se Dinah's baby boy," and kind-hearted Dinah rubbed Freddie's feet well, so he would not take cold; then, with fresh clothing, she made him just as comfortable and happy as he had been when he had started out shell hunting.

Chapter XI

DOWNY ON THE OCEAN

"Harry is coming to-day," Bert told Freddie, on the morning following the shell hunt, "and maybe Aunt Sarah will come with him. I'm going to get the cart now to drive over to the station. You may come along, Freddie, mother said so. Get your cap and hurry up," and Bert rushed off to the donkey barn to put Doodle and Dandy in harness.

Freddie was with Bert as quickly as he could grab his cap off the rack, and the two brothers promptly started for the station.

"I hope they bring peaches," Freddie said, thinking of the beautiful peaches in the Meadow Brook orchard that had not been quite ripe when the Bobbseys left the country for the seaside.

Numbers of people were crowded around the station when the boys got there, as the summer season was fast waning, so that Bert and Freddie had hard work to get a place near the platform for their cart.

"That's the train!" cried Bert. "Now watch out so that we don't miss them in the crowd," and the older brother jumped out of the cart to watch the faces as they passed along.

"There he is," cried Freddie, clapping his hands. "Harry! Harry! Aunt Sarah!" he called, until everybody around the station was looking at him.

"Here we are!" exclaimed Aunt Sarah the next minute, having heard Freddie's voice, and followed it to the cart.

"I'm so glad you came," declared Bert to Harry.

"And I'm awfully glad you came," Freddie told Aunt Sarah, when she stopped kissing him.

"But we cannot ride in that little cart," Aunt Sarah said, as Bert offered to help her in.

"Oh, yes, you can," Bert assured her. "These donkeys are very strong, and so is the cart. Put your satchel right in here," and he shoved the valise up in front, under the seat.

"But we have a basket of peaches somewhere," said Aunt Sarah. "They came in the baggage car."

"Oh goody! goody!" cried Freddie, clapping his little brown hands. "Let's get them."

"No, we had better have them sent over," Bert insisted, knowing that the basket would take up too much room, also that Freddie might want to sample the peaches first, and so make trouble in the small cart. Much against his will the little fellow left the peaches, and started off for the cliffs.

The girls, Dorothy, Nellie, and Nan, were waiting at the driveway, and all shouted a welcome to the people from Meadow Brook.

"You just came in time," declared Dorothy. "We are going to have a boat carnival tomorrow, and they expect it will be lovely this year."

Aunt Emily and Mrs. Bobbsey met the others now, and extended such a hearty welcome, there could be no mistaking how pleased they all were to see Harry and Aunt Sarah. As soon as Harry had a chance to lay his traveling things aside Bert and Freddie began showing him around.

"Come on down to the lake, first," Bert insisted. "Hal Bingham may have his canoe out. He's a fine fellow, and we have splendid times together."

"And you'll see my duck, Downy," said Freddie. "Oh, he's growed so big—he's just like a turkey."

Harry thought Downy must be a queer duck if he looked that way, but, of course, he did not question Freddie's description.

"Here, Downy, Downy!" called Freddie, as they came to the little stream where the duck always swam around. But there was no duck to be seen.

"Where is he?" Freddie asked, anxiously.

"Maybe back of some stones," ventured Harry. Then he and Bert joined in the search, but no duck was to be found.

"That's strange," Bert reflected. "He's always around here."

"Where does the lake run to?" Harry inquired.

"Into the ocean," answered Bert; "but Downy never goes far. There's Hal now. We'll get in his boat and see if we can find the duck."

Hal, seeing his friends, rowed in to the shore with his father's new rowboat that he was just trying.

"We have lost Freddie's duck," said Bert. "Have you seen him anywhere?"

"No, I just came out," replied Hal. "But get in and we'll go look for him."

"This is my Cousin Harry I told you about," said Bert, introducing Harry, and the two boys greeted each other, cordially.

All four got into the boat, and Harry took care of Freddie while the other boys rowed.

"Oh. I'm afraid someone has stoled Downy," cried Freddie, "and maybe they'll make—make—pudding out of him."

"No danger," said Hal, laughing. "No one around here would touch your duck. But he might have gotten curious to see the ocean. He certainly doesn't seem to be around here."

The boys had reached the line where the little lake went in a tunnel under a road, and then opened out into the ocean.

"We'll have to leave the boat here," said Hal, "and go and ask people if Downy came down this way."

Tying up the boat to a stake, the boys crossed the bridge, and made their way through the crowd of bathers down to the waves.

"Oh, oh!" screamed Freddie. "I see him! There he is!" and sure enough, there was Downy, like a tiny speck, rolling up and down on the waves, evidently having a fine swim, and not being in the least alarmed at the mountains of water that came rolling in.

"Oh, how can we get him?" cried Freddie, nearly running into the water in his excitement.

"I don't know," Hal admitted. "He's pretty far out."

Just then a life-saver came along. Freddie always insisted the life-guards were not white people, because they were so awfully browned from the sun, and really, this one looked like some foreigner, for he was almost black.

"What's the trouble?" he asked, seeing Freddie's distress.

"Oh, Downy is gone!" cried the little fellow in tears now.

"Gone!" exclaimed the guard, thinking Downy was some boy who had swam out too far.

"Yes, see him out there," sobbed Freddie, and before the other boys had a chance to tell the guard that Downy was only a duck, the life-saver was in his boat, and pulling out toward the spot where Freddie said Downy was "downing"!

"There's someone drowning!" went up the cry all around. Then numbers of men and boys, who had been bathing, plunged into the waves, and followed the life-saver out to the deeper water.

It was useless for Harry, Hal, or Bert to try to explain to anyone about the duck, for the action of the life-saver told a different story. Another guard had come down to the beach now, and was getting his ropes ready, besides opening up the emergency case, that was locked in the boat on the shore.

"Wait till they find out," whispered Hal to Bert, watching the guard in the boat nearing the white speck on the waves. It was a long ways out, but the boys could see the guard stop rowing.

"He's got him," shouted the crowd, also seeing the guard pick something out of the water. "I guess he had to lay him in the bottom of the boat."

"Maybe he's dead!" the people said, still believing the life-saver had been after some unfortunate swimmer.

"Oh, he's got him! He's got him!" cried Freddie, joyfully, still keeping up the mistake for the sightseers.

As the guard in the boat had his back to shore, and pulled in that way, even his companion on land had not yet discovered his mistake, and he waited to help revive whoever lay in the bottom of the boat.

The crowd pressed around so closely now that Freddie's toes were painfully trampled upon.

"He's mine," cried the little fellow. "Let me have him."

"It's his brother," whispered a sympathetic boy, almost in tears. "Let him get over by the boat," and so the crowd made room for Freddie, as the life-saver pulled up on the beach.

The people held their breath.

"He's dead!" insisted a number, when there was no move in the bottom of the boat. Then the guard stooped down and brought up—Downy!

"Only a duck!" screamed all the boys in the crowd, while the other life-saver laughed heartily over his preparations to restore a duck to consciousness.

"He's mine! He's mine!" insisted Freddie, as the life-saver fondled the pretty white duck, and the crowd cheered.

"Yes, he does belong to my little brother," Bert said, "and he didn't mean to fool you at all. It was just a mistake," the older brother apologized.

"Oh, I know that," laughed the guard. "But when we think there is any danger we don't wait for particulars. He's a very pretty duck all the same, and a fine swimmer, and I'm glad I got him for the little fellow, for likely he would have kept on straight out to smooth water. Then he would never have tried to get back."

The guard now handed Downy over to his young owner, and without further remarks than "Thank you," Freddie started off through the crowd, while everybody wanted to see the wonderful duck. The joke caused no end of fun, and it took Harry, Hal, and Bert to save Freddie and Downy from being too roughly treated, by the boys who were over-curious to see both the wonderful duck and the happy owner.

Chapter XII

REAL INDIANS

"Now we will have to watch Downy or he will be sure to take that trip again," said Bert, as they reached home with the enterprising duck.

"We could build a kind of dam across the narrowest part of the lake," suggested Hal; "kind of a close fence he would not go through. See, over there it is only a little stream, about five feet wide. We can easily fence that up. I've got lots of material up in our garden house."

"That would be a good idea," agreed Bert. "We can put Downy in the barn until we get it built. We won't take any more chances." So Downy was shut up in his box, back of the donkey stall, for the rest of the day.

"How far back do these woods run?" Harry asked his companions, he always being interested in acres, as all real country boys are.

"I don't know," Hal Bingham answered. "I never felt like going to the end to find out. But they say the Indians had reservations out here not many years ago."

"Then I'll bet there are lots of arrow heads and stone hatchets around. Let's go look. Have we time before dinner, Bert?" Harry asked.

"I guess so," replied the cousin. "Uncle William's train does not get in until seven, and we can be back by that time. We'll have to slip away from Freddie, though. Here he comes. Hide!" and at this the boys got behind things near the donkey house, and Freddie, after calling and looking around, went back to the house without finding the "boy boys."

"We can cross the lake in my boat," said Hal, as they left their hiding-places. "Then, we will be right in the woods. I'll tie the boat on the other side until we come back; no one will touch it."

"Is there no bridge?" Harry asked.

"Not nearer than the crossings, away down near the ocean beach," said Bert. "But the boat will be all right. There are no thieves around here."

It was but a few minutes' work to paddle across the lake and tie up the canoe on the opposite shore. Hal and Bert started off, feeling they would find something interesting, under Harry's leadership.

It was quite late in the afternoon, and the thick pines and ferns made the day almost like night, as the boys tramped along.

"Fine big birds around here," remarked Harry, as the feathered creatures of the ocean darted through the trees, making their way to the lake's edge.

"Yes, we're planning for a Thanksgiving shoot," Hal told him. "We hope, if we make it up, you can come down."

"I'd like to first-rate," said Harry. "Hello!" he suddenly exclaimed, "I thought I kicked over a stone hatchet head."

Instantly the three boys were on their knees searching through the brown pine needles.

"There it is!" declared Harry, picking up a queer-shaped stone. "That's real Indian—I know. Father has some, but this is the first I was ever lucky enough to find."

The boys examined the stone. There were queer marks on it, but they were so worn down it was impossible to tell what they might mean.

"What tribe camped here?" asked Harry.

"I don't know," answered Hal. "I just heard an old farmer, out Berkley way, talking about the Indians. You see, we only come down here in the summer time. Then we keep so close to the ocean we don't do much exploring "

The boys were so interested now they did not notice how dark it was getting. Neither did they notice the turns they were making in the deep woodlands. Now and then a new stone would attract their attention. They would kick it over, pick it up, and if it were of queer shape it would be pocketed for further inspection.

"Say," said Hal, suddenly, "doesn't it look like night?" and at that he ran to a clear spot between the trees, where he might see the sky.

"Sure as you live it is night!" he called back to the others. "We better pick the trail back to our canoe, or we may have to become real Indians and camp out here in spite of our appetites."

Then the boys discovered that the trees were much alike, and there were absolutely no paths to follow.

"Well, there's where the sun went down, so we must turn our back to that," advised Hal, as they tramped about, without making any progress toward finding the way home.

What at first seemed to be fun, soon turned out to be a serious matter; for the boys really could not find their way home. Each, in turn, thought he had the right way, but soon found he was mistaken.

"Well, I'll give up!" said Hal. "To think we could be lost like three babies!"

"Only worse," added Harry, "for little fellows would cry and some-one might help them."

"Oh! oh! oh! oh! we're lost! We're the babes in the woods!" shouted Bert at the top of his voice, joking, yet a little in earnest.

"Let's build a fire," suggested Harry. "That's the way the Indians used to do. When our comrades see the smoke of the fire they will come and rescue us."

The other boys agreed to follow the chief's direction. So they set to work. It took some time to get wood together, and to start the fire, but when it was finally lighted, they sat around it and wasted a lot of time. It would have been better had they tried to get out of the woods, for as they waited, it grew darker.

"I wouldn't mind staying here all night," drawled Harry, stretching himself out on the dry leaves alongside the fire.

"Well, I'd like supper first," put in Hal. "We were to have roast duck to-night," and he smacked his lips.

"What was that!" Harry exclaimed, jumping up.

"A bell, I thought," whispered Hal, quite frightened.

"Indians!" added Bert. "Oh, take me home!" he wailed, and while he tried to laugh, it was a failure, for he really felt more like crying.

"There it is again. A cow bell!" declared Harry, who could not be mistaken on bells.

"Let's find the cow and maybe she will then find us," he suggested, starting off in the direction that the "tink-tink-tink-tink" came from.

"Here she is!" he called, the next moment, as he walked up to a pretty little cow with the bell on her neck. "Now, where do you belong?" Harry asked the cow. "Do you know where the Cliffs are, and how we can get home?"

The cow was evidently hungry for her supper, and bellowed loud and long. Then she rubbed her head against Harry's sleeve, and started to walk through the dark woods.

"If we follow her she will take us out, all right," said Harry, and so the three boys willingly started off after the cow.

Just as Harry had said, she made her way to a path, then the rest of the way was clear.

"Hurrah!" shouted Hal, "I smell supper already," and now, at the end of the path, an opening in the trees showed a few scattered houses.

"Why, we are away outside of Berkley," went on Hal. "Now, we will have a long tramp home, but I'm glad even at that, for a night under the trees was not a pleasant prospect."

"We must take this cow home first," said Harry, with a farmer's instinct. "Where do you suppose she belongs?"

"We might try that house first," suggested Bert, pointing to a cottage with a small barn, a little way from the wood.

"Come, Cush," said Harry, to the strange cow, and the animal obediently walked along.

There was no need to make inquiries, for outside of the house a little woman met them.

"Oh, you've found her!" she began. "Well, my husband was just going to the pound, for that old miser of a pound master takes a cow in every chance he gets, just for the fine. Come, Daisy, you're hungry," and she patted the cow affectionately. "Now, young men, I'm obliged to you, and you have saved a poor man a day's pay, for that is just what the fine would be. If you will accept a pail of milk each, I have the cans, and would be glad to give you each a quart. You might have berries for dinner," she finished.

"We would be very glad of the milk," spoke up Harry, promptly, always wide awake and polite when there was a question that concerned farmers.

"Do you live far?" asked the woman.

"Only at the Cliffs," said Harry. "We will soon be home now. But we were lost until your cow found us. She brought us here, or we would be in the woods yet."

"Well, I do declare!" laughed the little woman, filling each of three pails from the fresh milk, that stood on a bench, under the kitchen window. "Now, our man goes right by your house to-morrow morning, and if you leave the pails outside he will get them. Maybe your mothers might like some fresh milk, or buttermilk, or fresh eggs, or new butter?" she asked.

"Shouldn't wonder," said Hal. "We have hard work to get fresh stuff; they seem to send it all to the hotels. I'll let the man know when he comes for the pails."

"Thank you, thank you," replied the little woman, "and much obliged for bringing Daisy home. If you ever want a drink of milk, and are out this way, just knock at my door and I'll see you don't go away thirsty."

After more thanks on both sides, the lost boys started homeward, like a milk brigade, each with his bright tin pail of sweet new milk in his hand.

Chapter XIII

THE BOAT CARNIVAL

"It didn't seem right to take all this milk," remarked Hal, as the three boys made their way in the dark, along the ocean road.

"But we would have offended the lady had we refused," said Harry. "Besides, we may be able to get her good customers by giving out the samples," he went on. "I'm sure it is good milk, for the place was clean, and that cow we found, or that found us, was a real Jersey."

The other boys did not attempt to question Harry's right to give expert views where cows and milk were concerned; so they made their way along without further comment.

"I suppose our folks will think we are lost," ventured Hal.

"Then they will think right," admitted Bert, "for that was just what we were, lost."

Crossing the bridge, the boys could hear voices.

"That's father," declared Hal. Then they listened.

"And that's Uncle William," said Bert, as another voice reached them.

"Gracious! I'm sorry this happened the first day I came," spoke up Harry, realizing that the other boys would not have gone into the deep woods if he had not acted as leader.

"Here we are!" called Hal.

"Hello there! That you, Hal?" came a call.

"Yes; we're coming," Hal answered, and the lost boys quickened their steps, as much as the pails of milk allowed.

Presently Uncle William and Mr. Bingham came up, and were so glad to find that Hal, Harry, and Bert were safe, they scarcely required any explanation for the delay in getting home. Of course, both men had been boys themselves, and well remembered how easy it was to get lost, and be late reaching home.

The milk pails, too, bore out the boys' story, had there been any doubt about it, but beyond a word of caution about dangerous places in deep woodlands there was not a harsh word spoken.

A little farther on the road home, Dorothy, Nan, and Nellie met the wanderers, and then the woodland escapade seemed a wild tale about bears, Indians, and even witches, for each girl added, to the boys' story, so much of her own imagination that the dark night and the roaring of the ocean, finished up a very wild picture, indeed.

"Now, you are real heroes," answered Dorothy, "and you are the bravest boys I know. I wish I had been along. Just think of sitting by a campfire in a dark woods, and having no one to bring you home but a poor little cow!" and Dorothy insisted on carrying Bert's milk pail to show her respect for a real hero.

Even Dinah and Susan did not complain about serving a late dinner to the boys, and both maids said they had never before seen such perfectly splendid milk as came from the farmhouse.

"We really might take some extra milk from that farm," said Aunt Emily, "for what we get is nothing like as rich in cream as this is."

So, as Harry said, the sample brought good results, for on the following morning, when the man called for the empty pail, Susan ordered two quarts a day, besides some fresh eggs and new butter to be delivered twice a week.

"Do you know," said Uncle William to Mrs. Bobbsey next morning at breakfast, when the children had left the table, "Mr. Bingham was telling me last night that his brother is at sea, on just such a voyage as little Nellie's father went on. And a man named McLaughlin went with him, too. Now, that's Nellie's name, and I believe George Bingham is the very man he went with."

"You don't tell me!" exclaimed Mrs. Bobbsey. "And have they heard any news from Mr. Bingham's brother?"

"Nothing very definite, but a vessel sighted the schooner ten days ago. Mr. Bingham has no idea his brother is lost, as he is an experienced seaman, and the Binghams are positive it is only a matter of the schooner being disabled, and the crew having a hard time to reach port," replied Mr. Minturn.

"If Nellie's mother only knew that," said Mrs. Bobbsey.

"Tell you what I'll do," said the brother-in-law; "just give me Mrs. McLaughlin's address, and I'll go to see her to-day while I'm in town. Then I can find out whether we have the right man in mind or not."

Of course, nothing was said to Nellie about the clew to her father's whereabouts, but Mrs. Bobbsey and Aunt Emily were quite excited over it, for they were very fond of Nellie, and besides, had visited her mother and knew of the poor woman's distress.

"If it only could be true that the vessel is trying to get into port," reflected Mrs. Bobbsey. "Surely, there would be enough help along the coast to save the crew."

While this very serious matter was occupying the attention of the grown-up folks, the children were all enthusiasm over the water carnival, coming off that afternoon.

Hal and Bert were dressed like real Indians, and were to paddle in Hal's canoe, while Harry was fixed up like a student, a French explorer, and he was to row alone in Hal's father's boat, to represent Father Marquette, the discoverer of the upper Mississippi River.

It was quite simple to make Harry look like the famous discoverer, for he was tall and dark, and the robes were easily arranged with Susan's black shawl, a rough cord binding it about his waist. Uncle William's traveling cap answered perfectly for the French skullcap.

"Then I'm going to be Pocahontas," insisted Dorothy, as the boys' costumes brought her mind back to Colonial days.

"Oh, no," objected Hal, "you girls better take another period of history. We can't all be Indians."

"Well, I'll never be a Puritan, not even for fun," declared Dorothy, whose spirit of frolic was certainly quite opposite that of a Priscilla.

"Who was some famous girl or woman in American history?" asked Harry, glad to get a chance to "stick" Dorothy.

"Oh, there are lots of them," answered the girl, promptly. "Don't think that men were the only people in America who did anything worth while."

"Then be one that you particularly admire," teased Harry, knowing very well Dorothy could not, at that minute, name a single character she would care to impersonate.

"Oh, let us be real," suggested Nellie. "Everybody will be all make-believe. I saw lots of people getting ready, and I'm sure they will all look like Christmas-tree things, tinsel and paper and colored stuffs."

"What would be real?", questioned Dorothy.

"Well, the Fisherman's Daughters," Nellie said, very slowly. "We have a picture at home of two little girls waiting—for their—father."

The boys noticed Nellie's manner, and knew why she hesitated. Surely it would be real for her to be a fisherman's daughter, waiting for her father!

"Oh, good!" said Dorothy. "I've got that picture in a book, and we can copy it exactly. You and I can be in a boat alone. I can row."

"You had better have a line to my boat," suggested Harry. "It would be safer in the crowd."

It had already been decided that Flossie, Freddie, and Nan should go in the Minturn launch, that was made up to look like a Venetian gondola. Mrs. Bobbsey and Aunt Emily and Aunt Sarah were to be Italian ladies, not that they cared to be in the boat parade, but because Aunt Emily, being one of the cottagers, felt obliged to encourage the social features of the little colony.

It was quite extraordinary how quickly and how well Dorothy managed to get up her costume and Nellie's. Of course, the boys were wonderful Indians, and Harry a splendid Frenchman; Mrs. Bobbsey, Aunt Sarah, and Aunt Emily only had to add lace headpieces to their brightest dinner gowns to be like the showy Italians, while Freddie looked like a little prince in his black velvet suit, with Flossie's red sash tied from shoulder to waist, in gay court fashion. Flossie wore the pink slip that belonged under her lace dress, and on her head was a silk handkerchief pinned up at the ends, in that square quaint fashion of little ladies of Venice.

There were to be prizes, of course, for the best costumes and prettiest boats, and the judges' stand was a very showy affair, built at the bridge end of the lake.

There was plenty of excitement getting ready, but finally all hands were dressed, and the music from the lake told our friends the procession was already lining up.

Mrs. Minturn's launch was given second place, just back of the Mayor's, and Mrs. Bingham's launch, fixed up to represent an automobile, came next. Then, there were all kinds of boats, some made to represent impossible things, like big swans, eagles, and one even had a lot of colored ropes flying about it, while an automobile lamp, fixed up in a great paper head, was intended to look like a monster sea-serpent, the ropes being its fangs. By cutting out a queer face in the paper over the lighted lamp the eyes blazed, of course, while the mouth was red, and wide open, and there were horns, too, made of twisted pieces of tin, so that altogether the sea-serpent looked very fierce, indeed.

The larger boats were expected to be very fine, so that as the procession passed along the little lake the steam launches did not bring out much cheering from the crowd. But now the single boats were coming.

"Father Marquette!" cried the people, instantly recognizing the historic figure Harry represented.

So slowly his boat came along, and so solemn he looked!

Then, as he reached the judges' stand, he stood up, put his hand over his eyes, looking off in the distance, exactly like the picture of the famous French explorer.

This brought out long and loud cheering, and really Harry deserved it, for he not only looked like, but really acted, the character.

There were a few more small boats next. In one the summer girl was all lace and parasol, in another there was a rude fisherman, then; some boys were dressed to look like dandies, and they seemed to enjoy themselves more than did the people looking at them. There was also a craft fixed up to look like a small gunboat.

Hal and Bert then paddled along.

They were perfect Indians, even having their faces browned with

dark powder. Susan's feather duster had been dissected to make up the
boys' headgear, and two overall suits, with jumpers, had been slashed to
pieces to make the Indian suits. The canoe, of course, made a great stir.

"Who are they?" everybody wanted to know. But no one could guess.

"Oh, look at this!" called the people, as an old boat with two little
girls drifted along.

The Fisherman's Daughters!

Perhaps it was because there was so much gayety around that these
little girls looked so real. From the side of their weather-beaten boat
dragged an old fishnet. Each girl had on her head a queer half-hood,
black, and from under this Nellie's brown hair fell in tangles on her bare
shoulders, and Dorothy's beautiful yellow ringlets framed in her own
pretty face. The children wore queer bodices, like those seen in pictures
of Dutch girls, and full skirts of dark stuff finished out their costumes.

As they sat in the boat and looked out to sea, "watching for the
fisherman's return," their attitude and pose were perfect.

The people did not even cheer. They seemed spellbound.

"That child is an actress," they said, noting the "real" look on
Nellie's face. But Nellie was not acting. She was waiting for the lost
father at sea.

When would he come back to her?

Chapter XIV

THE FIRST PRIZE

When the last craft in the procession had passed the judges' stand,
and the little lake was alive with decorations and nautical novelties,
everybody, of course, in the boats and on land, was anxious to know
who would get the prizes.

There were four to be given, and the fortunate ones could have
gifts in silver articles or the value in money, just as they chose.

Everybody waited anxiously, when the man at the judges' stand
stood up and called through the big megaphone:

"Let the Fisherman's Daughters pass down to the stand!"

"Oh, we are going to get a prize," Dorothy said to Nellie. "I'll just cut the line to Harry's boat and row back to the stand."

Then, when the two little girls sailed out all by themselves, Dorothy rowing gracefully, while Nellie helped some, although not accustomed to the oars, the people fairly shouted.

For a minute the girls waited in front of the stand. But the more people inspected them the better they appeared. Finally, the head judge stood up.

"First prize is awarded to the Fisherman's Daughters," he announced.

The cheering that followed his words showed the approval of the crowd. Nellie and Dorothy were almost frightened at the noise. Then they rowed their boat to the edge, and as the crowd gathered around them to offer congratulations, the other prizes were awarded.

The second prize went to the Indians!

"Lucky they don't know us," said Hal to Bert, "for they would never let the two best prizes get in one set." The Indians were certainly well made-up, and their canoe a perfect redman's bark.

The third prize went to the "Sea-serpent," for being the funniest boat in the procession; and the fourth to the gunboat. Then came a great shouting!

A perfect day had added to the success of the carnival, and now many people adjourned to the pavilion, where a reception was held, and good things to eat were bountifully served.

"But who was the little girl with Dorothy Minturn?" asked the mayor's wife. Of course everybody knew Dorothy, but Nellie was a stranger.

Mrs. Minturn, Mrs. Bobbsey, Aunt Sarah, Mrs. Bingham, and Mrs. Blake, the latter being the mayor's wife, had a little corner in the pavilion to themselves. Here Nellie's story was quietly told.

"How nice it was she got the prize," said Mrs. Blake, after hearing about Nellie's hardships. "I think we had better have it in money—and we might add something to it," she suggested. "I am sure Mr. Blake would be glad to. He often gives a prize himself. I'll just speak to him."

Of course Dorothy was to share the prize, and she accepted a pretty silver loving cup. But what do you suppose they gave Nellie?

Fifty dollars!

Was not that perfectly splendid?

The prize for Nellie was twenty-five dollars, but urged by Mrs.

Blake, the mayor added to it his own check for the balance.

Naturally Nellie wanted to go right home to her mother with it, and nothing about the reception had any interest for her after she received the big check. However, Mrs. Bobbsey insisted that Mr. Minturn would take the money to Nellie's mother the next day, so the little girl had to be content.

Then, when all the festivities were over, and the children's excitement had brought them to bed very tired that night, Nellie sat by her window and looked out at the sea!

Always the same prayer, but to-night, somehow, it seemed answered! Was it the money for mother that made the father seem so near? The roaring waves seemed to call out:

"Nellie—Nellie dear! I'm coming—coming home to you!"

And while the little girl was thus dreaming upstairs, Mr. Minturn down in the library was telling about his visit to Nellie's mother.

"There is no doubt about it," he told Mrs. Bobbsey. "It was Nellie's father who went away with George Bingham, and it was certainly that schooner that was sighted some days ago."

The ladies, of course, were overjoyed at the prospect of the best of luck for Nellie—her father's possible return,—and then it was decided that Uncle William should again go to Mrs. McLaughlin, this time to take her the prize money, and that Mrs. Bobbsey should go along with him, as it was such an important errand.

"And you remember that little pearl that Nellie found on the beach? Well, I'm having it set in a ring for her. It is a real pearl, but not very valuable, yet I thought it would be a souvenir of her visit at the Cliffs," said Mr. Minturn.

"That will be very nice," declared Mrs. Bobbsey. "I am sure no one deserves to be made happy more than that child does, for just fancy, how she worked in that store as cash girl until her health gave way. And now she is anxious to go back to the store again. Of course she is worried about her mother, but the prize money ought to help Mrs. McLaughlin so that Nellie would not need to cut her vacation short."

"What kind of treasure was it that these men went to sea after?" Aunt Emily asked Uncle William.

"A cargo of mahogany," Mr. Minturn replied. "You see, that wood is scarce now, a cargo is worth a fortune, and a shipload was being brought from the West Indies to New York when a storm blew the vessel out to a very dangerous point. Of course, the vessel was wrecked, and so were two others that later attempted to reach the valuable cargo. You see the wind always blows the one way there, and it is impossible to get the mahogany out of its trap. Now, George Bingham was offered fifty thousand dollars to bring that wood to port, and he decided that he could do it by towing each log around the reef by canoes. The logs are very heavy, each one is worth between eighty and one hundred dollars, but the risk meant such a reward, in case of success, that they went at it. Of course the real danger is around the wreck. Once free from that point and the remainder of the voyage would be only subject to the usual ocean storms."

"And those men were to go through the dangerous waters in little canoes!" exclaimed Aunt Emily.

"But the danger was mostly from winds to the sails of vessels," explained Uncle William. "Small craft are safest in such waters."

"And if they succeeded in bringing the mahogany in?" asked Mrs. Bobbsey.

"Nellie would be comparatively rich, for her father went as George Bingham's partner," finished Mr. Minturn.

So, the evening went into night, and Nellie, the Fisherman's Daughter, slept on, to dream that the song of the waves came true.

Chapter XV

LOST ON AN ISLAND

The calm that always follows a storm settled down upon the Cliffs the day after the carnival. The talk of the entire summer settlement was Nellie and her prize, and naturally, the little girl herself thought of home and the lonely mother, who was going to receive such a surprise—fifty dollars!

It was a pleasant morning, and Freddie and Flossie were out watching Downy trying to get through the fence that the boys had built to keep him out of the ocean. Freddie had a pretty little boat Uncle William had brought down from the city. It had sails, that really caught the wind, and carried the boat along.

Of course Freddie had a long cord tied to it, so it could not get out of his reach, and while Flossie tried to steer the vessel with a long whip, Freddie made believe he was a canal man, and walked along the tow path with the cord in hand.

"I think I would have got a prize in the boat parade if I had this steamer," said Freddie, feeling his craft was really as fine as any that had taken part in the carnival.

"Maybe you would," agreed Flossie. "Now let me sail it a little."

"All right," said Freddie, and he offered the cord to his twin sister.

"Oh," she exclaimed, "I dropped it!"

The next minute the little boat made a turn with the breeze, and before Flossie could get hold of the string it was all in the water!

"Oh, my boat!" cried Freddie. "Get it quick!"

"I can't!" declared Flossie. "It is out too far! Oh, what shall we do!"

"Now you just get it! You let it go," went on the brother, without realizing that his sister could not reach the boat, nor the string either, for that matter.

"Oh, it's going far away!" cried Flossie; almost in tears.

The little boat was certainly making its way out into the lake, and it sailed along so proudly, it must have been very glad to be free.

"There's Hal Bingham's boat," ventured Flossie. "Maybe I could go out a little ways in that."

"Of course you can," promptly answered Freddie. "I can row."

"I don't know, we might upset!" Flossie said, hesitating.

"But it isn't deep. Why, Downy walks around out here," went on the brother.

This assurance gave the little girl courage, and slipping the rope off the peg that secured the boat to the shore, very carefully she put Freddie on one seat, while she sat herself on the other.

The oars were so big she did not attempt to handle them, but just depended on the boat to do its own sailing.

"Isn't this lovely!" declared Freddie, as the boat drifted quietly along.

"Yes, but how can we get back?" asked Flossie, beginning to realize their predicament.

"Oh, easy!" replied Freddie, who suddenly seemed to have become a man, he was so brave. "The tide comes down pretty soon, and then our boat will go back to shore."

TOWARD THIS LITTLE ISLAND THE CHILDREN'S BOAT WAS NOW DRIFTING.

Freddie had heard so much about the tide he felt he understood it perfectly. Of course, there was no tide on the lake, although the waters ran lazily toward the ocean at times.

"But we are not getting near my boat," Freddie complained, for indeed the toy sailboat was drifting just opposite their way.

"Well, I can't help it, I'm sure," cried Flossie. "And I just wish I could get back. I'm going to call somebody."

"Nobody can hear you," said her brother. "They are all down by the ocean, and there's so much noise there you can't even hear thunder."

Where the deep woods joined the lake there was a little island. This was just around the turn, and entirely out of view of either the Minturn or the Bingham boat landing. Toward this little island the children's boat was now drifting.

"Oh, we'll be real Robinson Crusoes!" exclaimed Freddie, delighted at the prospect of such an adventure.

"I don't want to be no Robinson Crusoe!" pouted his sister. "I just want to get back home," and she began to cry.

"We're going to bunk," announced Freddie, as at that minute the boat did really bump into the little island. "Come, Flossie, let us get ashore," said the brother, in that superior way that had come to him in their distress.

Flossie willingly obeyed.

"Be careful!" she cautioned. "Don't step out till I get hold of your hand. It is awfully easy to slip getting out of a boat."

Fortunately for the little ones they had been taught to be careful when around boats, so that they were able to take care of themselves pretty well, even in their present danger.

Once on land, Flossie's fears left her, and she immediately set about picking the pretty little water flowers, that grew plentifully among the ferns and flag lilies.

"I'm going to build a hut," said Freddie, putting pieces of dry sticks up against a willow tree. Soon the children became so interested they did not notice their boat drift away, and really leave them all alone on the island!

In the meantime everybody at the house was looking for the twins. Their first fear, of course, was the ocean, and down to the beach Mrs. Bobbsey, Aunt Sarah, and the boys hurried, while Aunt Emily and the girls made their way to the Gypsy Camp, fearing the fortune tellers might have stolen the children in order to get money for bringing them back again.

Dorothy walked boldly up to the tent. An old woman sat outside and looked very wicked, her face was so dark and her hair so black and tangled.

"Have you seen a little boy and girl around here?" asked Dorothy, looking straight into the tent.

"No, nobody round here. Tell your fortune, lady?" This to Aunt Emily, who waited for Dorothy.

"Not to-day," answered Aunt Emily. "We are looking for two children. Are you sure you have not seen them?"

"No, lady. Gypsy tell lady's fortune, then lady find them," she suggested, with that trick her class always uses, trying to impose on persons in trouble with the suggestion of helping them out of it.

"No, we have not time," insisted Aunt Emily; really quite alarmed now that there was no trace of the little twins.

"Let me look through your tent?" asked Dorothy, bravely.

"What for?" demanded the old woman.

"To make sure the children are not hiding," and without waiting for a word from the old woman, Dorothy walked straight into that gypsy tent!

Even Aunt Emily was frightened.

Suppose somebody inside should keep Dorothy?

"Come out of my house!" muttered the woman, starting after Dorothy.

"Come out, Dorothy," called her mother, but the girl was making her way through the old beds and things inside, to make sure there was no Freddie or Flossie to be found in the tent.

It was a small place, of course, and it did not take Dorothy very long to search it.

Presently she appeared again, much to the relief of her mother, Nan, and Nellie, who waited breathlessly outside.

"They are not around here," said Dorothy. "Now, mother, give the old woman some change to make up for my trespassing."

Aunt Emily took a coin from her chatelaine.

"Thank the lady! Good lady," exclaimed the old gypsy. "Lady find her babies; babies play—see!" (And she pretended to look into the future with some dirty cards.) "Babies play in woods. Natalie sees babies picking flowers."

Now, how could anybody ever guess that the old gypsy had just come down from picking dandelions by the lake, where she really had seen Freddie and Flossie on the island?

And how could anybody know that she was too wicked to tell Aunt Emily this, but was waiting until night, to bring the children back home herself, and get a reward for doing so?

She had seen the boat drift away and she knew the little ones were helpless to return home unless someone found them.

Mrs. Bobbsey and the boys were now coming up from the beach.

What, at first, seemed only a mishap, now looked like a very serious matter.

"We must go to the woods," insisted Dorothy. "Maybe that old woman knew they were in the woods."

But as such things always happen, the searchers went to the end of the woods, far away from the island. Of course they all called loudly, and the boys gave the familiar yodel, but the noise of the ocean made it impossible for the call to reach Freddie and Flossie.

"Oh, I'm so afraid they are drowned!" exclaimed Mrs. Bobbsey, breaking down and crying.

"No, mamma," insisted Nan, "I am sure they are not. Flossie is so afraid of the water, and Freddie always minds Flossie. They must be playing somewhere. Maybe they are home by this time," and so it was agreed to go back to the house and if the little ones were not there—then—

"But they must be there," insisted Nellie, starting on a run over the swampy grounds toward the Cliffs.

And all this time Freddie and Flossie were quite unconcerned playing on the island.

"Oh, there's a man!" shouted Freddie, seeing someone in the woods. "Maybe it's Friday. Say there, Mister!" he shouted. "Say, will you help us get to land?"

The man heard the child's voice and hurried to the edge of the lake.

"Wall, I declare!" he exclaimed, "if them babies ain't lost out there. And here comes their boat. Well, I'll just fetch them in before they try to swim out," he told himself, swinging into the drifting boat, and with the stout stick he had in his hand, pushing off for the little island.

The island was quite near to shore on that side, and it was only a few minutes' work for the man to reach the children.

"What's your name?" he demanded, as soon as he touched land.

"Freddie Bobbsey," spoke up the little fellow, bravely, "and we live at the Cliffs."

"You do, eh? Then it was your brothers who brought my cow home, so I can pay them back by taking you home now. I can't row to the far shore with this stick, so we'll have to tramp it through the woods. Come along." and carefully he lifted the little ones into the boat, pushing to the woods, and started off to walk the round-about way, through the woods, to the bridge, then along the road back to the Cliffs, where a whole household was in great distress because of the twins' absence.

Chapter XVI

Dorothy's Doings

"Here they come!" called Nellie, who was searching around the barn, and saw the farmer with the two children crossing the hill.

"I'm Robinson Crusoe!" insisted Freddie, "and this is my man, Friday," he added, pointing to the farmer.

Of course it did not take long to clear up the mystery of the little ones' disappearance. But since his return Freddie acted like a hero, and certainly felt like one, and Flossie brought home with her a dainty bouquet of pink sebatia, that rare little flower so like a tiny wild rose. The farmer refused to take anything for his time and trouble, being glad to do our friends a favor.

Aunt Sarah and Harry were to leave for Meadow Brook that afternoon, but the worry over the children being lost made Aunt Sarah feel quite unequal to the journey, so Aunt Emily prevailed upon her to wait another day.

"There are so many dangers around here," remarked Aunt Sarah, when all the "scare" was over. "It is different in the country. We never worry about lost children out in Meadow Brook."

"But I often got lost out there," insisted Freddie. "Don't you re-member?"

Aunt Sarah had some recollection of the little fellow's adventures in that line, and laughed over them, now that they were recalled.

Late that afternoon Dorothy, Nan, and Nellie had a conference: that is, they talked with their heads so close together not even Flossie could get an idea of what they were planning. But it was certainly mischief, for Dorothy had most to say, and she would rather have a good joke than a good dinner any day, so Susan said.

Harry, Hal, and Bert had been chasing through the woods after a queer-looking bird. It was large, and had brilliant feathers, and when it rested for a moment on a tree it would pick at the bark as if it were trying to play a tune with its beak. Each time it struck the bark its head bobbed up and down in a queer way for a bird. But the boys could not get it. They set Hal's trap, and even used an air rifle in hopes of bringing it down without killing it, but the bird puttered from place to place, not in a very great hurry, but just fast enough to keep the boys busy chasing it.

That evening, at dinner, the strange bird was much talked about.

"Dat's a ban-shee!" declared Dinah, jokingly. "Dat bird came to bring a message from somebody. You boys will hear dat tonight, see if you doesn't," and she gave a very mysterious wink at Dorothy, who just then nearly choked with her dessert.

A few hours later the house was all quiet. The happenings of the day brought a welcome night, and tired little heads comfortably hugged their pillows.

It must have been about midnight, Bert was positive he had just heard the clock strike a lot of rings, surely a dozen or so, when at his window came a queer sound, like something pecking. At first Bert got it mixed up with his dreams, but as it continued longer and louder, he called to Harry, who slept in the alcove in Bert's room, and together the boys listened, attentively.

"That's the strange bird," declared Harry. "Sure enough it is bring-ing us a message, as Dinah said," and while the boys took the girl's words in a joke, they really seemed to be coming true.

"Don't light the gas," cautioned Bert, "or that will surely frighten it off. We can get our air guns, and I'll go crawl out on the veranda roof back of it, so as to get it if possible."

All this time the "peck-peck-peck" kept at the window, but just as soon as Bert went out in the hall to make his way through the storeroom window to the veranda roof, the pecking ceased. Harry hurried after Bert to tell him the bird was gone, and then together the boys put their heads out of their own window.

But there was not a sound, not even the distant flutter of a bird's wing to tell the boys the messenger had gone.

"Back to bed for us," said Harry, laughing. "I guess that bird is a joker and wants to keep us busy," and both boys being healthy were quite ready to fall off to sleep as soon as they felt it was of no use to stay awake longer looking for their feathered visitor.

"There it is again," called Bert, when Harry had just begun to dream of hazelnuts in Meadow Brook. "I'll get him this time!" and without waiting to go through the storeroom, Bert raised the window and bolted out on the roof.

"What's de matter down dere?" called Dinah from the window above. "'Pears like as if you boys had de nightmare. Can't you let nobody get a wink ob sleep? Ebbery time I puts my head down, bang! comes a noise and up pops my head. Now, what's a-ailin' ob you, Bert?" and the colored girl showed by her tone of voice she was not a bit angry, but "chock-full of laugh," as Bert whispered to Harry.

But the boys had not caught the bird, had not even seen it, for that matter.

Both Bert and Harry were now on the roof in their pajamas.

"What's—the—matter—there?" called Dorothy, in a very drowsy voice, from her window at the other end of the roof.

"What are you boys after?" called Uncle William, from a middle window.

"Anything the matter?" asked Aunt Sarah, anxiously, from the spare room.

"Got a burgulor?" shrieked Freddie, from the nursery.

"Do you want any help?" offered Susan, her head out of the top-floor window.

All these questions came so thick and fast on the heads of Bert and Harry that the boys had no idea of answering them. Certainly the bird was nowhere to be seen, and they did not feel like advertising their "April-fool game" to the whole house, so they decided to crawl into bed again and let others do the same.

The window in the boys' room was a bay, and each time the pecking disturbed them they thought the sound came from a different part of the window. Bert said it was the one at the left, so where the "bird" called from was left a mystery.

But neither boy had time to close his eyes before the noise started up again!

"Well, if that isn't a ghost it certainly is a ban-shee, as Dinah said," whispered Bert. "I'm going out to Uncle William's room and tell him. Maybe he will have better luck than we had," and so saying, Bert crept out into the hall and down two doors to his uncle's room.

Uncle William had also heard the sound.

"Don't make a particle of noise," cautioned the uncle, "and we can go up in the cupola and slide down a post so quietly the bird will not hear us," and as he said this, he, in his bath robe, went cautiously up the attic stairs, out of a small window, and slid down the post before Bert had time to draw his own breath.

But there was no bird to be seen anywhere!

"I heard it this very minute!" declared Harry, from the window.

"It might be bats!" suggested Uncle William. "But listen! I thought I heard the girls laughing," and at that moment an audible titter was making its way out of Nan's room!

"That's Dorothy's doings!" declared Uncle William, getting ready to laugh himself. "She's always playing tricks," and he began to feel about the outside ledge of the bay window.

But there was nothing there to solve the mystery.

"A tick-tack!" declared Harry, "I'll bet, from the girls' room!" and without waiting for another word he jumped out of his window, ran along the roof to Nan's room, and then grabbed something.

"Here it is!" he called, confiscating the offending property. "You just wait, girls!" he shouted in the window. "If we don't give you a good ducking in the ocean for this to-morrow!"

The laugh of the three girls in Nan's room made the joke on the boys more complete, and as Uncle William went back to his room he declared to Mrs. Bobbsey and Aunt Emily that his girl, Dorothy, was more fun than a dozen boys, and he would match her against that number for the best piece of good-natured fun ever played.

"A bird!" sneered Bert, making fun of himself for being so easily fooled.

"A girls' game of tick-tack!" laughed Harry, making up his mind that if he did not "get back at Dorothy," he would certainly have to haul in his colors as captain of the Boys' Brigade of Meadow Brook; "for she certainly did fool me," he admitted, turning over to sleep at last.

Chapter XVII

Old Friends

"Now, Aunt Sarah," pleaded Nan the next morning, "you might just as well wait and go home on the excursion train. All Meadow Brook will be down, and it will be so much pleasanter for you. The train will be here by noon and leave at three o'clock."

"But think of the hour that would bring us to Meadow Brook!" objected Aunt Sarah.

"Well, you will have lots of company, and if Uncle Daniel shouldn't meet you, you can ride up with the Hopkinses or anybody along your road."

Mrs. Bobbsey and Aunt Emily added their entreaties to Nan's, and Aunt Sarah finally agreed to wait.

"If I keep on," she said, "I'll be here all summer. And think of the fruit that's waiting to be preserved!"

"Hurrah!" shouted Bert, giving his aunt a good hug. "Then Harry and I can have a fine time with the Meadow Brook boys," and Bert dashed out to take the good news to Harry and Hal Bingham, who were out at the donkey house.

"Come on, fellows!" he called. "Down to the beach! We can have a swim before the crowd gets there." And with renewed interest the trio started off for the breakers.

"I would like to live at the beach all summer," remarked Harry. "Even in winter it must be fine here."

"It is," said Hal. "But the winds blow everything away regularly, and they all have to be carted back again each spring. This shore, with all its trimmings now, will look like a bald head by the first of December."

All three boys were fine swimmers, and they promptly struck off for the water that was "straightened out," as Bert said, beyond the tearing of the breakers at the edge. There were few people in the surf and the boys made their way around as if they owned the ocean.

Suddenly Hal thought he heard a call!

Then a man's arm appeared above the water's surface, a few yards away.

"Cramps," yelled Hal to Harry and Bert, while all three hurried to where the man's hand had been seen.

But it did not come up again.

"I'll dive down!" spluttered Hal, who had the reputation of being able to stay a long time under water.

It seemed quite a while to Bert and Harry before Hal came up again, but when he did he was trying to pull with him a big, fat man, who was all but unconscious.

"Can't move," gasped Hal, as the heavy burden was pulling him down.

Bit by bit the man with cramps gained a little strength, and with the boys' help he was towed in to shore.

There was not a life-guard in sight, and Hal had to hurry off to the pier for some restoratives, for the man was very weak. On his way, Hal met a guard who, of course, ran to the spot where Harry and Bert were giving the man artificial respiration.

"You boys did well!" declared the guard, promptly, seeing how hard they worked with the sick man.

"Yes—they saved—my life!" gasped the half-drowned man. "This little fellow"—pointing to Hal—"brought—me up—almost—from—the bottom!" and he caught his breath, painfully.

The man was assisted to a room at the end of the pier, and after a little while he became much better. Of course the boys did not stand around, being satisfied they could be of no more use.

"I must get those lads' names," declared the man to the guard. "Mine is ——," and he gave the name of the famous millionaire who had a magnificent summer home in another colony, three miles away.

"And you swam from the Cedars, Mr. Black," exclaimed the guard. "No wonder you got cramps."

An hour later the millionaire was walking the beach looking for the life-savers. He finally spied Hal.

"Here, there, you boy," he called, and Hal came in to the edge, but hardly recognized the man in street clothes.

"I want your name," demanded the stranger. "Do you know there are medals given to young heroes like you?"

"Oh, that was nothing," stammered Hal, quite confused now.

"Nothing! Why, I was about dead, and pulled on you with all my two hundred pounds. You knew, too, you had hardly a chance to bring me up. Yes, indeed, I want your name," and as he insisted, Hal reluctantly gave it, but felt quite foolish to make such a fuss "over nothing," as he said.

It was now about time for the excursion train to come in, so the boys left the water and prepared to meet their old friends.

"I hope Jack Hopkins comes," said Bert, for Jack was a great friend.

"Oh, he will be along," Harry remarked. "Nobody likes a good time better than Jack."

"Here they come!" announced Hal, the next minute, as a crowd of children with many lunch boxes came running down to the ocean.

"Hello there! Hello there!" called everybody at once, for, of course, all the children knew Harry and many also knew Bert.

There were Tom Mason, Jack Hopkins, August Stout, and Ned Prentice in the first crowd, while a number of girls, friends of Nan's, were in another group. Nan, Nellie, and Dorothy had been detained by somebody further up on the road, but were now coming down, slowly.

Such a delight as the ocean was to the country children!

As each roller slipped out on the sands the children unconsciously followed it, and so, many unsuspected pairs of shoes were caught by the next wave that washed in.

"Well, here comes Uncle Daniel!" called Bert, as, sure enough, down to the edge came Uncle Daniel with Dorothy holding on one arm, Nan clinging to the other, while Nellie carried his small satchel.

Santa Claus could hardly have been more welcome to the Bobbseys at that moment than was Uncle Daniel. They simply overpowered him, as the surprise of his coming made the treat so much better. The girls had "dragged him" down to the ocean, he said, when he had intended first going to Aunt Emily's.

"I must see the others," he insisted; "Freddie and Flossie."

"Oh, they are all coming down," Nan assured him. "Aunt Sarah, too, is coming."

"All right, then," agreed Uncle Daniel. "I'll wait awhile. Well, Harry, you look like an Indian. Can you see through that coat of tan?"

Harry laughed and said he had been an Indian in having a good time.

Presently somebody jumped up on Uncle Daniel's back. As he was sitting on the sands the shock almost brought him down. Of course it was Freddie, who was so overjoyed he really treated the good-natured uncle a little roughly.

"Freddie boy! Freddie boy!" exclaimed Uncle Daniel, giving his nephew a good long hug. "And you have turned Indian, too! Where's that sea-serpent you were going to catch for me?"

"I'll get him yet," declared the little fellow. "It hasn't rained hardly since we came down, and they only come in to land out of the rain."

This explanation made Uncle Daniel laugh heartily. The whole family sat around on the sands, and it was like being in the country and at the seashore at the one time, Flossie declared.

The boys, of course, were in the water. August Stout had not learned much about swimming since he fell off the plank while fishing in Meadow Brook, so that out in the waves the other boys had great fun with their fat friend.

"And there is Nettie Prentice!" exclaimed Nan, suddenly, as she espied her little country friend looking through the crowd, evidently searching for friends.

"Oh, Nan!" called Nettie, in delight, "I'm just as glad to see you as I am to see the ocean, and I never saw that before," and the two little girls exchanged greetings of genuine love for each other.

"Won't we have a perfectly splendid time?" declared Nan. "Dorothy, my cousin, is so jolly, and here's Nellie—you remember her?"

Of course Nettie did remember her, and now all the little girls went around hunting for fun in every possible corner where fun might be hidden.

As soon as the boys were satisfied with their bath they went in search of the big sun umbrellas, so that Uncle William, Aunt Emily, Mrs. Bobbsey, and Aunt Sarah might sit under the sunshades, while eating lunch. Then the boys got long boards and arranged them from bench to bench in picnic style, so that all the Meadow Brook friends might have a pleasant time eating their box lunches.

"Let's make lemonade," suggested Hal. "I know where I can get a pail of nice clean water."

"I'll buy the lemons," offered Harry.

"I'll look after sugar," put in Bert.

"And I'll do the mixing," declared August Stout, while all set to work to produce the wonderful picnic lemonade.

"Now, don't go putting in white sand instead of sugar," teased Uncle Daniel, as the "caterers," with sleeves rolled up, worked hard over the lemonade.

"What can we use for cups ?" asked Nan.

"Oh, I know," said Harry, "over at the Indian stand they have a lot of gourds, the kind of mock oranges that Mexicans drink out of. I can buy them for five cents each, and after the picnic we can bring them home and hang them up for souvenirs."

"Just the thing!" declared Hal, who had a great regard for things that hang up and look like curios. "I'll go along and help you make the bargain."

When the boys came back they had a dozen of the funny drinking cups.

The long crooked handles were so queer that each person tried to get the cup to his or her mouth in a different way.

"We stopped at the hydrant and washed the gourds thoroughly," declared Hal, "so you need not expect to find any Mexican diamonds in them."

"Or tarantulas," put in Uncle Daniel.

"What's them?" asked Freddie, with an ear for anything that sounded like a menagerie.

"A very bad kind of spider, that sometimes comes in fruit from other countries," explained Uncle Daniel. Then Nan filled his gourd from the dipper that stood in the big pail of lemonade, and he smacked his lips in appreciation.

There was so much to do and so much to see that the few hours allowed the excursionists slipped by all too quickly. Dorothy ran away and soon returned with her donkey cart, to take Nettie Prentice and a few of Nettie's friends for a ride along the beach. Nan and Nellie did not go, preferring to give the treat to the little country girls.

"Now don't go far," directed Aunt Emily, for Aunt Sarah and Uncle Daniel were already leaving the beach to make ready for the train. Of course Harry and Aunt Sarah were all "packed up" and had very little to do at Aunt Emily's before starting.

Hal and Bert were sorry, indeed, to have Harry go, for Harry was such a good leader in outdoor sports, his country training always standing by him in emergencies.

Finally Dorothy came back with the girls from their ride, and the people were beginning to crowd into the long line of cars that waited on a switch near the station.

"Now, Nettie, be sure to write to me," said Nan, bidding her little friend good-by.

"And come down next year," insisted Dorothy.

"I had such a lovely time," declared Nettie. "I'm sure I will come again if I can."

The Meadow Brook Bobbseys had secured good seats in the middle car,—Aunt Sarah thought that the safest,—and now the locomotive whistle was tooting, calling the few stragglers who insisted on waiting at the beach until the very last minute.

Freddie wanted to cry when he realized that Uncle Daniel, Aunt Sarah, and even Harry were going away, but with the promises of meeting again Christmas, and possibly Thanksgiving, all the good-bys were said, and the excursion train puffed out on its long trip to dear old Meadow Brook, and beyond.

Chapter XVIII

THE STORM

When Uncle William Minturn came in from the city that evening he had some mysterious news. Everybody guessed it was about Nellie, but as surprises were always cropping up at Ocean Cliff, the news was kept secret and the whispering increased.

"I had hard work to get her to come," said Uncle William to Mrs. Bobbsey, still guarding the mystery, "but I finally prevailed upon her and she will be down on the morning train."

"Poor woman, I am sure it will do her good," remarked Mrs. Bobbsey. "Your house has been a regular hotel this summer," she said to Mr. Minturn.

"That's what we are here for," he replied. "We would not have much pleasure, I am sure, if our friends were not around us."

"Did you hear anything more about the last vessel?" asked Aunt Emily.

"Yes, I went down to the general office today, and an incoming steamer was sure it was the West Indies vessel that was sighted four days ago."

"Then they should be near port now?" asked Mrs. Bobbsey.

"They ought to be," replied Uncle William, "but the cargo is so heavy, and the schooner such a very slow sailer, that it takes a long time to cover the distance."

Next morning, bright and early, Dorothy had the donkeys in harness.

"We are going to the station to meet some friends, Nellie," she said. "Come along?"

"What! More company?" exclaimed Nellie. "I really ought to go home. I am well and strong now."

"Indeed you can't go until we let you," said Dorothy, laughing. "I suppose you think all the fun went with Harry," she added, teasingly, for Dorothy knew Nellie had been acting lonely ever since the carnival. She was surely homesick to see her mother and talk about the big prize.

The two girls had not long to wait at the station, for the train pulled in just as they reached the platform. Dorothy looked about a little uneasily.

"We must watch for a lady in a linen suit with black hat," she said to Nellie; "she's a stranger."

That very minute the linen suit appeared.

"Oh, oh!" screamed Nellie, unable to get her words. "There is my mother!" and the next thing Dorothy knew, Nellie was trying to "wear the same linen dress" that the stranger appeared in—at least, that was how Dorothy afterwards told about Nellie's meeting with her mother.

"My daughter!" exclaimed the lady, "I have been so lonely I came to bring you home."

"And this is Dorothy," said Nellie, recovering herself. "Dorothy is my best friend, next to Nan."

"You have surely been among good friends," declared the mother, "for you have gotten the roses back in your cheeks again. How well you do look!"

"Oh, I've had a perfectly fine time," declared Nellie.

"Fine and dandy," repeated Dorothy, unable to restrain her fun-making spirit.

At a glance Dorothy saw why Nellie, although poor, was so genteel, for her mother was one of those fine-featured women that seem especially fitted to say gentle things to children.

Mrs. McLaughlin was not old,—no older than Nan's mother,—and she had that wonderful wealth of brown hair, just like Nellie's. Her eyes were brown, too, while Nellie's were blue, but otherwise Nellie was much like her mother, so people said.

Aunt Emily and Mrs. Bobbsey had visited Mrs. McLaughlin in the city, so that they were quite well acquainted when the donkey cart drove up, and they all had a laugh over the surprise to Nellie. Of course that was Uncle William's secret, and the mystery of the whispering the evening before.

"But we must go back on the afternoon train," insisted Mrs. McLaughlin, who had really only come down to the shore to bring Nellie home.

"Indeed, no," objected Aunt Emily, "that would be too much traveling in one day. You may go early in the morning."

"Everybody is going home," sighed Dorothy. "I suppose you will be the next to go, Nan," and she looked quite lonely at the prospect.

"We are going to have a big storm," declared Susan, who had just come in from the village. "We have had a long dry spell, now we are going to make up for it."

"Dear me," sighed Mrs. McLaughlin, "I wish we had started for home."

"Oh, there's lots of fun here in a storm," laughed Dorothy. "The ocean always tries to lick up the whole place, but it has to be satisfied with pulling down pavilions and piers. Last year the water really went higher than the gas lights along the boulevard."

"Then that must mean an awful storm at sea," reflected Nellie's mother. "Storms are bad enough on land, but at sea they must be dreadful!" And she looked out toward the wild ocean, that was keeping from her the fate of her husband.

Long before there were close signs of storm, life-guards, on the beach, were preparing for it. They were making fast everything that could be secured and at the life-saving station all possible preparations were being made to help those who might suffer from the storm.

It was nearing September and a tidal wave had swept over the southern ports. Coming in all the way from the tropics the storm had made itself felt over a great part of the world, in some places taking the shape of a hurricane.

On this particular afternoon, while the sun still shone brightly over Sunset Beach, the storm was creeping in under the big waves that dashed up on the sands.

"It is not safe to let go the ropes," the guards told the people, but the idea of a storm, from such a pretty sky, made some daring enough to disobey these orders. The result was that the guards were kept busy trying to bring girls and women to their feet, who were being dashed around by the excited waves.

This work occupied the entire afternoon, and as soon as the crowd left the beach the life-guards brought the boats down to the edge, got their lines ready, and when dark came on, they were prepared for the life-patrol,—the long dreary watch of the night, so near the noisy waves, and so far from the voice of distress that might call over the breakers to the safe shores, where the life-savers waited, watched, and listened.

The rain began to fall before it was entirely dark. The lurid sunset, glaring through the dark and rain, gave an awful, yellow look to the land and sea alike.

"It is like the end of the world," whispered Nellie to Nan, as the two girls looked out of the window to see the wild storm approaching.

Then the lightning came in blazing blades, cutting through the gathering clouds.

The thunder was only like muffled rolls, for the fury of the ocean deadened every other sound of heaven or earth.

"It will be a dreadful storm," said Aunt Emily to Mrs. Bobbsey. "We must all go into the sitting room and pray for the sailors."

Everyone in the house assembled in the large sitting room, and Uncle William led the prayers. Poor Mrs. McLaughlin did not once raise her head. Nellie, too, hid her pale face in her hands.

Dorothy was frightened, and when all were saying good-night she pressed a kiss on Nellie's cheek, and told her that the life-savers on Sunset Beach would surely be able to save all the sailors that came that way during the big storm.

Nellie and her mother occupied the same room. Of course the mother had been told that the long delayed boat had been sighted, and now, how anxiously she awaited more news of Nellie's father.

"We must not worry," she told Nellie, "for who knows but the storm may really help father's boat to get into port?"

So, while the waves lashed furiously upon Sunset Beach, all the people in the Minturn cottage were sleeping, or trying to sleep, for, indeed, it was not easy to rest when there was so much danger at their very door.

Chapter XIX

LIFE-SAVERS

"Mother, mother!" called Nellie, "look down at the beach. The life-guards are burning the red signal lights! They have found a wreck!"

It was almost morning, but the black storm clouds held the daylight back. Mrs. McLaughlin and her little daughter strained their eyes to see, if possible, what might be going on down at the beach. While there was no noise to give the alarm, it seemed, almost everybody in that house felt the presence of the wreck, for in a very few minutes, Bert was at his window, Dorothy and Nan were looking out of theirs, while the older members of the household were dressing hastily, to see if they might be of any help in case of accident at the beach.

"Can I go with you, Uncle?" called Bert, who had heard his uncle getting ready to run down to the water's edge.

"Yes, come along," answered Mr. Minturn, and as day began to peep through the heavy clouds, the two hurried down to the spot where the life-guards were burning their red light to tell the sailors their signal had been seen.

"There's the vessel!" exclaimed Bert, as a rocket flew up from the water.

"Yes, that's the distress signal," replied the uncle. "It is lucky that daylight is almost here."

Numbers of other cottagers were hurrying to the scene now, Mr. Bingham and Hal being among the first to reach the spot.

"It's a schooner," said Mr. Bingham to Mr. Minturn, "and she has a very heavy cargo."

The sea was so wild it was impossible to send out the life-savers' boats, so the guards were making ready the breeches buoy.

"They are going to shoot the line out now," explained Hal to Bert, as the two-wheel car with the mortar or cannon was dragged down to the ocean's edge.

Instantly there shot out to sea a ball of thin cord. To this cord was fastened a heavy rope or cable.

"They've got it on the schooner." exclaimed a man, for the thin cord was now pulling the cable line out, over the water.

"What's that board for?" asked Bert, as he saw a board following the cable.

"That's the directions," said Hal.

"They are printed in a number of languages, and they tell the crew to carry the end of the cable high up the mast and fasten it strongly there."

"Oh, I see," said Bert, "the line will stretch then, and the breeches buoy will go out on a pulley."

"That's it," replied Hal. "See, there goes the buoy," and then the queer-looking life-preserver made of cork, and shaped like breeches, swung out over the waves.

It was clear day now, and much of the wicked storm had passed. Its effect upon the sea was, however, more furious every hour, for while the storm had left the land, it was raging somewhere else, and the sensitive sea felt every throb of the excited elements.

With the daylight came girls and women to the beach.

Mrs. Bobbsey, Mrs. Minturn, Nellie and her mother, besides Dorothy and Nan, were all there; Flossie and Freddie being obliged to stay home with Dinah and Susan.

Of course the girls asked all sorts of questions and Bert and Hal tried to answer them as best they could.

It seemed a long time before any movement of the cable showed that the buoy was returning.

"THERE'S A MAN IN IT!" EXCLAIMED THE BOYS.

"Here she comes! Here she comes!" called the crowd presently, as the black speck far out, and the strain on the cord, showed the buoy was coming back.

Up and down in the waves it bobbed, sometimes seeming to go all the way under. Nearer and nearer it came, until now a man's head could be seen.

"There's a man in it!" exclaimed the boys, all excitement, while the life-guards pulled the cord steadily, dragging in their human freight.

The girls and women were too frightened to talk, and Nellie clung close to her mother.

A big roller dashing in finished the work for the life-guards, and a man in the cork belt bounded upon shore.

He was quite breathless when the guards reached him, but insisted on walking up instead of being carried. Soon he recovered himself and the rubber protector was pulled off his face.

Everybody. gathered around, and Nellie with a strange face, and a stranger hope, broke through the crowd to see the rescued man.

"Oh—it is—my—father!" she screamed, falling right into the arms of the drenched man.

"Be careful," called Mr. Minturn, fearing the child might be mistaken, or Mrs. McLaughlin might receive too severe a shock from the surprise.

But the half-drowned man rubbed his eyes as if he could not believe them, then the next minute he pressed his little daughter to his heart, unable to speak a word.

What a wonderful scene it was!

The child almost unconscious in her father's arms, he almost dead from exhaustion, and the wife and mother too overcome to trust herself to believe it could be true.

Even the guards, who were busy again at the ropes, having left the man to willing hands on the beach, could not hide their surprise over the fact that it was mother, father, and daughter there united under such strange conditions.

"My darling, my darling!" exclaimed the sailor to Nellie, as he raised himself and then he saw his wife.

Mrs. Bobbsey had been holding Mrs. McLaughlin back, but now the sailor was quite recovered, so they allowed her to speak to him.

Mr. Bingham and Hal had been watching it all, anxiously.

"Are you McLaughlin?" suddenly asked Mr. Bingham.

"I am," replied the sailor.

"And is George Bingham out there?" anxiously asked the brother.

"Safe and well," came the welcome answer. "Just waiting for his turn to come in."

"Oh!" screamed Dorothy, "Hal's uncle is saved too. I guess our prayers were heard last night."

"Here comes another man!" exclaimed the people, as this time a big man dashed on the sands.

"All right!" exclaimed the man, as he landed, for he had had a good safe swing in, and was in no way exhausted.

"Hello there!" called Mr. Bingham: "Well, if this isn't luck. George Bingham!"

Sure enough it was Hal's Uncle George, and Hal was hugging the big wet man, while the man was jolly, and laughing as if the whole thing were a good joke instead of the life-and-death matter it had been.

"I only came in to tell you," began George Bingham, "that we are all right, and the boat is lifting off the sand bar we stuck on. But I'm glad I came in to—the reception," he said, laughing. "So you've found friends, McLaughlin," he added, seeing the little family united. "Why, how do you do, Mrs. McLaughlin?" he went on, offering her his hand. "And little Nellie! Well, I declare, we did land on a friendly shore."

Just as Mr. Bingham said, the life-saving work turned out to be a social affair, for there was a great time greeting Nellie's father and Hal's uncle.

"Wasn't it perfectly splendid that Nellie and her mother were here!" declared Dorothy.

"And Hal and his father, too," put in Nan. "It is just like a story in a book."

"But we don't have to look for the pictures," chimed in Bert, who was greatly interested in the sailors, as well as in the work of the life-saving corps.

As Mr. Bingham told the guards it would not be necessary to haul any more men in, and as the sea was calm enough now to launch a life-boat, both Nellie's father and Hal's uncle insisted on going back to the vessel to the other men.

Nellie was dreadfully afraid to have her father go out on the ocean again, but he only laughed at her fears, and said he would soon be in to port, to go home with her, and never go on the big, wild ocean again.

Two boats were launched, a strong guard going in each, with Mr. McLaughlin in one and Mr. Bingham in the other, and now they pulled out steadily over the waves, back to the vessel that was freeing itself from the sand bar.

What a morning that was at Sunset Beach!

The happiness of two families seemed to spread all through the little colony, and while the men were thinking of the more serious work of helping the sailors with their vessel, the girls and women were planning a great welcome for the men who had been saved from the waves.

"I'm so glad we prayed," said little Flossie to Freddie, when she heard the good news.

"It was Uncle William prayed the loudest," insisted Freddie, believing, firmly, that to reach heaven a long and loud prayer is always best.

"But we all helped," declared his twin sister, while surely the angels had listened to even the sleepy whisper of the little ones, who had asked help for the poor sailors in their night of peril.

Chapter XX

THE HAPPY REUNION

A beautiful day had grown out of the dreadful storm.

The sun seemed stronger each time it made its way out from behind a cloud, just as little girls and boys grow strong in body by exercise, and strong in character by efforts to do right.

And everybody was so happy.

The Neptune—the vessel that had struck on the sand bar—was now safely anchored near shore, and the sailors came in and out in row-boats, back and forth to land, just as they wished.

Of course Captain Bingham, Hal's uncle, was at the Bingham cottage, and the first mate, Nellie's father, was at Minturn's.

But that evening there was a regular party on Minturn's veranda. Numbers of cottagers called to see the sailors, and all were invited to remain and hear about the strange voyage of the Neptune.

"There is not much to tell," began the captain. "Of course I knew we were going to have trouble getting that mahogany. Two vessels had been wrecked trying to get it, so when we got to the West Indies I decided to try canoes and not risk sails, where the wind always blew such a gale, it dragged any anchor that could be dropped. Well, it was a long, slow job to drag those heavy logs around that point, and just when we were making headway, along comes a storm that drove the schooner and canoes out of business."

Here Mate McLaughlin told about the big storm and how long it took the small crew to repair the damage done to the sails.

"Then we had to go back to work at the logs," went on the captain, "and then one of our crew took a fever. Well, then we were quarantined. Couldn't get things to eat without a lot of trouble, and couldn't go on with the carting until the authorities decided the fever was not serious. That was what delayed us so.

"Finally, we had every log loaded on the schooner and we started off. But I never could believe any material would be as heavy as that mahogany; why, we just had to creep along, and the least contrary wind left us motionless on the sea.

"We counted on getting home last week, when this last storm struck us and drove us out of our course. But we are not sorry for our delay now, since we have come back to our own."

"About the value?" asked Mr. Bobbsey, who was down from the city.

"The value," repeated the captain aside, so that the strangers might not hear. "Well, I'm a rich man now, and so is my mate, McLaughlin, for that wood was contracted for by the largest and richest piano firm in this country, and now it is all but delivered to them and the money in our hands."

"Then it was well worth all your sacrifice?" said Mr. Minturn.

"Yes, indeed. It would have taken us a lifetime to accumulate as much money as we have earned in this year. Of course, it was hard for the men who had families, McLaughlin especially; the others were all working sailors, but he was a landsman and my partner in the enterprise; but I will make it up to him, and the mahogany hunt will turn out the best paying piece of work he ever undertook."

"Oh, isn't it perfectly splendid!" declared Nan and Dorothy, hugging Nellie. "You will never again have to go back to that horrid store that made you so pale, and your mother will have a lovely time and nothing to worry about."

"I can hardly believe it all," replied their little friend. "But having father back is the very best of all."

"But all the same," sighed Dorothy, "I just know you will all be going home before we leave for the city, and I shall just die of loneliness."

"But we have to go to school," said Nan, "and we have only a few days more."

"Of course," continued Dorothy; "and our school will not open for two weeks yet."

"Maybe Aunt Emily will take you down to the city on her shopping tour," suggested Nan.

"Indeed I do not like shopping," answered the cousin. "Every time I go in a store that is crowded with stuff on the counters under people's elbows, I feel like knocking the things all over. I did a lot of damage that way once. It was holiday time, and a counter that stuck out in the middle of the store was full of little statues. My sleeve touched one, and the whole lot fell down as if a cannon had struck them. I broke ten and injured more than I wanted to count."

"And Aunt Emily had to pay for them?" said Nan.

"No, she didn't, either," corrected Dorothy. "The manager came up and said the things should not be put out in people's way. He made the clerks remove all the truck from the aisles and I guess everybody was glad the army fell down. I never can forget those pink-and-white soldiers," and Dorothy straightened herself up in comical "soldier's arms" fashion, imitating the unfortunate statues.

"I hope you can come to Lakeport for Thanksgiving," said Nan. "We have done so much visiting this summer, out to Aunt Sarah's and down here, mamma feels we ought to have a grand reunion at our house next. If we do, I am going to try to have some of the country girls down and give them all a jolly good time."

"Oh, I'll come if you make it jolly," answered Dorothy. "If there is one thing in this world worth while, it is fun," and she tossed her yellow head about like a buttercup, that has no other way of laughing.

That had been an eventful day at Ocean Cliff, and the happy ending of it, with a boat and its crew saved, was, as some of the children said, just like a story in a book, only the pictures were all alive!

The largest hotel at Sunset Beach was thrown open to the sailors that night, and here Captain Bingham and Mate McLaughlin, together with the rest of the crew, took up comfortable lodgings.

It was very late, long after the little party had scattered from Minturn's piazza, that the sailors finished dancing their hornpipe for the big company assembled to greet them in the hotel.

Never had they danced to such fine music before, for the hotel orchestra played the familiar tune and the sailors danced it nimbly, hitching up first one side then the other—crossing first one leg then the other, and wheeling around in that jolly fashion.

How rugged and handsome the men looked! The rough ocean winds had tanned them like bronze, and their muscles were as firm and strong almost as the cables that swing out with the buoys. The wonderful fresh air that these men lived in, night and day, had brightened their eyes too, so that even the plainest face, and the most awkward man among them, was as nimble as an athlete, from his perfect exercise.

"And last night what an awful experience they had!" remarked one of the spectators. "It is no wonder that they are all so happy to-night."

"Besides," added someone else, "they are all going to receive extra good pay, for the captain and mate will be very rich when the cargo is landed."

So the sailors danced until they were tired, and then after a splendid meal they went to sleep, in as comfortable beds as might be found in any hotel on Sunset Beach.

Chapter XXI

Good-By

"I don't know how to say good-by to you," Nellie told Dorothy and Nan next morning. "To think how kind you have been to me, and how splendidly it has all turned out! Now father is home again, I can hardly believe it! Mother told me last night she was going to put back what money she had to use out of my prize, the fifty dollars you know, and I am to make it a gift to the Fresh Air Fund."

"Oh, that will be splendid!" declared Nan. "Perhaps they will buy another tent with it, for they need more room out at Meadow Brook."

"You are quite rich now, aren't you?" remarked Dorothy. "I suppose your father will buy a big house, and maybe next time we meet you, you will put on airs and walk like this?" and Dorothy went up and down the room like the pictures of Cinderella's proud sisters.

"No danger," replied Nellie, whose possible tears at parting had been quickly chased away by the merry Dorothy. "But I hope we will have a nice home, for mother deserves it, besides I am just proud enough to want to entertain a few young ladies, among them Miss Nan Bobbsey and Miss Dorothy Minturn."

"And we will be on hand, thank you," replied the joking Dorothy. "Be sure to have ice cream and chocolates—I want some good fresh chocolates. Those we get down here always seem soft and salty, like the spray."

"Come, Nellie," called Mrs. McLaughlin, "I am ready. Where is your hat?"

"Oh, yes, mother, I'm coming!" replied Nellie.

Bert had the donkey cart hitched and there was now no time to spare. Nellie kissed Freddie and Flossie affectionately, and promised to bring the little boy all through a big city, real fire-engine house when he came to see her.

"And can I ring the bell and make the horses jump?" he asked.

"We might be able to manage that, too," Nellie told him. "My uncle is a fireman and he can take us through his engine house."

Nan went to the station with her friends, and when the last good-bys were said and the train steamed out, the twins turned back again to the Minturn Cottage.

"Our turn next," remarked Bert, as he pulled the donkeys into the drive.

"Yes, it seems it is nothing but going and coming all the time. I wonder if all the other girls will be home at Lakeport in time for the first day of school?" said Nan.

"Most of them, I guess," answered Bert. "Well, we have had a good vacation, and I am willing to go to work again."

"So am I!" declared Nan. "Vacation was just long enough, I think."

Mr. Bobbsey was down from the city, of course, to take the family

home, and now all hands, even Freddie and Flossie, were busy packing up. There were the shells to be looked after, the fish nets, besides
Downy, the duck, and Snoop, the cat.

"And just to add one more animal to your menagerie," said Uncle
William, "I have brought you a little goldfinch. It will sing beautifully
for you, and be easy to carry in its little wooden cage. Then, I have
ordered, sent directly to your house, a large cage for him to live in, so
he will have plenty of freedom, and perhaps Christmas you may get
some more birds to put in the big house, to keep Dick company."

Of course Freddie was delighted with the gift, for it was really a
beautiful little bird, with golden wings, and a much prettier pet than a
duck or a cat, although he still loved his old friends.

The day passed very quickly with all that was crowded into it: the
last ocean bath taking up the best part of two hours, while a sail in Hal's
canoe did away with almost as much, more time. Dorothy gave Nan a
beautiful little gold locket with her picture in it, and Flossie received the
dearest little real shell pocketbook ever seen. Hal Bingham gave Bert a
magnifying glass, to use at school in chemistry or physics, so that every
one of the Bobbseys received a suitable souvenir of Sunset Beach.

"You-uns must be to bed early and not go sleep in de train," insisted Dinah, when Freddie and Flossie pleaded for a little more time
on the veranda that evening. "Come along now; Dinah hab lots to do
too," and with her little charges the good-natured colored girl hobbled
off, promising to tell Freddie how Nellie's father and Hal's uncle were
to get into port again when they set out to sea, instead of trying to get
the big boat into land at Sunset Beach.

And so our little friends had spent all their vacation.

The last night at the seashore was passed, and the early morning
found them once more traveling away—this time for dear old home,
sweet home.

"If we only didn't have to leave our friends," complained Nan,
brushing back a tear, as the very last glint of Cousin Dorothy's yellow
head passed by the train window.

"I hope we will meet them all soon again," said Nan's mother. "It
is not long until Thanksgiving. Then, perhaps, we can give a real
harvest party out at Lakeport and try to repay our friends for some of
their hospitality to us."

"Well, I like Hal Bingham first-rate," declared Bert, thinking of the friend from whom he had just parted.

"There goes the last of the ocean. Look!" called Flossie, as the train made a turn, and whistled a good-by to the *Bobbsey Twins at the Seashore.*

END OF

"The Bobbsey Twins at the Seashore"

BY LAURA LEE HOPE

END OF

"The Bobbsey Twins Collection, Volume 1"

FLYING CHIPMUNK PUBLISHING
Fairy Tale Collections
The Andrew Lang Fairy Book Series:

The Blue Fairy Book - 978-1-60459-547-5   The Red Fairy Book - 978-1-60459-544-4
The Green Fairy Book - 978-1-60459-549-9   The Yellow Fairy Book - 978-1-60459-545-1
The Crimson Fairy Book - 978-1-60459-759-2   The Grey Fairy Book - 978-1-60459-756-1
The Violet Fairy Book - 978-1-60459-548-2   The Pink Fairy Book - 978-1-60459-751-6
The Brown Fairy Book - 978-1-60459-758-5   The Lilac Fairy Book - 978-1-60459-794-3
The Orange Fairy Book - 978-1-60459-797-4   The OliveFairy Book - 978-1-60459-795-0

The Joseph Jacobs Folk and Fairy Tale Series:

English Folk & Fairy Tales - 978-1-60459-870-4
More English Folk & Fairy Tales - 978-1-60459-871-1
Celtic Folk & Fairy Tales - 978-1-60459-869-8
More Celtic Folk & Fairy Tales - 978-1-60459-876-6
Indian Folk & Fairy Tales - 978-1-60459-877-3
European Folk & Fairy Tales - 978-1-60459-878-0

Joseph Jacobs' English, More English & Indian Folk & Fairy Tales
978-1-60459-903-9 (Hardcover), 978-1-60459-895-7 (Paperback)

Joseph Jacobs' Celtic, More Celtic & European Folk & Fairy Tales
978-1-60459-904-6 (Hardcover), 978-1-60459-896-4 (Paperback)

Other Fairy Tale Collections

The Red Indian Fairy Book, by *Frances Jenkins Olcott* - 978-1-60459-753-0
The Japanese Fairy Book, by *Yei Theodora Ozaki* - 978-1-60459-754-7
Irish Fairy and Folk Tales, by *William B. Yeats* - 978-1-60459-796-7

Collections for
Adults and Children

Halloween Games and Ghost Stories - 978-1-60459-483-6
Charles Dickens' Other Christmas Stories - 978-1-60459-488-1
Charles Dicken's Christmas Stories - 978-1-60459-490-4
          (*Collected from* Household Words *and* All the Year Round)
Thanksgiving, An American Holiday - 978-1-60459-750-9
The One-Hoss-Shay, How the Old Hoss won the Bet, & The Broomstick
          Train, by *Oliver Wendell Holmes, Sr.* - 978-1-60459-872-8
Mr. Richard Hannay's War Adventures, by *John Buchan* - 978-1-60459-905-3
          (The 39 Steps, Greenmantle, & Mr. Standfast)
Ghost Masters, Volume 1 - Victorian ghost stories - 978-1-60459-486-7
Ghost Masters, Volume 2 - Victorian ghost stories - 978-1-60459-485-0

All available from Amazon.com

FLYING CHIPMUNK PUBLISHING

FOR CHILDREN 7 - 12

THE BOBBSEY TWINS

by Laura Lee Hope

One of the longest running story series for children is *The Bobbsey Twins*. Follow the adventures of two sets of young twins at the turn of the Twentieth Century when there were no telephones, radios, and televisions, and horses and carriages were common. The twins enjoy wonderful days filled with sunshine and love with their playmates, Grace, Nellie, and Charlie, and get into and out of trouble as only little kids can manage. Their cat, Snoop, (and after book #4, "*The Bobbsey Twins at School*," their dog Snap, too) goes along on many of their adventures as they build snow houses, ice boats and kites, explore islands and boats, help their friends, and even save chickens from a flood! First pubished in 1904, each volume includes the original illustrations.

THE BOBBSEY TWINS, VOLUME 1 — 978-1-60459-980-0
> *The Bobbsey Twins, Merry Days Indoors and Out*
> *The Bobbsey Twins in the Country*
> *The Bobbsey Twins at the Seashore*

THE BOBBSEY TWINS, VOLUME 2 — 978-1-60459-982-4
> *The Bobbsey Twins at School*
> *The Bobbsey Twins at Snow Lodge*
> *The Bobbsey Twins on a Houseboat*

THE SIX LITTLE BUNKERS

by Laura Lee Hope

Another famous series is *The Six Little Bunkers*. Delightful stories for little boys and girls which sprang into immediate popularity when they first appeared in 1918. To know the six little Bunkers is to take them at once to your heart. Each story has a little plot of its own—one that can be easily followed—and all are written in a most entertaining manner. Join the fun, and mischief, as two parents try to keep track, and control, of six small children who are always exploring everything around them. Each volume includes the original illustrations.

THE SIX LITTLE BUNKERS, VOLUME 1 — 978-1-60459-983-1
> *The Six Little Bunkers at Grandma Bell's*
> *The Six Little Bunkers at Aunt Jo's*

THE SIX LITTLE BUNKERS VOLUME 2 — 978-1-60459-984-8
> *The Six Little Bunkers at Cousin Tom's*
> *The Six Little Bunkers at Grandpa Ford's*

All available from Amazon.com

FLYING CHIPMUNK PUBLISHING
JUVENILE STORIES FOR TEENAGERS!

THE MOVING PICTURE GIRLS
By Arthur M. Winfield

"*The Moving Picture Girls*" are the adventures of Ruth, age 17, and Alice age 15, DeVere, two young girls who live with their father, a widower and a theater actor, who is forced to leave his profession for the "Silent Movies." Both girls aid him in his work and visit the many localitiesthese pictures are filmed at, as well as act in the movies themselves. This is what it was like when Hollywood was still a dream-in-the-making, and every stunt was performed live in front of a camera without computer-graphics. First published in 1914-15, each volume includes the original *frontispiece* illustrations.

THE MOVING PICTURE GIRLS, VOLUME 1 — 978-1-61720-028-1
 ...First Appearances in Photo Dramas
 ...At Oak Farm—Queer Happenings While Taking Rural Plays

THE MOVING PICTURE GIRLS, VOLUME 2 — 978-1-61720-029-8
 ...Snowbound—The Proof on the Film
 ...Under the Palms—Lost in the Wilds of Florida

THE MOVING PICTURE GIRLS, VOLUME 3 — 978-1-61720-030-4
 ...At Rocky Ranch—Great Days Among the Cowboys
 ...At Sea—A Pictured Shipwreck that Became Real

THE SUBMARINE BOYS
by Victor G. Durham

A voyage in an undersea boat! What boy has not done so time and again in his youthful dreams? "*The Submarine Boys*" did it in reality, diving into the dark depths of the sea, then, like Father Neptune, rising dripping from the deep to sunlight and safety. Yet it was not all easy sailing for the Submarine Boys, for these hardy young "undersea sailors" experienced a full measure of excitement and had their share of thrills, as all who sail the seas are certain to do. The author knows undersea boats, and the reader who voyages with him may look forward to an instructive as well as lively cruise as *the Submarine Boys* fend off spies, saboteurs, and jealous rivals. First published in 1909, this volume includes the original illustrations.

THE SUBMARINE BOYS, VOLUME 1 — 978-1-61720-031-1
 ...On Duty—Life on a Diving Torpedo Boat
 ...Trial Trip—"Making Good" as Young Experts

All available from Amazon.com

FLYING CHIPMUNK PUBLISHING

JUVENILE STORIES FOR TEENAGERS!

UNCLE SAM'S BOYS

H. Irving Hancock

These stimulating stories are among the best of their class. They breathe the life and spirit of our army of today (or at least, as it was in 1910), and in which Uncle Sam's Boys fought with a courage and devotion excelled by none in the World War. This series tells the story of a soldier's life from the rookie stage until he has qualified for an officer's commission. First published in 1910-12, each volume includes the original illustrations.

UNCLE SAM'S BOYS, VOLUME 1 — 978-1-61720-032-8
  ...In the Ranks—Two Recruits in the United States Army
  ...On Field Duty—Winning Corporal's Chevron

UNCLE SAM'S BOYS, VOLUME 2 — 978-1-61720-033-5
  ...As Sergeants—Handling Their First Real Commands
  ...In the Phillippines—Following the Flag against the Moros

---

THE ROVER BOYS

By Arthur M. Winfield

No stories for boys ever published have attained the tremendous popularity of this series. Since the publication of the first volume "*The Rover Boys At School*", over three million copies of these books have been sold. They are well written stories dealing with the Rover boys in a great many different kinds of activities and adventures. Each volume holds something of interest to every adventure loving boy. This series, in fact, provided the template for other famous series such as the *Hardy Boys*, *Nancy Drew*, and *Tom Swift*, to name just a few. First published beginning in 1899, each volume includes the original illustrations.

THE ROVER BOYS, VOLUME 1 — 978-1-61720-034-2
  ...At School—The Cadets Of Putnam Hall
  ...On The Ocean—A Chase For Fortune

THE ROVER BOYS, VOLUME 2 — 978-1-61720-035-9
  ...In the Jungle—Stirring Adventures In Africa
  ...Out West—The Search For The Lost Mine

THE ROVER BOYS, VOLUME 3 — 978-1-61720-036-6
  ...On the Great Lakes—The Secret Of The Island Cave
  ...In the Mountains—A Hunt For Fun And Fortune

All available from Amazon.com

FLYING CHIPMUNK PUBLISHING
Classic Fiction from Charles Dickens

Oliver Twist, or, The Parish Boy's Progress—Oliver Twist, an orphan, escapes from a workhouse and joins a gang of pickpockets in London before being rescued. The novel is one of Dickens's best-known works. With the original George Cruikshank illustrations.   Softcover - 978-1-60459-484-3

A Tale of Two Cities—The story of two men, Charles Darnay and Sydney Carton, two cities, London and Paris, the French Revolution, and love. With the original illustrations of Hablot K. Browne (Phiz) and F.O.C. Darley. Charles Dickens' 17th novel.   Softcover - 978-1-60459-487-4

David Copperfield, or, The Personal History, Adventures, Experience, & Observation of David Copperfield the Younger, of Blunderstone Rookery— The most autobiographical of his novels "David Copperfield" follows the protagonist from childhood to maturity in the mid-1800's. Features the original 39 illustrations by Hablot Knight Browne (Phiz).   Softcover - 978-1-60459-489-8

Other Fiction

The Confidence Man, by Herman Melville—His last major novel and the first to portray that American icon - the con-man. More than just a thief, the con-man uses the victim's own greed (or desperation) to trick or trap the victim into giving the con-man what he wants.   Softcover - 978-1-60459-550-5

The One-Hoss-Shay, How the Old Hoss won the Bet, & The Broomstick Train, by Oliver Wendell Holmes, Sr.—One of the best regarded American poets of the 19th century. Here are three of his most famous poems. Features the original illustrations by Howard Pyle.   Softcover - 978-1-60459-872-8

Richard Hannay's War Adventures: The 39 Steps, Greenmantle, & Mr. Standfast, by John Buchan—One of the earliest examples of the "man-on-the-run" thriller, follows Richard Hannay, "an ordinary man" who puts his country's interests before his own safety during World War I. Softcover - 978-1-60459-905-3

Non-Fiction Works of Interest

Behind the Scenes — 30 Years a Slave, and 4 Years in the White House—The true story of the black slave Elizabeth Keckly, her meeting with the Lincolns, her experiences in the White House, and the sad end of her friendship with Mrs. Lincoln.   Softcover - 978-1-60459-808-7

Bundling & More About Bundling, by Henry Reed Stiles, M.D., and A. Monroe Aurand, Jr.—A curious custom, usually as a part of courting behavior-- essentially, dating in bed. Originated either in the Netherlands or in the British Isles, and was common in Colonial America.   Softcover- 978-1-60459-543-7

Geronimo's Story of his Life, in his own words, by S.M. Barrett—One of the most feared Indians in the American Southwest, with 28 vintage photos.
                    Softcover - 978-1-60459-985-5

Three Translations of The Koran (Al-Qur'an)—One of the most important religious books in the world, translated by three Islamic scholars into English. The verses are side-by-side for easy and accurate comparison.
          Hardcover - 978-1-60459-809-4   Softcover - 978-1-60459-873-5

All available from Amazon.com

CPSIA information can be obtained at www.ICGtesting.com
Printed in the USA
BVOW08s1849061113

335644BV00003B/151/P